PRAISE FOR
THE CAIRO CODEX,

the first novel in The Justine Trilogy and winner of the Silver Nautilus Award and the Bronze IPPY Award, 2014

" . . . A rather remarkable diary—one with profound implications for religious communities already roiling with discontent . . . the novel delivers a tautly suspenseful historical tale. In particular, Lambert sharply ties together early Christian beliefs with the plight of females in traditional societies, and effectively depicts the fears unleashed when entrenched beliefs are challenged . . . She keeps a sure hand on the romance plotline, letting it percolate and flare . . . An engaging thriller/romance, and a smart evocation of modern Egypt."

—Kirkus Review

"This page-turner will keep you on the edge of your seat! The contents of the codex are so startling to both Christian and Muslim faiths that their disclosure triggers violent reactions. The Muslim Brotherhood is further provoked to action as it prepares to take over the political reins of the country. This discovery will challenge accepted belief in history and religion. It will also raise questions of just how much knowledge the world deserves—or is prepared—to receive. THE CAIRO CODEX is the first in what will be THE JUSTINE TRILOGY."

—Arab Vistas Today

"The author of THE CAIRO CODEX shows a surprisingly in-depth, and even prescient, knowledge of modern Egypt and the conflicts between the Muslim Brotherhood and other segments of society."

—Historical Novel Society

"THE CAIRO CODEX is a riveting novel that portrays the unique bonds between two powerful women separated by millennia. Their relationship foreshadows a seismic shift in the Egyptian landscape. A splendidly researched and original historical novel that evokes the beautiful prose and exotic setting of *The Red Tent*."

—Jeffrey Small, best-selling author of
The Jericho Deception and *The Breath of God*

"Lambert's life in Egypt was the stimulus for this multilayered historical novel. It combines the three great religions of the Middle East with modern and historical characters, suspense, and the challenges of life and politics in present-day Egypt. This creates an altogether fascinating narrative that is hard to put down!"

—Dr. Waguida El Bakary,
former Associate Dean, American University, Cairo

"The most rewarding experience for any author is to *know* that you have written a great book and that perceptive readers will be able to share your story and enjoy your talent. Such is THE CAIRO CODEX—a spellbinding novel of Egyptian history, religion, romance, and politics."

—David Appleby, composer,
author of *Bravo Brazil!* and *Music of Brazil*

"I loved THE CAIRO CODEX. After reading the prologue, I was hooked and immediately felt propelled into Cairo. The writing is strong, as are the characters and story. Brava! I'm looking forward to the next adventure of Justine Jenner."

—Paul Williams, archaeologist,
US Department of Interior

A
RAPTURE
OF
RAVENS

AWAKENING IN TAOS

Also by Linda Lambert

Novels in The Justine Trilogy:

The Italian Letters
The Cairo Codex

Non-fiction in Leadership:

The Constructivist Leader, Editions 1 and 2
Who Will Save Our Schools
Women's Ways of Leading
Building Leadership Capacity in Schools
Leadership Capacity for Lasting School Improvement
Liberating Leadership

A
RAPTURE
OF
RAVENS

AWAKENING IN TAOS

LINDA LAMBERT

WEST
HILLS
PRESS

West Hills Press
Atlanta • San Francisco

...In the magnificent fierce morning of New Mexico one sprang awake, a new part of the soul woke up suddenly, and the old world gave way to a new.

—D. H. Lawrence, *New Mexico*

Ebony-blue cinder descends from the sky;
Emblem of night, obsidian eye;
Circles of ash floating from space;
Lighting the earth, soul of shining grace.
A Rapture of Ravens.

—Janice Razo, Taos poet

DEDICATION

‒‒‒∞‒‒‒

I dedicate this novel to Bill Haller, President of the Friends of D.H. Lawrence, Taos, New Mexico. Bill is a dear friend, Lawrence scholar, and generous soul. His love of Lawrence is personal, having encountered his work while in the Peace Corps in Africa. Like many Taoseñas, he lives in Taos because Lawrence is buried there. His tireless efforts to make the D.H. Lawrence Ranch on Lobo Mountain available to fans, scholars, and media are vital to the legacy and legend left by one of the greatest writers of the 20th century.

I could not have written this novel his assistance.

PROLOGUE

～∞∞∞～

I will never forget one thing. In Winter time, when you go to Wounded
Knee, never dig deep into the snow. All you will do is find the blood left
by your family before me. Think only of them and say, it is a good day
to die!

—Tashunkala (Little Horse), SihaSapa Lakota

FEBRUARY 3, 2011

JUSTINE STOOD AT THE FROSTED WINDOW in flannel pajamas, an Indian blanket curled around her like a cocoon, curtains drawn to reveal an island of
lights on the Taos campus of the University of New Mexico a half-mile away.
A meteor streaks by and disappears into a palette of stars, a mere sliver of
moon hung in the eastern sky. Barely 5:30 a.m., she hadn't slept since Amir's
2:30 call. In a couple of hour, the mantle of snow on the Sangre de Cristo
Mountains would turn shades of mauve in the early morning light.

Revolution day all over again. She held her steaming coffee cup with both
hands, the noise of the television in the background. Without turning, she
listened to the sounds of men and women flooding into Tahrir Square in
Cairo. It was Wednesday.

All Amir had said before the line went dead was, "I love you, Justine. It
could be today. Then I'll be home . . . ." *It could be today*, which could only
mean one thing: Mubarak was expected to step down. The revolution would

achieve its goal: the end to a brutal thirty-year dictatorship. Justine felt a tension in her gut—*could it be so easy? Could Mubarak be brought down in less than two weeks?* Perhaps, but not likely.

The possibilities were promising, yet she was gripped by deeply unsettling fears for Amir, his leadership role with the youth of Egypt placing him at great risk of being arrested. The turmoil in the Middle East was unprecedented, clearly, so perhaps none of the old rules applied. *This is a new game, in a new world bursting from the ground up, a popular revolution quickened by social media. But then what?* She knew that if Mubarak were removed, Egyptians would still have the military and the Brotherhood, since no one else was as organized. Perhaps with Amir's help, those who led the January 25th revolution would form themselves into a focused political movement. *Perhaps.*

Justine gripped the blanket more firmly around her chilled body and returned to the kitchen for the last dregs of coffee. On the couch, she curled her stocking feet under her and stared at the screen. Tahrir Square was crowded with thousands of Egyptians chanting, "Down with Mubarak," arms flailing the air, placards in Arabic demanding the president's resignation. The crowd throbbed, like a singular heart beating in concert.

Her vision was captured by a familiar-looking figure in the throng. While the images were nearly indistinct, she recognized his gait, his posture, even his profile. *Amir!* She smiled involuntarily to see that he was wearing the Kokopelli scarf she'd given him for Christmas. *It must be Amir.* She couldn't be wrong, could she? He was facing west, toward the burned-out Hilton, leaning into a small group of four or five men.

From the edge of the screen, men rode swiftly into sight on sturdy Arabian horses and lanky camels, clubs swinging above their heads, then coming down to strike indiscriminately into the swarm of young people.

Suddenly, one of the camel riders rushed in his direction, charged with intent as though he knew his target. Amir didn't see him. Justine jumped to her feet, spilling her coffee, turning over the coffee table. "Amir! Amir!" She was with him in the middle of the grassy square, screaming, warning him. Two men in the crowd pointed frantically and raced to pull the hoodlum from his camel, but too late. The club crashed against Amir's head. She imagined blood spurting into the electrified air. As the rider lifted his club for a second blow, he was pulled from his camel and beaten into the ground.

Bloody Wednesday had begun.

Blue Lake

To Taos
Ski Valley

D.H.
Lawrence
Ranch

64

64

Taos Pueblo

N

Mabel Dodge
Luhan House

Kit Carson Rd

64

Witt Rd

Old
Taos
Guesthouse

Plaza

Cruz Alta

Fernandez

BLM

Church

68

Paseo de Cañon

585

To
Llano Quemado
&
Santa Fe

Visitor
Center

CHAPTER 1

—∞∞∞—

**FIVE MONTHS EARLIER, SEPTEMBER, 2010,
LLANO QUEMADO, NEW MEXICO**

ON THE HIGH ARID DESERT OF THE Taos Valley, where the Red Willow
people make their home, the rain shadow on the leeward side of the
13,000-foot Sacred Mountain steals any scarce moisture that might make its
way into the soil. Without clouds or humidity, the intense heat of the day re-
linquishes its reign at night, giving way to freezing temperatures. In spite of
such extremes on this Aeolian plane, it is home to kangaroo rats and prickly
pears, coyotes and desert holly, jackrabbits and juniper. Ravens commune
with each other. Life insinuates itself into a rugged presence.

Justine Jenner stared at the vast, arid landscape adjoining her rented home
in Llano Quemado, just south of Ranchos de Taos. She stretched her arms into
the dry, sage-scented air, her hands gently encircling her neck, lifting her
long, tawny hair toward the sky and releasing it. Taking a deep breath, she
smiled—the sheer beauty of the mesa reminding her of the pristine deserts of
Egypt.

From Egypt to Taos had been a rugged trek of thousands of miles, accompanied by her demanding traveling companions, anxiety and regret. Notwith-
standing all this, she took immense satisfaction in the moment. Although she
was far from family and friends, alone in new surroundings—a pleasurable
warmth swept through her body.

Images of the past four years floated through her mind, a caravan of people and events. Returning to Egypt in the spring of '07 for her first real job, with a fresh Ph.D. in hand, she'd claimed the coveted role of an anthropologist team member in the UNESCO Community Schools for Girls. She held high expectations for herself, yearning to be in charge of her own life, to learn who she was in the process. Yet on her third day back in Egypt, the entire region slipped on its plates and the earthquake nearly buried her . . . . but not without leaving a precious codex at her feet.

She stood, stilled by her last observation, her wide-set golden eyes, their well-trained lenses absorbing the morning splendor of the Taos Valley. She shouldn't have been surprised when she was kicked out of Egypt. After all, she wasn't hired to launch a revolution. Justine turned, her lithe body moving sensuously under lavender satin pajamas, picking up her still warm coffee, returning her attention to the ravens.

Temporarily letting go of the dramas that punctuated her life for the past four years, Justine reminded herself that it was D. H. Lawrence who brought her to Taos. She desperately wanted to understand Lawrence's passion for Taos and his ranch. Frieda's ranch really. How he'd found his spiritual center there. Letters from the author to her great-grandmother Isabella she'd found in Italy, written during the last three years of his life, often mentioned a ferocious longing to return to the ranch, a longing sadly left unfulfilled at the time of his death in France from tuberculosis in 1930. He was only forty-four. Once again she trembled at the loss of such a talent in a world on the brink of another devastating war. *What had he found here that was different from any other place? Will I find my own spiritual center?*

Eighty-five years had passed since Lawrence left Taos, never to return, yet it is said that his spirit still lives in the curvatures of this high desert landscape. Justine wondered how that was possible. She knew that the answers to these questions would not come today, for this was the first day of the celebration of the return of Blue Lake.

In Albuquerque Justine had purchased a blue 2007 Prius, hoping it would be sturdy enough for the terrain, the harsh weather. The elevation. She discovered in the local *Santa Fé New Mexican* that in two days a 40th celebration honoring the return of Blue Lake would be held at the Taos Pueblo. A partial history of the determined quest for the return of Blue Lake explained that the mystical Sacred Mountain and its hidden gem were taken from the Taos peoples by President Teddy Roosevelt in 1906 and given to what would become the Carson National Forest. Soon, the mountain witnessed unwanted intrusions by sportsmen and hunters in search of game. Unable to accept such a loss, Taos leaders launched decades of dogged pursuit for the land, driven by a longing that could only be satisfied by the return of the Sacred Mountain and the Blue Lake in 1970. Forty years ago.

Even before 7:00 a.m. on Friday, St. Jerome Church at the Taos Pueblo was crowded with local Indians, Hispanics and a few Anglos for the special Mass opening the Blue Lake ceremonies. Justine found a narrow seat next to a family of four near the center of the church; almost in concert, the family slid toward the far end of the pew to give her more room. Mother and daughter in matching rainbow shawls of lavender, pink and powder blue thrown over ankle-length dresses and moccasins, stared straight ahead with expressionless faces, as though separating themselves from the man and boy next to them. The father and son wore uniform male attire: patched jeans, scuffed tennis shoes and plaid shirts. Restless even before services began, the young boy of about five squirmed, kicking the seat in front of him. Picking up the ragged hymnal, he wrinkled the first page in his fist. The older sister broke her stoic stare, frowned down at him and grabbed the songbook out of his hand. His father reached out, laid his hand firmly on the boy's shoulder; he immediately sat up straight and grew quiet. Justine smiled, remembering without pride what a good girl she was; even when her knee and arm itched from poison oak, she'd sat quietly. The Berkeley Unitarian church wasn't even stuffy, but Justine was proper, wishing above all to avoid criticism from Mom and Dad who shared traditional ideas about proper church behavior.

The family drama—and her own thoughts—under control, Justine glanced around the crowded room, growing warmer as the parishioners snuggled into pews, pressing together. The overcast sky allowed only muted light to sneak through the blue windows topped with white doves and crosses. Even though there were a few electric lights and candles near the altar, the room was still nearly dark. An empty loggia perched above the back of the church, and a few parishioners gathered in the back near a small balcony overlooking the Pueblo and the crystal clear Rio Pueblo below. Gnarled hands arched above the piano keys, beginning to play "Be Still, My Soul, The Lord Is On Thy Side."

Justine observed the range of expressions on the faces of practitioners: distracted and bored; beatific, almost saintly; confused and dismayed; un-readable. She wondered if it would be any different in a Catholic church in Omaha—or are there fierce tensions here that are usually suppressed? She reasoned that inner conflicts must surface in some way, in some behaviors. *But what kind?* Justine pondered that question and shifted her eyes to the front of the church.

Carved statues of Jesus, of the Virgin Mary and Saint Jerome, and of a young Indian woman, were scattered across a table between two candelabras and near a replica of a miniature white church lit from within. Above the table stood the crowned, life-sized Virgin Mary in an alcove between two painted corn stalks. Dressed for fall in lavish yellow satin, Mary was the centerpiece nestled in a wall of niches housing statues of saints. Mary—or Mother Earth as she is known to the Indians—appeared in different forms in many of the niches. From the codex or diary of Mary of Nazareth Justine had found in Egypt, she knew them as though they were family—their lives, their relation-ships, their conversations. She knew that Mary had taught her son about values and reflection, history and what it meant to be Jewish. In spite of this intimacy, Justine personally resisted traditional religion, reserving knowledge of the Holy Family for her life as an anthropologist. Instead, she was seeking a new spirituality, a discovery that she was convinced Lawrence had made on the side of Lobo Mountain.

Justine drew in a deep breath, sighed, and turned from her turbulent thoughts to the presence of a large casket sitting to the right of the altar, draped in yellow and crowned with artificial flowers. She had learned that it was intended to symbolize the body of Jesus laid to rest. More than four hundred years ago, the Spanish had unsuccessfully insisted that the Indians bury their dead in caskets. But the locals had resisted the corruption of their sacred burial ceremonies: a warm blanket was all that was needed for protection when they lowered their loved one into a shallow grave, making it easier for Mother Earth to reclaim her servant. Jesus' casket was the only one on the Pueblo. For the peoples of the pueblos, Jesus was a Western individualist; after all, he saved people one at a time, not the clan or the community. Catholicism had insinuated itself into the culture, but had not displaced their deeply held beliefs.

The young priest spoke to the congregation gently, bound to his message of sin, yet reaching for hope, determined not to dampen the spirit of the day. "Let me remind us that God is good," he said. "He wants the best for us, his children." The cloaked man, his glasses reflecting candle light, paused, permitting his eyes to survey the seemingly attentive audience. "Yet we cannot deny that this is a sinful world—we see it everywhere. We are all sinners, sins for which we atone as we pray together today, ask forgiveness, and promise to live the good life. Let us pray."

Adults and children alike received his familiar, yet sorrowful, message without reaction. They prayed, sang, rose and sat down, rose and sat down. Justine detected no significant shifts in facial expressions, and wondered if they were reflecting on their own sins—whatever they might be. Or perhaps they simply came for ritual and music and a sacred place for their own private prayers. For her, it was a familiar story, heard often in the churches of Europe where she attended with her grandmother. Raising his voice in gratitude and exaltation, the young priest concluded by asking for guidance for President Obama and thanking God for the return of Blue Lake to its original people.

The double doors to the rear of the church opened noisily with the fanfare of arriving royalty. Five Indian men in full regalia, including feathered headdresses, entered the back of the church grasping drums bound in elk hide. Chanting and dancing, they moved in undulating rhythm to the front and took their assigned places alongside the priest, continuing their performance.

Justine felt an energizing shift in the mood and attentiveness among parishioners as her own body moved in concert. Ancient cultures side by side, Indians
sharing the stage with the Hebrew disciple, and the priest of the Abrahamic
religion. She watched the feet of a young girl swing to the irresistible
rhythms.

Justine had encountered the integration of native and Catholic beliefs before—of nature and spirits and the white man's universal abstract god—all
well orchestrated. Since 1540, when Capitan Alvarado rode into Taos Valley,
peoples who lived alongside one another had come to terms with the discrep-
ancies between the two faiths. Whatever beliefs could not be integrated were
often ignored. Plurality—practicing two faiths alongside each other—didn't
seem to concern the Taos peoples. For a few, it was troublesome; for most, it
was just the way things were. Similar motifs and metaphors animate all religions, Justine understood well, providing common ground for understanding
nature, life everlasting, and one's relationship to the gods.

At this moment, in response to the priest's invitation, parishioners lined up
between the pews to receive communion, the blood and flesh of Jesus Christ.
The patient line progressed slowly toward this transmutation, heat from the
morning sun radiating intensely through the pale blue windows, drawing soft
halos around the heads of those who waited.

A young girl of about seven, with blue-black braids and large ebony eyes,
watched Justine, smiling broadly when their eyes met. Justine wondered if the
little girl, or adults for that matter, understood this ritual. She bowed slightly
to the girl who could barely stop herself from breaking into a spontaneous
giggle at the tall stranger. The woman and girl, a generation apart, felt like co-
conspirators when they looked up into the grandmother's gentle, amused face.

Several lively young men moved with dispatch to the front of the church
and proceeded to dismantle the altar, removing statues, candelabras and
cloths from the tables and handing Saint Jerome, Jesus, Mary, the Indian girl,
and other saints of blurred identity into the arms of the waiting women and
children. Scrambling onto the now empty table, the men reached for the
nearly five-foot tall statue of the Virgin, carefully lowering her to other men
who stood her erect on a homemade platform with four handles.

A parade was forming. Justine filed into line behind the towering Virgin as it wound out the church gate and circled the grounds of the thousand-year-old pueblo. Others standing in the open plaza joined the parade as it moved sinuously through the plaza, the numbers growing into the hundreds.

Justine felt welcome, although separate and apart, a conflicted feeling she frequently experienced in cultures other than her own. Part of her wanted to overcome this strange feeling of separateness, although it served her well in her observational role as anthropologist. Swept along by the mounting energy and press of Indians and Anglos alike, she knew she would not be separate today.

CHAPTER 2

⊶⊷

THE SKY WAS INDIGO BY THE TIME Justine's feet traversed the path leading home. Fortunately, she had left the house lights on or she might have overshot the turn, ending up in the ditch that bordered highway 110. In spite of the cooling night, her skin radiated the warmth of a stinging sunburn, for the brim of her new lavender bonnet hadn't adequately shaded her neck and shoulders during the parade and speeches at the pueblo. Her thoughts were elsewhere now. In Egypt, after finding the diary of the Virgin Mary, she came to know her thoughts—her persona. Now, halfway around the earth, Justine marched in the pueblo parade, the Virgin Mary again leading her. It was as though Queen Isabella of Spain had orchestrated history from that medieval tent in the ancient village of Santa Fe just beyond the Alhambra. Without the conversation she'd had with the young upstart Christopher Columbus, and her sponsorship of his exploits, Taos would be quite different today. The Queen's goals, piety and spreading the gospel; Columbus' goals, adventure and riches. The Blessed Mary—decked out in luscious fall colors —would not have ridden high at the head of the parade. She wondered how Mother Earth would have been represented if the Taos peoples had their way?

The irony amused her—the invention and reinvention of the Virgin. But that was not her reason for being in Taos. For moving to Taos. It was D. H. Lawrence who drove her passions for discovery. Who was he and what had he found here? But Lawrence would have to wait. Today she would return to the pueblo.

That night she slept well, waking at the first glimmer of light, meeting the day with a warm sense of pleasure that spread through her limbs. Languishing across her comfy bed, her taffy hair flowing across multiple pillows, Justine explored the prism of color moving across the ceiling of vigas and timber. A sense of calm washed over her. *I'm in my element here,* she mused, *a Petri dish for a cultural anthropologist . . . a climate and terrain to please the senses—what more could I want?*

—∞∞—

Justine parked and walked some distance into the vast, open pueblo plaza where tan canvas covers spread over aspen poles offered protection from the sun. The recently erected traditional grandstand in front of the five-story pueblo was crowded with council and government leaders, guests and visitors. She settled into her green-striped lawn chair under the eastern lean-to and withdrew her water bottle and writing materials for a second unforgettable day.

Guest speakers filed onto the podium to explain their commendable roles in the efforts to secure the return of their treasured lands. Regional governors and legislators, assistants to President Nixon, senators, the assistant director of the Bureau of Indian Affairs, and children of legendary leaders of the past spoke passionately and proudly of the struggle. These long and often discouraging years of Indian solidarity had brought confidence to the Taos.

Pueblo Governor Lujan was introduced by the only woman on the stage, apparently the facilitator of the day's festivities. As she stepped forward, the middle aged Indian woman with a sculpted, stilled expression deftly moved the microphone to her mouth for a crisp introduction. The governor spoke eloquently of the fierce fight against all odds, sixty-seven years of persistence. "We can all identify with the need to protect that which gives us meaning, to preserve the precious cycle of life," he said. Hundreds of on-lookers nodded solemnly.

Then the governor spoke briefly and lovingly of his grandfather, Tony Luhan, who had married a white woman named Mabel Dodge. The tribe had opposed the match, but Mabel had brought in outsiders who retold the story of the Indians who helped save their land and dignity. Today, Tony was forgiven for his violation of tribal law. Justine listened with intense interest since she knew that Mabel could help lead her to Lawrence, for it was Mabel who had brought him and his wife Frieda to Taos in the early 20s.

Justine removed her denim jacket, for the morning chill was quickly giving way to rising temperatures. The powder blue sky would soon be washed into a glare of white light, reminding her of the vast, cloudless skies of Egypt. Whether blanketing the Nile or the sprawling Sahara, no boundary line separated land and sky. She glanced up to find eight drummers in red and gold Indian blankets, eagle-feathered headdresses, and beaded moccasins moving into the enormous plaza of packed soil in front of the grandstand. When the Friendship Dance was announced, the drummers created a rhythm that permeated the warm, dry air and reverberated in the pulsing bodies of onlookers. As though on cue, residents and visitors alike joined together in an ever-widening circle in the center, holding hands and moving slowly clockwise in time with the drumming. Without hesitation, Justine donned her khaki hat and joined the dancers, moving in time to throbbing drums, a sense of palpable unity flooding through her agile body. The circle grew larger and larger; eventually, hundreds danced. Indians and Anglos holding hands, swaying to the drumbeat, faces upturned to the sun.

Suddenly, Justine felt it was twilight and could again feel Amir's arm encircle her waist as they danced at the edge of the pool at Cairo's Marriott. They were the only dancers, or perhaps it just felt as though they were, floating there above the shimmering azure pool, enveloped by the dark indigo sky, the orchestra violins casting a magical spell that penetrated her warm body. Amir in his white dinner jacket—that lock of ebony hair curling across his forehead.

She was not aware that the drumming had stopped, but felt the stillness in the moist skin still clasping her hands. Then her hands emptied, the dancers turning to return to their original places, if not their original roles. Justine knew only too well that people who dance together subtly alter their identities as well as their relationships. She had been changed by many dances, but never more than the one with the man she had known in Egypt, then loved in

Italy. She smiled at the young man in ragged western dress at her side, an expression of mild confusion turning to pleasure on his bronze face.

—∞∞—

By 2:00, the announcers invited the crowd to follow young guides to homes spread throughout the pueblo for lunch. Justine left her chair and jacket, grabbed her backpack, and accompanied several visitors as they crossed a bridge over the Rio Pueblo and walked among the red willow trees to homes where tables and chairs had been set in the shade. On this side of the river, just beyond the original pueblo, families were allowed running water, electricity, and indoor plumbing—not so in the pueblo itself, kept sacred in its original state.

Justine heard a low whistle coming from the cluster of trees, the kind of whistle that was not unfamiliar. She turned to observe three young boys staring at her, one taller than the others, muscular, with deep auburn hair pulled back into a long braid, and a half smile that was more of a smirk. As she stared in their direction, the whistle became a laugh, low and guttural, sinister. She trembled slightly and shook her head, trying to dispel images of her sexual assault on a Cairo street racing through her mind.

She quickly turned back to join the line winding among tables, bicycles, plastic toys, and sketchy lawns into the back door of a kitchen where several women endured the sweltering heat from huge pans of simmering brisket of beef, corn and squash calabacitas, beans, and corn pudding. Pots of red chile. Chopped vegetables and large slabs of warm Indian bread stood in baskets on a side table with plastic ware and napkins, near a table of water, sodas, lemonade and coffee.

"I'm Justine Jenner." She smiled warmly at two Indian women seated across from her at the picnic table. She reached for their welcoming hands. The women introduced themselves as Lucinda and Martha. "I'm honored to be invited into your homes," Justine said. "I knew so little about the Blue Lake struggle."

Lucinda smiled in gratitude. "We do this a lot," she said. "We cook for special occasions and invite visitors. San Geronimo Day. Christmas. On All Saints Day we cook for our Spanish neighbors and our dead. It's what we do."

"Yet today is different?" probed Justine. "A 40th anniversary."

"Yes. Different," agreed Martha. "We celebrate the Blue Lake Return every ten years. My grandfather was governor in 1970. He went to Washington to accept the signing pen from President Nixon." She ripped her Indian bread in half and folded it to scoop up some beans. Her pupils expanded and a soft blush of light pink appeared on her tan temples. An undeniable expression of pride.

"You must be very proud," said Justine, copying Martha, scooping her own beans with the Indian bread.

Martha just nodded, humility preferable to pride.

"Tell me about the person who was today's facilitator . . . is it common to have a woman in such an important role?"

"This is the highest role ever given to a woman here," said Lucinda. "Suzanne is very accomplished. Contributes a lot to our people. She worked in a health project in Tucson, then came back home."

"We're happy she did," continued Lucinda, more open with her feelings than her neighbor. "She inspires us, pushes us really. Her role in the ceremonies is unusual because women usually have no opportunity to lead our people, unlike some other pueblos. Many of us are unhappy. We want more for our daughters."

Martha gave her friend an almost indistinguishable glance of disapproval.

Lucinda challenged her friend. "Well, why send our girls to college if we can't expect them to come back and be leaders in our community? Do you want them to move to Albuquerque, like Georgia's daughter?" She glanced around and fell silent.

Justine asked herself if such criticism could bring reprisal. "Tell me about the corn and squash dish," she said, poking at the dish in question. "It's so delicious!"

Lucinda let her grin linger, admiration swept across her face. "It's called 'calabacitas,' one of our favorites. Just fry up the onions and add chopped squash, corn and cheese—lots of it. An old Anasazi recipe."

"Anasazi?" asked Justine. "Weren't the ancient peoples from Chaco and Mesa Verde called Anasazi?"

"A part of the Great Migrations, hundreds of years ago. The desert grasses dried up, water was scarce," offered Lucinda, her voice dropping as she saw a tall man approach and stand near Justine's shoulder.

"Dr. Jenner?" he asked.

"Yes," she replied, staring into the sun at the darkened outline of a towering man with full hair and deeply tanned skin, both hands grasping the brim of a western style hat.

"May I have a few words with you?" he asked without formalities, apologizing for the interruption. The two Indian women grew silent, their shoulders stiffened.

Justine rose, excused herself, deposited her dishes on a nearby tray, and followed the man she barely recognized as Mike Sandoval from his photo on the New Mexico Office of Archaeology website. His brown eyes flickered with life, an animated mouth giving him an expression of eagerness. Ears threatening to protrude from under his longish hair. They meandered among the tables and willows back toward the Rio Pueblo.

CHAPTER 3

—◦◦◦—

JUSTINE AND MIKE FOUND THE MEAGER shade of two red willows where they
could hear the gurgling of the river and crowds moving back from lunch
across the bridge. As they settled onto the barren ground, Justine recalled the
process that had prepared her for this encounter today. Her interest in D. H.
Lawrence—her obsession really—required that her time in New Mexico
would not be short; after all, she was in pursuit of an eighty-five year old
mystery—for Lawrence had left Taos in 1925.

She would need a job. Her grandmother's inheritance had been substantial,
but it was against her principles to use it for living expenses. In response to
one of her three job applications, the Director of the New Mexico Office of
Archaeology had responded: "Your credentials are excellent. Although you
have become a controversial player in the field, we would like to invite you
to join us." *Controversial player* she repeated to herself. In a way, she cherished the depiction of herself as a notorious woman. She'd had few illusions
about the consequences of her actions when she had submitted what had become one of the most provocative articles of the new century to the journal,
Archaeology, announcing major revelations found in the diary of the Virgin
Mary.

"Your interest in the issue of community intrigues us," the Director had written. "Mike Sandoval, one of our staff, has written extensively in the field, so a
collaboration might be in the offering. Unfortunately, we need to ask that you
secure your own funding once the project becomes more fully defined." Finding

funding would not be easy, especially since she had only a loose grasp of the research question. Her undergraduate alma mater—UC Berkeley—where her father was still a professor of archaeology, had offered some possibilities. Still, she had to write the grant proposal, and she couldn't begin until she had a better grasp of Mike Sandoval's thesis. Although reluctant to interrupt the conversation with the Taos women, she was pleased that Mike had found her.

Justine could hear Suzanne introducing the next speaker on the other side of the plaza, but turned her attention to observing her new colleague: a husky man in his late 50s or early 60s with wide-set, high cheekbones, and a full head of salt and pepper hair—his tanned skin toughened by the life of an archaeologist in the scorching sun.

Mike asked a flurry of questions: What were her interests in community? Where was she living? Why had she *really* been expelled from Egypt? What did she do in Italy? He had read the critical reviews questioning the provenance of her work in *Archaeology*. As he spoke, his animated features formed fluctuating masks: an eager child, an intense scientist, a sarcastic critic, a curious muse. Justine wondered which he was, anticipating that she would learn of the many faces of Mike Sandoval in the months to come.

Initially amused by his questions and eagerness to pursue them, Justine revealed her interests in community by explaining her graduate studies with the Hopi in Arizona and the UNESCO Community Schools for Girls in Egypt. "So," she continued, "these communities hosted the schools, providing space and a governing council, usually chaired by one of the mothers. The UNESCO project provided the curriculum and the teacher."

"Do these schools work? Do parents allow the girls to attend school? I wouldn't have thought so . . . . " He challenged her.

Quickly noticing Mike's propensity to drop punctuation from his lively speech, she responded, "They were strikingly successful. Community members solved problems together and took ownership of the schools. Then a tragedy happened. An earthquake caused one of the schools to collapse, killing three of the girls, so I thought everything would change."

He grimaced. "I would think they would consider the quake an act of God. A message about the education of girls." Mike was insistent.

"That's what I thought. I was sure the disaster would be viewed as a sign that God was against educating girls. And, it was seen that way by a few, but not by enough to close the school." She chose not to tell him that she was nearly buried in the same earthquake in an old crypt fifty miles away.

"Incredible!" exclaimed Mike, obviously skeptical. "I'd think that the education of young girls is a difficult sell, particularly in the Middle East. And relying on the locals can be misleading. They often survive on myths and stories that give meaning to their lives." He stopped himself, as though he knew he might have gone too far in a first conversation. After all, he didn't know Justine.

Justine was surprised at what appeared to be a sweeping condemnation of native peoples. Silence hovered between them for a few moments. "I find that a surprising statement for an archaeologist, Mike. Perhaps I misunderstood. It sounded as though you were questioning the value of involving native voices in our work ." She let her sentence linger, inviting his response.

"Well," he said more slowly, "I've been burned more than once when locals would use myth and legend to explain data, and it turned out to be distorted, or slanted. For instance, not long ago we discovered Comanche encampments along the Rio Grande. The locals, whom my team members insisted on including, got it wrong. They described the Comanches as plains Indians, hunting, passing through, while we found undeniable evidence that the tribe was here to raid and plunder—take whatever they could, including women." Mike perspired heavily as he watched Justine closely, picked up a small willow branch, and held it between his teeth, as though it held a secret serum.

Justine studied his intense rumination. His outrage sounded personal. She blinked and decided to answer his most elementary question: Where she was living. "I'm renting a house owned by my friend Emily. It's near the University of New Mexico campus in Llano Quemado."

She sized him up: intelligent and curious, loquacious. While she prized her capacity to read people quickly, she knew there would be more surprises ahead with this man.

CHAPTER 4

—οοο—

SUNDAY MORNINGS IN TAOS REMINDED her of childhood. Sleeping in, the Sunday papers, a generous breakfast with her parents, a short run in Berkeley's Tilden Park with her mother. These images came back to her swiftly. What had she been dreaming? Justine couldn't remember this time, yet it must have been pleasant, peaceful for a change. Too often, her dreams were nightmares about the earthquake in Cairo, being trapped in the crypt, that feeling of helplessness flashing back to her.

The nightmares came less frequently now, yet they worked at her mind like a virus, finding undefended cavities in which to hide, ready to jump into dreams like bit players. Fed by random instances, like the three boys in the willows yesterday. Whistles of admiration followed by contemptuous laughs. Chilling.

She opened her eyes, stretched and rolled over in bed, staring at the massive pine beams, the morning light forming a kaleidoscope of images dancing across the ceiling like the prism her mother once hung in her bedroom window.

Justine's amber eyes danced across floating bubbles of light. She closed her eyes and imagined Amir's hand touching her bare waist, moving toward her breasts. His face nestled in her hair as he placed his chin lightly on her shoulder, that unruly black hair tumbling across his eye, the smell of musk filling her nostrils. How she missed him; how she missed their lovemaking. She breathed deeply, shuddered, and opened her eyes.

After a quick shower, Justine sipped her tea, picked up her old valise and made her way out the back door onto the chilly patio, situating herself in one of the green wrought iron chairs near the table. She surveyed the expansive landscape that would surround her in upcoming months. Or, years. She just didn't know. Flowers bordered the patio: several beach roses snuggled up against a lamb's ear and scattered lilies; towering hollyhocks shaded two yarrow plants. Courageous creatures of nature, braving the daily swings in temperature.

The musky aroma of dust and grasses reminded her of the end of summer at her paternal grandparents' barren farm in Nebraska. A solitary raven watched her closely, as though reading her mind. Thirty feet to the west, a barbwire fence ran north to south. Farther on, a pulsating wall of water caught the morning sunlight as it moved back and forth across the golf course.

At 10:00 a.m., the chill of the land was being transformed into rising steam. Two black-chinned hummingbirds fluttered around the feeder by the kitchen window, one clearly propitious. "I'm going to love it here," she declared aloud, her feet firmly planted on the cement flagstones, hugging the valise to her chest. The air, the landscape, the mountains—this sweep of grandeur that holds so many secrets. *Whatever this next adventure holds, I already feel a serenity that I haven't felt in years. Is it because I'm far from the madding crowd of critics who had sought to discredit my work? From parents who love me a little too much?*

Justine wiped the condensed moisture from the table and laid her old valise in front of her. Opening it slowly, she withdrew two large bundles of letters tied with blue satin ribbons. She placed a hand on each bundle and sat in meditative posture for several moments. These were letters from D. H. Lawrence to her great grandmother, Isabella—treasures that have occupied her mind for two years, turning it into a playground she found difficult to leave.

Justine lifted the second bundle and extracted the letter on the bottom of the pile; as far as she knew, this was the last letter he had written to Isabella. She examined the signature once again. *No one knew D. H. as David—but Isabella did.* She read aloud, for at least the hundredth time:

Hotel Beau Rivage, Bandol, France, 18 September 1929

My dearest Isabella,

Your news fills me with a joy greater than I've ever known. I was sure the fates had decided that I would never have a child of my own. Undeserving. With little to offer another. I'm afraid that I may have to leave fatherhood to your fine husband. Does he suspect? Surely not.

This French doctor is as useless as the others. I overheard him tell Frieda that there is little chance of improvement. The air is damp here; all my strength goes to pulling in what air I can. And I write when I can. I need you at my side, my darling, but know that is not possible. Even if you changed your mind and wanted to come to me, you shouldn't travel with little Lawrence in your womb.

I beg of you to consider these thoughts when raising our child. I wish him to have your lightness of spirit and innocence about the world rather than his father's cynicism. Give him freedom and choices early, and love him without suffocation. Let him spread his wings wide. Protect him from the life of a writer! Terrible lot. And science and politics. Almost as bad. They steal away life's mysteries. But I digress. I am excited beyond words by your news. My one regret in this short life has been the absence of a child of my own. And now that my child is to be given life by the woman I truly love, what more could I want?

So, for us, a God-be-with-you. I have lived as vividly as I have written—and because I have left with you, dear woman, the seed of my deepest self, I will die with a gladness and fulfillment in my belly, worshiping the son in yours. How brief, yet how important, you have been to me. As if God had said, "Wait!---there is someone you must meet."

> *If you need anything, my love, remember you can trust*
> *Lady Brett. She is living at the ranch. Stay well and carry*
> *my seed with care.*
> *Love always, David*

The eagerly awaited child hadn't been a boy, but a girl whom Isabella named "Laurence" replacing the "w" with a "u," as was the custom in Egypt. Justine held the letter as it fluttered in the warming morning breeze. Again, her nervous system sent currents to her extremities. Her whole body responded to the romance—and yes, the truths—in this last letter from Lawrence to Isabella.

History turned on this letter, the infamous author without a child, he now possessed a legacy biographers had not discovered. How this would alter the course of literary history! *How I wish I could have met him.* A rightful heir to his talents and his significant body of work—like herself—might have shaped his legacy with more empathy. Avoided the troubled path his reputation and writings traveled. Few took the time to understand Lawrence; accusations of obscenity and misogyny abounded. Now he is a literary god.

Justine's identity turned on this letter as well, for this was the letter that had told her who she was—partially at least. This knowledge brought her to Taos. But there was more to her story than her relationship to D. H. Lawrence, as profound as that knowledge was.

Isabella's father had been the Egyptian ambassador to the Vatican in the twenties and he, as was the custom, had chosen a young Egyptian diplomat to be her husband. In turn, Isabella and her husband made sure that Laurence married an Egyptian as well—Justine's grandfather, who was killed at El Alamein in northern Egypt in the struggle against Rommel's German army during World War II.

Laurence was D. H.'s daughter, sensuous and determined. After the death of her first husband at El Alamein, with whom she'd had her daughter Lucrezia, she married an Italian named Cellini. Benvenuto Cellini adopted Lucrezia, Laurence's daughter and Justine's mother.

Lucrezia grew up to be as headstrong and passionate as her mother. More, she chose to change family history by marrying an American, from Berkeley by way of Nebraska. Lucrezia had expected the Berkeley influence would override the indoctrination of his Nebraska roots, at least where men and women were concerned. She was wrong. Her husband Morgan proved to be overprotective and controlling.

Little did Justine know, until that day she found the Lawrence letters in a trunk in her grandmother's attic in Fiesole, that her complicated geographic heritage included the British Isles. D. H. Lawrence's Nottinghamshire, to be exact, he the son of a coal miner and a rigid Protestant mother who spent his life distancing himself from his roots.

Lawrence referred Isabella to Lady Brett at the end of this last letter. *What do I know about Lady Brett?* Pretty much what everyone knew. She was a nearly deaf artist from a royal British family who had followed Lawrence to Taos at his request. Disgusted by the state of the world during and after World War I, Lawrence had sought to establish a self-sufficient, utopian, community in Taos called Ramaman. But "The Brett"—as he called her—was the only person to accept his invitation. Lawrence loved Taos, and in time Frieda came to love it as much as her husband.

After Lawrence's early death in France at forty-four, Frieda returned to Taos and lived there for the rest of her life.

For a man who trusted few people, Lawrence trusted Brett. Why?

A long-eared jackrabbit leapt into Justine's line of sight. He leisurely wiggled through two prickly pear cacti, turning toward Justine. The rabbit and the woman keenly eyed one another. Lush gray fur pivoted on his neck, reminding her of a family photo on her mother's Baroque walnut bureau. Isabella Hassouna in a gray fox stole standing in front of the Vatican, her crimson velvet hat resting on that plump gray fur stole. Large, sad eyes stared intently at the photographer, seemingly not an acquaintance. Justine had asked her mother about the photo when she was a girl, but she'd been given only evasive answers. Except that the photo was taken in 1931. What was happening then? Of course! D. H. had died the year before and Isabella had given birth to their daughter Laurence. Mussolini was challenging the authority of the Vatican and Justine's Egyptian great-grandfather and his family would soon be expelled. But Isabella couldn't have known all that at the time.

Justine's mind froze, as did everything around her—the air, the clouds, the rabbit. Is it possible, she asked herself, that Isabella traveled to New Mexico to speak with Lady Brett? *Did Isabella yearn to know more about his life here, like I do? Was theirs an unfinished story for my great grandmother as well?* Her thoughts lingered on Isabella—and Lawrence— her mind traveling along the path of imagination to the moment they first met. *Did the enchantment occur then? Did they recognize it?*

Chapter 5

—ᴇᴇᴇ—

FEBRUARY 23, 1927, FIESOLE

"Mr. Lawrence, I would like for you to meet my daughter, Isabella," said Ambassador Hassouna. He and his family were guests at the Medici Palace.

Lawrence turned from the Ambassador to his daughter, extending his hand, meeting hers in mid-air as it moved toward him. He stood still, as though stilled by time, his striking sapphire eyes growing intense. "Signora Isabella." He paused and bowed slightly in slow motion, long enough for the Ambassador to be drawn away by a demanding guest. "Delighted. Your home is near Villa Borghese and the Vatican, I am told." Lawrence reluctantly released her hand, detecting that was her wish. He trusted his intuitive powers which enabled him to appraise people quickly, to size them up.

"This is true," she said, placing the empty hand tenderly into her other, as though a strange warmth emanated from it. "The winter can be quite damp in Rome. Yet the fragrances are sweet, the air buoyant. And you, Mr. Lawrence, what brings you to Fiesole? Another book perhaps?"

Lawrence found himself momentarily without words. He observed her confident demeanor, her jewels . . . an Oriental prin-

cess with Italian shoes extending from under a burgundy lace gown. Old world aplomb, yet with an unmistakable modern flair. He was mystified. Further, she knew of his work. "Quite perceptive," he said, "We are staying at the Villa Mirenda nearby. I just finished The Virgin and the Gipsy and am struggling with the third draft of a novel about a Lady Chatterley. Set in Nottinghamshire, where I grew up. A few random poems. Your observations on the sweet fragrances and balmy air may lend some thoughts to my poetry." He paused again, his eyes lingering, gazing into hers. "Do you write?"

She didn't look away, but returned his gaze, pondering his words. "A few modest poems. Nothing, really. Not publishable. You know of the work of St. Vincent Millay? From New York, I believe." Isabella had read some of Lawrence's work and harbored a great regard for the author. Yet, she had not admired what she'd heard about Lawrence, the man. Egotistical. Arrogant. Easily outraged. Well, let's see how he responds to a good jostling, she thought. She grinned at her own mischievousness.

"I've read Millay, yes, with great favor. Perceptive woman, able to capture the wanton times in America. In Paris."

"Why 'wanton'?" she challenged, black eyes flashing.

Once again Lawrence was caught off guard. Rarely had he been challenged by a woman—except Frieda, of course. Never by a well-born, exotic beauty. "The new creative breed are reckless, without direction. Willful. Take Fitzgerald and Hemingway, for instance. Pound."

"Gertrude Stein. Brave people. Searching, it is true. Not all of us have the freedom to be careless, Mr. Lawrence." Her gaze was intent, matching his own; for several moments two wild cats scrutinized one another.

It wouldn't have surprised him if they had begun to circle. Am I out of my depth? he mused. I've not encountered such buoyant intensity in an Oriental woman. How far may I go before she withdraws, recoils? He loved challenge, the unknown, was easily bored by the predictable. Isabella was captivating. Novel. "Will you be here long, Signora Isabella?" he smiled, choosing to break the spell, pursuing the better part of valour, or so he thought, even though energy swirled between them.

"My husband and I accompanied my parents here for the month. My father and Anwar will be traveling to Egypt tomorrow, and my mother and I will remain here until they return. The Medicis are most generous with their hospitality."

"Perhaps we will see one another again before you leave," he said as Frieda approached, glancing from one to the other.

"Perhaps," Isabella said, inexplicably. A Mona Lisa smile, a pale, almost indistinguishable blush.

CHAPTER 6

⊰∞⊱

FOR THE PAST TWO PLUS YEARS, Justine had read many of the biographies and autobiographies of the central characters of Taos in the 1920's and realized that Mabel Dodge Luhan would probably have known whether her great grandmother Isabella had visited Taos. If anyone knew how the stories all came together, Mabel would have. Yet, she hadn't read anything about Isabella Hassouna in Mabel's many autobiographies. If she had come to Taos and Mabel didn't mention it, there would be a reason. What reason would cause her to conceal such information?

Justine had to ask herself a question that would arise many times in the year to come: Why did it matter if her great grandmother came to Taos? After all, she was in pursuit of what Lawrence found out about himself on the side of Lobo Mountain. But she knew the answer immediately, and would need to remind herself again and again. She was fascinated with everything about Lawrence. After all, as an anthropologist, she wanted the entire mosaic—every shade and fiber, every texture and color—of his life. Only then could she understand who he was, could she deduce how his mind and heart worked.

She knew that Mabel was much more than the wife of Taos native Tony Luhan. From a wealthy banking family in Buffalo, the young and attractive Mabel had made her way to New York City and Florence right after World War I. Mabel held salons with the flamboyant political and literary figures of the day in New York and, much like Justine's mother Lucrezia, in Florence—

activities that included a prolonged affair with communist John Reed and two men who would become her husbands.

By the time Mabel arrived in Taos with husband number three and her only child, John, she was determined to find the personal peace that had eluded her, as well as pursue her vision of how the world should work.

Her vision of such a world was not so different from mine, Justine mused. For Mabel, the individual draws insights from life's experiences, enriches herself by attributing meaning to these experiences, and evolves into ever-expanding states of consciousness. She realized that this was not so different from Lawrence as well, who believed that the soul finds expression through the will, and emerges into social activism—fighting the human shallowness borne of capitalism.

"The noise of war," Mabel pronounced in one of the columns she wrote for the Hearst papers, "violates the soul, for only in peace can individuals and societies attain higher forms of consciousness." Further, in an expression especially dear to Justine, Mabel believed it was women who could best vocalize these essential, breathless truths. Soul, will, and intuition blended in this vision: the individual created community and in turn, community created the individual. "A reciprocity of tenderness," Lawrence would later call it.

Eventually, Mabel would author several autobiographical volumes. Still craving a salon that would offer the intellectually rich conversations that Tony couldn't offer, Mabel used her resources and personal will to gather key figures of the time around her: D.H Lawrence, Georgia O'Keeffe, Robinson Jeffers, John Marin, Willa Cather, Ansel Adams, Mary Austin. Friend Jaime de Angulo invited Carl Jung—and he came.

Deep in thought, Justine fixed her stare on the barbed wire fence, peripherally observing a man and his golden retriever moving slowly along the path, being passed by a woman, shoulders thrown back, marching militaristically with two brown and white terriers. While her eyes wandered along the horizon, her thoughts meandered among the letters and speculated about Mabel's persona. Lawrence and Mabel had a conflicted relationship at best. More obsession on Mabel's part, Justine suspected. After all, Mabel needed to be important to Lawrence—to be his muse. *Can one be in love with another's mind? I believe so. Certainly, in love with his worldview.*

One of her many autobiographies, *Lorenzo in Taos,* included an exchange of letters that revealed a relationship between Mabel and D. H. to be both sympathetic and critical. While public opinion about Mabel's talents varied, Justine admired her knack for self-revelation and examination, with occasional flares of fine writing. She pulled another letter to Isabella from the stack and removed the lavender post-it.

> *You ask of Mabel,* **Lawrence wrote.** *Her ego reins over her intellect and fills her with insistencies. Yet she is not without sympathies or generosities. I told you that she gave Frieda the Ranch in '24. Not that I didn't want it for myself, but indebtedness to Mabel would not sit well with me. Frieda gave her Sons and Lovers in exchange. Worth a lot someday, I should imagine. She is married to a red man from the pueblo. Tony Luhan by name, Mabel's red trophy. Tony has a quiet, sacred place inside his heart. I learn from him.*

What did this passage tell her? Lawrence's feelings about Mabel, the Ranch, the Sons and Lovers manuscript, Tony. She grinned at her great grandfather's efficiency with words, a habit he rarely practiced in literary fiction.

She carefully stuffed the letters back into the peeling valise, opened the screen door and stepped back into the kitchen. She poured herself another cup of tea, dropped a slice of whole wheat bread into the toaster and peeled a banana. Leaning against the kitchen cabinet to eat, she pondered the dynamics that were part of those fiery relationships of the 20's, many of them lasting into the 60's, morphing into . . . what? Frieda, Mabel and Brett lived on in Taos for many decades after Lawrence died. Justine suspected that they grew into strong women together, confident in their own powers, without a need to compete. And, they were joined by other powerful women, Millicent Rogers and Alexandria Fechin, the wife of the Russian artist Nicolai Fechin, among them.

Justine stepped into a black and gray quilted skirt that promised to brush the tops of her buckskin boots as she moved, a white cotton blouse, silver belt and earrings for her drive to Mabel's. She hadn't been to the Luhan property as yet, although she'd been told at the Visitor's Center how to find it. Stopping at Walgreen's to pick up the *Times*, shampoo and toothpaste, Justine followed the leisurely line of Sunday traffic into the center of Taos and turned right onto Kit Carson Road.

The renowned home and museum of Kit Carson sat on the left and three blocks further east she found a small dirt road called Morada. "Morada" she knew, meant a small chapel used by the Penitents, a group of intense believers who sought to emulate the suffering of Jesus, especially at Easter. She had heard that they were very active in Northern New Mexico where they had kept the church alive, strengthening their numbers, after priests were withdrawn in the 1800s.

Following along the looming latilla fence of aspen poles for a quarter mile, she found the marked entrance to the Mabel Dodge Luhan properties, several acres scattered about with cottages for guests, a conference center built in the 70's, and off to the right, a three-story structure that Tony had built as their personal home. *Impressive,* observed Justine, as she parked. This must have been considered a grand estate in the 20's—the center of artistic life in Taos. Famed artists Ernest Blumenschein and Bert Phillips arrived before the war and put Taos on the map artistically, Blumy traveling back and forth until his wife came, yet it was Mabel who created the next wave of creative life here.

Justine briskly climbed the wooden stairs past an arbor, aging, peeling, furniture and a swing. A stone pathway led to the front of the house and connected a long line of single-story rooms extending south, all part of the original structure. Facing the end of the slender extension were four large storybook pigeon houses with scores of miniature windows and nearly as many pigeons. She observed the birds socializing in the morning sunlight, wondering what they had to say to one another. Turning back toward the house, her eyes followed the full length of the roof: wooden beams extending from the ochre adobe exterior.

Opening the lavishly carved yet exceptionally narrow front door, she stepped into the living room decorated with wine velvet-covered furniture and supported by mammoth pillars of twisted walnut rising like chocolate candy canes. Two pillars rose from the sides of a massive bench, undoubtedly hauled in from a nearby church. More steps took her up into a personal parlor opening to the west, with low ceilings, bookcases and family photographs. Mabel and Tony, as an aging couple, stared intently out from their seated positions in this room. Distinguished and self-assured, Mabel seemed to be asking, "You have a question?" In earlier photographs, she appeared less distinctive with her hair styled in a simple pageboy bobbing above loose gingham dresses that Justine remembered pleased D. H. Tony had grown quite heavy, yet his dignified, stoic face was unchanged. Justine glanced with pleasure at the Black Orchid poster by O'Keeffe above the bookcase. Then, unexpectedly, she found herself face to face with a diminutive woman of around sixty.

"May I help you?" asked the woman who introduced herself as Cheyenne. Her tanned, unadorned face showed laugh lines around her eyes and thin vertical lines above her upper lip. Vivid hazel eyes sparkled with an expression of earnest curiosity. A woman secure in herself, forthright. Approachable, thought Justine. "I'm looking for Mabel," said Justine, distracted by her own observations.

"We all are," grinned Cheyenne, "These days you'll find her in the Kit Carson Cemetery. In the meantime, make yourself at home. There's coffee, tea and muffins in the dining room."

They laughed with ease, an immediate familiarity.

"Thanks," said Justine, continuing to absorb this pleasant woman with a pencil behind her ear and a forefinger tucked into a copy of Mabel's *Winter in Taos*. "Tell me, how did you make this house look like Mabel's home again. I understand that Dennis Hopper and friends treated it quite roughly."

"You're right about Dennis. When he bought it from Mabel's estate in the early 70's, he hosted many visitors who had little regard for its history. Guests were hanging around like pigeons. I was one of them, I'm afraid. Dennis and I were quite an item for awhile."

"You knew him? You knew him well?" Justine raised an eyebrow and waited for Cheyenne to continue.

"Very well, I'd say. We did leave the house in a bit of a mess. My work here now is a form of penance." They both laughed. "However, the next owners refurbished the home and grounds for seminars on global education and the current owners host conferences and events about Mabel and her friends. So, it became Mabel's home again. Many of the books and artifacts you see here came from Dorothy Brett's home—given to us before everything was shipped off to the University of Texas. There are also a few of Frieda Lawrence's possessions that she couldn't part with. All three lived to become friends—eventually."

"Nice to have that confirmed. Women seem to have a way of working things out, don't you think? Even jealousies." Justine perused the room with fresh eyes.

"That they do," agreed Cheyenne, "although those years were not without struggles—often over little things."

"Little things?"

"Oh, like who would drive Lady Brett. Who was invited to Millicent's parties. Who was over- or under-dressed for an occasion."

"Sounds like typical squabbles."

"Just so." Cheyenne paused and glanced back toward the office. "I need to finish up a couple of things. Come with me and then we'll have tea."

The dining hall might have been a western bunkhouse in a Roy Rogers movie: heavy multi-colored vigas painted to resemble a Navajo rug, clay and black tiled floor, red plaid table cloths in a room large enough for at least sixty ranch hands. Abstract paintings of Mabel and Tony guarded the entry while muted morning light caressed lace curtains, casting streamed shadows on the adobe walls below—an ethereal set re-enacting its glorious history. Dual French doors painted turquoise opened onto the tile-studded patio beyond. Justine could imagine Mabel and D. H. arguing fiercely over fresh geraniums. Frieda slowly stirring sugar into her coffee, ready to pounce if tension turned to intimacy.

Cheyenne and Justine walked to the long serving table and helped themselves. The blueberry muffins were still warm, although there weren't other guests around to enjoy them. "This room is generous enough to hold large events," Justine observed, filling a white ceramic coffee cup, topping it off with cream, and placing a warm muffin on a napkin, recognizing once again that if she ever gave up running she'd have to give up muffins too. They settled into two high-back wooden chairs facing the corner fireplace.

"Natalie Goldberg teaches her "Writing Down the Bones" here once a year," said Cheyenne, concentrating on the blueberry muffin. "I'm trying to watch the sugar, but the cook here is merciless. In addition to Natalie," she continued, "an array of other writers come and go. Occasionally a design workshop. Tee shirts to couture. In a few weeks, we'll host a literary conference on D. H. Lawrence. And, the Taos Writing Conference has become a national event."

"It looks as though my arrival in Taos is timed just right," Justine said. "I attended Blue Lake ceremony at the Pueblo during the last two days."

"Quite a show, I understand. I had to work or I'd have been there. I heard that Tony's grandson spoke about his grandfather and the annoying white woman."

"He did. But lovingly, pointing out how helpful some of Mabel's guests had been in maintaining Taos lands and rights."

"Just so." She paused. "Tell me a little about yourself. What's your interest in the history of Mabel and friends? Are you a writer?"

"No, not really. I keep a diary from time to time. And publish articles about my work. I came to Taos to accept a job with the New Mexico Office of Archaeology. I'm an anthropologist—and a bit of a historian—interested in Native Americans and the literary world of Taos. I like to know the history, the culture, wherever I am." She had decided not to reveal her relationship to Lawrence as yet. That time would come.

"I'm surprised that you didn't choose Santa Fe—most people do, especially if their office is there."

"Understandable, but Taos history fascinates me more. I'm drawn to the Pueblo, Mabel—especially Lawrence. . . ." She let her voice trail off.

"I see," said Cheyenne simply, smiling in recognition. "I've talked with hundreds of visitors who come here to visit Lawrence. Especially the

Japanese in recent years. You'd be surprised at the number of people who live in Taos just because Lawrence is here. Or Kit Carson. Or Georgia O'Keeffe."

"Why the Japanese?"

"In the 60's there was a major obscenity trial in Japan over Lawrence's works—and of course, that set off a run on the books! What I find surprising is that fifty years later the interest still remains."

"Intriguing indeed! Why do you think Lawrence fans live here? Eighty years after his death??"

"I'm not really sure I know. We all have our reasons, yet all roads seem to lead to Taos. Art Bachrach owns the bookstore and is a Lawrence scholar. David Farmer compiled the Cambridge edition of Lawrence's *Women in Love*. Dean Stockwell played the part of Lawrence in the original *Sons and Lovers*. Dennis Hopper was buried in Ranchos De Taos this past June." Her voice trembled. She paused in her recitation.

Justine gazed at Cheyenne and waited.

After several moments, Cheyenne swallowed hard and continued. "Nearly the entire faculty of Black Mountain College came here when it closed in '56. And, then there's John Collier's grandson, Robin. He's planning a new radio station in town. I don't know Sam Richardson's story, but he will chair the Lawrence meeting. Biographers for Mabel, Frieda, and Brett come and go. Bill Haller 'met' Lawrence while in the Peace Corps in Africa. You must meet Bill; he'll tell you the story. He works at Cid's. Then there's you . . . and hundreds before you . . . as there will be hundreds more."

Justine was genuinely surprised. "The spirit of place? Lawrence thought the valley had a soul—a place where he found his own." She opened the sugar-brushed muffin, watching the steaming blueberries to ooze out.

"Well put. Yes, this place definitely has a spirit, a life force. Some say Lawrence never left. We'll go over to the pink house before you leave."

Justine raised an eyebrow. "The Pink House?"

"That's where the Lawrences lived before they got the ranch. It's now owned by a sculptor and musician."

"I'd love to see it! Why do you think Mabel really gave the ranch to the Lawrences? Hadn't she already given it to her son?"

"She gave it to her son in '23, but took it back the same year. As you can imagine, John was not happy about that, but he knew that his mother often made abrupt and arbitrary decisions that were usually part of a larger agenda. She had wanted to give it to Lawrence. To keep him close."

"But he wouldn't take it?" Justine probed.

"He didn't want to be beholden to Mabel. But Frieda had no such reservations."

"And, of course, Lawrence came with Frieda."

"As well as the idea of "community property" and the manuscript of *Sons and Lovers*."

"Do you think either of them had any idea of the value of the manuscript?" asked Justine.

"I don't. Even though Frieda behaved as though it was equal to the value of the ranch—and Mabel let her think it was—they both knew that the manuscript had nothing to do with the exchange. Or, so they say. I tend to think otherwise."

"Why?"

"I'm not really sure. . . just a feeling I have from reading Frieda's autobiography. The book is in the glass bookcase if you want to check it out."

"I'll do that. Thanks." She paused. "I understand that Mabel gave the manuscript to her psychiatrist in New York. A man named A. A. Brill."

"That's right. For a favor Brill did for a friend apparently. For several years, Mabel had gone to New York to see him and he had become a friend and confidante, as well as her psychiatrist. Yet, she clearly didn't have a grasp of the value the manuscript would claim in later years when it was purchased by U.C. Berkeley. "

So the original manuscript was in her father's school. "Perhaps you can help me with another question." She paused. "Dorothy Brett returned to the ranch before Lawrence's death. One of his letters asked her to look for old manuscripts left behind. Did she find any?"

"I don't think so, but there were rumors of a key, a strong box perhaps. I don't know what happened to that part of the story."

Justine was pensive. She watched the sunlight dance across the checkered tablecloths, rendering the lace curtains translucent. "I imagine that

Mabel resented Brett's return as well. I understand she wasn't fond of her."

"Mabel saw Brett as an intruder from the git go. There she was at every gathering, holding Toby close to Lawrence. She didn't want to miss a word."

"Toby?"

"That's what she called her hearing device, it resembled a trumpet."

Justine laughed. "That must have been most annoying! Now there were three women vying for his attention."

"At least." Cheyenne stood, picking up her coffee cup, ready to return to work.

Justine nodded and paused, gazing out the window at the gazebo and swing. She called after Cheyenne, "Do you know how to get to the Kiowa Trail?"

Cheyenne turned, "Mabel's cave?"

"Yes. Mabel's cave."

CHAPTER 7

⸺⸙⸺

J USTINE WOULD ENTER THE KIOWA trail just outside Arroyo Seco, a lazy little town of shops and cafes, boasting the best ice cream in the West. So they claimed. Following Cheyenne's rough directions to the Kiowa trail, she drove straight through town north into a '70's housing development running up the hill where she confronted a barbed wire fence barring further progress by car. From there, she would hike to the trail crossing near the floor of the infamous cliffs and cave. "Infamous" because they had served as the setting for the climactic scene in Lawrence's *The Woman Who Rode Away*. Justine had read the story soon after happening upon Lawrence's letter to Isabella saying he had used Mabel Dodge Lujan as his leading character in the story. *One of his best pieces*, she thought. *I find myself liking his short stories and poetry best. Abstract and powerful—more like a novella.* The story chronicles the sacrifice of a woman to the gods by "savage" Indians—intended perhaps as a parallel to Mabel's marriage to Tony.

The cliffs and cave loomed before her as she crested the rise. Unlike the ice-covered mountain confronted by the woman in the story—that "dazzling California girl from Berkeley" as Lawrence had called his leading character—Justine found no ice, or even flowing water. Her plan was to examine the cave, then jog to the ranch, which she estimated to be perhaps seven miles to the northwest. The Kiowa trail actually originated in Taos lands near the Pueblo, but Justine didn't feel comfortable requesting entry at that trailhead, assuming the Tribal Council would turn her down. These sacred lands, once well-trodden by sportsmen when they were part of the National Forest Service, are held inviolable unless outsiders are invited in for a ceremony or feast day. *As it should be*, she thought.

The waterfall had dried by late September, yet she could see evidence of the deep crevices into the mountain made by winter ice and a fierce spring runoff from Taos Mountain. Since snow, like rain, had been scarce this year, the land was parched and she doubted that the waterfall had been plentiful or lasted long. She checked her watch: 7:30. Sunrays caught the fragmented granite along the edge of the cliff. Cat's claw vines and clumps of grass clung to rock walls. The cliffs reminded her of the tufo mountains in western Italy where she and Amir had first made love. They were in search of an Etruscan tomb that day, but found each other instead. Her skin tingled, her body warmed by the sensuous memory.

From above, a smattering of rocks tumbled from the ledge, inches away, she jumping aside. What made them fall? She searched for a clumsy bear, a mountain lion—something less threatening.

Once again, stones crashed to the ground alongside the path. Justine cupped her hand over her brow, straining to see what had precipitated the collapsing stones. At first she saw nothing unusual; if it were a predatory animal, she had no intention of meeting it face to face. While camping in the Sierras once, she had discovered that she could outrun a bear, but she knew well enough she could not outrun a mountain lion. At any rate, she had no intention of trying.

More crumbling stones, until finally, a helpless cry. Justine searched the edge of the cliff, seeing first the teetering toes of moccasins and bare ankles, hands reaching forward, flowing black hair hanging loose. Much too close to the edge for comfort. No face nor features that could be deciphered from two hundred feet.

"Wait!" Justine yelled. "Hold on! I'm coming to get you." She didn't wait for a reply, but moved swiftly to the dry waterfall, and began to climb.

"No!" screamed the voice in return. "Please, no. Let me be."

Justine talked rapidly as she climbed. "I'm Justine. I want to meet you. Wait for me. . . ." She didn't care if her words made any sense, as long as they delayed the woman's fall. *Jump?* Her scrambling climb up the two hundred foot sheer cliff was not easy, but she found the energy that comes with urgency. Minutes later she reached the ledge, placed both hands on the grass-carpeted edge and catapulted her body to the flat rise above. She lay on her stomach for several seconds, gratefully gulping the thin air at more than eight thousand feet.

The young woman watched as though mesmerized. Was she transfixed by the stranger's presence, or heroic climb? Justine rolled on her side and stared at the young woman, sizing her up. Around fifteen or sixteen, she thought. Lovely high cheekbones that Justine had observed among the Hopis; stringy, oily black hair that looked as though it hadn't been washed in weeks. Penetrating black eyes registered a blend of terror and curiosity. They stared at one another for some moments, Justine finally breaking the silence, "What's your name?"

The teenager remained silent, her eyes flitting from side to side.

The older woman began to chatter again. "I'm Justine," she repeated, "I'm new here and living by myself south of town. I don't know Taos very well. I like to run and this seemed like a good place. My parents live in Italy. I came here to work—take a job." She paused; the girl hadn't moved. "Will you help me up?"

The young girl hesitated, then moved forward, timidly extending her hand.

Justine grabbed it, then did something spontaneous. Risky. Standing, she pulled the girl into a firm embrace. The girl started to shiver, then weep softly; the cry, finally, breaking into thunderous sobs.

Holding her firmly, Justine said, "You have to be careful up here, you could fall." The slight body convulsed further in her arms. They stood intertwined for a time, until she could feel the girl sigh, begin to still. "Can you tell me your name?" she asked again.

"Taya," the girl said in a nearly inaudible voice.

"Taya," repeated Justine, keeping her voice soft and soothing, stroking the girl's back. "Beautiful. Shall we go? Is there another way out of here? I didn't care for the climb too much."

The girl gazed at Justine with a shy half-smile. Her tear-streaked face was round and beautiful. She nodded and pointed east along the ridge.

Justine took hold of Taya's hand. Looking around to see if anything had been left, she spied a photo lying on the grass near the ledge. When she bent down, she saw a photo of a handsome young man whose ethnicity she couldn't discern. She picked it up—still holding tight to the girl's hand—and asked: "Yours?"

Taya nodded. Justine handed it over to the girl, who shoved it into her pocket. She then guided Justine east along the ledge path that led down to the Kiowa trail. When they reached the car, Justine helped her into the passenger seat, buckling the seatbelt; the girl slumping like a deflated doll, as though wanting to shrink into personal oblivion.

Justine decided to take Taya to her own home for the time being. She would figure out what to do from there. She drove back through Arroyo Seco, and continued straight at the blinking light, turning left onto Blueberry Hill, the ridge road above town. *Is this hill the source of the song by the same name*? she wondered, fascinated once again by how irrelevant trivia can unexpectedly pop into mind. The terrain was stunning. Golden cottonwoods flowed across the desert landscape dotted, with earth tone adobe homes. According to the map, this road would make a wide girth around town and come out at the Ranchos post office. It did, depositing the two women close to Highway 110 and Justine's house on Sand Storm.

—ɷ—

Justine filled her bathtub with very warm water, found a fluffy towel and sat the shampoo and soap within reach. She returned to the living room to find Taya where she'd left her, wrapped in an oversized beach towel, sitting in the reclining rocker. Her tear-streaked face gave her the appearance of a sad clown; she seemed numb. Justine practically lifted the girl out of the chair, leading her to the warm bath.

She turned away while Taya stood as though numb, then wordlessly undressed herself and climbed into the tub. At first, she stared at the slippery soap Justine handed her as though she didn't know what to do with it. Then she began to wash herself slowly.

Justine was not about to leave the room and find a drowned girl at the bottom of her tub on her return. Pulling the shower curtain across and turning away, Justine sat on the toilet stool and continued talking. "I was born in Berkeley, where my father worked. My mother was from Egypt."

"Egypt?" asked Taya, without affect.

"In North Africa—where the pyramids are. My dad was from Nebraska originally, part Lakota. Our family was happy; at least I thought so. I was an only child and my grandparents lived far away, so I didn't see them much. I missed my grandmothers," she said, remembering those fond moments in childhood when her grandmother Laurence gave her a warm bath after they had worked in the flowerbeds all day.

Taya stared at Justine from around the shower curtain, an expression of sorrow in her ebony eyes. "You must have been lonely," she said so softly that Justine struggled to hear.

"I was. Yes. I was a fat little girl too. I felt invisible. I was pretty miserable." She paused. "Thank you for understanding."

"Invisible?"

"As though I wasn't there. People would look right through me. I felt like nothing."

"Oh."

"Do you have any brothers or sisters?" Justine asked.

"Three sisters. All grown."

"No brothers?"

Taya's face darkened. She turned away, letting the shower curtain fall back into place, a wall of plastic.

Justine surmised that she did have a brother. "I actually came to Taos when I was eight," she said. "In the spring of 1989, my father brought me to one of his meetings in Taos. I saw petroglyphs in the caves along the Rio Grande rift. It was so exciting. I thought I wanted to do the same thing my dad did, look for old things—pueblos, art, pottery, people who have disappeared."

"Can a girl feel invisible just because she's a girl?" Taya's voice was flat.

"Sure, even beautiful girls like you can feel invisible. In most parts of the world, boys are considered more important, so they and others often treat girls as though they're invisible. Women have felt invisible for hundreds— thousands—of years."

"My mom and gramma don't feel that way. They're strong. They always know what to do."

"I'll bet they felt that way when they were younger."

Taya began to shiver. "I'm cold."

"Stand up," Justine told her, quickly wrapping her young guest in a large pink fluffy towel, using a second towel to swathe her hair into a turban. "Now," she said, "you look like a princess."

A flicker of amusement, appreciation moved through Taya's eyes, but didn't stay long. "Can I stay here?"

What's going on with her brother? Who's in the photo? "I don't want your family to think you've disappeared or been kidnapped."

Taya frowned, "They won't care."

Justine shook her head. "It often feels that way, doesn't it? For now, I can't let you stay unless I call your mother. While your clothes are in the dryer we'll have something to eat."

⸻

"Hello, Mrs. Acosta? This is Dr. Justine Jenner. Taya and I met when I was on a run east of town. I offered her a ride."

"East of town? Why wasn't she in school?" the woman demanded.

"Taya will need to answer that. We're both exhausted and she is a little upset. I would like to have her stay the night, if that's okay. I'll bring her home in the morning."

"Doctor, you said? Is she all right?" Her voice turned from anger to concern.

"She's fine. Just a little rumpled and tired. Taya and I were both a little lost today, so we helped one another. Her clothes are in the washer and we're going to have something to eat."

"Let me talk to my daughter."

Justine handed the phone to Taya, who grimaced at the thought of talking to her mother. "Yes. . . Okay. . . I'm fine, but I just couldn't go to school today. . . I'm sorry I didn't let you know. Mom, I'm okay!"

As she listened, Justine remembered the times she had worried her parents through her own mildly rebellious behavior, deliberately not getting home on time, disappearing occasionally. She felt a sudden wave of regret.

Taya abruptly handed the phone back to Justine. "She wants to talk to you."

"Well, okay, Dr. Jenner. Justine. I guess it's all right," said Taya's mother. Uncertain, perhaps, and clearly confused; nonetheless, she had given her permission.

"Thank you. My cell is 510-338-4343," Justine said slowly. "Call if you have any questions. Since tomorrow is Saturday, is it alright if I bring her home by ten in the morning?"

Justine turned around to find Taya standing in the kitchen. She was grinning. The towels hung loose on her head and body, turning her into a blur of pink. She looked like a seven-year old waif.

CHAPTER 8

⁓⁓⁓

TAYA SLURPED HER CHICKEN NOODLE soup as though it were a gourmet delicacy. Whenever Justine was sick or just feeling down as a child, her mother would warm up Campbell's soup and make tea. "Better than antibiotics," her mother had assured her. Justine smiled at Taya, who glanced up with a weak grin. *How delicate we are*, Justine thought. *We girls, a family unto our own.* She sat quietly, nursing her own soup, until Taya finished hers. "More?"

Taya shook her head and reached for her tea. Through the window, a deep orange ribbon lay lazily on the landscape. The sun was almost down. Where had the day gone?

Justine knew their life experiences had not been similar—yet, somehow, they were developing a kinship. *How is that so? Did gender supersede culture? Genetics? Worldviews? Female brains are hard-wired for communication and collaboration, empathy and compassion.* Yet, she knew that these attributes could smother a woman in softness if she didn't also discover her strong voice. A woman could enable victimhood if she tried too hard to please, as a consequence neglecting her own needs. She knew this all too well for she'd been down this road before.

Taya ran her hand over the sea foam quilted bedspread in the guest bedroom. Even though the sky was still barely aglow, Justine drew the shades and turned on the reading light. "It's 8:00, not too early to go to sleep," Justine suggested, tucking the blanket under the young girl's chin and sitting down on the side of the bed. "I'm tired too. I could use a good night's sleep." She paused briefly. "Who is the young man in the photo, Taya?"

Taya paused, answering hesitantly. "My boyfriend, Ricardo. He loves me, " she said as an after thought, as though it explained everything. Justine could feel the anxiety in Taya's voice, desperately wanting those simple words to be true.

"Handsome young man," Justine said, leaning forward to kiss her young guest on the forehead and smooth her hair. "Do you love him back?" Taya nodded. "We'll talk more tomorrow."

Relieved that it had been a friendly face in the photo, Justine wondered what love meant to Taya? A crush? Thoughts of her sophomore year at Berkeley High flooded her mind. *Jack Granger. I fell hard,* she mused. *I was so sure I was desperately in love, but he didn't know I was alive.* She was surprised that it still caused her heart to flutter. She turned off the reading light, picked up her Mac laptop off the desk, and returned to the kitchen to wash dishes, answer her e-mail, and then take a shower.

What does love mean to me? As the warm water massaged Justine's body, she sighed, closing her eyes, imagining Amir's fingers touching her back in the small Italian town. He'd slid into the narrow shower stall behind her, his naked body pressing against her back and buttocks. She didn't flinch as his hand reached for her breasts, the other encircling her waist, pulling her toward him. He kissed her neck and shoulders. Trembling in his grasp, she arched her back to press more fully into his body. Shampoo floated down her shoulders and onto his chest, silkened flesh sliding smoothly together. Steam surrounded them as their breathing quickened.

Justine opened her eyes and shook her head to loosen the memory, to put it away. She trembled when she let her body remember his touch. His touch had provoked her even more than his striking good looks. Amir possessed a subtle humor, a tension of desire that radiated from his body as though he was desperately attracted to her, yet held back the reins of advance, trembling on the brink of a sexual precipice. She found the anticipation palpable. The way he would tilt his head and stare at her with those compelling black eyes.

—∞—

Taya slept nearly twelve hours. Having stayed up later, Justine was still in bed at 8:00, watching prism rainbows dance across the ceiling, lounging in her memories, when she heard her guest close the bathroom door. She thought about the day ahead. At 1:30, she would meet with Mike Sandoval about their project. This morning she would take Taya home. But first, she wanted to learn more about the girl's life and motivation for attempting suicide. Might she encourage the family to agree to counseling or intervention? Would they consider such a suggestion as a violation of privacy?

Justine sat up and ran her finger along the long scar on her right leg, a souvenir from the Cairo earthquake. Throwing back her down comforter, she wore only a light nightgown since she had given Taya her flannel one. The morning air was very cold. She grabbed her velour robe, walked into the hallway and turned up the heat, nearly bumping into Taya coming out of the bathroom. "Good morning!" Justine said cheerfully, handing over the robe. "Did you sleep well? Are you hungry? How about some scrambled eggs?"

Taya shook her head mournfully. "Not much," she said, rubbing her red eyes. "Scary nightmares."

Justine wrapped Taya in the robe and gave her a gentle hug. She wanted to ask about the nightmares, but that could wait. "Your clothes are in the dryer so let's get dressed and have breakfast. Okay?"

"Okay," Taya agreed, her voice reedy and weak, nearly inaudible. Brimming with apprehension.

Half an hour later, they met in the kitchen. Justine sipping her coffee, stirring the eggs.

"May I have some?" Taya asked.

"Some?"

"Coffee," Taya clarified, sitting on the island stool.

Justine placed a small cup of coffee, cream and sugar on the island nearby, handing Taya a teaspoon and watching as she heaped three mounds of sugar into the steaming cup. Justine carried two plates of scrambled eggs, whole-wheat toast, and strawberries to the table. From the small buffet under the silver Mexican mirror, she drew out napkins and motioned Taya to join her.

Taya picked at her eggs with her fork, as though exploring strange terrain. "I don't eat breakfast much," she admitted without making eye contact.

Justine let several moments pass. "Tell me about your nightmare."

Taya's eyes clouded over. "I don't remember much. I was running after Ricardo—my boyfriend—but I couldn't catch him and a wolf was running after me. I couldn't breathe."

Justine considered the implications of such a nightmare—who was the wolf? Why was Ricardo running away? Taya clearly feared losing him. "Very frightening," she acknowledged, reaching across the table to touch the girl's small hand, "especially when you can't breathe. I have nightmares too—about when I was trapped underneath a church during an earthquake." Taya's eyes grew large. "Tell me more about Ricardo."

Taya shifted her focus to the window, then returned her gaze to Justine. "I met him at school. I go to Taos Community School. Two boys were teasing me and Ricardo made them stop."

Justine remembered hearing that TCS was the continuation school, where kids are sent who just don't fit in. "He protected you."

"He's very nice."

"Do your parents approve?"

Taya looked surprised by the question, a dark veil sinking over her face. "No. . . not now."

"Why not?"

"My brother and Ricardo had a fight. He. . . uh. . . I mean Ricardo, knocked out my brother's tooth."

"What's your brother's name?"

"Shilaw."

"And. . . ."

Shilaw was all bloody. My parents are still mad. They said I couldn't see Ricardo any more."

"Why did they fight?" They both stopped eating and watched each other closely. Justine sensed that this might prove a pivotal point in Taya's fears.

Taya grew very still, staring at her plate, as though she would find answers among the folds of her now-cold eggs.

Justine let time pass, debating whether to back off, ease the tension in the girl's face. "Tell me only if you want to."

Taya looked terrified. "I told Ricardo that I was afraid of my brother."

Justine took a deep breath. "Why are you afraid of your brother?"

Taya started to cry, moving her head back and forth, refusing to speak further.

Justine paused, watching Taya's eyes expand with fear. "Do your parents know you are afraid of your brother? Have you told them?"

"No, no. I can't tell them. Shilaw said he would hurt Ricardo if I told. Besides, it's my fault."

"What's your fault?"

"Whatever happened. . . all my fault," she began to cry. "Shilaw is a boy. He is better than me. He's preparing for the races."

Justine knew that it was not unusual for a victim, particularly a young girl to blame herself. "The races?" she decided to ask.

"For San Geronimo Day. The races. He's a man."

Justine knew of these races, but had never seen them. "I see," she said simply. She unconsciously gulped, felt a tightening in her throat.

"You can't tell, Miss Justine. Please."

Justine smiled at her reassuringly. "Taya, I wouldn't do anything to hurt you."

———

They left for the pueblo at 9:30. Justine understood Taya's motivation better now, her fears and sense of hopelessness. She was unsure how to approach the family.

"Why did you come to Taos?" Taya asked as they drove past Cañon Road and the Visitor's Center.

"I'm sure it seems strange with my family so far away, but I came here for what seemed like two reasons to me: to take a job and to find my great grand-father, D. H. Lawrence."

"Who?"

"Lawrence was a famous writer," Justine explained. "He wrote many po-ems, short stories and novels—even textbooks." She knew she would have to start at the beginning. Few young people knew of Lawrence, and the high schools seemed to avoid him. One English fellow, Mr. Shakespeare, was enough for a literary course of study. "You haven't read any of his stories in school?"

"I don't think so," Taya said. "Does he live here?"

"No, not really. He died in France eighty years ago. His ashes are buried here. At a ranch on Lobo Mountain."

Taya twisted in her seat and turned toward Justine, eyes wide, mouth open. Then she started to giggle.

"All right, smarty pants. You think I'm crazy?"

Taya nodded. "Yes!" she laughed.

"Well, let me tell you a little more. It's a story told in old love letters. I found them in a secret compartment in a trunk in my grandmother's attic in Italy. Very secret! They were written by D. H. Lawrence to my great-grand-mother, Isabella. They had a child together, my grandmother Laurence."

Taya listened attentively. "So romantic! Sounds like a movie! But he's not really *here,* Miss Justine."

Justine slowed for the Sunday traffic and grinned. "I know. . . ." At the stoplight in front of the Kachina Inn, they looked at each other and started to laugh. They couldn't seem to stop. They were still giggling when they pulled into the yard of dried grasses and golden aspen, Taya's home east of the main Pueblo plaza.

CHAPTER 9

JUSTINE EXPLAINED TO TAYA'S mother Sharon how the two of them had met, leaving out the assumption that the young girl was preparing to take her own life. As agreed, it was Taya who told her mother how sad she was and that she had wanted to hurt herself. That was all she would say, but it gave Justine an opening to ask, "Is there a counselor at the local clinic with whom Taya could talk?"

Sharon's calm doe eyes stared at Justine, appearing to understand. "I know a woman at the clinic," Sharon said, her full mouth relaxed, "my neighbor's cousin and a counselor. We might be able to see her this week." She paused and gazed at her daughter, asking no further questions.

Justine trembled at the fear in Taya's face, the look of being cornered. The young girl sat with her shoulders slumped, looking down. She wondered whether the family would seek out a counselor, but she knew well it was not her business to intrude further into Taya's family life. She said to Sharon, "If there is anything I can do, I would like to help. With your approval, I would enjoy seeing Taya from time to time. Perhaps we could go for a run after school sometime this week. I'll be in Santa Fe a few days on my new job, but I'll work it out. Would that be okay?"

Sharon looked at her daughter who nodded slightly, then she followed Justine to her car. "Let's plan to talk again soon. Please," Sharon pleaded, her hand on Justine's forearm. Then she turned and walked back into the house. Justine watched her go. Long burgundy-black hair flowed down to her thighs;

her feet touched the earth with reverence. Justine knew that Sharon was an intuitive woman, who understood and loved her daughter. *But will either of us discover why Taya fears her brother so?*

—∞—

Mike had offered to pick her up and drive her to the office in Santa Fe for her first day of work on Monday. Although she would sometimes be working at sites around Taos, and often out of her home, Justine's official office and supervisor would be in Santa Fe. As Cheyenne had suggested, she had considered getting a place in Santa Fe, but chose to be near her great grandfather's ranch and burial site. It was nearly impossible to believe that Lawrence was only in New Mexico for about sixteen months total. When she'd read his letters to Isabella there was such a strong yearning to return to the land he called home. Justine knew she'd keep searching until she deeply understood his motivations.

She had agreed to work as an unpaid intern, then, as the project took form, to write the grant that would pay her salary and provide the necessary overhead to the New Mexico Office of Archaeology. This could be a win-win situation, if somewhat risky for her, since there were no guarantees. She reminded herself that jobs were scarce, especially in anthropology and she was considered a risky investment.

Justine expected Mike around 7:30. Awake before 6:00, she grabbed a cup of coffee and reread his paper on "Community." It was nearly 7:00 when she mixed a half-cup of blueberries with Greek yogurt, eating it as she made for the shower.

Slowly Justine returned her attention to Mike's paper, trying to concentrate, realizing that he would be here before she was ready. The paper was well constructed and researched, she thought, forcing her attention into academia. The size of communities, he described, determined the governmental and living structures: the larger the group, the more subdivisions, the more complexity. The leadership was male, the governing council as well. Much like the Taos pueblo today. The study involved communities from the ancient Anasazi to the current Pueblo tribes, but no mention of what Lucinda referred to as the "Great Migration."She grabbed a towel and dried herself roughly. Not her cup of tea, this paper. It served its function well, but lacked attention to the connecting fibers that anthropologists look for in community formation, especially relationships; social dynamics, especially power struggles and gender roles. No mention of women at all. In her opinion, in a paper on community, women would be front and center. But then she knew her own feminist propensities.

Justine was especially sensitive to women's issues. Some would even think her radical. It had sometimes gotten her into deep water, especially in Egypt. But New Mexico isn't Egypt and she was older and wiser now. Her own father had once accused her of narcissism—but then he'd qualified his comment with, 'If that isn't the pot calling the kettle black. You came by it honestly, Honey.' She confessed a certain degree of self-indulgence, and a tendency to evaluate events based on how they affected her. *But that time is over, isn't it? Italy changed everything.* She stood talking to herself in the mirror, wrapped in the damp towel. Glancing at her watch tilted on the bathroom counter, she unwrapped the towel and lifted it to her dripping hair, rubbing furiously.

⸺◦∞◦⸺

Mike Sandoval was warm and gracious from the moment he knocked on the door, as though trying to gloss over his challenging comments on the first day they met. Since Justine could not see a car enter her driveway—no windows on the east side of the house—he waited inside until she found her jacket and turned out the lights and coffee pot. "Ready!" she said, and they walked silently to the car.

"Has your family been in this area a long time?" Justine asked, opening the door of his '99 Ford pickup, and placing her coat and briefcase behind the seat. She was soon to discover that one question could cause this loquacious man to talk with drama and fluidity.

The intense morning sun penetrating the windshield cast Mike as a darkened profile without distinguishable features. "A very long time," he began, the gravel in her driveway churning as he turned the pickup around. "My father's family came from Mexico through El Paso in the 1800's. They moved to the Chimayo area, to take up farming. Land was available then. Became very devout—not that he wasn't before. A good Catholic. When the miracles started to happen, my grandfather switched from farming to carving."

"Miracles?" she asked.

"The miracles of Chimayo. Quite well known. The word "Chimayo" came from a pool of water sacred to the Tewa Indians. This is a good example of what is called syncretism."

"The mixture of different beliefs," she inserted. Justine listened attentively, while watching the changing view along the Rio Grande gorge, the rushing waters carving a curving path through the land. Golden cottonwoods sparkled in the sunlight, trading posts and a few local wineries appeared from time to time. The Sangre de Cristo Mountains to the east intermittently shadowed the car from the rising sun. Thoughts of dancing landscapes—that notion that everything is interdependent—went through her mind as she listened. *When one thing changes, everything changes.*

"Christian miracles and Indian magic," Mike continued. "One and the same. Started in 1810 with the Penitents Brotherhood. It seems that a wooden cross, a crucifix, was found half buried in the earth. They tried to move it to a local church three times, but it always magically returned to its original spot. Then they got the message: there was something sacred about this place, which the Pueblo Indians had always known. One of the Brothers—Don Abeyta, as I recall, built a small shelter to house it, and that was the beginning of the legend. He was cured of something and the stories began to teach that the dirt was magic, a healing miracle."

"Is this the place where people go to eat the dirt?" Justine watched his profile closely. "I've heard of it, but doubted its existence."

"The same. The room is lined with crutches left behind by those who are healed. In 1816 a chapel was completed on the Chimayó site by Father Otocio, and it became a mission. Today you can buy the dirt, which miraculously replenishes itself." His voice adopted a sarcastic tone. "One of these days we'll drive by there on our way back from the office."

"So your grandfather took up carving. . . ." she encouraged.

"Carving sacred images. He was a Santero, a carver of Saints. He was good, but not as good as my father. Dad moved his business into Taos right after World War II." Mike fell silent.

"But his son became a scientist, an archaeologist. A skeptic," she challenged gently.

"A realist." He laughed. "Never believed in miracles myself."

Justine grinned to herself. "And your mother? Is that where you got those green eyes?"

"My mother was Italian, but that is another story." Mike barely paused before announcing the name of the working town at the end of the gorge road. "Española! I'll tell you two conflicting stories. A fierce tornado once hit this town and did three million dollars worth of improvement." He paused, only briefly, to ensure that she got the joke.

She couldn't help but laugh, yet felt a bit embarrassed for doing so.

". . . now the good story. Espanola is essential to northern New Mexico. A very reasonable place to live for those who can't afford Santa Fe, Los Alamos, Taos, and Abiquiu valley. And for the many casinos you've no doubt noticed. More of those to come, including Buffalo Thunder, one of the largest in the country. Locals find basic government services and shopping here. No frills. A fine town with reasonable people."

Justine looked at the town with new appreciation. She, too, could become judgmental of a town with so little evidence of history, of aesthetic effort. A rambling Wal Mart, corner McDonalds, small cafes, Walgreens, River Rock Casino, Radio Shack, Mexican grocery stores, many, many empty and abandoned buildings. Clearly, the economy was not booming.

They passed the Los Alamos turnoff without comment, then a few miles ahead took the off ramp into Santa Fe at St. Francis. Continuing on the road as it turned into Guadalupe and passed the Railroad plaza, he turned onto Galisteo. Still listening to Mike, Justine paid little attention to the town itself this time. They parked on the west side of the building housing the archaeology offices. She looked up to read the building's name: The Bataan Memorial Building. The former state capitol. She would have to ask him about Bataan one of these days, why the name was so ubiquitous. She gazed at Mike and nodded. She liked this man, and in spite of his prejudices and occasional rigidity, hoped to encourage him to keep an open mind. About her at least.

CHAPTER 10

⊷⊶

"WHAT IS COCONUT BLISS ice cream?" she asked no one in particular. After returning from Santa Fe, Justine stood in front of the freezer chest at Cid's, the health food store in El Prado, just north of Taos.

"All organic, made with coconut milk and agave. My favorite is Cherry Amaretto," said the tall man standing by her side. "They said you were looking for me?" A question wrapped in a statement.

Justine turned to meet this slender man with sandy hair, a baseball cap, gentle blue eyes, and serene demeanor. She couldn't help but compare his aura with the Buddhist cleric, Thich Nhat Hanh, whom she had encountered that summer in Berkeley. "Bill Haller?"

"That's me," he said. "How can I help you?"

"Well, hi. I'm very glad to finally meet you. I was told that you could help me get into the D. H. Lawrence Ranch. I understand it's closed."

"Temporarily, we hope. But if you like, I can call the University and get you in. Would Wednesday work? I'm off at 12:30."

"Perfect," she said, amazed that Bill was so helpful when he knew nothing about her. For all he knew, she could have been an ordinary tourist. *Not quite*, she mused. "I'm working at home on Wednesday. But I don't want to bother you. I could just drive out there. . . ."

"No bother. That's what I do with visitors. How did you get interested in Lawrence?" It was a simple question without any flavor of interrogation.

"We all have our stories, don't we? Let's just say I'm a fan." She gave him an enigmatic smile, which he readily accepted. She already felt that she didn't need to explain herself to Bill, which of course would prompt her to do so. Grabbing two containers of Cherry Amaretto Coconut Bliss, Justine accompanied Bill to the front of the store.

———⚬⚬⚬———

On Wednesday afternoon, Bill set two bottles of pomegranate juice in the passenger side of his old Dodge pick-up and held his own coffee mug. Justine left her Prius on the northern end of Cid's parking lot. He'd told her to dress warmly, bring a hat, and wear sturdy shoes. She had obeyed. In jeans, black sweatshirt with red lettering announcing her a San Francisco Giants fan, and her caramel-toned ponytail spilling out of her baseball cap, she looked much younger than her years. Bill appeared in his red St. Louis Cardinals tee shirt. They glanced at each other and laughed.

Driving north, they fell easily into conversation as Justine asked about Bill's story. She learned that he was from St. Louis and had lived for twenty years in San Francisco after the Peace Corps.

"So how did you come to live in Taos?"

"When I was in the Peace Corps in Africa, I ran out of things to read. A friend gave me Lawrence's *Women in Love*. It changed my life." His face was almost beatific.

"Changed your life?"

"It brought me out of my depression and taught me to love. In a way, it freed me from myself. The way Lawrence described relationships between men and women. The language he chose. It all touched me in some deep inexplicable way. Even now, I can't explain it. All I knew was that some day I had to live where he was."

"Taos," she said simply.

"Taos."

Justine was so moved by Bill's story that for a time she didn't speak. They rode in silence. Leaving El Prado they traveled west along Highway 128 toward Hondo. "Mine is a love story too," she began. "A story that began in 1927."

Bill shot an unbelieving glance at her. "1927?"

She tilted her head, watching him closely and explained about her great-grandmother, her relationship with Lawrence. Italy. She paused, unscrewed the cap on the pomegranate juice, and took a drink, letting the pungent taste sit on her tongue for a few moments. "She became his friend during the last three years of his life. And his lover. They saw each other infrequently; his letters tell the story. "

"Are you sure? I know nothing about this." Bill's skin turned a shade of grayish white. His muscles tightened around his eyes and mouth. He was stunned.

"There are letters. I have them with me. In his last letter to her he speaks of the child, who was my grandmother. She was named Laurence."

"We turn here," he said quietly, as though he was entering a sacred place. Unspoken thoughts appeared to wrinkle his forehead, he pulled onto the road near the Lawrence Ranch and remained quiet as the paved corridor gave way to a rough, gravel road leading straight uphill to a locked fence.

CHAPTER 11

⟨⟨⟨

JUSTINE SAT ON A BENCH in the Bent Street Plaza awaiting Mike and a surprise guest, someone he wanted her to meet. She stared across the street at the Bent House Museum, the home of Charles Bent, the first governor of the New Mexico territory. History tells that Bent was appointed governor in 1846 and murdered during an insurrection the next year. He was captured, killed, and scalped in front of his wife and children. U.S. troops took vengeance, shelling the Catholic Church at Taos Pueblo and killing more than a hundred Indians who sought sanctuary inside. Justine shivered as she recalled the heartbreaking history of Anglos, Hispanics, and Indians in this troubled time.

She became aware that Mike was standing near her, although she could only detect his outline framed by sunlight and see that another man had come along. She rose to greet them. "Justine, meet Pablo. He's with the Bureau of Land Management. An old archaeologist, like me," said Mike.

Pablo was at least six foot five. *A giant teddy bear.* At five eight, Justine came only to his shoulders. A slight breeze ruffled her hair like slender plant tentacles, blowing it into her open mouth; she tucked it behind her ear as they walked toward the tall white coyote cutout lurking under the Bent Street Deli and Café sign. The lascivious canine held a board announcing the day's lunch specials.

Inside, orange, yellow, and turquoise chairs hung from towering rafters across from a mammoth blackboard announcing wine and beer specials. A large painting of a stately Holstein cow signaled the homey character of this local gathering hub. The waitress quickly recognized Justine, picked up a third menu, and led them through the café's glassed-in porch into the patio. "I've asked for an outside table," she said. The three maneuvered among uneven flagstones, finding chairs around a stone table shaded by a green canvas umbrella.

"I brought Pablo along because he and his kids do a lot of local field work. And he works with Severn in the early summer. You know, the man from Columbia University I told you about. Thought he might be helpful," said Mike. "This big guy is retiring soon but that won't mean anything. . . can't keep him out of the field. Right, Pablo?"

"Right," mumbled Pablo, staring at the menu. He grinned slightly, clearly expecting to say little at this gathering. He'd come along for lunch. And to meet Justine.

Justine observed the new acquaintance and ordered the spinach quiche. Both men asked for burgers and sweet potato fries. "Tell me about some of your projects near Taos," she asked of Pablo.

Mike started to answer for him, and Justine gave him a quick glance that arrested him before he began.

Pablo couldn't miss the gesture. He looked mildly surprised, as though saying 'How could she know Mike so well already?' His beard and graying mop of hair moved softly in the breeze. "Well, over the years I've worked with hundreds of middle and high school kids. We look for petroglyphs—the technology for recording and categorizing has become very advanced. They catch on real quick," he said, his eyes tearing up, "I'm proud of the kids. They inspire me."

"Super project!" interjected Mike. "Been out myself a few times. Smart kids...."

"Next week, I'm meeting a group of fifty seventh graders from Santa Fe at the Hupobi site near Ojo Caliente," explained Pablo. "You could join us if you want."

"I'd love to," Justine grinned, blinking with pleasure as she realized that Pablo reminded her of Gary Cooper. Style rather than looks. She paused and turned to Mike. "Would that work for our schedule?"

"I supposed so. . .sure," said Mike. "We'll be in Santa Fe at the first of the week, then I'll be working on a report at home. So sure. Pablo claims it's bigger than Pueblo Bonito at Chaco, but I have my doubts. Been there a couple of times myself."

"He doesn't want to admit it, but it's amazing," said Pablo, his eyes sparkling like a kid with a new bike. "Huge kiva, plaza outline, pottery sherds everywhere, evidence of dry farming. Deep river valley below."

"Pablo has outlandish theories. Pure speculation. I say, 'Show me the evidence. Just show me the evidence,'" said Mike. "My friend here has quite an imagination."

"Mike requires a sworn affidavit from God," teased Pablo. "Too hard to please. *No* imagination, if you ask me."

Justine was having a grand time. Clearly these men had a long and tangled history of mutual respect and affection—taking pleasure in poking fun at each other. "What theories, Pablo?" she urged. "What are your speculations about this Hupobi site?"

"Whoa..." interrupted Mike. "Wait 'til you get there and judge for yourself. I think you'll support my skepticism. No real evidence to support this old coot's ideas."

Pablo nodded and held up both hands, palms out. "Okay, Justine. We'll wait. Meet me at the Bureau offices at eight on the third. Turn east at Walgreens and go past the Kit Carson Electric offices. Can't miss it. BLM."

—⊶∞⊷—

Later that evening, Justine arrived at the Taos Community Theater for the viewing of *Easy Rider*, a 1969 film introduced to her by her father before she was sixteen. She hadn't understood it then; she couldn't feel the cultural impact others around her felt. Now, seemingly a lifetime later, she would try again. *Easy Rider* brought Dennis Hopper, Jack Nicholson and Peter Fonda to Taos in the late 60's, their characters feverishly moving through disjointed lives on motorcycles, drugs, and frenetic music, seeking undefined freedoms. The counter culture film energized the "hippie" movement in New Mexico by creating an array of communes in the Sangre de Cristo Mountains where dropouts raised goats for milk and cheese and planted alfalfa while temporarily steering the art community into psychedelic media. All of which raised local ire. Hopper purchased Mabel Dodge Luhan's home, and established what he considered the heart of the movement, drawing visitors from the hills above.

Justine had been advised that getting a ticket for *Easy Rider* would be a problem, and yet she had made no effort to secure one ahead of time. Starting a new job, getting settled into an unfamiliar place—and Taya—had kept her incredibly busy. She parked in the lot adjacent to Kit Carson Park and headed for the concrete terrace that ran the length of the theater, surprised to find that the terrace mosaics could have been painted during Hopper's era. More Hindu than American Indian, with the exception of the Masonic emblem on the far left.

Justine's eyes found those of a slender woman with curly black hair and pixie face with freckles. Playful eyes and a classic Romanesque nose in a devilish elf-like face. *Italian? Jewish? Russian?* Her denim skirt and flowered blouse under a short western vest bespoke the blended Southwest style of Taos that Justine was beginning to admire. Giovanna Paponetti stepped forward and introduced herself, handing Justine a flyer, an announcement for a book talk at the Moby Dickens Bookstore on Saturday for *Kateri, Native American Saint: The Life and Miracles of Kateri Tekakwitha.*

"Who's Saint Kateri?" asked Justine without formalities.

"Kateri Tekakwitha isn't really a saint –not yet," Giovanna answered, "but she has a chance to be the first real Native American saint. She was beatified thirty years ago and is now awaiting the Pope's approval of a recent miracle in order to be canonized. We are hopeful."

"Remarkable," said Justine, "I had no idea. I'd love to know more about Kateri—I'll be at the book talk. Now if you will excuse me, I'd better get a ticket before they're all gone."

Giovanna grinned. "Actually, that's the real reason I was standing here. I have an extra ticket," she said, digging it out of her purse and handing it to Justine.

"Thanks," said Justine, claiming the ticket as she drew a ten-dollar bill from her wallet. She looked up to see a vanishing Giovanna walking rapidly toward the park.

Justine entered the crowded theater and found a single seat near the center just as Cheyenne, the woman she'd met at Mable Dodge Luhan's home, climbed the stairs onto the massive stage and stepped to the lectern. Apparently, there was no need to introduce herself; Justine would later learn that Cheyenne served on the community theater program committee.

"Since the death and burial of Dennis Hopper in Ranchos de Taos in June," Cheyenne began, "our community has honored our friend and resident 'bad boy' who directed and starred in the film, *Easy Rider*. Like myself, many of you in this audience are old enough to remember the feeling we had when we first saw this provocative movie. Personally, I felt camaraderie and shock; fascination and aversion; a desire to be a part of such a counter-culture rebellion, and yet a real fear of doing so. I was devastated and alarmed by the ending. Many of us felt as though voice was being given to a deep sense of disquiet in the shadow of the Viet Nam war and a decade of tragedy as well as liberation. Tonight we will revisit Dennis and his friends in the most famous film of his career. Thank you for coming and please stay for the conversation at the end of the showing."

Lawrence and Hopper, Taos' bad boys, she thought. At sixteen, Justine had been bored by the film, but now she blinked in anticipation and settled back in her chair. Her dad had tried to explain it to her, but she just couldn't feel it in her personal ethos. Born in 1980, she'd had her own iconic films—*Thelma and Louise, Pulp Fiction, Wag the Dog*—and generational struggles. Her paternal grandmother, Grace, spoke of Ozzie and Harriet, Doris Day, and the confinement of the '50's, the liberation of the '60's—then the assassinations of two Kennedys and Martin Luther King shook the world.

Justine never had a love affair with government, unlike her parents who had come of age in the days of Kennedy and the race to the moon; the Cold War and Iron Curtain held only intellectual, rather than emotional, currency for her. Clinton's high tech boom and Bush's wars of choice didn't quite do it either, although 9/11 did bring her face to face with the failures of 20th century foreign policy. At the University of Chicago, interpreting history through a cultural lens, she began to understand how human behavior was shaped. How culture, environment and genetics conspired to create the humans we study. Whether in Berkeley, Chicago, Egypt, Italy or New Mexico, similar factors were in play.

Tonight, *Easy Rider* took on new meaning, ironically becoming a metaphor for the clash of cultures that still existed in Taos, although more peaceably now. Parallel lives. Strangers to each other. Indian and Chicano, Spanish and Anglo, farmer and artist, Taoseño and others, all negotiating their own spaces and roles. Many cultural territories, often overlapping, but infrequently corresponding. If the community ever united, it wouldn't be an easy ride.

CHAPTER 12

———

"**R**UN LIKE A WILD MUSTANG," Justine told Taya. "Be a mustang." The two women stood on the edge of the raw desert west of the Casino. A tangerine-tinted sky cradled the setting sun, a chill swept the barren soil. "Hey, wait for me," she called as Taya took off, her black mane streaming away from her shoulders.

Already in flight, Taya couldn't hear her. To the north, the sacred Taos Mountain towered above the desert in undulating hues of lavender.

But Justine soon caught up with the younger woman. They didn't speak, running side-by-side, Taya's moccasins a blur. *She's a natural*, Justine realized.

After a couple of miles Taya's breath became more pronounced; she stopped abruptly, slumping onto the cooling ground. "Look, I can hardly see the pueblo! I can't believe how far we've come!" cried Taya, stretching her slim legs out in front of her. She giggled. "Indians run all the time, but not just for fun! We women dance. Our dancing prepares the earth to receive the seeds. Very important."

"I find that fascinating. Women preparing the earth, waking it up to grow."

Taya nodded, her chin moving slightly upward. "Why do you run?"

"Well. . . " Justine began. "Many reasons. Running is like a quest. When the endorphins in my brain are released, I see things more clearly, feel a sense of well being, lightness. I feel good."

"But I hurt all over. That's good?" Taya raised an eyebrow in a disbelieving stare.

"Ah, good. Yes. The hurt will pass. And the more we run, the more we feel our beautiful selves. Your body will lose its stiffness and you'll get a sensation of inner strength. Confidence in yourself."

"I'd like to feel stronger! But I'm not comfortable talking to people, telling them what I think. What I want."

"Do you always feel like that?"

"At home. At school. When I'm with Ricardo."

"Whew. . . ." Justine released her breath slowly. "Lots to talk about. But for now, we'd better run back; it's almost dark. Can you make it?" She extended a hand to Taya who gratefully grasped it, then took off, a graceful young filly running into the night.

Justine met Lucinda at Elevation, a popular coffee house in El Prado. She had so many questions, yet didn't want to shape the conversation; she had learned by trial and error that the natural flow of genuine interaction was the best way to learn what she wanted to know. *In fact, humans construct themselves through relationships.* When she'd first met Lucinda at Blue Lake celebration, she'd experienced an immediate connection that would eventually transcend mere acquaintance. Today, she hoped to learn more about this Tiwa woman and share herself as well.

In truth, she also yearned to make sense of her own spirituality, such as it was—or wasn't. Justine had never been traditionally religious. If anything, her studies in anthropology had led her further away from religion, casting its claims as mythology and metaphor, yet opening the door for spirituality. *Woman, you are full of contradictions!* She convinced herself that she had no intention of guiding this conversation.

Like her mother's family, Justine had been drawn to Epicureanism, but her father was raised in a Midwestern Methodist church, occasionally attending a Unitarian service. Some of her friends and lovers insisted that Epicureanism meant pleasure, indulgence. For her it meant balance, happiness, avoidance of fear of death and whimsical gods. Yet, too, she felt a profound respect for friends in Egypt and Italy who seemed to find wholeness in faith. She was spiritually hungry and wanted to find what Lawrence found here. Admittedly, she hadn't yet been significantly tested, although life had been challenging in recent years. And she wasn't sure that her interest in spirituality wasn't more academic than personal. *I do tend to intellectualize.*

Lucinda smiled broadly as she saw Justine in the back of the room. Stopping by the counter to order a cup of Elevation's tempting brew, she walked to the table, placing her notebook and computer on a chair, gave Justine a hug, then moved across the room with the aplomb of a dancer. Short and stocky, her black hair flowed down her back and moved in rhythm with her stride.

So like Taya's mother.

"I hope you're feeling welcome in Taos," Lucinda offered with a smile, seating herself across from Justine. Her clear, mocha skin and wide-set eyes made her seem timeless. "You said that you're an anthropologist."

Justine thought she detected a suspicious tone. Amir was initially suspicious of her when they met in Cairo. He called anthropologists arrogant, condescending, thinking they knew all about cultures other than their own "Yes, I'm an anthropologist," Justine said gently. "My work will be out of the Santa Fe Anthropology office, primarily with archaeologists. I'll be working with a few colleagues to map out some new sites of petroglyphs on private lands and help create a new project on defining community. I'll be listening a lot, learning about cultures here. I try to come without preconceived notions." "That must be hard," Lucinda grinned, as though realizing she'd been more transparent than she wanted. She paused, "Defining community? I would have thought that community was a well-established idea."

Justine studied Lucinda for a few moments. "So true," she grinned. "Community is a well-established concept in your eyes and mine. Of course, as an anthropologist, I've studied communities for years—and you live in one. We understand that reciprocity holds communities together. Archaeologists claim a different challenge."

"Different how?" asked Lucinda.

"Well, since they don't study living communities, they must find artifacts and structures that tell a story about how communities were formed and operated at the time. Evidence that they can accept—that's sometimes the dilemma."

"Do you think they'll ever ask us? Ask my people. Ask you?"

Justine laughed fully and Lucinda joined in. They gazed into one another's eyes as they laughed, sensing the beginning of a friendship. Laughter was like that—it opened the mind and body to bonding.

Justine relaxed as she pushed back into her slender wooden chair. She wasn't really sure whether her colleagues planned to ask the original peoples for their histories and thoughts, but she suspected that Mike didn't plan to do so. This will be an uphill battle. "Lucinda, the day we met you mentioned the Great Migration. What migration were you referring to?"

Lucinda paused and stared into her coffee.

Justine waited patiently, then, "If this is a secret, please tell me so."

"The truth is woven among secrets. I am pulling them apart." She grinned and continued, "Our people say that very long ago the sun began to drink our water. Not the great lake from which we came, but the moisture in Mother Earth. Crops died, our people of the northwest became parched. This misfortune did not visit the Red Willow peoples of our Pueblo, but our neighbors began to move. They came to the peoples of Santa Clara, Ohkay Owingeh, Tesuque, our own Taos. They were gentle and adopted our ways. That is the story."

"Does that include the peoples of Mesa Verde?"

"Mesa Verde. Yes."

"I see. You must be aware that this is provocative information. The disappearance of the peoples of Mesa Verde is still one of the great mysteries in archaeology. I wonder why."

Lucinda just laughed. "That's because no one listened to us, so we stop telling the story. We don't say much to the other side of the world anyway, although we are always ready to remember what our ancestors told us."

Justine studied Lucinda thoughtfully, narrowing her eyes. "Well phrased. More coffee?" Justine knew the stubbornness of archaeologists surrounding Mesa Verde. No baggage, they contend, no physical evidence that the peoples of the north ever migrated here. No pottery, rituals, structures that would convince a scientist that major tribes had moved into the area. She didn't yet know what the local conflicts were. She took both coffee cups, returned to the counter, and asked for refills.

When she returned to the table, Lucinda challenged her. "You're not sure what to believe either?"

Justine tilted her head in a half smile. "Being able to work in this area—and keeping an open mind—will make me ripe for new discovery. I look forward to the challenge." She paused and Lucinda grinned back. "By the way, do you know of Kateri?"

"Sure." Lucinda blinked. "Our Native American Saint. Many miracles. My aunt was very sick, ready to die, and then she put a picture of Kateri under her pillow and prayed. She was well in two days. The doctors couldn't explain it. Faith is powerful."

"No wonder she's a saint to the Tiwa."

"Not only Tiwa. Kateri is a saint to all Indians. We don't need to wait for the Pope to tell us she's a saint. I'm not a strong Catholic, but I'm a believer."

"What makes her a saint? Did she perform miracles during her short life?"

"Many miracles upon her death. Kateri was horribly scarred by smallpox, yet when she died, the pox marks immediately disappeared. She was beautiful. And the blue blanket she was wrapped in was used to heal many. Many others reported healings."

"I see. And Giovanna. Do you know her as well? We just met last night."

"Of course I know her. Good friend to our family. She made paintings of Kateri's tribe by going to Canada and finding real models. She designed and created the art for an altar screen in Ohkay Owingeh—that's where my daughter lives. You know it?"

"The old San Juan Pueblo?"

"The same—they threw off the Spanish name and returned to their original selves."

"I see. Bold."

"Well, Ohkay Owingeh means 'land of strong people.' Is that what you mean by bold? Strong?" She paused.

"I suggested 'bold' because Ohkay Owingeh seems to be among the first to reject the Spanish heritage, to take the lead."

"Well, they've rejected the name. In many ways, we chose to blend cultures—a pragmatic approach. St. Jerome, San Geronimo. One and the same, but originating from quite different cultures. We are no longer one or the other." Lucinda gave her a patient smile, as though she was observing a plant blooming in front of her.

Justine regarded Lucinda's playful eyes. *Those dancing eyes are reading me like a book.* Rarely so transparent, Justine temporarily felt a wave of discomfort, then relaxed into silence. Moments passed. Eventually, she nodded and asked, "Do your people still have tribal healers?"

Lucinda paused and took a sip of her still warm coffee. "That's a sad story," she began. "My grandfather was a healer, a very good one, but the tribe began to ostracize him, began to lose respect. You see, healers are no longer seen as useful. Indians are now drawn to Anglo medicine."

Justine was surprised once again. "Really?"

"For us, everything comes in fours. . .four seasons, always in balance. . . ."

"The four directions. . . east, south, west, and north. . . a lovely balance," Justine added in verbal rhythm and smiled.

Lucinda nodded. "And when someone dies we spend four days with them. We talk and eat and pray and grieve with our dead family member," she explained. "This is how we do things."

"How does the adherence to fours relate to healers and western medicine? I don't understand."

"Our people found that antibiotics could often cure our children in four days—healers cannot. Sadly, we too have entered modern times. But at what cost?"

"At what cost indeed. Your people must be concerned about losing their ways, voluntarily relinquishing their powers to the white man."

"Ironic, isn't it? We fought for so long and lost so much, only to willingly give up more of our ways."

"Yet, your efforts to regain the Sacred Mountain and Blue Lake must inspire your confidence, keep you strong."

Lucinda's lips curled into a grin. "That was forty years ago and we still ride on that achievement. But we are strong, especially our women. We are a private people who hold onto the past and its many secrets. Our language and rituals, our beliefs. Unlike the Hopi, we have not been told that we may share our ways."

Justine raised an eyebrow. She knew the Hopi had been given such permission to share their philosophy, for the Hopi ways are written about and taught. The Elevation was filling up. Middle-aged women with open computers, pairs of men in dungarees deep in conversation. A young Hispanic mother with a stroller full of wriggling twins. One man in a suit and tie sipping a frothy cappuccino. For the first time, Justine saw Anglos, Indians and Hispanics going about their day in the same room. She grinned to herself. *And coffee shall bring us together.* "I respect your secrets," she acknowledged, returning Lucinda's gaze.

"That doesn't mean that I can't share my personal thoughts and ways, only that I can't share the ways of the Tiwa." Lucinda opened another door.

"Spiritually, I'm a seeker," Justine said, taking quick advantage of the offer. "Our family has few common beliefs and I'm not a member of any organized religion, but I do yearn to define my own spirituality." She paused, searching for the right words, but decided to ask directly. "What guides you?"

Lucinda didn't hesitate. "When I die I will join the great spirit world with my ancestors. For now, I have my guides—some would call them angels—who are with me, who make me feel safe and help me take the right paths."

"What's that like?" pressed Justine. "Do you see your guides?"

"I don't see them. It's more like a presence, a reassuring warmth. As though they are standing near my shoulder. I never feel alone," Lucinda said, a beatific gaze enveloping her face.

"How do you know when they are with you?" Justine experienced a rush of indistinguishable emotions: attraction, skepticism, curiosity, envy. *Could I ever allow myself to believe in guides?*

"They are always with me, Justine." A warm affection radiated from her eyes, embracing her young friend once more. "Would you like to come to my home on San Geronimo Day," she asked. "We invite our friends."

CHAPTER 13

TODAY, JUSTINE WOULD RETURN to the Lawrence Ranch alone. Once she left the paved road running half-way up the mountain, her low-slung Prius occasionally scraped on the ridges rising parallel to deep ruts. Justine flinched, pondering whether she should have invested in a mini-SUV. Spindly trees leaned across sagging barbed-wired fences; irises and lilies struggling to outlast their season, mingling among jersey cows and an occasional mare. Her lungs told her she was climbing, reaching nearly nine thousand feet at the ranch. She drove through the gate left open for her arrival, continued upward another quarter mile and parked in front of the big house, built for Frieda by her Italian partner in the early '30's.

Nico, a short Hispanic man, with a barely discernable chin, graciously welcomed her. Admittance had to be secured through the Maintenance Department at the University of New Mexico in Albuquerque. Bill Haller had made the call. On her first visit Bill had accompanied her and given her a first class tour. *Such a generous man,* she thought. She was moved by Bill's story of discovering his capacity to love in Lawrence's *Women in Love.*

Justine could imagine her great-grandfather standing just where she now stood on this ranch, observing this magnificent, fierce morning, a vast landscape in shades of muted rose for as far as he could see. In front of her now, his tan adobe cabin, turquoise window frames, and a tin roof from which the heavy winter snows would slide off, keeping it from collapsing from the weight. The majestic Ponderosa pine, "Lawrence's Tree," as Georgia

O'Keeffe had named it, towered over the meager yard. O'Keeffe and Lawrence had met only once, at a dinner party in New York in 1925 on his way back to Europe. She had been captivated by him, his spirit, which Justine sensed most markedly here at the ranch. *It was difficult to know either of them*, she admitted. *Such internal people, alone in their talents, somewhat out of sync with the world. Ahead of their times? Outside of time? The world has come to understand and appreciate their art, but rarely the artist within. Perhaps they preferred it that way. Mysterious, even incomprehensible.*

Turning southeast, Justine stared beyond the thin wooden sheep fence at pockets of mist snuggling into the lush contours of the land. Rivers of aspen flowing like honey down the encircling mountains. The air was chilly. *Why did he refer to the mornings here as fierce?* she wondered. *Ferocious, wild, untamed, no doubt. Natural. But, too, didn't the thin air sting his delicate lungs? Lawrence yearned for the untamed in nature and in friends and lovers, a reflection of his own ferocity. Am I ferocious? Untamed? I hope so. As much as my upbringing and experiences will allow. I strive to be mysterious, yet trusted. Can I be both?*

Years after Lawrence died, Frieda bequeathed the ranch to the university in her will. For many years it was used for writing retreats and gatherings around issues of the day. Neglected in recent years, the property was in poor condition, although clean up appeared to be underway. A huge flatbed truck half loaded with debris was backed into the yard: rusted machinery, coils of wire, broken toilet bowls. To the west of Lawrence's cabin sat the miniature doll-like house that had been Lady Brett's home, and to the northwest a dilapidated barn, barely standing, that must have housed their horses and Susan, the beloved Jersey cow.

University personnel claimed the closure was related to the hantavirus, a treacherous lung disease caused by the feces of local mice. Board members of the Taos-based Friends of D. H. Lawrence and the Taos Community Foundation had their doubts. Tensions had developed between the university and those interested in having Lawrence's home available to his admiring public. Visitors came from all over the world, especially Japan and England, and when formal tours were offered, hundreds flocked to the revered site. Even though the ranch was closed, names kept appearing on the sign-up roster in the chapel. Unfazed by the locked gate, visitors hiked the mountain to pay their respects. For the University, the ranch was a low priority, silently competing with more vocal demands on limited resources. This was not an age of preservation for the university, but survival. Yet, the institution consistently refused to carry out the intent of Frieda's will as Justine understood it. Surely there was a recourse.

Justine stepped onto the porch of Lawrence's cabin and rattled the wobbly knob unlocked for her by Nico. In the entryway, she was met by a large poster of Georgia O'Keeffe's "Poppy" hanging in front of the kitchen of peeling pine wooden cabinets and a rusting sink. Wooden plank floors creaked under her buckskin boots. She turned right to enter the living area with a stone fireplace painted white, its bay window opening onto Lawrence's massive pine, the majestic view beyond. Her eyes wandered across the plastered walls and shredded curtains, a wobbly table and chairs much like the ones in the Pink House. The lone bedroom hosted two single beds, far from one another, covered with thin blankets. Cracking white paint turned the cupboard into a road map. She imagined Lorenzo—as others called him—and Frieda ensnared in each other's bodies, crowded into one of the twin beds, fiercely making love, he with his face snuggled into her full breasts. Frieda claimed that their lovemaking was no longer possible toward the end of his life. *But how about here? In late '23? Whatever Lawrence found on this mountain reawakened his desires, enabling him to consummate his love with Isabella.*

Isabella, that fiery Egyptian woman who captured Lawrence's sensibilities and sympathies in Italy, enabling him to burst forth in a torrent of creativity. Unique in character, never needy nor demanding, she shaped a space between them, mutually occupied in pleasure and imagination. Isabella was his muse.

Justine felt a tremor of her own desire. She could feel Amir's hands searching her body. She turned away. The burden of desire was more than she wanted to encounter right now.

Justine stepped back into the living room area, forcing her mind to clinically survey the non-descript chamber. Someone apparently went wild in here with white paint, *When would that have been?* It was difficult to determine whether these skimpy furnishings and hapless efforts at decor were left from the writing retreats of the 60's and 70's, or the Lawrences. Probably the former.

Returning to the alabaster fireplace, she placed both hands on the mantelpiece and leaned forward, stretching her back muscles while reflecting on the lives of those who had given so much meaning to this bare, rustic cabin. Ghosts creaked the floorboards, loud and boisterous, leaving the lingering fragrance of Frieda's perfume. Tensions of arguments were still palpable, as well as the pleasured screams of competitive charades and singing. Then, her eyes caught sight of an even, rectangular incision notched on either side, carved into the cement hearth. Odd, she hadn't noticed it before. *A hiding place?? For what? Frieda's jewels? Precious documents? Manuscripts?* In one of his letters to Brett, Lawrence asked her to scour the property for remaining manuscripts. This cement cutout was so obvious that surely it was searched long ago. Even so, adrenalin surged through her body as she scanned the room for some sort of lever to pry it open. Finding none, Justine returned to the clean-up site to look for a crowbar, running into two workers chatting near a toolbox.

"May I ask a question?" she interrupted. The two men stopped talking. Her gaze was drawn to the stubby hands of the man whom Nico introduced as Jack.

"You a writer?" Jack interjected, shoving his hands into his pockets.

Justine smiled, "Not really" she said. "Well. . . sometimes." She didn't want to go there. Not when she was newly obsessed with a mystery.

"I write," said Jack, a smile washing across his unshaven face.

"That's good," she replied in an encouraging voice. Turning to Nico, "Has anyone pried open the cement plate in front of the fireplace in Lawrence's cabin?" She kept her voice casual, flat.

The two men looked at each other, puzzled at first, then Nico pulled at his non-existent chin. "I haven't, but it was probably opened years ago. Who knows?" His lack of interest was overt; he turned away, ready to continue his conversation with Jack. No doubt he was weary of visitors full of curiosities, questions he'd heard many times before.

"I see," Justine said, pausing to stare at the ground near her feet. "Thanks for your help," she said, smiling and shaking hands with Nico. Jack kept his hands in his pockets, but nodded repeatedly. "I'll be going now. But I'll be back."

CHAPTER 14

⌘

As she walked toward her car, Justine glanced back at the barn that had housed his cow, Susan, and imagined Lawrence and Brett, a strange relationship indeed.

APRIL, 1924, THE LAWRENCE RANCH (AKA THE KIOWA RANCH)

Still cold in the early mornings, Lawrence slipped on his jacket and gloves and set out for the barn, collecting Brett from her cabin as he went. She had taken the time to slip on her boots, chaps and ten-gallon hat, the look she savored ever since attending the Buffalo Bill Wild West show in England as a child. It had turned cold on the mountain, but he was used to severe weather in Europe and knew it would get worse when the snows came. Susan lazily turned her head as the two arrived. Revealing neither surprise nor expectation, she returned to munching hay while the man patted her damp nose and pulled up a small stool near her veined, full utter. Patting her flank, "How are you today, Susan?" he asked, with a respect reserved for animals and small children. "Decided not to run away this morning?" Susan had made a habit of wandering down the road to the Hawk ranch.

Brett sat on a hay bale nearby so that she could gaze directly at her old friend. "Does she answer you, Lorenzo?" she inquired irreverently, cold fingers grasping the chilled metal of her hearing trumpet. "You'd think she was a better friend than me." Brett's voice was uncharacteristically petulant this morning.

"She knows who takes care of her," Lawrence answered, looking directly at Brett, immediately sensing the testiness. "And she knows who she is. A cow. No need to feign affection or indignation." He became silent as his hands found their rhythm and milk spurted melodically into the dented metal bucket, his facial expression meditative. Then, "What's going on with you this morning, Brett? You look glum."

"After last night, Frieda is angry with me again."

"You shouldn't have taken my side. It upsets her."

"But you asked me too! You said, 'What do you think, Brett? Do you think Frieda is being unfair?' You wanted me to side with you. You always do."

"I'm not responsible for what happens between you and Frieda, Brett. Don't put it on me."

Brett remained quiet as she always did when his argument didn't make sense. Or when he was enraged. Exasperated all the same, she knew their friendship depended on her calibration of his moods, a powerful role that Frieda understandably resented. "I'm going to paint today," she declared flatly.

"We'll paint," he confirmed, viscerally aware of the cadenced change in their talk. It amused him. "I've to finish my landscape."

CHAPTER 15

‑‑‑◈‑‑‑

J USTINE DROVE HER NOW grimy vehicle down the mountain toward the entrance gate and pondered what she knew of the relationship between Lawrence and Brett, in whom he clearly felt a rare trust. Brett's memoir of her relationship with Lawrence described an awkward attempt to make love. Lawrence could be a generous protector of wounded animals and children; he even paid for the surgery to correct a hair lip on a child in Italy. She assumed that Brett's hearing handicap accounted for some of the empathy he felt for her. Yet, even as deep as his relationship was with Brett, why had he needed to alert Isabella to his trust in Brett in the ending paragraph of his last letter? Was this a signal for some action he expected Isabella to take? And, did she? Justine felt compelled to find out. Surely there was more than is known—yet Brett's papers housed at the University of Texas make no mention of Justine's great-grandmother, Isabella Hassouna. Nor does Brett's autobiographical account of her friendship with Lawrence. And the writings of Huxley and Brewster, the two men who would have known if he had an Italian lover, were silent on that account. Yet she knew that these were the men who could be trusted to conceal any information that he didn't want made public. If Lawrence were determined to keep his relationship with Isabella a secret, it was undoubtedly his desire to protect her. *After all, in the Egyptian culture an illicit affair could be catastrophic. Yet, how could such secrets be protected for so long?*

Justine didn't find it surprising that Frieda resented Brett, although there were accounts of friendship between the two women when they were alone together, laughing together as women, shopping in the markets, preparing food. Seemingly, it was Lawrence who poisoned the mix, with his occasional fits of outrage and the jealousy he provoked from both women. It had all come to a head in Mexico when Frieda was finally fed up with Brett's constant presence and defense of Lawrence, her taking sides against Frieda. The blasting fights finally forced Brett to travel alone from Oaxaca back to the Hawk family ranch in New Mexico, where she was given a cabin to stay in until the Lawrences returned. *After being rejected so, sent away, why hadn't she gone home to England? I would have. I did, didn't I?* she thought, recalling her return to her mother's home in Italy after she was expelled from Egypt.

CHAPTER 16

⸙

SEPTEMBER 30, 2010, SAN GERONIMO DAY, TAOS PUEBLO

FIFTY BAREFOOTED RUNNERS stepped up to the starting line, the men behind them rubbing their backs with feathers to help them fly. Runner bodies were white and clay-colored with paint, their brightly decorated loincloths of red velvet, blue and purple satin, and flowered rayon. Eagle down spread across their chests running up into their hair. They whooped and yelped—women trilled—each new runner took the place of one returning to cross the branches marking the finish line. One small boy tripped and fell as he sprinted out, but regained his footing and continued, an expression of humiliation flashing across his young face. Runners began in a fast sprint, but returned slowly, some walking the last few yards.

By 7:00 a.m. Justine was situated at the base of the five-story pueblo towering alongside the bower near the starting line. The chilly air and emerging light guided her steps that morning. "Race" didn't quite describe this ancient Indian ritual for the men, ages seven to seventy, for they ran in tandem, one behind another. No competition. This essential ritual keeps the seasons, as well as the sun, rotating around Mother Earth, the source of all life. "And what if you didn't perform these rituals," Carl Jung asked of Chief Mountain Lake in 1925. "The earth would become dark and everyone would die," Mountain Lake had replied.

The sun sprayed across the line of Pueblo women in colorful shawls sprouting up along the edges of the towering adobe, a layered birthday cake.

Justine thought she saw Lucinda standing on the third story. Anglos, lined up on the south side of the running area, jockeyed for a good view. A makeshift bower stabilized by upright beams eight feet above the ground was encircled by tree limbs abundant in golden aspen leaves. A cross wrapped in the most red aspen leaves towered over the enclosure like the crown of a church, inside of which sat two priests, the leader of the Penitents, and three Indians. Statues from the nearby St. Jerome Church had been paraded around the Pueblo after the 6:00 a.m. mass and planted on the platform. The Virgin Mary–dressed in her seasonal gold-colored satin– was joined by St. Jerome, the Indian saint Kateri, and Jesus.

A darkened cloud slipped silently across the rising sun like a closing shutter on a camera. "That's my brother, Shilaw," said Taya, standing alongside Justine, pointing toward the impressively tall and muscular young man preparing to run, intense resolve as vivid as the paint on his face.

"He looks determined," said Justine.

"This is important to him—to all of them. Our running ritual is sacred. My father says it's been with us since the beginning of time."

As much as Justine wanted to further pursue the meaning of the ritual, she knew it was not considered appropriate to ask such questions. Yet she knew that ritual connects the conscious with the unconscious by surfacing our deepest beliefs and assumptions. Further, she knew that rituals allow us who practice them to participate in our myths, the stories that connect us to our worldview, ensuring that they endure. "You must be proud of him," she suggested tentatively.

Taya hesitated. "Yes, yes, we're proud of all the runners. I must go now, but I will be back."

"I'm going to join Lucinda's family for lunch," Justine said, reaching for Taya's arm. "Do you know where she lives?"

"I will take you there when it is time. It's across the river in the willows." She pointed toward the east where the full limbs of reddening leaves smothered rows of scattered homes.

Justine turned back toward the races, fascinated, revisiting her own marathon races. Boston. Chicago. Competitive all, churning in her the obsessive desire to win. Yet there were exceptions, she knew, like the time in Chicago when a man ran side by side with the blind runner, until the last moment when his partner pointed him in the right direction and let go. Even now, cold chills ran up her arms when she revisited that compelling moment.

Preoccupied, Justine overstepped the line separating the crowd from the runners. An elder warned her not to cross the feather perimeter of the race arena. She grinned weakly and stepped back, attending more closely to relationships among the runners. They demonstrated care for one another, rubbing dust on the legs of returning runners, kissing their hands, patting shoulders, massaging each other with feathers, brushing hands with open palms. When the race was finally over, the men ran in unison toward the east, turned and came back to stand for prayer. The crowd showered small candies on them as those in the grandstand scrambled down the ladder, parading the paint-chipped religious statues back to the church.

She waited for Taya, wanting to connect with the girl again, feeling real affection for her. Perhaps she was looking for a younger sister. Or a child? As an only child, Justine had sometimes longed for a sibling to care for—to care about.

"Ready?" Taya asked walking toward Justine.

Justine noticed quite a different young woman from the one she'd rescued from the cliff. *Radiant*. A fringed pink and purple woven shawl around her shoulders, her gleaming black hair a striking contrast. Two feathers crowned her head. Even the way she carried herself projected greater self-confidence. *What has happened?* Justine wondered if her mother had taken her to the counselor—or perhaps she had confided in her mother. When they ran recently the transformation appeared to be already in process. Justine observed a more confident posture, eyes that did not dart around in confusion. "I'm ready," said Justine, taking Taya by both shoulders and gazing into her eyes. The girl's eyes glistened with an excitement that bordered on mania. But something was also causing the muscles around her eyes to throb in fear, although she was clearly thrilled by the ceremonies.

The two women crossed the plaza and the arched bridge over the Rio Pueblo. As they walked, Justine asked, "How about another run tomorrow in the early evening. I'll be in Santa Fe during the day, but should be home by 6:30."

"Yeah. Sure. Okay," Taya said eagerly. "I can meet you near the Casino." Stopping short of Lucinda's house, she pointed, "That's the house. Over there."

—◦⬞◦—

Lucinda's traditional Indian adobe home was set off a dusty road nestled in red willows, close to the place where Justine met her the day of Blue Lake celebration. Busy in the kitchen, Lucinda introduced Justine to her daughter, Amitola, who led their guest into the backyard, offering some ice tea as she explained the history of the house. Like many of the homes just outside the Pueblo, it was built in 1945, right after her grandfather returned from World War II. Before that, most families lived in the Pueblo itself. "A big improvement," said Amitola, "here we have electricity, running water—even indoor toilets." She laughed. "Of course, I don't really remember the old days."

"That must have been difficult, especially for women. I can hardly imagine it," admitted Justine. She estimated that she and Amitola were about the same age. "Amitola. A beautiful name."

"My grandmother named me. She said she could tell when I was only a few days old that I would be a free spirit. It means 'butterfly.'"

"Ah, yes. I do wish Anglos paid more attention to the relationship between character and names. Do you live here with your mother?"

"I live in Ohkay Owingeh with my husband and son. I'm the financial officer for the tribe's casino near Española. We're just visiting Mom for San Geronimo Day."

"I've heard great things about Ohkay Owingeh. Don't you have one of the larger churches in New Mexico? And a new altar screen created by Giovanna Paponetti?"

"You know of it? I'm surprised. Not many do. It is quite new, and beautiful. The panels on the screen tell the story of Kateri. Just last week a group came from Denver on a pilgrimage. They were seeking a healing for one of their people."

"Watch out! Run!" shrieked the elderly woman seated across the patio. She had been leaning on her cane and dozing off. "Help! Help," she screamed again, throwing her head back, her hands trembling.

Amitola ran to her side, kneeled and took her in her arms. "There, there Grandma," she said, caressing the older women's thin gray pigtails. "It's alright. They're gone and you are safe. No one is hurt."

The elderly woman began to calm, leaning forward on her cane once more.

Amitola stood and turned to Justine. "My Grandma Thelma," she said. "She was a naval nurse in the war. A kamikaze plane dove into her ship while she was topside. The medical center took a direct hit and all the other nurses and doctors were killed. She was told later that her closest friend, another nurse, was apparently standing between two oxygen tanks. She saw so much…too much suffering and death. She hasn't been quite right since."

Tears came into Justine's eyes. Thoughts of her grandfather being bombed out of a foxhole in Mersa Matruh, in North Africa, flooded her mind, a wave of pain moving through her. She shivered. "I'm so sorry. Is she Lucinda's mother?"

"Yes, my maternal grandmother. She lives with Mom. Shall we go in?"

Amitola helped her grandmother to stand up and straightened her cane. Taking her by the arm, she led the way into the house.

Justine followed, making her way through the home supported by carved wooden columns, furniture adorned with colorful weavings, paintings and photos of tribal events, Indians dressed as they were portrayed in early western movies. Two bows and a pair of weathered moccasins hung on the wall along with Navajo serapes. She stepped over three little girls watching Roadrunner cartoons on television and joined Indian and Anglo guests at the large dining table in the kitchen. Heaping plates of turkey and dressing, ham, salads, chile stews, homemade breads, posole, cakes and pitchers of lemonade spread across the table. Great coffee, homemade biscotti.

Justine recognized one of the young boys who had raced that morning— the one who had tripped, then gotten back in the race so quickly. He sat at the head of the table of ten people, all older than himself, and was asked to say the blessing. Justine watched his flushed face radiant with pride, wondering what would it mean to make such a contribution, to be treated with such honor at age seven. Justine knew well that such roles, played out at a young age, caused faith and tradition to be instilled in one's mind and body for a lifetime. Yet even at seven, boys received much more respect than girls. She smiled and nodded at the boy who stared back at her.

As she ate, Justine occasionally watched Grandma Thelma seated across from her, lost in her own world. Amitola had filled the old woman's plate and she now picked at it as though she wasn't sure what it was, or that she trusted its safety. In that moment, her eyes cleared, a strong voice came forth. Everyone stopped eating and turned to the elder. "Oh, Great Spirit," she began, "whose voice I hear in the winds, and whose breath gives life to all the world, hear me, I am small and weak, I need your strength and wisdom." She ceased talking as quickly as she had begun, and fell into silence.

Justine's eyes welled up as she watched the elder across from her. *Lakota,* she thought as she heard the ancient prayer. Lucinda laid her hand on her guest's forearm. "I've been thinking a lot about our conversation last week. . . ." She spoke privately.

Justine set her fork down and turned to her host. "Yes?"

"You got me thinking more about my guides. They've been with me since I was my grandson's age. I think they were given to me by my grandmother who told them to take care of me. I'm not sure that everyone has guides."

"I imagine guides are very personal and I will have to find my own," said Justine, unsure whether she could ever believe in something so mystical.

"They must find you. You just need to be open to them. Be patient," said Lucinda, patting Justine's hand, then turning back to her guests. "More ice tea?"

They must find you, Justine repeated Lucinda's words to herself. *I must remain open. I'm not always good at that,* she admitted to herself. "I'd love more ice tea," she said, scooping chili onto her fork.

—◦∞◦—

At the plaza after lunch, Justine witnessed the ten sacred Tricksters, often referred to as Dark Eyes, emerge over the top of the five-story Pueblo. The sight gave her shivers. Painted with black and white horizontal stripes, feathers springing from headdresses and loin cloths, they looked menacing, like prowling animals slithering across the top of the towering structure on all fours. Powerful medicine. The ancient Pueblo came alive with the natural wildness of the Indian gods, Tricksters who would honor no boundaries, could transcend every rule, could do anything they wanted. Arising even before the creation of other Tiwa, and channeling straight talk from the unconscious, the Tricksters represent an archetypal god resembling the Greek Pan, later court jesters, and the fools of the Renaissance.

An ominous sight. Justine was flushed with excitement. Of course she had read about them in textbooks—and their meaning—but never encountered one in the flesh. She stared at the kaleidoscope of faces radiant with delight and mischievousness, knowing she too could be a target for a Trickster prank.

With graceful stealth the Tricksters sliced through the crowd, teasing, whooping, touching. Improvising at every turn. In the plaza, vendors from the other nineteen Pueblos covered their wares to protect them from the marauding Tricksters, who could steal their turquoise and silver, blankets, and precious artifacts: baskets, arrowheads, belt buckles. But the gods must be satisfied, so the vendors placed distracting tokens —food, water, woven reed bracelets—atop the covers. Merchants believed that gifts to the Tricksters brought blessings to themselves and sustained their own youthful spirits, yet their generosity had limits.

Two Tricksters approached a circle of small, trembling boys, each picking up a child to throw into the river situated a hundred feet to the south. One boy of about five began to wail in fear, yet behind him stood his proud father, complicit in this rite of passage. One after another, boys were thrown into the frigid water, most wading out to run rapidly back to their mothers—others basking, splashing one another, in the sheer pleasure of getting wet, of paddling about in a river off limits during the rest of the year.

A rotund, comical Trickster prowled through the crowd, passing near Justine, then rapidly turning to face her. He grinned lasciviously. Heart pounding, she returned his grin with little-girl innocence. He extended his hand and motioned to Justine that he wanted to take her to the Sacred Mountain beyond. Puckering and smacking his lips, he pointed to his cheek, insisting on a kiss. When she coyly resisted, he took firm hold of her hand and pulled her toward him, reaching to take her backpack from her back and flinging it into the river. The crowd gasped as they and Justine followed the arc of the backpack flying through the air. A young Indian girl quickly waded into the river, pulling the backpack out of the cold, rushing river, setting it on the bank. *Taya.* Relieved to not worry about her belongings, she turned back to her tormentor and reluctantly stepped forward to kiss him. Whooping with delight, the Trickster became a jumping jack. The crowd roared with delight.

Suddenly, Justine was being pulled north toward the mountain, when another man burst out of the crowd, a stranger significantly larger than the hefty clown. For a moment, she thought he was native, but no, more Mediterranean, his dark, oval face marked with dimples. He stared playfully at the Trickster, wrestling Justine's hand from his grasp, pulling her away, his eyelids sinking into a sultry stare. But the Trickster was quick and ran after them, grabbing the unclaimed hand. For several moments, Justine felt as though she was being stretched on a rack. Amused, a bit giddy, she turned to the stranger and whispered, "It's really okay, but thank you." She knew that to resist the will of this divine creature was a bad omen. The interloper winked, bowing to the omnipotence of the Trickster, released her hand and stood back, a slight grin forming in the corners of his mouth.

The Trickster now reclaimed her and resumed his march north toward the Sacred Mountain. As soon as they were out of sight of the crowd, he kissed and freed her hand ceremoniously, speaking to her in Tiwa. She nodded graciously and followed some distance behind as he returned to center stage, stomping and pounding his chest in victory. Picking up his abandoned bottle of orange soda, he shook it and sprayed the laughing crowd. Nearby, Taya handed Justine her backpack and said, "You were a good sport, Miss Justine."

Some of the marauding Tricksters corralled women of all ages into a circular dance, some leaving the dance to climb the grandstand and furiously tear it apart, handing limbs of gold to nearby Indian women.

As the afternoon began to fade, several Tricksters gathered at the base of the sixty-foot greased ponderosa pole erected in the plaza just for this celebration. Near the top, gift bags, and a sheep hanging from thin wooden poles. Justine turned into the sun, shading her eyes, just as the first Trickster attempted the climb. He came very near the top, then began to slide, losing his footing. He fell several feet to the ground and lay there winded for several moments before jumping up, opening his bloody palms, and prancing before the crowd to display his trophies of suffering. The next Trickster barely made it to the top, straddled the protruding branches, then used loops of rope to lower the gifts. The successful climb would bring health and prosperity until next year's events. The pulsing crowd scrambled toward the bundles, a climactic end to the day of celebrations. The crowd dispersed slowly; some aimed toward the vendors or sought out a Navajo taco, its makings piled high on fried bread. Taya was nowhere in sight, so an exhausted Justine walked back to her car, failing to notice a Chevy pickup perched under a nearby tree, the occupants awaiting her return.

CHAPTER 17

⸻⸻

THE NIGHT FROST BLANKETING Lobo Mountain evaporated under the rays of the morning sun, sparkling like scattered diamonds. Moisture darkened the ends of her hiking boots. Once again, the beauty nearly took her breath away, yet she forced several deep gulps of thin air into her lungs. It was Saturday, September 28, the day after San Geronimo Day, and Justine was returning to the ranch alone. This time in secret; she hadn't even mentioned it to Bill for she knew that he was such a decent man, he would not approve of her entering the ranch without explicit permission. Yet it was Bill's comment during their visit about hidden manuscripts or letters that compelled her to return.

She knew that Nico's son served as the ranch's caretaker and resided in the house Frieda's Italian lover had built for her. Justine parked on the side road leading up to the Hawk Ranch and waited until she saw him drive his battered pickup down off the mountain. Bill had mentioned that the young man went for the mail in San Cristobal each morning. As she began her ascent on foot to the ranch, she found Taya sitting under a sycamore tree just off the road, picking patiently at dandelions. When Justine had unwisely shared her mission with Taya, the young girl had insisted on coming along. Justine had been emphatic, "No, absolutely not." *Getting myself arrested for trespassing would be bad enough—but I could hardly defend getting Taya arrested as well.* But here she was, gazing up at her mentor, glowing at the thought of an adventure.

The two women climbed the last hundred yards to the Lawrence Ranch, a crowbar protruding from Justine's heavy backpack. Taya carried a satchel with water and lunch snacks strapped to her back. Justine wondered again how the young girl could be so agile in moccasins, then realized how ridiculous the question was. Indians had negotiated difficult terrain in moccasins for thousands of years.

Justine's passion, to pry open the cement slab in front of the fireplace, could not be extinguished. Ever since she'd noticed the carved-out slab on her last visit just a few days ago, she couldn't stop thinking about it. While she didn't expect to find anything, she had to know for sure. The caretakers seemed disinterested, as they had been when she'd asked if there hadn't been more possessions left behind in the cabin…books, a typewriter, pictures? It seemed unreasonably bare.

"Not much of a ranch, Miss Justine. Looks like it's falling apart," Taya said as they crawled through the barbed wire. She jumped when a black lab-mix mutt stuck its head through the roof of a dilapidated outhouse and barked ferociously. "That's weird!" she exclaimed. "Can he get out?"

"Don't mind the dog. He's harmless," said Justine, touching the girl's shoulder. "And, you're right about the ranch, Taya. It's very old, and falling apart. Lawrence's cabin is back here," she pointed, walking west around the house and shed. The mutt watched them go, barking intermittently. "See this little house? It was used by Lawrence's friend, Lady Brett. And, there's the main cabin. Our goal for today."

Taya stopped to admire the hand-painted buffalo drawn on the south side of the cabin. "Painted by a Tiwa, I bet," she said. "Why didn't your great grandfather live in the big house. He was very important, right?"

"Right you are about the buffalo. Lawrence had several Indians who worked for him. He considered them friends. But he didn't live in the big house because it wasn't there at the time. After he died, his wife Frieda had her new husband, Ravagli, build it for her." Justine didn't mention that the two hadn't married until 1950, twenty years after Lawrence died and only six years before her death. "She moved back from Europe and lived here for the rest of her life."

"In this house?"

"No, they lived here for a few winters, then built another house near town, on the road to the Millicent Rogers museum."

"Oh." That's all she said. She'd never heard of Millicent Rogers.

"Millicent was a rich socialite who designed extraordinary jewelry and collected Indian artifacts," Justine explained. "They're now housed in her museum north of town."

"Does she still live here?"

"No. She died in 1953 of complications from a childhood illness. Rheumatic fever, I think. You see, she only lived in Taos for six years. Her sons created the museum."

Taya nodded, fascinated—and a little confused—by Justine's interest in all these dead people.

Justine grinned as she watched Taya's face contort in puzzlement, turning to lead the way to the northern door of the cabin, one that was rarely used, although it opened into the living room. Digging a small metal file out of her backpack, she proceeded to jimmy open the locked door.

Taya's eyes grew into perfect orbs. "Wow! Miss Justine, you could be a safe cracker! Rob a bank!"

Justine was embarrassed and disconcerted, her cheeks reddening. "I don't make a habit of this, Taya. I do know this is University property, but in a way it belonged to my great-grandfather," she said, weakly justifying her actions.

Taya just grinned.

"We're in! Now, let me show you the carved-out piece on the hearth. It is so obvious that I don't expect to find anything. But yet. . . ." They stepped into the living room, the fireplace directly in front of them. Justine dropped her backpack on the wood plank floor and withdrew the crowbar. "See what I mean: a deliberate cut-out." She leveled the crowbar into one of the notches and pushed down. Nothing happened. "Ummm, it's going to be tougher than I thought." She withdrew the metal tool and re-situated it into one of the other three notches. "Come here, Taya, and sit on this handle."

Taya enthusiastically placed her bottom on the crowbar and began to bounce.

"Careful!" cried Justine. "We don't want to break it into pieces. Just push down slowly and firmly and I'll push too." Justine placed both hands on the end of the crowbar and the two of them brought their full strength to bear on the lever.

The slab squeaked as though it was suffering from the assault. Slowly, it began to lift on one end. "Now, just sit there, Taya. Don't move. Keep it suspended."

Taya did as she was told, holding her breath and easing her eyebrows into a look of intense concentration. No words passed between them.

Justine drew a metal trowel out of another backpack compartment and frowned as she found it not up to the job. She reached for a short metal rod in the same compartment and inserted it. Slowly the weighty cover, about three inches thick, began to lift. Leaving the rod wedged between the cover and the hearth, Justine looped a bungee cord over the slab and pulled it away from the opening—then slid it onto the hearth.

Taya and the rod fell to the floor. Still wordless with excitement, both women crawled on their knees and peered into the opening. "Darn!" said Justine. "Nothing! Only the ground below. There might have been something once, maybe a strongbox of manuscripts, but they're long gone." Not yet fully accustomed to the altitude, she sat back against the hearth and breathed deeply.

"Don't give up so easily," urged Taya, dangling her head into the opening, black hair covering her face, falling toward the earth below. One hand carefully patted the underside of the opening on all sides. "I found something!" she cried, withdrawing her hand, and prying it open for Justine to see. A large, furry wolf spider crawled across her hand and leaped from her fingers onto the hearth near Justine, who jumped as though on cue. Taya giggled from sheer pleasure.

"You devil!" accused Justine.

Taya resumed her search while Justine watched her with new appreciation. Minutes passed and Justine leaned back against the hearth, her attention wandering to Lawrence's giant pine outside. *How prolific he was*, she mused, a sense of wonder and pride moving through her. One of the most productive writers of all times, and all by hand. Then she noticed Taya sitting upright and looking thoroughly smug. One hand was closed.

"Another spider?"

"Better than that," Taya said proudly. "A key!" she said, holding up a small, rusty object that barely resembled a key.

"A key!!" cried Justine. "How? Where?"

"On a ledge inside. It's very rusty. What do you suppose it is for?"

"I have no idea," said Justine. Then, hearing sounds of a truck rattle up the drive, both women stiffened. "Well, it's time to go," she said calmly. Taya helped slide the cement cover back into place and stuff the tools into the backpack. They made for the door, closing it quietly behind them. "This way," motioned Justine, "we'll have to go around." They ran to the sheep fence on the eastern side of the property, jumped the fence and scurried down the hill toward the gate and parked car.

"Judy Lynn," answered the voice on the other end of the line.

"Judy. Bill Haller suggested that I call you. I asked him to recommend an attorney who might be interested in my dilemma . . . which ties in with the Lawrence Ranch. Actually, my issues concern the estate of D. H. Lawrence," said Justine.

"Judy Lynn," she corrected. "Actually, it would have been Frieda Lawrence's estate. Go on. I'm listening...." The heavy accent conjured up an image of the blustery Texas governor, Ann Richards, but Justine ignored that impression and explained her interest in D. H. Lawrence, her reasons for coming to Taos. She managed to summarize her position in less than three minutes, accurately anticipating that she would have little air time. She didn't have to wait for Judy Lynn's response.

"Whew! I have so many questions, but can't talk further now. How about meeting me at Graham's today, around 12:30? Great Sunday brunch. I often go there after church."

Justine entered the rear of Graham's restaurant through the kitchen, walked past the bar and into the main dining room. A banner on the wall of the connecting hallway announced the "Best of Taos" award for best restaurant three years in a row. She spotted the diminutive redhead popping up from one of the booths.

"Judy Lynn?" Justine asked, standing by the table and gazing at the woman who had told her to look for red hair.

"You're tall!" Judy Lynn exclaimed, her freckles glowing above a little girl grin.

Justine quickly slid into the seat across from the attorney, eager to reduce her height and get on an even footing. "So I am! Got it from my dad."

"Do you like dogs?" Thus began a recitation that went on for several minutes. "I have a dinner today for the SPCA. I'm on the board. Can't eat much today. How do you get your hair that color?" She paused long enough to take a sip of ice water.

Is she for real? Justine blinked. "My hair is naturally this color—at least for now," she grinned. "And, yes, I like dogs—most of them anyway." She picked up the menu and held it in both hands without opening it. Bill had said she was different, but he didn't say she talked in non-sequiters.

"I have four dogs. Unconditional love, I say. And a couple of horses. Do you ride?" Judy's eyes were globes of innocence, the wonderment of a child.

"I love to ride. My grandparents in Nebraska kept a horse for me when I was a kid. A beautiful bay." She returned Judy Lynn's smile and opened the menu, briefly staring at the list of salads.

"That's lovely. We'll have to ride at my place. Out of town." She pointed over her shoulder to the west. "Almost off the grid, near the Earthships, but we like it. Can be a difficult drive in winter—but this is a lovely time of year. No problem now. " Justine listened while Judy Lynn continued without taking breaths, or using punctuation. "I was thinking about your case, or maybe I should say, your interests. Amazing story! Can hardly believe it. What are you really looking for?"

Justine wasn't sure which part of Judy Lynn's oration to respond to first. "I know, amazing. It does seem unbelievable—but I can assure you—it's true.

I don't really know what I'm looking for. Old manuscripts. Letters to Lawrence from my great-grandmother . . . perhaps whether he ever owned any property in New Mexico."

"Only the last thing you listed could come under my areas of expertise. If it concerns his estate or probate. Whether he owned any property here. Where was his will probated? Do you like blue cheese?"

"His will was probated in England where he was from. Well, sort of. A will was never found. And, yes, I like blue cheese," she grinned again.

"Never found? Then as far as New Mexico is concerned, he died intestate—without a will. If he had owned property here, that condition would have to have been registered with the court. Do you think he owned any property here? The ranch was Frieda's, I understand."

"True. Mabel gave the ranch to Frieda. In '24, I think," said Justine.

"Were Frieda and Lawrence married then?"

"Yes. For several years."

"Ummm . . . sounds like community property to me. If they were married, all property in New Mexico is community property. Unless it was a gift."

"It was a gift." Disappointment washed over Justine's face. "Well, just about. Frieda gave Mabel D. H.'s original manuscript of *Sons and Lovers* in return."

"I see. Perhaps a case could be made. How much was it worth?"

"I don't know. Probably not much then."

"We'll go to the courthouse sometime this week. The information we want must be in the records with the county's Eighth Judicial District Court. Everything—well, almost everything—is on microfilm. We need to see the deed. And Frieda's will. Let's order."

Justine decided on the spinach salad with strawberries and pecans. "We could find these records eighty years after his death?" She knew she was less interested in the estate than in what Lawrence found for himself on Lobo Mountain, but she wanted to know everything she could find about his motivations. His life.

"I like strawberries in my salad," Judy Lynn said, as though reading Justine's mind. She turned to the patient waitress and ordered. "And ice tea. Lots of lemon." She paused long enough for Justine to order.

Both Justine and the waitress were thankful for the reprieve. "Eighty years is a long time . . . " Justine said, drawing her lunch partner's attention back to the subject at hand.

"Not too long, really. You said that the will was never found? How did Frieda get everything?"

"Long story. But to put it briefly, their mutual friend Murray—one of Frieda's lovers—testified at the hearing that he and D. H. had written their wills at the same time. Murray brought his along and said he had read D. H.'s. He said it left everything to Frieda."

"Why would Lawrence be so careless? He knew how sick he was."

"He did and he didn't. I think he was in denial. So many times before he had come to the edge of death, then recovered. Since he had little use for the medical profession, I suppose he didn't believe much of what they said."

"Love these strawberries," pronounced Judy Lynn, poking them with her fork. "Wherever do they get them out of season?" She savored the taste, chewing slowly.

"Well, now. We'll just have to find out about this estate. You know Frieda left the ranch to the university. They've let it go to ruin I hear."

"There's something else," Justine said, digging a small, gleaming copper key out of her purse and handing it to Judy Lynn. "Here."

"Connoisseurs?" the attorney asked, energetically stabbing her pecans. "Connoisseurs??"

"I use Connoisseurs Jewelry Cleaning Gel. Surely the key didn't look like this when you found it."

Justine laughed. She was beginning to enjoy this quirky woman. "I used Stain Rx," she admitted. "What do you think?"

"Wherever did you find it?" Judy Lynn narrowed her eyes and wrinkled her nose; her mouth twisted to the side.

What an expression. Every feature on her face moves in concert. A real pantomime actor. "I found it under a plate of cement carved into the hearth in Lawrence's cabin at the ranch." *No need to involve Taya.* Justine managed to look sheepish.

Judy Lynn's face relaxed into a full grin as she gazed at Justine with amused respect. "You are adventurous, girl!" she said, turning the key over and over in her hand.

"Looks like a safety deposit key to me," she said. Without blinking she asked, "Do you have a dog?"

CHAPTER 18

———⟨∞⟩———

"WE'LL DRIVE TO THE FOOT of the plateau," Pablo explained, "then climb. The Hupobi Pueblo remains are up there." He pointed to the top of a mountain, more like a mesa, evenly flattened across a mile or more of a nearly treeless, rocky terrain. The climb looked challenging, but no more than the road ahead that snaked up the side of the mountain.

Carmen, a woman Justine met at the Taos Archeological Society, was not new to such adventures. Small and sinewy, she was an athletic and well-prepared eighty-year old. Nevertheless, even Carmen was momentarily deterred by the rushing waters of the Rio Ojo Caliente that had washed out the road. The last time Pablo was here the river was shallow enough to drive through and continue to the base of the mesa. He keenly examined their options, his forehead a washboard of puckered skin, and declared: "We'll cross on foot."

"Along with fifty seventh graders?" Justine asked, slightly incredulous, staring at him.

He grinned. "They'll love it."

"If they don't get swept away," declared Carmen, her eyes betraying trepidation.

Pablo studied Carmen's anxious face for a few moments, sizing up her hesitancy. "I think I can drive the pickup backwards across the river and take you both," he said finally. "No problem." This husky mountain man rarely encountered problems that deterred him.

No problem, Justine thought, recalling the endemic Arab phrase '*mish mumpkin.*' Whenever 'no problem' is used, it is sure to be quite a problem. "No problem," she repeated, and grinned at Pablo as she climbed up into the rear of the pick-up truck. She held out her hand to Carmen, who spritely scrambled up the side. "We're ready," Justine shouted.

"Hold on!" shouted Pablo as he jammed the gears into reverse and began to slowly back into the river. They were no more that a few feet into the rushing water when the back of the pickup sunk into a hole, allowing the river to rise above the wheels. *This truck is going nowhere,* Justine realized, taking off her shoes and tying the strings together, flinging them around her neck. Carmen followed suit. They would get soaked, but fortunately the early October sun was warm—unlike the chilling river.

As the two women slid into the rushing waters, the school bus from Santa Fe arrived with fifty wriggling, giggling seventh graders and three teachers. Pablo crawled across the passenger seat and waded out of the river to welcome the students along with a young archeological apprentice, Hannah, whose blond ponytail stuck out from under a khaki baseball cap. She had left her own car near the entry to the property and jumped onto the school bus. Justine searched the faces of the children with their heads and gangling arms hanging out the bus windows, listening to Pablo explain that they would need to forge the river on foot. *Pablo was right—they're delighted,* she observed, standing in the river and holding onto the fender of the sunken truck. The rapidly moving water swirled around her thighs. She shivered.

"We'll form a chain," shouted Pablo after he'd further explained the dilemma to the teachers, who looked both obliging and worried. "Take off your shoes and tie them around your neck. Hold hands! And leave your lunches and backpacks on the shore."

The human chain moved toward the river with the three teachers and Hannah interspersed among the students, nearer to the shorter ones—those most in danger of being washed away.

Carmen and Justine now stood on the opposite bank. "I wonder how good their insurance policy is?" Carmen said casually. "Drowning may not be covered."

Justine stared at Carmen's stoic face, then turned to watch the water parade. She plowed back into the river, standing firmly in the middle with feet anchored wide apart, providing extra support as each child in the chain passed along. One small, frightened girl with moist eyes looked up gratefully as Justine began to sing "My Favorite Things" from *Sound of Music*. The teachers and Hannah enthusiastically joined in, accompanied by Pablo's baritone and Carmen's lilting soprano. How many times had she seen the 1965 film? Twenty? Thirty? The little girl sniffed back a tear and began to sing just as a Plain-Bellied water snake crossed her forearm. When she screamed, every youngster followed suit. Screaming, wiggling, laughing. Justine picked up the snake by its tail automatically and flung it into the air. A hundred eyes watched the olive green snake with a pale yellow stomach fly through the air and land in the back of the sunken pickup. The children laughed in relief. Now they would have a snake-occupied, sinking truck to deal with when they returned. She was amused, Pablo relaxed.

"It's larger than Pueblo Bonito at Chaco Canyon," Pablo called out as fifty-six hoarse explorers scrambled to the top of the four-hundred foot mesa. Coming alongside Justine, he whispered, "You know those Plain-Bellies bite and keep biting,," he said. "Just thought you should know." He gave her his customary little boy grin.

Justine turned white. "Poisonous?" Her voice trembled. Although she considered herself brave in traumatic moments, she was actually terrified of snakes—of all kinds. Her mother could work in the garden with a snake wound around her neck, but not Justine.

"Naw," he said. "Just feisty." A big man, light on his feet, Pablo scurried up the crest to keep pace with the children.

As Justine topped the mesa, it nearly took her breath away. It wasn't flat like it seemed from a distance, but the rocky soil undulated in the shape of the former civilization, the breasts of a woman rising through a wet tee shirt. A long rise here, mounds there, dry garden patches surrounded by rocks on a somewhat higher plane. It was as though history lay asleep, dozing under the earth. This terrain, the subtle rises, without the protrusions extending upward from the earth like on Easter Island, or Rome, or Egypt where great monuments reach for the sky. After all, Indians came from below, under Mother Earth's mantle—from Blue Lake, the Colorado River in the Grand Canyon, a solitary lake in southern Colorado, all connected below the surface.

On its northern edge, the mesa fell away into the Rio Chama valley, far below, the river weaving among thousands of golden cottonwoods. The view was framed by rolling hills nearly high enough to be called mountains, although not quite, but rather a painted landscape hanging in a Taos gallery. The students swarmed over the surface like excited lemmings.

"You can pick up the sherds and examine them," Pablo offered the students, "then put them back on the ground." Justine lowered her eyes, surprised to find the surface covered with sherds of pottery, although she shouldn't have been because she knew the earth percolates as though it is alive—churning everything to the top eventually. Such small discoveries, these sherds, like the key burning a hole in her backpack. She walked gently to avoid stepping on the treasures, bending toward the earth repeatedly to examine dozens of pieces just lying unprotected in the open. She stooped to photograph the stunning sherds; she recognized Biscuit ware—fired but not glazed--using organic paints to create black and white geometric designs, small tick marks along the edges. Most of the sherds were miniatures, about two by two inches. Justine found them familiar. *Plains Indians? Sikyatki from the First Mesa?* Similar to the black on white found at Chama from the Four Corners. Yet, she didn't find the designs bold enough.

Long roots from three scrub trees grew along the sides of a deep, circular kiva. The largest she had ever seen. Pablo shouted and waved his arms to gather everyone around the edge. The students shuffled up slowly, some sitting along the side of the great Kiva, dangling their feet into the yawning crevasse.

"The population in Northern New Mexico expanded greatly in the late 13th century, right about the time the Four Corners peoples disappeared. How many of you have heard of Mesa Verde?"

Nearly all hands sprang into the air. He had their undivided attention.

"Good for you. Well, I think they moved here to Hupobi, and to other pueblos along the Rio Grande in the Tewa basin, settling themselves into the many communities," continued Pablo.

What did he just say? Justine asked herself, startled. *Did he suggest that the Mesa Verde peoples came here? One of the greatest mysteries in archaeology solved just like this? Like Lucinda said?* She stared at Pablo intensively, eager to hear more.

"The dry farming techniques are similar, as are the black and white geometric designs on the sherds. The timing is right, the distance is doable," Pablo continued, lowering his brim against the sun.

"But why would the Mesa Verde people leave their homes?" asked a wiry boy who had been constantly on the move around the mesa. "I liked their cliff dwellings. My dad took my sister and me there last summer."

"A beautiful place," agreed Carmen, standing nearby, fanning herself. Her clothes were nearly dry, although steam rose from the folds in her jeans. "Many archaeologists and anthropologists claim it was the climate. Records show that the climate became too hot and dry."

"I understand that tree-ring dating tells us that there was a 50-year drought around 1130 and another from about 1275 to 1300," added Justine, sitting on the edge of the kiva among the children, her long legs hanging free. "Around that time, Chaco, Mesa Verde and Kayenta were all abandoned and their residents scattered. Is that right, Pablo?"

"Right!" he said, grinning at his colleagues, his easy-going style inviting participation. "And there's another theory I'm fond of. An intriguing mystery. My colleague Scott Ortman at the Santa Fe Institute argues that they moved precisely so they *could* leave their old culture behind. That could explain why we haven't found much of their 'baggage.'"

"Baggage?" laughed a lovely Latina girl hanging on every word.

"Yeah, that's what we call the art and tools and other stuff migrants bring along, leftovers from their own cultures. Scott thinks there was a sharp division among the Mesa Verde inhabitants. Most were just subsistence farmers, while the leaders lived in luxury. Rich and poor."

"Like Santa Fe today!" quipped another girl.

Pablo nodded. "The more affluent were buried in luxury too. Like Egypt. So…just maybe they moved to form a more equitable form of society, such as the Tewa. They formed new forms of living together after they moved." He was a little breathless, becoming more animated as he shared his theories.

A bit of a stretch, thought Justine. Although Lucinda had called them gentle and adaptive. She wanted to think that humans had a natural inclination toward equality. Yet the Taos peoples aren't equitable—certainly not toward the women. "Without baggage," she asked, "what evidence does Scott use to say these were Four Corners people?"

"Well now, that's the interesting part! One of the sources of data Scott used was the structure of the faces of the new immigrants into Tesuque and Ojo Caliente areas—like here—are very similar to the faces of Mesa Verde peoples," said Pablo. "Technology is giving us more information than we've had in the past."

"Wow! Where did he get the human skeletons?" said one of the taller girls with a big hat shadowing all but her chin. Justine noted how much taller girls were than boys at this age. Her mind wandered back into the classrooms in the Community Schools for Girls in Egypt. *So like these girls*, she thought. *There are some things that are universal, that can't be hidden under culture.* She felt a pang of regret, regret that she hadn't been able to watch the Egyptian girls grow up before she was expelled.

"Not skeletons, but special photos. Tribal elders oppose the use of human remains and most excavations, which led to the Native American Graves Protection Act more than twenty years ago." Pablo answered.

"What about DNA? Couldn't they use DNA?" insisted the wiry boy, shifting from foot to foot. Impatient to understand the world, so smart.

Justine nodded encouragement toward the boy.

One of the teachers replied, "Indians have been reluctant to allow DNA testing as well. They've been stung a few times when the information was misused. But that will come, especially as more Native Americans become archaeologists and join in the hunt."

Pablo nodded. "That's about right. Archaeology is still a young science. We have a lot of growing to do. How many of you would like to become archaeologists?"

Several students waved their hands vigorously. Carmen, now settled on the ground next to Justine, whispered, "It's not as glamorous as people think. A lot of grueling, hard work."

"So true," Justine whispered back. Then turning to Pablo, "Why hasn't this great kiva been explored? There are amazing stories to tell here. At Chaco, when they began to dig, they found stone walls and a floor, and another kiva below that. Maybe that's true here."

"Resources. Very limited these days. Archaeology is a slow business. Not always satisfying to funders who want quick results."

"So what happened to these people?" asked one of the older teachers, tilting her hat toward the sun and dabbing her face with a lace handkerchief. "Why did they want to leave?"

"We think it was disease," said their guide.

"But that was before the Spanish—the carriers of all the great scourges," responded the teacher. "I thought it was the Spanish who brought the devastating diseases."

"Generally true," said Carmen, noting the lace with a curious stare. "But a large number of graves have been found here together, seemingly dug around the same time."

"Or they were murdered about the same time," the wiry boy added cryptically.

Pablo chuckled, thoroughly enjoying the boy's enthusiasm. "Well, anything is possible, young man . . . let's get moving. First the dry farming area, then the petroglyphs. And, lunch." The whole group moved *en masse* toward the higher mesa.

An hour later, the troop scampered down the path and made their way back to the river. By now, the rushing water nearly topped the pickup's fenders. Pablo held out his hand about five feet off the ground. "Okay kids, if you're as tall as my hand, step over here." The children rushed to measure themselves, to meet Pablo's test, even without knowing the purpose. When he had a cluster of around twenty, he announced, "We are forming a brigade, teams of five, to push the truck out of the river. Are you game?" The chosen ones nodded vigorously, the short students registered disappointment. "But watch out for Justine's snake!"

Justine shuddered, amused that it was now her snake. She walked into the river and headed for the pickup. "Wait till I get the snake out," she announced. Of all the terrifying adventures she'd had in the last four years: burial by an earthquake, kidnapping, death threats, digging her way out of a tomb—this was at the top of her list. Her mother told her that fears were there to be conquered. *Well, Justine, let's give it a try.*

CHAPTER 19

⊸⊶⊷

"**A**MIR?!" JUSTINE'S VOICE nearly sang into the phone. "Where are you?"

"I'm still in Egypt, *Habibti*. How are you doing?" His deep voice was remarkably clear, as though he were in the next room.

"When will I see you? I'm doing well—the new job is underway." She avoided saying it was still vague; and she was still just a volunteer. Instead, Justine chose to imagine her handsome Egyptian archaeologist intertwined with her on the couch.

"Things are moving fast here. Since April I've been advising a group of young activists working with Wael Ghonim. He's with Google, North Africa."

"I don't know Wael. Sounds like a youth movement of some kind. About time. What's it about?"

"Wael and his supporters are forming a political party to challenge Mubarak. The Middle East is a seething caldron, Justine."

"I know it is, Amir, but good luck with challenging Mubarak!" she exclaimed, kicking off her boots and curling her legs under her. She had just walked in the door from the Hupobi trip. "As long as he controls elections, and follows past practice, he's apt to jail whatever candidate you choose." Noting her own cynicism, she asked herself, *Who am I to be telling him about Egypt?*

"That's what I say. Some days I think they're just Pollyannas, but on others...many youth are with him. Educated young men and women talking constantly through the social media. It could be different this time. I know politics isn't my field, but everything is political here, even archaeology."

"Especially archaeology. I still have frightening images of Omar Mustafa." *Mustafa. The Supreme Director of Antiquities who masterminded the first theft of the Virgin Mary's diary.* "How could I ever forget his arrogant stance, his syrupy grin?"

"Well, he's still the Supreme Director of Antiquities, in spite of his involvement in thievery, lying, misusing funds . . . but enough about my charming life. How is my Justine?'

My Justine. She rolled it over in her mind, caressed it. "Truthfully, not much is taking off with the archaeology office, but I just got back from an unexcavated pueblo with Pablo William from the Bureau of Land Management and a couple of his colleagues. He's convinced that it's a site to which the Mesa Verde peoples migrated."

"Pablo?" Amir asked, a slight tension creeping into his voice. "Bureau of Land Management? I don't know of it."

"Pablo is an archaeologist," Justine had started to say 'older' or 'near retirement,' but decided not to assuage his imagination. "with the Bureau, a government agency charged with protecting public lands. Along with fifty 7th graders from Santa Fe. Great kids."

"Mesa Verde, huh? Sounds a little far-fetched. One of the greatest archeological mysteries of all time. Wouldn't we have heard more about it if there were any substantial evidence? Of why they left, that is." He softened his voice, dropping instead of lifting it at the end of the sentence.

"I would imagine so, and there is less contention about the migration than why they left and exactly where they went, but the evidence sounds persuasive." Justine was immediately aware of his self-editing, catching himself in the midst of a cynical response. But the resonance of that rich, slightly British-accented voice reached her senses and she began to lose her train of thought. A compelling wave of desire flowed through her body. "I've missed you, Amir," she whispered seductively.

He paused, quietly absorbing the changing moment, as though desire could float through cyberspace. "I'm coming to Taos for Christmas, Darling. Will you be there?" he asked, his thickening Arab accent taking precedence. A British-educated Arab.

"Of course I'll be here," she replied. "I've so much to tell you. Amir—you'll love it here—the high desert reminds me of Egypt. The people are just as warm." She paused. "Amir, I lie in bed and imagine your touch. Remember Cerveteri?"

"The day we found the tomb? How could I forget? You wore my good white shirt and tucked in the tail for underwear!" He laughed softly. "I want to see you so badly. Gaze upon you. See your eyes, your smile. I can Skype you next week from Wael's office. Would Tuesday night work?"

———

What a full day, Justine mused, as she lay in bed, hair splayed out across double pillows, legs propped up in front of her. Moonlight beamed through a small opening in the muslin curtains. *Hupobi and the kids. That snake scared the hell out of me. Amir.* She scrunched down into the sensuous comforter and the honey-colored satin sheets and closed her eyes. Not to sleep, but to review what had brought them here, to this place in their relationship . . . a short journey in cosmic time, a lifetime in experiences.

She silently voiced her thoughts to Amir as though he were there next to her. *When we met on the felucca that first day I arrived in Cairo, I fought against my immediate attraction, considering you rude and arrogant. Then as the intense work on Mary's diary brought us closer, that view slowly began to change. At first, I think it must have been the respect and affection you showed for your elderly grandfather. Of course, when you rescued me from the kidnappers, you were somewhat more appealing.* Eyes still closed, she grinned to herself. In spite of her lust for this delicious man, she was not about to marry an Egyptian. Her mother had nearly guaranteed that decision. After all, even as an Egyptian herself, she knew she could never have a liberated life if she did so. Ironically, her own father, the celebrated Berkeley archaeology professor, turned out to be unable to break with his conservative Nebraskan roots and his need to protect—or control—the women in his life. She shouldn't have been surprised that they divorced when she went off to graduate school. She'd accepted her mother's reasoning and remained clear that she would never marry an Egyptian. However, when Amir showed up in Italy she couldn't resist a torrid affair.

Yet when Amir returned to Italy after the trial of his grandfather's murderer in Cairo, he was more distant. They were both cautious, intent not to get too serious again. Tossing and turning as she tried to relax her muscles, sore from climbing the Hupobi mesa. She missed him in a way she didn't anticipate. The intimacy of a closer friendship, as well as the pleasure of being lovers. Gradually, the tension between them had heightened until last June when they drove to the Amalfi coast. She halted her thoughts momentarily as a wave of desire moved through her. Even though they had re-ignited the passion, they also agreed that marriage wasn't in the picture. *Thankfully, it's a question I don't have to resolve because he'll never ask me.*

Opening her eyes, she stared at the log vigas, barely visible in the dim moonlight, and traced the timbers end to end, wondering where her relationship with Amir stood now. The men in her life demanded so much attention— her father, Amir. Lawrence.

It would take another Carl Jung to figure it out. She turned and sank into a dream-filled sleep.

CHAPTER 20

THE MABEL DODGE LUJAN HOUSE, TAOS, APRIL, 1925

"Mabel is gone to New York, some sort of surgery," Lawrence says to the tall stranger helping himself to a cup of coffee in the massive dining room.

"So Tony told me. I am, of course, disappointed to miss her. You must be D. H. Lawrence. She speaks highly of you."

Lawrence is silent for a few moments, keenly observing the stranger's face, carriage. *"You're the psychiatrist from Switzerland. Student of Freud, I believe."*

"Jung. Carl Jung. Hardly a student of Freud's. We were colleagues at one time, but we went our separate ways."

"But a psychiatrist still," Lawrence insists, his fiery turquoise eyes flashing. The two men walk to a long wooden table without ceremony. *"Mabel is captured by some of your ideas. Not for me, I say."*

"Psychiatry isn't for everyone, but novelists sometimes tell me that archetypes help them understand and develop their characters."

"Humph. Archetypes are little boxes. Man alive cannot be diagnosed, analyzed, and explained. He is whole, yet ever-changing."

"*Ever-changing, yes,*" *agrees Jung,* "*but tied to fate. Arche-types arise from the collective unconscious—your 'instinct,' if you will. The unconscious accompanies us into life. Unavoidable.*"

"*What is fate?! Fate is pre-conceived by psychiatrists like yourself. Philosophers and scientists as well. You take a little piece of man—the mind, in this case—and think you have him. You don't have him. You seek to still our souls so you can label us.*"

"*Isn't that what a novelist does? 'Still our souls.' Affix us on the page?*"

"*A novel is a living instrument. The characters are whole and live out their lives in the context of the novel,*" *Lawrence insists.* "*They take on a life of their own and live beyond the man who holds the pen. Man is indescribable except as he comes alive in the novel. If you want to understand the living, read a good novel or play...Homer, Tolstoy, Shakespeare.*"

"*And D. H. Lawrence?*" *Jung's eyes twinkle.*

"*And Lawrence,*" *he nods, amused by the perceptiveness of the man.* "*Modesty is not one of my virtues.*" *Lawrence observes the morning light enter the eastern casement windows, coming to rest on Jung's coffee cup. Lace shadows dance on the table.* "*What are you looking for?*" *he finally asks.* "*Why do you come here when Mabel is gone?*"

"*I want to understand the Indians. Their ways. Their beliefs. They are the most ancient of peoples and have much to teach us,*" *Jung continues searching Lawrence's openly curious face with something like amazement. Here is a man with many an-swers, yet who seeks to know more.*

"*Ah, we find a common interest. The Red Man is a religious man. Not that he can't be annoying, even savage at times, but when he enters his reverence, he is with nature. He is whole, one with his body. Movement is prayer to the Red Man,*" *declares Law-rence with the assurance of a man who trusts his own insights.*

"He needs no intermediary."

"Quite right. No god or gods to do his bidding. No Jesus to intercede with God for his salvation."

Jung nods and stares at his large hands, pondering whether he should share his meeting at the Pueblo. "I met with Mountain Lake yesterday. You know him?"

"Tony introduced me. A wise man."

"Mountain Lake claims that their rituals keep the sun moving in the sky, the seasons coming and going. Our very existence depends on them. What meaningful lives!"

"San Geronimo Day is in the fall. You can see it all on display. Will you stay?"

"I cannot. I'm expected in Bern in a couple of weeks."

Lawrence prepares to leave, stepping toward Jung and offering his hand. "For a psychiatrist, you're not such a bad sort." He grins.

The towering Jung smiles in return and rises to take Lawrence's hand, patting the shorter man on the shoulder, then sits back down to finish his breakfast as Lawrence takes his leave. They never meet again.

CHAPTER 21

━━⟨∞⟩━━

JUSTINE DROPPED OFF A summary of the Hupobi trip she'd volunteered to write at the Bureau of Land Management office. It was the end of the workday and Pablo wasn't around, so she left it with the receptionist and returned to her car. She suspected that she'd offered to write this report, not only to keep a record of the adventure for herself, but in hopes of breaking the writer's block keeping her from writing the grant proposal. She also wanted to discover what it was about Hupobi that fascinated her. The hidden secrets just below the surface, yet riddled with clues. A metaphorical terrain for everything that fascinated her: subterranean, subtle, historical. *Yes, I must go back.*

She still struggled with how to define community from an archeological point of view—or perhaps her belief that understandings could be greatly enhanced by an interdisciplinary approach and recognizing that community was about reciprocity. *A "reciprocity of tenderness," as Lawrence described?* Writing the summary had helped, so she'd decided to write the grant proposal the way she wanted and let the chips fall where they might.

As she turned left out of the parking lot, Justine noticed a beat-up blue Chevy pickup of early 90's vintage parked at the curb. The driver quickly made a U-turn and pulled up behind her at the stop sign. The Chevy full of young boys—three in the front, two in the bed of the truck, passing a bottle of beer back and forth through the window—turned right as she did and kept a close distance behind.

Being followed was not new to Justine, so she became instantly vigilant. What others may attribute to coincidence, she didn't. Of course, it was possible that she was imagining that they were tailgating, but she didn't think so. The driver sat tall in his seat, and his deep auburn hair was undeniable. She recognized him from her first day on the pueblo, before she met Taya. Every fiber in her body was on alert and she trusted those experienced nerves. The pickup followed eight or ten feet behind. She speeded up, then slowed down; it was as though the Chevy were connected to her bumper by a tow bar. Fully formed memories of a similar situation vividly appeared: being followed on the desert road between Cairo and Alexandria. She glanced into the rear view mirror and saw five young Hispanic boys laughing with each other.

Justine pulled into the Casino parking lot as the Chevy sped by, spinning its wheels, throwing up gravel. Taya was standing under the awning.

"What kind of car does Ricardo have?" Justine asked Taya as she stepped from her own. Her voice was soft and unrevealing.

"An old Chevy pickup. I just saw him go by! I wonder where he is going so fast? I know it's not to my house!"

"Ready to run?" Justine asked, careful not to register her concerns about being followed. She didn't want to worry Taya with the misadventures of her boyfriend—at least not yet.

"Sure," Taya nodded, yet her eyes searched the road ahead. She was distracted.

Justine pulled her running shoes and a sweatshirt out of the car, and sat down on the bright green concrete ledge around a planted area in front of the Casino. "Ok, what's going on? Something with Ricardo? School?"

"I go to school okay—that's the only time I see Ricardo."

"Did you tell him about me?" Justine asked casually.

"Sure. I told him you were helping me."

"And . . . what did he say?"

Taya looked away, hesitating.

Justine waited. "I want to hear your voice. Tell me directly."

"He said, 'Fuck. Why would you want help from a rich white lady! She'll just mess up your mind! Take my word for it.' He thought he was done, finished. That I would listen to him. Do whatever he said." Her tone was sarcastic.

"And you said?"

"I told him that I liked you. You were my friend and it was none of his business."

"I'm proud of you, Taya. You stood up for yourself." Now she knew why Ricardo and friends were following her. Did he plan to do her harm or just scare her? It was hard to tell.

"I did, and it felt good, but now he's mad at me and won't talk to me. I feel bad again, Miss Justine."

"Tell me how you felt when you told him it was 'none of his business.'"

"I felt strong. Confident. I could feel all this energy in my arms. But . . . ."

Justine gently interrupted, "It's the new you, Taya. The person who is sad because Ricardo is mad at you is the old submissive, obedient you. The invisible one. Does that make sense? Hang onto those feelings of strength."

"It does, but it's hard, Miss Justine." Taya jumped up and started to run onto the path west of the Casino. "Catch me if you can," she called over her shoulder.

"I'm coming," Justine laughed, running to catch up. The two sped into the early evening, the cooling breeze catching their long hair. A sea of sage dancing in the air.

∞∞∞

Back home with no Chevys in sight, Justine made herself a thick tuna sandwich on whole wheat and poured a glass of ice tea, cut up an apple, even though she'd had a generous lunch with Mike and Sam at Café Pasqual's in downtown Santa Fe. They had discussed the grant and the community project. Justine introduced the story of the trip to Hupobi Pueblo. That conversation had not gone all that well.

"Pablo's a romantic, God bless his soul," said Mike, expecting support from his boss. "I love the old coot, but there's no real evidence for these migration myths. Don't you think so, Sam?"

"Well," Sam started. "I just talked to Scott Ortman out at the Santa Fe Institute the other day and he thinks he may be on to something."

"Hogwash," exclaimed Mike. "Let's order."

—✕—

Justine had a struggle on her hands. So did Pablo. She wondered if she should just forget Hupobi and Mesa Verde and try not to get herself into trouble again. *Ah, but that is not my custom.* The last low rays of the setting sun were coming through her kitchen window. She chewed her tuna slowly, methodically turning her attention to Ricardo and friends. Were they a gang? Involved in drugs? She got up from the table, locked both doors and called Judy Lynn.

"Judy Lynn?" Justine asked when a voice came on the phone.

"Right. Justine? I've been thinking about you. I may have a theory about your key. Been out with the horses. Wait. I need to wash this dirt off my hands." The phone went silent for several moments.

Justine waited patiently, amused once again by Judy Lynn's quirkiness.

"Hi. I'm back. Sorry to keep you waiting. Ah, yes, the key. I've been trying to find out if any of the banks were around in the 20's so that we could find a safe deposit box—although I guess it could be a post office key. No luck finding a bank. Earliest one here was built in the 60's. But," she paused, "there's a rumor about a bank on the plaza in the 20's."

"On the plaza?" Justine managed to slip in. "Do you know where?"

"I'm working on it. Have you ever heard of the tunnels? Under the plaza?"

"No. For real?"

"Well, every man I ask says 'no,' and every woman says 'yes.'"

Justine laughed. "No way! What's your theory?"

"What I heard from the Historical Society is that it ran under the plaza, west under the Alley Cantina, under Don Fernando to the Red Cat Melissiana and Antiques on La Luz, turned right to Antonio's, which was then a cat house—excuse the pun—and east under Church of Our Lady of Guadalupe. Whew, quite a mouthful!"

"I thought the church was north of Antonio's."

"Not at that time. The church sat in the parking lot in front of the Red Cat. The cemetery too. Story has it that all roads, tunnels, from both directions ran to the cat house. Father Martinez was a well-known womanizer, leaving many progeny in the community. Part of Taos' rich heritage." Judy Lynn guffawed sarcastically.

"Some story. But why the Red Cat."

"I don't really know. In the basement, right in front of the tunnel entrance, is a mammoth fireplace, big enough for a major conference center. Some big doings went on down there."

"Could that have been the bank?"

"I don't think so. Not really on the plaza, and not that big. Hey, wait! You called me. What's up??"

Justine had almost forgotten why she called. "I've been followed. An old Chevy full of boys, and I know one of them: a young man named Ricardo." She explained Ricardo's connection to Taya and his probable motive.

"Ummm. Could be serious business. Tell you what. You call the Chief of Police, a friend of mine. Name's Paul Martinez. Good man. Tell him all about it and ask his advice. Okay?"

"Will do. Thanks, Judy Lynn. I'll let you know what happens. Please get back to me about that old bank."

———

Justine stood in front of the giant Mexican mirror in her dining area, brushing her hair and straightening her collar. Her Mac sat on the table behind her, ready for the Skype conference with Amir. At 10:00, it was pitch dark outside; 7:00 a.m. in Cairo. How long had it been since he had seen her? Nearly six months. She wondered if her appearance had changed? Longer hair; more tan. *Oh my god, I'm as nervous as a cat!* She turned and opened her computer, staring into the scene saver, the photo of Lawrence's cabin.

She'd decided not to tell Amir about being followed, although she was sure of it. She certainly didn't want him to get on a plane and come to her before he was ready—before his planned visit. No, she would just tell him about Lawrence, the job, Taya.

The Skype screen buzzed from an incoming call. She answered and enlarged the scene. There he sat in a cramped office piled high with newspapers and books. A single bulb hung overhead. He looked macabre, ghastly, the light and shadows giving his face a morgue pallor.

"You look great!" he said, his face transformed as he smiled and winked at her.

"I wish I could say the same for you, my friend. Are you getting any sleep?"

"A little. As your favorite poet, St. Vincent Millay put it, 'I've lit the candle from both ends.' Exciting work."

"My candle burns at both ends," she corrected and grinned. "It sounds as though you're feeling satisfied, successful. It must be going well with your rebellious young friends."

"Well, as you know, I'm a Greek aficionado. Last night I told them how the Greeks got democracy and how they lost it."

"Very helpful! Did you also bring those thoughts into the 21st century?"

Amir laughed. "But of course! They do listen. We talked about institutions, the rule of law, participation, economic freedom. You know, Egypt never experienced an Enlightenment. Even though these ideas are appealing, they don't know how democratic systems could work. And, then there's the Muslim Brotherhood."

"Ah yes, the Brotherhood. After nearly sixty years of oppression, don't you think they're bursting at the seams to take control?"

"You can't really blame them."

"No . . . . "

His comment gave her pause. *No, you couldn't blame the Brotherhood for wanting to burst forth after decades of oppression. Many of them are professionals. Well educated. Organized. But what is behind Amir's statement? Is he buying their propaganda that they've become moderate?* She was ready to ask, then realized that his safety might be at stake. *Perhaps he is being extremely cautious with what he is willing to say on-line.*

After a long pause, Amir ventured. "How is your hunt going, Justine? What are you finding out about your great-grandfather? How's the job? The house?"

She was relieved to let go of the Brotherhood conversation, and proceeded to describe her frustration with her new job and her two trips to the Lawrence ranch. Taya. Judy Lynn. The key.

"A key? To what?" Amir loved mysteries, that's what made him a clever archaeologist.

She smiled. "Judy Lynn thinks it's a safe deposit box or post office box. Could be lost manuscripts. More letters. Who knows."

"Be careful, Justine. You know, you've gotten yourself into trouble before. . . . " The lights went out behind Amir and she heard a voice tell him they needed to close and hide the computers. "Got to go, Justine," he said lightly. "I'll e-mail you later in the week and see you before Christmas." The screen went black.

Justine sat staring into the blank screen for several moments. *Security police? Hiding computers. Black out. He is in real danger—anything can happen in Egypt.* She closed her computer, stood up, stretched, and headed for the bedroom. She temporarily lost her balance in the hallway. As she caught herself, tears streaked her cheeks. Amir could be arrested, tortured, disappear. Her mind reeled. She knew that sleep would be hours in coming.

CHAPTER 22

B EING ALONE IN THE WILD helped her to think. When she pondered the dangers facing Amir, her heart pounded and echoed inside her head. She had resisted and rationalized her feelings for Amir for several years now. Like her mother, she was determined to not get drawn into a culture that suffocated women. Justine wondered how much longer she could remain vague about their future.

Bill Haller had shown her the way to the Hawk Ranch and beyond, to Lobo Canyon. As president of The Friends of D. H. Lawrence, he had taken her under his wing, helping her to understand even more about Lawrence's idiosyncrasies, his moods, and put his outbursts of rage into perspective. Bill was forgiving with genius, as were others in Taos. "D. H. lived in a different world," he'd insisted, "a world that few of us ever see."

Once again, Justine turned her low-slung Prius onto the deeply potholed road that ended at the barbed wire fence surrounding the abandoned Hawk property. Sunday morning: the land as quiet as a cemetery, except for the low rustling of cottonwood and aspen, a gentle breeze crawling in from the west. She parked and walked twenty yards along the faux fence line to where it had collapsed, entangled in grass and fallen branches. The ranch was accessible, although few knew it. An old wooden ranch house sat within sight, a rusting tricycle and two unraveling wicker chairs on the porch as though waiting for their owners to return. She imagined Lawrence sitting in that old chair, bouncing the two-year old Walton Hawk on his knee, each keenly eyeing one another. Both possessed that unfiltered power of observation most often found in young children.

This morning she would follow the path taken often by Lawrence, sometimes with Brett on horseback, other times with an Indian guide, but most often alone with just his walking stick to visit his neighbors, the Hawks, and ride up toward Lobo Canyon. They were good friends, indulgent of his moods, helpful during that first harsh winter on the mountain. He was drawn here, she knew, by the wildness of the place, the cream copper cliffs, dense forest, secret gullies. The promise of unknown dangers. *Surely he conjured up plots for his prose, lines for his poems, during these sojourns into the mountains.*

Nagging thoughts nudged at Justine's consciousness as she jogged past the cabin and headed across the meadow toward the rise leading to the canyon. Amir. The key, Judy Lynn, the threatening young men who had trailed her in the truck. Even though she'd tried to contact Amir the following day, she hadn't any luck. Then, yesterday, a brief e-mail, cheery and lacking in any substantial news. *He can take care of himself, girl!*

Across a vast open meadow of red wild spinach and cactus she ran, spotting a dry man-made reservoir at the foot of the mountain. Trees were closer together now, slowing her down, forcing her to weave in and out like a thoroughbred in a steeple-chase. Justine paused at the crest of the hill, turned and extended her arms to the sky, stretching the muscles in her back, her eyes following the nearly cloudless sky arcing toward the towering cliffs to the northwest. The cliffs were nearer now, close enough to see small caves poxed into the smooth ruby rock.

This place reminded Justine of the day she and Amir were in search of circular tombs in the caves of the Maremmia in Italy. Reliefs were carved into the walls—angel wings, grotesque faces with swollen lips, animated snakes winding around the base of rocks. They made love for the first time that day, pressed against the tufa cliffs carved into a frozen sea by wind and water millennia before. The mauve hues of those mountains so like these cliffs on Lobo Mountain. Her body quivered.

Justine turned and continued the ascent, more slowly now; her heartbeat quickening with excitement as she climbed toward the high canyon that few ever saw—a spot untouched by progress, by centuries past or present. Finally, feet wide apart, she stood on the rim of the canyon, reaching for her water bottle tucked into her fanny pack. Justine stared at the mountain behind her, water trickling down her neck, cooling herself against the searing sun. Sweat crawled along her hairline as she wiped her hand across her neck and up into her damp ponytail, shifting her eyes to gaze into the canyon ahead. *It must be more than nine thousand feet here*, she thought, breathing deeply and adjusting her pack for the descent.

Glorious. The excitement of discovery pulsed in her veins, as though she were the first to capture this view, this land. But so many had come before: for thousands of years the Indians explored and hunted here; then trackers like Kit Carson, and alien visitors like Lawrence honored the land, this sanctity of nature. The Hawk family lived here for nearly a century. Yet it looked so pristine, untouched.

Justine found a ledge near the bottom of the canyon wall and sat down, drawing an apple from her pack and biting gratefully into the crisp, refreshing orb. Delicious, cooling. She sat quietly, closing her eyes, breathing deeply, clearing her mind to a meditation state. She stretched out on the warm stone, using her fanny pack for a makeshift pillow. Soon, she was asleep. A deep, dreamless sleep.

How much time passed? She had no idea. Allowing consciousness to seep back in like a lazy creek filling with the first spring rain, eyes closed, she mentally scanned her body. The warm stone and her body had melted into one. The air was still. A soft cacophony of sounds—a breeze rustling leaves, the flapping of a hawk's wings soaring above. Breathing. *My own?* She realized in that moment a presence, a nearly inaudible purr. An unfamiliar wild, earthy fragrance. Her face, heated from the unguarded sun as she slept, was now in shadow.

She slowly opened her eyes. Unnervingly close to her face, wide almond eyes of gold stared back at her. The outsized stranger's clear eyes expressed a tenderness, a calm embedded in wildness. Curiosity. Justine felt his warm, damp breath moving in and out across her flushed face. For several moments they breathed almost in concert, the rhythm coming as naturally as she and Taya running in tune with one another, or lovers moving synchronistically as one.

The mountain lion arched its back in a stretch, the two prescient beings regarding one another. Justine felt no fear, nor an impulse to move, mostly just a reverence for this magnificent animal. She moved only her eyes, slowly, feeling as though she was in a spell, hypnotized by this powerful, yet unthreatening, predator. After licking its paws one at a time, the tawny lion turned and lumbered further down into the canyon. His steps were deliberate, silent, as though he, too, hadn't wanted to disturb their intimacy. He glanced back, just once, finding Justine's eyes. She nodded.

MID-OCTOBER, LOBO MOUNTAIN, 1923

Lawrence feels the strain on his slim frame, muscles contracting, pressing to cooperate with their master. Relying heavily on the walking stick, he grasps it desperately, his knuckles white. Spruce and balsam scent his climb; water trickles from a small spring, soon to be enhanced with the runoff from an early snow. He is intent on making this climb alone one more time before he, Frieda and Brett leave for Mexico. He cherishes these sojourns alone, rare as they are. He thinks uninterrupted, words bubbling into his mind, taking form. The necessary journey for a writer, immersed in sensuous nature, the ultimate inspiration for art, fermenting before he takes pen into hand.

Lawrence understands his own restlessness, his need to move on, to find the next unfamiliar experience. Yet here life sings of surprises, so he returns again and again.

Suddenly, two Mexican men carrying guns approach. Guns. Why? he shouts silently. He knew the answer, yet wished he didn't. Men are the most dangerous of animals.

What is he carrying? Lawrence asks himself as the men near. Yellow. A calf? An old yellow dog exhausted by the hunt?

The men smile gently, as though they were quite innocent of any wrong doing. The natural way of men. With guns. A mountain lion, long and slim and yellow, across the buckskin shoulder of the larger of the two men.

At first, they don't speak of it. Lawrence can't speak of it.

"Caught her in a trap," one of the Mexicans says, smiling foolishly, "this morning."

His friend looks at the lion, and back at the stranger. Expectantly. Lawrence walks forward and lifts the cat's beautiful, round head. So perfect in its symmetry, he thinks. Dead eyes, with perfect little Chinese fans for lashes. Limp ears.

They walk on and Lawrence says nothing. He looks up into the blood-orange cliffs and spots her lair, a little cave. Where she'll never walk again.

Lawrence thinks that in this shallow world there is room for him and the mountain lion. Perhaps fewer humans. "Yet what a gap is left in the world by the missing white frost-face of that slim yellow mountain lion."

CHAPTER 23

⸎

"WHAT'S A MIRACLE?" asked Justine as she and Giovanna pounded the pathway arcing into the foothills just south of the University of New Mexico campus.

"Do you mean my definition or the Vatican's?" Giovanna asked without taking her eyes off the alternating light and dark moving across the landscape. The path curled upward toward the south, then twisted to the west. The rising sun at their backs cast giant shadows stretching as they moved.

"Let's start with yours," said Justine. Her breathing was smooth; she realized she had acclimated to the elevation.

"Well…let me make a distinction between mine and the Vatican's. They are more demanding of evidence, and rightly so. For me, I intuitively consider the many miracles attributed to the Blessed Kateri and say to myself: yes, this is a miracle. You are asking about the Blessed Kateri—right?"

"Yes, Kateri, specifically."

"Well, the major criterion is being saved from death by a prayer to Blessed Kateri—or another person or saint. A doctor has to certify that there is no other explanation. That the person would have died without the saint's intervention. Saint nominee in this case."

"Of course. Is there a special miracle being considered in the Blessed Kateri's case—or many?"

"You'll remember from my book presentation that the Blessed Kateri died from complications from self-flagellation in 1680. There have been many miracles since—all sorts of them—including the miracle at her own passing when, within fifteen minutes of her death, her horrible smallpox scars disappeared. Then, the blue blanket she'd wrapped herself in was used to perform miracles for others. But the most recent miracle under consideration is of a six-year old boy named Jake Finkbonner who fell and cut his lip on a metal fence in the closing moments of a basketball game. In Washington State, I think. Overnight, Jake's face swelled up and he had a high fever. Doctors determined that a flesh-eating bacteria, necrotizing fascitis or Strep A, was actually devouring his face! The doctors had to operate daily to remove the damaged flesh.

Justine was startled, her eyes growing into round discs. "I've heard of such things, but didn't know they were for real."

"They're for real alright. Doctors said they couldn't save him...that there was nothing they could do. So a family friend, Reverend Sauer, asked his congregation to pray to the Blessed Kateri on Jake's behalf. The priest chose Kateri because of her facial scars and Indian heritage – Jake is half Lummi Indian. The prayers started coming in from all over, and a representative from the Society of the Blessed Kateri Tekakwitha went to the hospital and placed a pendant of Kateri on Jake's pillow. The very next day, the bacteria stopped growing and Jake recovered."

"But you said it's already been four years. Doesn't that mean they've rejected the miracle?" Justine asked.

"Not necessarily. The Vatican doesn't accept miracles lightly—the way they did in the Middle Ages—they investigate for years. We are waiting." Giovanna stopped running and turned to Justine. Her breathing was labored. Beyond the rise in the mesa now, they couldn't see the campus.

Justine stopped, standing in place to stretch, "Did you send your book to the Vatican investigating committee?"

"I did; the group is called the Congregation of Saints. A copy was also sent to Pope Benedict XVI. I received a letter of receipt. I'm hopeful and excited. But canonization comes slowly, if at all." She sat down on a gathering of gray stones framing the drainage pipe.

Justine sat down beside her. "I had something amazing happen a couple of days ago—it felt like a miracle to me."

Giovanna stared at Justine, leaning forward with her hands on both knees. "What?"

Justine told Giovanna of waking up on Lobo Mountain with the mountain lion gazing into her eyes. "It felt as though I was staring wildness—life—in the face. Exhilarating …then he just stretched and walked away."

"You were alone?" asked Giovanna, a soft rebuke intended, "You should know better!"

"I was. And, yes, I know that isn't wise. Bill taught me as much. 'Don't go into Lobo Canyon alone,' he'd insisted. He also taught me how to know if lions or bears were close—tracks, scat, claw marks on logs—how to enlarge my stance if I needed to fight. But really, no one could have taught me how to deal with a lion a few inches from my face."

Giovanna let her breath out slowly, shaking her head. "That's for sure. Weren't you scared to death?"

"Amazingly not," Justine grinned, drawing in the cool air and allowing herself to re-experience those moments. "The expression in the cat's eyes was so tender, unthreatening, as though we knew one another."

"Well, that's a miracle in my book!" Giovanna exclaimed, "as well as the dancing morning shadows ahead of us. All God's miracles."

Justine envied Giovanna her faith, her simple acceptance of miracles. *I wish it were so easy for me.* The two women jogged on silently, amid shadow and light, each deep in thought.

Justine was reminded of the boat trip from Sicily to Sardinia she'd taken with Amir—seeking to repeat her great-grandfather's journey—the ship in rhythm with the undulating waves, disappearing and reappearing with each crest. *The sea's shadowy dip, swallowing the ship and sailors, then regurgitating these strangers into its midst, only to be swallowed up again. Man's relationship with the sea and its shadows releasing control to indifferent nature. Melville's Leviathan. The Sea and Sardinia,* Lawrence's most well-known travel book, the one that persuaded Mabel Dodge Luhan that he was the one to write about the Tiwa, told the story Justine chose to re-experience. *Now the shadowy waves of light and dark on the barren land mimic the sea, burying meager plant life and exposing it once again. The desert becomes the sea. What do I consider a miracle?* Justine asks herself. *The sea? The desert? Life itself?*

—∞∞∞—

Justine drove into the parking lot behind the renowned San Francisco de Assisi Church in Ranchos de Taos, parking near the Ranchos de Taos Grill. She stepped lightly from the car, buoyed by just completing the grant proposal for the Archaeology office. She let her eyes sweep the clean lines of the church. *Like a Benny Bufano sculpture,* she thought once again, *one of my favorite Italians.* The smooth-skinned, angular structure is known as the most painted and photographed church in the world, repeated in the work of Georgia O'Keeffe and Ansel Adams. In fact, Yahoo touts it as one of the major sights to see before you die. Its legend is kept alive by such recent events as the June memorial service for Dennis Hopper attended by Jack Nicholson, Peter Fonda, and other Hollywood notables.

She had been told that the entire Ranchos de Taos community is involved in perpetuating its fame, raising monies every year by way of community bazaars to resurface the church with fresh mud generously spread by hundreds of eager hands. Justine lingered for several moments before slowly turning toward the Grill where she would meet Giovanna and her friend, Maria, a descendant of one of the original Spanish families.

Her eyes lighted on a familiar battered pickup parked just to the south of the Church. The young men who had followed her before peered ominously through the dirty window shield. While she couldn't make out the figures, she assumed they were the same boys who'd followed her several days ago as she was leaving the Bureau of Land Management. *What do they want?* she asked herself again, then decided to find out. She slammed her door and walked rapidly toward the truck. She wasn't surprised when the driver slammed the transmission into reverse and sped backward, spinning around in a whirlwind of dust, before racing out the alley toward the elementary school. Dangerous, not only for Justine, but for any children in their path. At least this time she got the license number.

—∞∞∞—

Justine opened the iron gate leading through the patio into the Ranchos de Taos Plaza Grill. Every outdoor table was occupied with people enjoying Saturday lunch. The well-maintained building had been a hub since 1858, a part of contiguous structures surrounding the church. Established as a restaurant in 1999, just before the turn of the millennium. Everyone knew it was the best place in the area.

Justine followed the waitress through the ancient adobe structure with the familiar log vigas into a room where she found Giovanna and Maria, a lovely Spanish woman with an open, engaging smile. "Sophisticated" was the word that came to mind as Justine observed Maria's stylish outfit in shades of fuchsia. Her erect posture added an air of confidence; charm radiated from her chocolate brown eyes. She reached for Justine's extended hand. "Giovanna has told me so much about you. I'm delighted to have a chance to meet you in person."

Justine held Maria's hand for a moment. "Thank you," she replied. "My pleasure."

"My favorite dish here is the stuffed sopapillas," offered Maria, after they had settled in their seats. "Little pillows, but the word in Spanish really means 'holding soup.' They're filled with chicken, rice and beans, then coated with a rich cheese sauce. Hard to imagine the flimsy little things actually holding soup. Delicious, but not good for my waistline." Maria delicately patted her stomach with both hands and turned to Giovanna. "You didn't tell me Justine was so lovely...those golden eyes, and tanned skin." She paused in appreciation. "By the way, have you heard anything from the Vatican about Kateri?"

Justine was usually disconcerted by such open praise, particularly from a stranger, yet it was offered in such a soft, authentic voice, she just smiled easily and reached for the menu.

All three women ordered the stuffed sopapilla and raspberry iced tea. "I wanted Justine to be my surprise," Giovanna confessed. "And no, no word about Kateri's canonization as yet. We are hopeful."

"It takes time, sometimes years." Maria said, turning to Justine. "Tell me about yourself. What brought you to Taos?"

Justine smiled at the familiar question. By now, she had a rehearsed, yet sincere, answer that seemed to satisfy. She explained her parentage, the journey from Egypt to Italy, the search for a lost Etruscan tomb, then her new job with the New Mexico Office of Archaeology. Her pursuit of D. H. Lawrence. While Giovanna knew the story about the diary, Justine wanted to get to know Maria better before venturing into this highly charged territory, that could be shocking to any good Catholic woman. As she finished, Giovanna nodded, slightly amused, more by what she left out than what was included.

"That's incredible," exclaimed Maria. "What an adventurous life you've had already. I envy you. I'd no idea Lawrence had a child, but then we know very little about him in this community."

"I find this curious," Justine said, genuinely puzzled. "One of the most famous writers in the world is buried here, yet many aspects of his life seem like a well-kept secret. But then the letters to my great-grandmother remained a family secret for decades. Lawrence is surrounded by mystery."

"So true." Maria tilted her head as though she wanted to talk further about the letters, but chose another tack. "As far as I remember from my experience and that of my four children, his books are not discussed in school here and his followers come and go silently. I think the only book I've read of his is *Lady Chatterley's Lover*—when it was prohibited. I have to admit I was shocked, but I was young and sheltered," she said, selecting an unfilled sopapilla from the basket to scoop up the generous overflow of cheese sauce and beans. "That was a long time ago. I'm a little less sheltered now—at least I hope so." Maria grinned as though treasuring her own secrets.

"Maria grew up right here in this Plaza," offered Giovanna, stabbing into the center of her stuffed pillow causing steam to rush into the air, tickling her nose.

Maria obliged. "We were Catholic when I was a young girl, but then my mother became angry with the priest—I can't even remember why—and we moved to the Presbyterian Church until the priest died. 'Churches are all the same,' she told us at the time, 'we all pray to Jesus.' That was when the community was almost entirely Christian. But things have changed now, fortunately; we're much more diverse. We have two Muslim temples and Buddhists as well. But in time our family missed the Virgin Mary. Protestants don't give her enough attention, you know."

"I agree. Mary is worshipped much more in the Catholic Church and the Coptic Christian Church of Egypt," confirmed Justine. "Otherwise, did you find the churches similar?"

"Not so different. They're all looking for God. But I like the Catholic rituals. At any rate, I went off to business school in Santa Fe and met this girl who talked me into becoming a nun. I thought it a lovely idea at the time. So I went along. For awhile."

Giovanna turned to Justine. "An easy career choice," she laughed, "like becoming a teacher."

"Giovanna doesn't let me forget that I made a big decision rather casually." Maria playfully boxed her friend on the arm, more a show of affection than rebuke. "But it turned out well, didn't it?"

"It did," admitted Giovanna, leaning backward to avoid the heat still bubbling from her plate. "You met Greg."

"We were sent off to Minnesota for training and that's where I met Greg."

"Greg?" questioned Justine, leaning forward.

"My husband. He was preparing to be a priest. But the order ran out of funds and we were all sent home for the summer. He, too, was from Taos. We'd known each other slightly in high school, but I hadn't paid him any mind. Before that summer was over, we were engaged. Four children and forty-five years later, here we are."

"I love it," said Justine. "I understand that your own family was one of the original Spanish land grant families in the area. And Giovanna tells me you're related to Kit Carson."

"True, although that's a mixed blessing. Jaramillo was my maiden name. My great aunt was Josefa Jaramillo, Kit Carson's third wife. That would make Carson my great uncle, I guess. The Jaramillos were a prominent family in Taos at that time, and they objected to their daughter marrying this illiterate Indian Scout, with half-breed children, whose first two wives were Indian. Josefa and Kit were married by Father Martinez who managed to bring Carson into the church, mostly to please his wife's family."

"A fascinating history. Romantic. Do you know any of the other Carson descendents?"

"Not really. We're not in touch. Most of the other family members live in southern Colorado, in the Arkansas Valley, although grandfather Jaramillo was quite a character, I understand. I never really knew him. He was a trapper, self-proclaimed vet and owned a bank on the plaza."

"A bank on the plaza?" Justine leaned forward, her eyes sparkling with possibilities. "When would that have been? Where was it?"

"Early in the last century. But it went broke and closed during the depression. Hard times." She paused and watched Justine, whose cheeks were flushed. "I believe it was near the La Fonda Hotel where the chocolate store is now."

Justine picked up her fork and slowly swirled the beans on her plate. With little intention of eating them. "You knew this, didn't you?" Justine aimed her gentle accusation at Giovanna.

Giovanna stabbed at her puffy sopapilla once again and grinned, wrinkling her elfin nose. "Ask her about the tunnels."

"You want to know about the tunnels?" Maria asked, glancing from one woman to the other, clearly intrigued by the interchange. "Of course they exist. The descendants of Father Martinez would prefer to keep them a secret, but they're there all right. They start under the Red Cat."

"The Red Cat...the shop west of the Plaza?" Justine picked up another sopapilla from the basket, tore open one end and filled it with honey. As she drew it toward her mouth, the honey squirted from one end and ran down her forefinger. Absorbed by the trickle of stickiness, she almost didn't hear Maria say, "But the La Fonda Hotel owner will never agree to blowing the safe, if there is one."

CHAPTER 24

———

I N ONE HAND, Justine held a bowl of blueberries and granola for the ravens—in the other, her coffee cup. On the table lay a small book of poems she had been reading earlier, by local poet Janice Razo, stuffed with poems about these blissfully fascinating birds. Justine looked up in time to see the seventh raven swoop onto the patio with a golf ball in its mouth.

"Shouldn't you be in church this morning?" Justine asked, surprised to find Taya lounging in one of the green wrought-iron chairs. Taya started to laugh as she watched the raven with the ball join six others for their morning ritual. "Ravens like meat, Miss Justine. But they'll like berries too," she said simply without a hint of judgment. "I went to early mass over here in the plaza this morning. With my aunt...it was okay. I just let myself in the side gate. Is that okay? Can she eat that ball?"

"Ravens are terrible thieves; but, no, she won't eat the ball. Actually, I prefer balls to the dead mice they sometimes drag in. The golfers may not agree with me. Would dog food do, or do I have to chop up mice and road-kill?" Justine grinned and proceeded to place the breakfast bowl near the center of the circle of ravens.

"Dog food will do." Taya had that enchanting smile that never failed to captivate her host. "They get married too."

"Married? Ah, you're just teasing me!"

"No. They do, Miss Justine. Couples stay together for life. They love each other."

Justine observed the ravens with new appreciation. "Then they accomplish something that humans can't...." A tinge of pain held over from her parent's unexpected divorce moved through her chest. "I'm glad you went to church with your aunt this morning. That's good."

Appearing quite pleased with herself on all counts, Taya stood and walked into the kitchen, helping herself to a cup of coffee with loads of cream and three spoons of sugar. Justine had continued buying sugar for Taya, whom she was trying to break of the habit. *One thing at a time*, she'd decided.

"Look! Miss Justine! You have one of those special trees!"

"What special tree?" Justine followed Taya's eyes to a scrawny fruit tree in the northeast corner of the yard.

"A Manzanita Mexicana—little Mexican Apples. Very special. From Chihuahua. Makes good, sweet pies. A gift of the land. Of the Great Spirit."

"Ah, those little green apples no bigger than a tennis ball?"

"Sometimes they're red, or even yellow. My Gramma says they came from Asia a long, long time ago, then through Spain. Can I take some home?"

"Of course," Justine said, pleased to hear that Taya knew more of her own Native history than she had thought. "All you want...it seems to be the end of the season. Not many left." She paused. "I think your boyfriend has been following me."

"Oh, my God, Miss Justine! I'm so sorry. It's my fault 'cuz he's really mad at me. He says I'm real selfish now."

Justine listened in amazement. "Selfish? How so?"

"Well, he used to be able to do whatever he wanted. Now, I tell him to stop."

"Do you mean he could touch your body whenever, wherever he wanted?"

Taya blushed, the tips of her ears turning pink. "Yeah, sort of. I guess. I told him last week he needed to use a rubber. The school counselor gave me one."

"And...what happened?" Justine spoke casually, careful not to project authority or expectations.

"He blew up! Yelled at me. Threw my purse and everything out the window. I was scared." Her enlarged pupils shone against the white. She hadn't touched her coffee.

"The window? Where were you?"

"In the car. Up by Seco. I jumped out and ran. It took me a long time to get home." Tears formed like small bubbles on tan cheeks. She looked at her mentor expectantly.

"I'm proud of you, Taya," Justine said, her voice even, soft. "You stood up for yourself. Took a risk. Did you tell him that both of you were too young to have a baby?"

"Yeh, I did. But he said not having a baby is the girl's job, not his. He has no intention of putting one of those rubbery things on his . . . his . . . body."

"I see. Taya, do you enjoy sex?"

"It's okay." She looked away. "Ricardo wants it so bad. He says boys are different that way."

"Girls can enjoy sex too. It feels good. But having sex is a really big responsibility. You're playing with life: your life, Ricardo's life, maybe a baby's life."

" . . . I'm not sure I understand . . . it's hard to . . . . "

"Let me put it this way. Sex is the most personal of all human connections. Nothing is more intimate. Before having sex with anyone, it's important to at least be friends. Do you like each other?"

Taya's mouth hung partly open; she held her cup in mid-air. The ravens chattered on, taking turns stabbing blueberries with their beaks, stabbing at the round blue morsels, in friendly competition with each other.

Justine continued. "Friends respect, trust, and care for the other, listen to each other's concerns. Ask yourself if this is the kind of relationship you have with Ricardo."

The blood drained from Taya's cherubic face. "I didn't think about it that much. Girls talk about sex all the time. Teasing. Making fun. Like . . . like it's just what you do."

"Everyone doesn't do that, Taya, especially at your age. It's a serious commitment. You have stood up for yourself—that was good and brave. Now, you are the person who can decide what you will and will not do with Ricardo, or anyone else. If you decide to have sex with him, you need to protect yourself from getting pregnant. Ask your mom to help you get birth control pills if necessary." Justine concluded, her eyes projecting a deep affection for this young woman who reminded her of herself at that age. *I was so unsure of myself. If a boy spoke to me kindly, I wanted to be with him, please him. Fortunately, I could talk to my mother.* She smiled fully at Taya, patting her hand.

"If you think so, Miss Justine. I guess," she said, weakly at first, then staring directly into her mentor's eyes, a new resolve replacing meekness. Her chin moved forward as her body relaxed under Justine's touch.

Justine noted the shift in Taya's demeanor. "How about a run? We could return the golf ball to the club."

Taya giggled. "Sure!"

——∞∞——

Justine drove Taya back to the Pueblo after their run, with the intention of stopping by to see Giovanna on her way home. But she was interrupted. While passing the casino on her way from the pueblo, the familiar Chevy pickup full of boys pulled in behind her. *Don't they have anything better to do?*

Justine's discussions with the local police had been unsatisfactory. They said until something actually happened, some kind of illegal offense, she had little basis for charges. *Déjà vu!* When she was followed in Egypt no one would take it seriously either. Until she was kidnapped. She shivered at the memory. While she was not afraid of these boys, since she didn't think they intended her any real harm, she also knew it wasn't wise to underestimate threats.

She sped up and slowed down, turning north from the Pueblo road, then left again onto Camino del a Placita, taking the less traveled road running parallel to downtown. Justine wanted to make sure she wasn't imagining things. Now on the side street, the Chevy sped up and bumped into her rear bumper several times. *Now, that makes me really angry!* She decided to pull up in front of the police station on Civic Drive.

When it appeared that no one was in the station—*where are they? Out chasing heroin peddlers?* She had another thought: The Red Cat. She circled onto Bent Street, crossed Placita on to Dona Luz, and spun into the parking lot in front of the Middle Eastern café next to the Red Cat Melissiana and

Antiques. The same parking lot, she had heard, that was built over the location of the original Catholic Church and cemetery. The pickup parked less that thirty yards away and three menacing boys scrambled out of the cab.

For a moment, the boys and Justine stood their ground, staring at one another. She examined each young man in turn. *I assume that's Ricardo,* she thought, he being taller and more self-assured than the others. His eyes didn't waver as they sustained contact with Justine; the others looked down and away, clearly unsure of their mission. Two shorter Anglo boys looked to be brothers. The fourth, a classic Taos multi-ethnic mix. *Spanish? Mexican? Indian?* Each wore ragged jeans, tee shirts, sweat jackets, as though they had consulted each other about wardrobe. *Standoff at OK corral*, she mused. Then, Ricardo yelled at her, "You stay away from her, you Anglo bitch!"

"I'm afraid I can't do that. Sorry." Justine said softly, turned and walked into the Red Cat. She struggled to appear casual. Stepping into the shop was like stepping back in time—a twenties collection of antiques and novelties in a cacophony of colors animated by stuffed, ceramic, and crocheted cats in all shapes and designs. She wandered aimlessly for several minutes, watching the boys in her peripheral vision.

They still stood in the parking lot, as though waiting for a signal. Then, they began to run toward the Cat. As though someone had given the order, they broke rank, and followed the taller boy.

Her breath quickening, Justine turned and walked the twenty feet to the woman at the desk at the rear of the shop. "Hello, Melissa," she said, sounding as relaxed as she could manage. "Our mutual friend, Maria, tells me you have a tunnel in your basement that stretches under the plaza. I'm Justine, by the way." She recognized the shop owner from Maria's description: a glamorous woman in her mid-fifties, dressed in layers of woven lavender chamois adorned with bangles of estate jewelry. Her striking ebony hair was highlighted with a broad platinum streak folding back from her forehead above porcelain skin and extremely large black eyes.

Melissa gave Justine a blank stare at first, then seeming to put the puzzle together, a smile curved onto her coral lips, her eyes becoming animated in recognition, as though she had met Justine before. "I'm Melissa . . . and yes,

I do have a tunnel. Would you like to see it? Kit, keep an eye on those boys," she said to her assistant.

"That would be most generous of you," said Justine, surprised to find fear gripping the muscles of her stomach. The boys had been slowed by cars crossing Doña Luz, but now stood inside the shop, pretending to examine a few lovely ceramic dishes in vivid shades of red and yellow. Handling them roughly. Three of the boys looked quite lost. Confused. "Why are we here?" was written all over their faces.

While slightly amused, Justine had begun to fear for her own safety, that of Melissa, and particularly, the condition of the shop stuffed with delicate artifacts and glass treasures. *What damage they could do if they chose to*, she thought, turning to follow Melissa down the narrow stairwell into the cellar. Two short flights, a landing decorated with cryptic icons for the Day of the Dead: a bleached steer's skull and horns in a cowboy hat sitting in an ancient wooden window frame, a makeshift shadow box. Pumpkins sat on either side of the display.

At the bottom of the stairs, Justine was amazed at the size of the fireplace, large enough to adorn a banquet room—just as Maria had described. Throughout this main low-ceilinged room, worn wood slats provided support, while three smaller rooms sprung off to the side. Clearly, this had been one big meeting room at one time. Walls were hand-plastered, serving as a back-drop for ancient, rusted tools and window frames.

"This is it," said Melissa, pointing to a door near the fireplace that could have qbeen the covering for a Midwestern tornado cellar, wood slats battened down with cross hatches. She glanced furtively back up the stairs. A padlock hung from the metal latch.

"Could I see inside?" asked Justine casually, hearing the heels of heavy boots on the wooden floor above them as the boys approached the stairs leading into the cellar.

"There's really nothing to see," said Melissa. "I use it for storage, keep a few boxes near the entrance . . . but if you'd like . . . " She drew a set of keys from her pocket, searched through them and chose the smallest to insert into the brass padlock.

Justine noticed how similar the key was to the one she had in her pocket, realizing that it could fit into thousands of padlocks. What secret strongholds are there for Lawrence's unknown treasures. What could she possibly find? But then, Lawrence never returned to Taos after he met Isabella, so anything found couldn't tell her much about the relationship.

Melissa pulled open the little-used door to the tunnel, now stuffed with numerous cardboard boxes and stepped back. "As you see, I just use it for storage. But I've been assured that this is the infamous tunnel. Many don't believe it ever existed."

"Have you been in there?" asked Justine. "Explored it?"

"Actually, no. It's small for me, and there's water seepage, a little muddy. It's probably collapsed in places. Not very inviting." She turned to confront the young men as they clomped into the room. "Can I help you boys?" Melissa asked with trepidation as well as authority. She was fully aware of a sense of urgency and confusion on the boys' faces—young men rarely found her shop of interest.

"Ma'am," mumbled the tallest of the four boys. "Just looking around. Thank you, Ma'am." Ricardo's eyes darted around the room, then rested on Justine who was quickly clearing boxes from the tunnel. The other boys gazed intently at the toes of their own boots, as though they expected to decipher some secret message written in the leather.

"Ma'am," Ricardo said for the third time, pushing Melissa aside and racing toward the tunnel entrance.

Melissa turned just in time to see Justine disappear. "Stop! Justine! Don't go in there—it's not safe!" She ran toward the tunnel, colliding with Ricardo and veering into the stone fireplace, scrapping her shoulder.

Ricardo reached the opening and grabbed for Justine's boot, grasping the heel. She kicked hard against his skull. Momentarily stunned, his forehead beginning to bleed, he yelled out, "Cunt! Stay away from Taya. You get me?"

Melissa stood dazed, her face grimaced, eyes wide, shocked by the young man's actions and words, but even more by Justine's disappearance into the tunnel.

A faint, echoing voice called back, "Afraid I can't do that, Ricardo." Shakened and alarmed that she had used Melissa, Justine turned her full attention to the tunnel ahead of her. Giant iron pipes and a plastered wall towered in front of her. She had a choice: to the right or left. She took a right turn. For now the tunnel was as tall as she was, but it didn't last. The walls looked as though they had been dug out with an ice cream scoop. Muddy water dripped from the top and sides, making the going wet and slippery.

No more than twenty feet into the dark tunnel, Justine came to another fork; one path leading straight ahead toward Antonio's, the original "cat house," the other turned east toward the plaza. She sat down next to a collected pool of drainage, curled her feet under her, and fished out her small flashlight, wondering if Melissa would wait for her.

The light flickered on and she turned east, determined to get to the plaza and the probable location of the bank. It was almost easier to crawl than to bend her five foot eight frame into dwarf size. An odor of sewer drifted into her nostrils; she gagged. By now, she thought she must be under Doña Luz— the street running in front of the Red Cat—as she could feel the vibration of cars passing above. Ahead, three splintered wooden corners protruded into the passageway. *Caskets!* she exclaimed to herself, assuming that all of the bodies had been removed from the old cemetery. The thought of decomposing bodies sent shivers down her spine. She sat down to consider the path ahead. *Is this worth it?? Could the tunnel collapse with me buried alive? After a few hundred years, it's not likely to collapse now,* she concluded, *unless I do something stupid, like knock out a critical brace.* She shivered again.

Justine rose to her muddy knees again, holding the flashlight in her teeth as she crawled, occasionally slipping and sinking into the soft soil, cutting her finger on a pottery sherd. *Damn!* Ignoring the cut rather than sticking the muddy finger in her mouth, she was now more watchful for broken glass, sherds, bottles.

I'll have to burn these clothes when I get out . . . If I get out. Further ahead still, the passageway became a puzzle, running right alongside a remaining section of the stone foundation of the old Our Lady of Guadalupe church.

She could hear rumbling from Placitas Road above, after which the floor of the passageway began to rise slightly, moving closer to the surface. New odors—old bacon grease, garbage—coming from the kitchen in the corner gallery. From here to the plaza is still several hundred feet. *Can I make it?*

And, then, that most grateful of sights—light. She saw a few rays of meager light. Her lungs sniffed a small burst of air. A rusting metal stairwell protruded three feet into the passageway, apparently leading up into the back of the gallery on the southwest corner of the plaza. And, the owner had told her there was no tunnel under Taos. Why did so many consider the tunnels a myth? What do they have to lose—after all, a credible rumor of tunnels would only heighten the mysteries of Taos. *Like the Taos Hum. Good for tourism.*

Abruptly, a large tawny cat appeared in the stairwell, reminding Justine of the mountain lion, but more menacing. "Hello there," she said, slowly moving her arm through the metal rungs toward the tabby feline. She drew her hand back quickly, scraping her knuckles, when she realized the cat had a large rat in its mouth. She hadn't bargained for vermin, shuddering as she recalled the plague—the Black Death—contracted by a man in the Northwest when he tried to take a rat from the throat of a strangling cat. She sat back, pressing her lithe frame against the tunnel wall, bleeding with crimson earth, watching the cat tease and then finally devour the struggling varmit. She wanted to turn around and crawl as fast as she could back in the opposite direction.

'Self talk' was usually helpful in a situation like this. Justine mulled over this action, deciding to give it a try. She had talked herself down before. *All right, Justine, there is no real danger here. You're in control of the situation. If you slow down your breathing, relax your muscles, your brain will follow.* She felt her body relaxing, stomach muscles loosening, her mind slowing. She allowed herself to remain seated until her breathing was regular, deep, slow.

Another junction appeared and she took the right fork, aiming toward the west side of the plaza where the hotel was located. Justine had a fairly good sense of space now, her visceral sensitivities fully tuned in. At the next juncture there was no choice, for the tunnel turned to the left. As she had heard, it was built to circle the plaza.

The next two hundred feet seemed like a thousand, her knees aching with each crawl. Slow. She was tired, short on oxygen; her brain demanded that she turn around. Her mind began to swim. She was sitting at their kitchen table in Berkeley, talking to her father—*where was mom?—at an art class? Dad was describing his days at the university in Santa Cruz with Gregory Bateson. In the '70's. Their walks on the beach... conversations over coffee. Connectedness, relationships, that is what he'd learned. Ideas, even truth, reside in the spaces among us, the patterns of culture. No one is complete; rather we are a part of everything else. What did he say?? We exist in relationships. I saw this up close among the Hopis: no one exists independent of culture.* Her mind felt muddled, unclear. Just as she felt as though she was passing out, she grinned at the influence of those very thoughts on her emerging spirituality. *Notions of community. Is this part of what Lawrence found too?*

Finally, Justine could see the tunnel ahead widening, the ceiling rising, like a vast cavern opening into a grotto. Another sniff of oxygen lightly brushed her face; her pulse quickened with excitement, bringing her brain back into consciousness. She was almost there. Twenty more feet and she could stand up. And breathe.

Once there, she saw an old battened down door of darkened wood. *Thank God! I can get out without crawling back through the tunnel!* She moved faster now, so consumed with reaching the looming door that she forgot about her search for a bank. She was foggy, near unconsciousness.

Reaching the door, she first tried the simplest of acts: grasping the iron handle, and pushing it downward, intent on opening it. No luck. *Come on, Justine, what did you expect? The proprietor with a hot cappuccino in hand?* She stepped back and examined the entire structure. Greek lettering flashed across the top of the frame; she couldn't read it. She didn't read Greek, after all. Not about to give up, she tried to unlatch the lock, loosen the frame—then she started to pound on the door. "Hey! Anyone there! Help me! Get me out of here."

She pounded until she was spent and slid to the ground. Not moving for several minutes, she breathed deeply again, letting the strength seep back into her arms and legs. There was more air coming through into this enlarged cavity than in the tunnel itself, probably around the door jam. She sat back on the soggy soil and looped circles on the cobweb embroidered wall with the flash-light, searching for another outlet, looking for bats—and bugs, rats, snakes. Finding none, she began to bring her breathing back to normal, relax into her thoughts, as she continued to project the light around the cavern. She wondered why her Dad couldn't apply his knowledge of relationships and culture to his marriage with her mother. *After all, in regard to women, Nebraska and Egypt are not all that different.*

Abruptly, unexpectedly, the light of her flashlight came to rest on a smooth silver surface to the south, to her right. This time, she held her breath as her imagination gave way to mindfulness. She could physically feel her mind calculating the options. *A silver wall? Mine? Sculpture? Machine of some kind? Aha . . . .*

There it was. A safe the height of the crevasse, taller even. She could see the markings and the round compass-like dial on the vault door. She rose and walked toward the mammoth silver hulk. It appeared in pristine shape. Just filthy and worn. Certainly the Greek owner of the hotel knew it was here. She reached up and wiped the dirt off the indentations above the door. "Bank of Jaramillo." She smiled and ran her arm across her sweating brow.

It was well after dark when Justine stepped out of the tunnel, back onto the wooden plank floor of the Red Cat cellar. She hoped that Melissa would be waiting for her. No doubt, she would be angry. Not about to take a chance of passing out again from lack of oxygen, she had assumed an awkward bent position and nearly ran back out of the tunnel, tripping and falling into the mud several times. Her tawny hair was brown and stringy with moist dirt. In spite of the ordeal, she was grinning with the mischievous, guilty expression of an errant child.

Several candles and one electric lamp reflected on the figure of Melissa curled up on the blue velvet couch facing the unlit fireplace. "Justine! I thought you were probably dead by now," she exclaimed. "Maybe the tunnel had collapsed, or you'd gotten lost, or, Lord, who knows. I was giving you until 11:00 and then I was going to call the fire department. What in the hell is this about?"

"I'm glad you didn't!" Justine collapsed on the floor, aching all over from being bent over for nearly four hours. Melissa stared at her in amazement. "Were you running away from those boys?? What did you find? What did you do for light??"

"Thanks for waiting for me, Melissa. Actually, no, I wasn't just running away from those boys. I needed to get into the tunnel and this seemed like an opportune time. I had a flashlight." Justine slowly, painfully pulled off her boots, then leaned back against the white adobe fireplace, breathing deeply. "Not much oxygen in there," she said, still gasping.

"Hold on a minute," said Melissa. She ran upstairs to her apartment in the back of the store and returned with a wet towel and a couple of bottles of Evian. "Here, first drink—then wash your face so I can see who I'm talking to."

Justine laughed in appreciation, accepted the towel and proceeded to wash her face, hands, and forearms. "I'm sorry, Melissa. Sorry for barging in on you, sorry for going into the tunnel without your permission."

Melissa waved off the apology. "Well, did you find what you were looking for—whatever that is??" asked Melissa, settling back into the blue divan and drawing her feet up under her.

Justine didn't look as comfortable. "Yes and no."

"Okay. Shoot. I think I deserve the full story, don't you?"

Justine grinned and nodded as she finished off the Evian. Melissa handed her another, as she began to weave the narrative leading up to her actions today. Her host joined the circle of close friends who knew Justine's story. Nearly all of it: Egypt, Italy, D. H. Lawrence and her reason for coming to Taos. Even her love for Amir. Melissa dug out a bottle of red table wine, but couldn't find the opener, so Justine used the method she'd learned from a felucca helmsman in Cairo: pound the bottom steadily with the heel of your shoe until the cork pops out. It works every time.

"So, did you find the bank? The safe? The deposit box that could be opened by the key?" Melissa was on her third glass of wine. She hadn't heard such a story since her ex-husband gave his reasons for serving ten years in an Arizona prison for armed robbery.

"Yes. Yes. And no. Under the corner gallery—I think—I took the south fork toward the La Fonda. There's a lot of junk down there. A gold mine really. Anyway, I eventually ran into the safe. A really big safe, partly buried in mud, with the name splashed across the top: Bank of Jaramillo. But, of course, I couldn't open it. It was probably under the chocolate store as Maria thought, since I came to a locked door that I think must lead into the La Fonda cellar. There were Greek letters over the door."

"Put there by Saki Karavas, the dashing Greek owner no doubt!"

"No doubt. I couldn't read them."

"So, where do you go from here?"

"I don't know. But one thing I do know is that I have to go to work tomorrow and I have to get home. Thanks for your hospitality!" Justine nearly crawled toward the stairs.

"Anytime, Justine. Anytime!"

CHAPTER 25

JUSTINE COULD HARDLY GET OUT of bed the next morning. Her thighs, back and shoulders cried out, whining about the unnatural positions she'd assumed wiggling through the tunnel under Taos plaza. She let herself fall back into the comfort of the cotton womb, rehearsing a few scenarios for her forthcoming conversations: the meeting later this morning in Santa Fe on her draft grant proposal, the discussion later in the day with Scott Ortman about her interest in the population migration of the peoples of Mesa Verde, and—if she could find time—discovering if Maria's family might be willing to excavate the old safe under her grandfather's bank. *A blur of uncertainty*, she mused. It seemed as though she had been swimming through blurs for several years now. Or maybe it was just the uncertainty of the grant and her pursuit of Lawrence.

She rose progressively, nearly crawling into the bathroom, lifting her legs one at a time into the hot shower, as though they didn't belong to her at all, but to some feeble, elderly woman in the final throes of life. Justine let the hot water massage her body for a good long time, then made her way back into the bedroom, laid herself flat on the floor and began to stretch. Her body fought back, but gradually relented, reluctantly releasing tightness and pain like a child petulantly releasing sharp scissors. She stared up into her closet, choosing a lavender silk blouse and tan linen slacks—her preferred work uniform for many years. While she'd flirted with high fashion at Ferragamo's in Florence, she preferred fine fabrics and simpler styles.

Rather than riding with Mike as usual, Justine drove herself to Santa Fe since she had an appointment at the Santa Fe Institute in the late afternoon. She desperately wanted to know more about Ortman's theories on migration from Mesa Verde, and the ideas she'd learned about from Pablo on the Hupobi trip—and Lucinda in their private conversations.

By mid-morning, a more limber Justine pulled into the north parking lot of the Bataan Memorial office building in Santa Fe. A small review team—consisting only of Sam and Mike— planned to give her feedback on her grant application. This was office routine—a review before final signatures. She felt puzzled by her apprehensions about the meeting. More than feeling like hell, aching all over, she knew her heart wasn't entirely in it. Still she'd added a few conditions to the community investigation that made the project more acceptable to her. Based on earlier discussions, she braced herself for Mike's objection to including at least one Tewa archaeologist, and preferably a Tewa or Hopi anthropologist as well, to the team mixture.

"I'm afraid I would have trouble approving this grant application, Justine," said Mike, his lower lip curled in mild distain. The office suite was an engorged, airless basement, reminding Justine of the old wing of Berkeley High School— yet homey and intimate. Papers and artifacts everywhere; staff stuffed into small cubicles, personal photos and mementoes tacked to bulletin boards. She'd been shown the plans for the new archaeology building on a mesa west of town, but the engineers hadn't yet solved the water shortage problem.

"I've some issues with the grant as well, but they may be different from Mike's. I don't find the objectives crisp enough, clear enough. Too general." Sam spoke straightforwardly, sounding very rational. His self-confidence and clarity were hard to describe . . . perhaps it was the direct, uncompromising eye contact, the persuasive tone. Still, there was something else, an air of surety without arrogance. His demeanor encouraged Justine to want to meet his high expectations.

Trying not to appear vapid, Justine hid behind intense note taking. Her head began pounding; she needed air.

"I see what you mean, Sam. Yes. Too general," agreed Mike. "One of my major objections is the team composition. Indians often confuse stories with evidence. Not a good mix." Mike was convinced that he wasn't biased—after all he was part Indian—and as a scientist, he considered himself practical, pragmatic.

Justine asked herself again, *What experiences caused him to keep Indians at arms' length—at least professionally? Why does he feel threatened?*

Sam stared at Mike, who was quiet, as though he were balancing several scenarios at once. "You have to let go of that bias, Mike. It's time. The profession has moved on and you need to move with it. The team composition stays in, Justine. Now let's talk about specificity." His voice was flat, leaving little room for argument.

Mike rolled his eyes and threw up his hands. Sam ignored him. Mike may have felt angry, insulted, but, he'd known this day would come. He and the local natives still bristled about the illegal dig he'd undertaken on Tiwa land in '82. Little did he realize at the time that he'd been on sacred land—but the taking of the pot, now that was questionable. Memories can stretch a lifetime—several lifetimes. He'd never be comfortable teaming with the locals. For now, he'd just need to let it go and allow these two to learn from experience. Fall into their own traps. He smiled to himself, as though temporarily satisfied with his plan.

Relieved at not having to argue her case, Justine observed Mike's self-satisfied grin with amusement, inferring accurately that he would bide his time, wait for her to shoot herself in the foot. She only hoped she wouldn't have to struggle through their differences at every turn. Her eyes fixed on a Navajo weaving on the windowless wall behind Sam until the fibers began to blur.

Sam was talking. "Justine, you've included several lines of evidence that have merit: community plaza design, resources, kiva placement, even gender roles." At the mention of gender roles, Mike rolled his eyes again. " . . . cultural artifacts, population movement . . . but you need to tighten those descriptions, as well as the definition of community. Give a few examples. I'd like to ask Jeff Boyer to join the team. He is well steeped in community research and native culture. Been here all of his life. What do you think, Justine?"

"Very doable, and Jeff would be a welcome addition. I can have a revision to you by Monday, still in plenty of time for the November deadline. Thanks for your careful reading and feedback." Her headache was easing. *Perhaps the Tylenol has kicked in or the stress of this morning was passing. At any rate, this damn meeting is almost over and I can quietly creep back to my desk and meditate for a while.*

"Done," said Sam. "Mike, are you on board?"

"Sure," he said, pressing both palms on the dusty table. "We'll be set to go by the first of the week. Want to do a little work now, Justine?"

Oh, god, must I?

The work session with Mike seemed interminable. He pontificated, while she wrote; some of his ideas she would use in the proposal, others she wouldn't. Finally, around 1:00, Mike took out his tuna sandwich and home-made chocolate chip cookies.

—∞—

Justine excused herself to walk down to Starbucks on San Francisco Street. Stepping out of the airless offices of the massive adobe building, she felt a rush of welcome fresh air enter her nostrils. A garden area of succulents flourished in the gravel along the sideway. Justine turned north along Galisteo, across from the Old Santa Fe Inn that claimed "hospitality from a simpler time." Dodging the rotating sprinklers spraying the lush lawn in front of the building, she stopped to consider the giant, circular New Mexico Veterans Memorial erected in 1912 and dedicated to U.S. soldiers in the armed services. Above the Memorial flew three flags: the U.S., New Mexico State Flag, and flag of the territory. On her right, the Inn offered a simpler life; on her left, recognition of one of the most complex and tragic periods of history. *Paradoxical,* she mused, *like so much of life. Nowhere else is American history more penetrating, more revealing of human struggles.*

Continuing north, Justine crossed De Vargas, the Santa Fe River, and the Alameda. She knew she could have done better on the grant, and she didn't like falling below her own expectations, or Sam's. She lingered briefly in front of Seret's—the phenomenal assortment of ancient doors, windows, and gates—and Maya's, one of her favorite clothing stores. An azure silk jacket caught her eye, but not enough to relieve her self-accusations.

The line was inordinately long as she waited patiently to order a tall latte and yogurt parfait, admiring the original brick wall and mahogany benches and wainscoting. Once outside, she claimed a table, feeling a rush of unexpected pleasure at the adobe skyline and church bell tower, Santa Fe's evident respect for history preserved in architecture. Santa Fe, Ogha Po'oge in Tewa, "Holy Faith" in Spanish, was established as Ogapoge by the Pueblo Indians around 900 C.E., the Spanish claiming ownership seven hundred years later.

Justine spread the *New York Times* across her sidewalk table, glancing at the headlines: "In Appeal to Hispanics, Obama Promises to Push Immigration Reform." She hoped so, the article reminding her of the tunnel and the Jaramillo Bank. She picked up her phone and dialed Maria.

The phone rang slowly, eight times. Justine shuddered at the thought of the new Arizona laws seemingly designed to punish Hispanics, regardless of whether they were illegal or not . . . and the forthcoming New Mexico election. She had just registered to vote in New Mexico. *Susana Martinez. She wondered if a Republican woman, funded by Tea Party Texans, could be elected Governor.* "Maria, hi. It's Justine."

"Oh, hello Justine. Lovely to hear from you."

Justine barged ahead, "I got into the tunnel last night and found the bank, at least the safe. It was right where you said it would be: under the chocolate store next to the La Fonda."

"That's exciting! I want to see it. Are you going back in?" Maria replied. Her voice held a child-like exhilaration.

"Well, that might depend on you. Does your family still own the property?"

"No. No, we sold it to the hotel a generation ago so you will need to talk with Kosta, the owner. He's an adventurous soul, but I don't think you can entice him to blow open the safe."

"Thanks for the advice. I'll go see him soon. May I use you as a reference?"

"Of course. Justine, I read your article in *Archaeology* on-line last night. I had trouble dealing with it. I've always felt a special connection to the Virgin

Mary. When you wrote that she wasn't a virgin, about her intimacy with Joseph, well . . . . " Her voice cracked.

Justine could hear Maria whimpering softly and she was at a loss for words. *What a day*, is all she could think. "Maria, you know this article wasn't based on personal opinion, but on the translation of the diary I found in Cairo. Several experts deciphered the meaning." Her voice was gentle, soothing. Three young women in western dress sat down at the table next to her, talking loudly about a forthcoming divorce.

"I know, Justine, I know. It's just that . . . ." Maria's voice was drowned out by the laughter at the next table.

"Just like a man," said the young woman with turquoise hanging in triplicate from her ears, multiple necklaces around her neck, bracelets on her wrists, and one around her bare ankle. Justine rose from the table and walked several feet away where tourists quickly surrounded her, chattering on about the many-colored leather purses arranged on a sidewalk table.

"It's too loud here, Maria. Not a good place to talk. Meet me for coffee tomorrow morning at the Wired Café?" Justine felt herself pleading. "Please."

"I'll be there by 9:00." She hung up.

—∞∞—

By the time Justine pulled into the Santa Fe Institute's parking lot in the foothills above town, her expectations were minimal, mood dark. Physically, she still felt like hell and had fallen short of Sam's expectations for her work. Then Maria. She wasn't sure what to expect from Scott, but decided that she preferred to be surprised than disappointed. Her dusty car was not out of place in this warren of vehicles owned by eccentric scientists.

Justine walked to the front desk and announced that she had an appointment with archaeologist and Omidyar Fellow, Scott Ortman. She recycled the compelling words from Pablo about Mesa Verde migration through her mind. Excitement rose in her chest as she anticipated this encounter.

Light from towering windows and skylights washed over intimate spaces, creating pools of openness and warmth. Just outside, patios were surrounded by mesquite pine. *I could be creative here,* she mused; her eyes swept the connecting spaces and clusters of cozy corners, rich carpeting, and sunken rooms.

Scott stood in front of her. Tall, lanky, young. Sandy hair, large eyes framed by rimless glasses. Handsome in a rugged, little boy way—not unlike his photo on the web. He led her through a maze of cubicles into the workroom, where they grabbed a cup of tea, continuing into one of the meeting spaces with a small round table.

"I've read about some of your adventures in Egypt and Italy, Justine. Quite a ride!" Scott leaned back, relaxed, crossing his ankle across his faded jeans.

She pushed her chair back and crossed her legs, laughing at his directness. "So it has been! And, from what I understand from Pablo, your research into the migration of Mesa Verde peoples into the Tewa Basin is no less startling. I must admit, I was stunned."

Scott grinned in return. "You're not the only one. If the evidence for the migration of Mesa Verde people into the Rio Grande were considered conclusive, there wouldn't be so much disagreement. Tensions run high around this thesis."

"I'm sure! I'm told your evidence includes genetic, linguistic and cultural background about the Tewa and you've concluded that these peoples—at least their identity and practices—originated with a large scale population movement from the Four Corners area."

"I'd say that's a good summary."

"Yet I'm puzzled by the absence of baggage. Archaeologists with whom I've talked—except Pablo, of course—are adamant that there would be signs of the Four Corners culture: similar kiva construction, pottery, village layout, transport. But there really isn't, is there?" Her question floated in the air.

"This conversation is going to take awhile," said Scott. "Are you in a hurry?"

"Not at all," she said, grateful for the time.

"There was substantial migration from the Mesa Verde region to the Tewa Basin, the northern Rio Grande, primarily during the 13th century. Of that I'm sure and most would agree."

"My Tiwa friend, Lucinda, said as much. She called it the Great Migration."

"I'm gratified to hear that. My Tewa friends say the same. The evidence is clear: biological, archeological, linguistic, oral traditions . . . they all point to that conclusion. But, as you suggest, the fundamental mystery lies in the lack of clear evidence that migrants brought their own culture with them— 'baggage,' if you will. And, if not, why not? Except for some of the sherds at Hupobi, there are no signs of new methods of building homes or kivas; pottery, wells, even the layout of the pueblos are distinctly indigenous. I imagine it had something to do with the quickness with which they left."

"Exactly. Why not?" Justine repeated, raising an eyebrow, her body relaxing as the warm tea seeped into her tired limbs.

"The mystery lead me to religious revolt, charismatic leaders and emergence stories." He paused, slowly sipping his tea, observing her face as she registered his comment, more puzzled than ever.

Justine listened. Most of the staff had gone for the day, only two individuals focused intently at their computers. She recognized Melanie Mitchell from Portland State whose work on artificial intelligence and cellular automata was gaining national attention. A vacuum cleaner whined in a back office.

Scott began to unravel his story like a thread being pulled from an elaborate tapestry. "I'm primarily talking about the 13th century, when the major abandonment of Mesa Verde took place, and the population of the Tewa Basin swelled rather dramatically. This was not a straightforward, unmodified lineage, but a hybrid of cultural practices by the indigenous of the Rio Grande, earlier Mesa Verde, and jointly invented new practices. A melting together so that today we cannot fetter out anything distinctly Anasazi. We must then ask why and how could this happen."

"Good question." Justine pondered this, brow furrowed. She loved it when he posed his own questions. "Why would a people willingly integrate with another tribe and re-invent themselves in the process? Give up their own identity? This isn't a natural process, Scott."

"Right. At least I thought so. This is where religious mythology and charismatic leadership comes in. As you know, in Indian lore, to 'emerge' means to go back to the origins and continue their ancient beginnings."

"Are you suggesting an earlier migration—two waves—from Mesa Verde, even that life might have originated there as well as in Africa??" She blinked. "When I reminded my Tiwa friend that anthropologists say the Indians originated in Asia, her reply was: 'It was the other way around.'"

Scott just grinned. "I am suggesting two movements, provoked by religious revolution. By this, I mean a rejection of new or imposed ways, such as those of the Spanish, and a return to ancient ways.

"Like the Pueblo Revolt of the 17ᵗʰ century."

"Exactly. That revolt, led by the charismatic leader Po'pay, was patterned after the 13ᵗʰ century revolt led by P'oseyemu against Mesa Verde inequalities...in lineage, status, class, wealth." Scott shuffled among his papers. "Here, listen to these words by Po'pay reported by Juan, a Tewa:

'. . . Po'pay came down in person with all the war captains and many other Indians, proclaiming through the pueblos that the devil was very strong and much better than God, and that they should burn all the images and temples, rosaries and crosses...discard the names given to them in holy baptism . . . leave the wives whom they had taken in holy matrimony . . . .'"

"And you think the Mesa Verde leader promoted the same rejection of the life that had been imposed upon them? In one case, by native dictatorial leaders—in the other, by the Spaniards?"

"P'oseyemu promoted the southeast movement to correct the inequalities he saw—that they all felt. When they moved into the Tewa Basin they found peoples who were less advanced, who adhered to the old ways—the old ways that represented the past they yearned for."

"Thereby allowing emergence back into the ancient ways of life. I see. How do you describe a charismatic leader? I've read some of Lincoln's work."

Scott nodded, appearing appreciative that she was keeping pace with his explanations. "Bruce Lincoln suggests a few characteristics of charismatic leaders. For instance, these leaders are from outside the major faction and possess the personal authority to point out inequities, those sustained by the elite to benefit themselves. More powerfully, they draw direct revelations from some deity, or source, suggesting a transcendent reality."

"As I recall, Lincoln talked about the charismatic leader as someone who could draw out suppressed discontents and offer hope in overcoming them. I guess we could apply that insight to any age." She grinned as she thought of her personal reaction to President Obama's hopeful message.

"So true," Scott nodded, the corner of his mouth turning up in a sideward grin. "So what we have in legend and in history are two similar charismatic leaders, P'oseyemu and Po'pay, who was a Tewa, each influencing their peoples to revolt against the causes of their discontents, class struggles, and emerge back into the old ways of life. This is the life P'oseyemu and his followers found in the Tewa basin."

"So they were willing to give up their traditions, practices imposed by those leaders in the Four Corners and seek out more equal and natural lives, even willing to create a new identity to do so."

"Today's Tewa identity," Scott concluded.

She was overwhelmed by the meanings of such a conclusion. She rose and walked to the window, staring at the empty patio shadowed by the setting sun. A few ravens convened for a late afternoon summit. Justine turned to find Scott standing beside her. She stared into his soft brown eyes for several moments, her face serious, intent. "It seems logical—yet a bit far-fetched. Very speculative," she said.

Scott grinned, laugh lines around his eyes furrowing with pleasure. Obviously, intrigued by her challenge. He was accustomed to critics, skeptics; in fact, he enjoyed the debates. If anyone accepted his arguments too easily, he questioned their legitimacy as scientists. "Would you like to read the full manuscript?"

Justine nodded. "I would." She found she was surprisingly alert, refreshed.

"Now, how about dinner? I want to hear about Egypt and Italy."

CHAPTER 26

—⚬⚬⚬—

TUESDAY, OCTOBER 26, 2010

JUSTINE FELT CONSIDERABLY better by morning. The aches and pains from crawling thorough the tunnel had subsided. A stretch, a run, and a hot tub dip do wonders for the body, as well as the psyche. Nearly convinced that Scott Ortman was right about the Mesa Verde migration, it would be a tough up-hill battle to convince the skeptics at the office, especially Mike. She knew that her struggle to believe his thesis still centered on the startling perspective that Ortman advanced regarding the lack of "baggage"—the absence of cultural artifacts from the Four Corners in the current Tewa basin. Further, she knew that nearly ten lines of evidence were required to "prove" direct lines of descent: Mesa Verde to Tewa. While Ortman had persuasively presented biological, genetic, linguistic, archeological, and historical lines of evidence, it still took a leap of faith to entertain the "religion of resistance" motive in arguing that the immigrants were ready to relinquish their old ways, to accept and integrate into the Tewa culture.

More, the Hupobi Mesa had not even been excavated. If Mesa Verde Indians were the first inhabitants there as well, would they have voluntarily given up many of their cultural markers and invented new ones? *This seems like a stretch.*

These compelling issues were on her mind as she pulled up in front of the Wired Cafe, a coffee house situated just behind Albertsons on La Posta Road.

Justine turned off the engine, grasped the steering wheel with both hands, and laid her forehead on the top of the wheel. She thought about Maria and her emotional response to the article in *Archaeology*; she harbored no assumption that she could convince Maria that the translation of the Virgin Mary's diary was accurate—although she had little doubt that it was. *Why shake this woman's faith further?*

Justine entered the shaded garden of the funky Wired Café. Railroad ties formed miniature Stonehenge structures topped with potted plants. A fountain spilled into a stone-framed pool; crowded lily pads boasting one lone lily were nearly overgrown with algae. Approaching the café's pine French doors, she saw Maria through the screened-in porch, staring thoughtfully into her coffee cup.

Maria looked up and smiled warmly as Justine slid into the seat across from her. "I'm embarrassed by my behavior yesterday," Maria began. "While my personal feelings have not changed, I know you are a professional scholar, reporting your findings as you saw them."

"It is I who feels apologetic for any offense…Mind if I order?" Without waiting, Justine rose and walked to the café counter in the adjoining room. "A banana-pineapple smoothie, please," she told the young man. His tee shirt announced: "Taos, a world apart." *It certainly is, although some things are certainly universal*, she thought, peering back at the serious Maria, seeking a way to separate the investigative findings from interpretations. From her beliefs as well.

"Not exactly my findings," Justine said as she returned to the table, as though the conversation had not been interrupted. "My colleagues and I reported on the findings after the diary was translated by two expert linguists. I'm personally confident of the findings. But that is beside the point, isn't it?" A deep red translucent canvas arched over the porch, projecting a soft vermillion glow over the makeshift porch and its inhabitants.

Maria grinned. "In a way. You'll remember, I was brought up in a religious family and almost became a nun. The Virgin Mary is untouchable to me. Belief requires that certain ideas, stories, remain whole. She is an important part of my life, which is the way I want it."

"And that is the way you should keep it. I have no intention of compromising your faith, even if it were possible." Three suspended Casablanca fans moved the warm air while two elderly men played chess at the end of the elongated room undisturbed by the movements of air or people.

"You understand, there are certain questions I just don't allow myself to ask." Maria sat quietly for a long while, a relaxed expression washing over her face. Her eyes wandered through the familiar multitude of workspaces. Another log-braced porch perched above them, extending southward toward a small Victorian sitting area and additional garden in the rear.

"In a way, I envy you," said Justine to the spoken and unspoken words. "It must surely be a gift to be able to keep a part of your life inviolable. I didn't have that opportunity, so I don't know quite how it feels. I was taught to ask questions, to accept nothing at face value." The fans swayed wooden Chinese chimes, adding to the muted sounds of conversations and recorded music.

Eyes widening, Maria looked alarmed. "How difficult that must be for you—if everything must be open to examination. What is your core? What defines your relationship with the world, this one and the next?" They were silent now, soft rock music filling the spaces between them.

Justine was pensive, lost in thought for several moments, reading some of the titles of books by Kurt Vonnegut lining the bookshelves against the wall. *Cat's Cradle, Slaughterhouse Five, Breakfast of Champions.* She hadn't expected Maria to go so deep. "My values, I would say. My parents felt that values come from being human. They—and I—reject the notion that morality comes from religion."

"I can understand that. It is freeing in a sense, allowing you to select from a world of values, not needing a religious narrative to explain your behavior."

"Umm. You could put it that way, although it's not like a smorgasbord. I believe there are a few values that emerge as humans grow and mature. These I seek. Cherish. Among them are truth, compassion, a yearning for social justice. Caring."

Maria's eyes sparkled like bubbles in champagne. "It would seem, my dear friend, that we are seeking the same things. I just find it in my church, my faith. I *know* that certain stories don't make sense. For instance, how could a woman be both a virgin and a mother? I just don't go there."

Justine laughed and drained the last of her smoothie. "I'll admit, there are many things I don't understand about faith, Maria, but I admire and respect your clarity. We share a desire for compassion and truth. For me, religion—I prefer the word 'spirituality,' lends itself to exploration, testing. I resist truth that comes solely from authority."

Maria reached across the table and patted Justine's hand, holding her gaze. "I need to get back to my granddaughter. She's expecting to work in the garden today and I don't disappoint her." She rose, picked up her purse, hugged Justine, and started to leave, then turned around, "Oh, yes. About the safe and the key. Tell Kosta that the Jaramillo family will intercede with the city council if necessary."

"Thanks, Maria. I'll tell Kosta—I'm headed over there now." As Justine watched her go, she pondered the similarities among the women she'd met in Taos and her Nebraskan grandmother. Other women she knew in Egypt and Italy. *These women of faith are strong, tenacious and they have something that I don't have as yet. What is that?* She grinned to herself, collected her belongings and headed for the La Fonda.

—⁂—

Justine stood at the reception desk waiting for the fleshy man at the computer to turn around. *Unlikely that this is Kosta.* She didn't expect the owner to be working at the reception desk. He turned and stared at Justine, holding her surprised gaze for some time.

He smiled broadly, "May I help you—again?"

She laughed; they both laughed. "I hope I wasn't rude, it's just that I wanted to play along with the Trickster."

Kosta's eyes twinkled. "I fully understood. I was just playing out a fantasy: beautiful damsel in distress. Dashing prince to the rescue."

"I'm Justine Jenner," she grinned and extended her hand. "Perhaps you'll have a chance to rescue me yet."

"Kosta Papamanolis. I own this hotel, such as it is. A long line of Greeks. Not much of a businessman myself . . . can't even keep a restaurant going in here." He pointed to the space in the back of the hotel that once contained a highly successful dining destination.

"Kosta! How serendipitous! I really do need to thank you for trying to rescue me on San Geronimo Day. I hope not recognizing you here at the hotel earlier will not color our next adventure."

"Ah. Adventure. What a charming word. What can I do for you?"

"May we speak privately?"

Kosta motioned to a young woman from the back office to take over for him. Then, he led Justine into his small office behind the reception desk.

She expected to find a mountain of clutter, chairs piled with debris, a desk where nothing could be found, so was surprised at finding it exceptionally neat and orderly. He'd made efficient use of limited space. *Ah, once again my experiences with Mediterranean men have conjured up faulty assumptions.* Justine told him the story of her great-grandfather D. H. Lawrence—that was enough to capture his attention and cause his jaw to drop. She continued. The key. Her journey through the tunnel initiated at the Red Cat. The conversation with Maria about the bank. She paused and grinned innocently as though she had just discussed their dinner menu.

Kosta sat immobile as a stone, his face flushed; a shocked stare had drawn his full eyebrows up as though they were blinds on a pulley. Finally he spoke, "And you want what?"

"You must know of the safe in the tunnel under the shop next door. There is a door leading into your hotel. Am I right? Greek words across the top. I'd like you to blow open the safe and see if we can find a safe deposit box belonging to Lawrence. I have no idea what I'm expecting to find . . . . "

Kosta began to laugh. "Of course I know of the safe, but on whose authority am I to blow it open?"

"You've never opened it? It belongs to the hotel, right?"

"Right," Kosta admitted. "My dad opened it in '72 for a couple of families from Los Alamos who happened to have deposit box keys, but then he couldn't remember where he hid the combination. He's gone now. Hasn't been opened since."

"Would you consider opening it again?" she asked.

"Using dynamite underground in Taos is against city ordinance. And good sense. Could cause trouble." Kosta's eyes grew leery; he clearly didn't want to become entangled in city politics.

"A bit tricky," she admitted. Pausing, she said, "Could I see the paintings?"

"Sure!" Kosta jumped up, relieved to change the topic. "I'll go with you."

———

Kosta thumbed through a cluster of keys and found the one that opened the door to a large, rectangular room with a deep mahogany table and chairs in the southwest corner of the hotel. R.C. Gorman paintings of Indian woman dotted the southern walls; an enlarged portrait of Lady Brett in her later years adorned the wall nearest the door.

"I haven't been here since I was eight," she said. Not much had changed, except for the Gorman paintings. "Wandered in here when my dad was at a conference and peaked behind the curtain."

Kosta raised a quizzical eyebrow. "These paintings must have felt a little confusing to such a young girl." He drew back the heavy curtain covering the north wall.

"You bet!" Her eyes widened as she watched the familiar images burst from the canvases. *Familiar, yes, but projecting an entirely different meaning now. No longer mystifying, more like a family album.* She stared at the *Holy Family*: a young boy with a sly smile sitting at the table surrounded by circles, half circles—bowls, cups, a window, the arc of the chair. A man with his arm wrapped around a woman, supporting her circular, bare breasts. Halos or luminous clouds encircling the standing couple.

"Do you think he was religious?" she asked without shifting her eyes from the painting.

"Certainly not in the traditional sense. He was too pagan, too irreverent," Kosta said. "The circles, I've been told, represent balance, completeness. "

"For Lawrence, balance was blessedness. Balance between man and woman, parent and child, man and his environment," Justine said.

Kosta nodded. "Sounds like the first peoples to me—and very Eastern as well."

"Lawrence started painting in earnest in '26 after he left the ranch," Justine said, "a new life force seemed to spring forth. Then he began to write Lady Chatterley's Lover in early '27, right after he met my great-grandmother."

Kosta turned and caught Justine's eye, an expression of understanding alive in their gaze. "And, the *Red Willow Trees*. What do you see there?" he asked.

"I see layers of green pines dot the horizon of the canvas, like little umbrellas I saw on the beach at the Red Sea. Clumps of orange willows sit in the foreground. One nude male bather sits in a willow, branches positioned to suggest he has antlers. Two other nudes sit by the river."

"Nudes are classic Lawrence," Kosta observed.

"Yes. For him, the human body is the subject, sacred, at one with the environment," she said. "He used motifs similar to Cezanne's. But I think I like this one the most." She pointed to *The Flight Back into Paradise*. "Eve is sneaking back into Paradise while Adam and the angel fight it out." She laughed.

Kosta grinned and looked at his watch. "I need to get to a meeting," he said. "Take your time."

"Thanks." Justine pulled up one of the heavy wooden chairs, sat down, and turned her attention to *Flight with an Amazon*.

CHAPTER 27

‹––––⊗⊗⊗––––›

THE BALLOON FESTIVAL, OCTOBER 30, 2010

THE AZURE SKY CAME alive with dozens of vividly colorful balloons being launched from the Taos Mountain Balloon Rally. Thick woven baskets hung from each, cables rising to envelope each side of the protruding orbs. Occasional flames blasted hot air into the balloons. The intensifying sun turned the immense balls into dazzling kaleidoscopes dangling above one of the most beautiful landscapes on earth. Justine found the event at the corner of Gusdorf and Albright Street, across from *The Taos News* offices.

She had not heard back from Kosta. It had been several days. Justine had confirmed that the property and everything in it had technically belonged to the hotel for decades. In the meantime, she found herself consumed by work, running with Taya and Giovanna, and occasional conversations with Amir. Reading everything she could find locally about Lawrence. Life had settled into a routine punctuated by daily visits from her ravens.

But today, she would witness the Balloon Rally up close. While the giant Albuquerque Balloon Festival was more famous, Justine decided that the unfolding palette of the Taos Rally would do just fine. The event was organized by a non-profit group of citizens who work all year to sponsor nearly fifty balloons in flight. As she drove, she stretched her head toward the windshield to keep track of the floating parade, quickly concluding that this sight probably exceeded the larger festival, since the setting against the Sangre de Cristo range was unparalleled.

Justine parked in a large field across from the launching area, noting a greater number of balloons still on the ground, firing up. In various stages of readiness, the blazing torches filled dozens of inflatable heavy silk balloons, flames rising from generators in the center of the baskets. A few riders surrounded the gas generators, holding on to the outer rims of the baskets to escape the heat. Supporters on the ground encircled the immense globes, holding ropes to keep them steady while they filled. The crisp mountain air a sharp contrast to the escalating heat and expanding balloons.

Justine had dressed warmly, layers of sweaters topping her Napa Triathlon tee shirt; her hair spilled out of her favorite orange and black ball cap imprinted with "San Francisco Giants."

More and more bobbing balloons of every color and size colored the sky. *What an exquisite site*, observed Justine, *I wish my mother could see this. She's such an aesthetic; the combination of light, mountains, and balloons would surely bring forth a new painting or poem.* The thought of her mother Lucrezia drew her thoughts back to the Marin county fair her family attended when she was a young girl. Color and music and costumes. And rides. She'd loved the animals, especially the lambs, reminding her of the baby llama and angora rabbits at the Wool Festival earlier this month. Sheer delights.

Thoughts filling her, she turned slowly, holding her Canon camera, taking photos from all angles. A balloon adorned with a giant Tweety bird rose, surrounded by excited children in warm, hooded coats. Another boasted an advertisement for Harley Davidson, one announced "Fiesta," but most were uncluttered by commercialism.

A young girl, arms hanging loose in a demeanor of defeat, entered her camera frame. *Taya.* Justine lowered her camera and ran toward her.

"Taya!" she shouted to the girl who had not yet noticed her. "Over here!"

"Miss Justine," the young girl answered weakly, turning away.

Justine grabbed her by the shoulders, rotating her body so they faced each other. "What is it?"

"Nothing . . . ," Taya said, "Oh, nothing."

"It's not 'nothing,' Taya. I know you. You came here for a purpose. Let's sit down." They sat on the grass on the eastern side of the grounds, backs to the rising sun. Justine's mind raced, imagining every possible problem, crisis, tragedy. Had she flunked out of school? Broken up with Ricardo? Been kicked out of her own home? Further abused by her brother? She didn't imagine what she was about to hear.

"I think I'm going to have a baby, Miss Justine." Her voice was flat, without affect, eyes down. The clouds over the Sangre de Cristos darkened, foreboding trouble for the balloonists if they flew east.

Justine could feel the blood drain from her face. She shivered as though a cold wind had enveloped her. She stared at Taya, observing pain move through the girl's eyes, tightness in the small muscles near her mouth. Tension stiffened her slight body.

"Who's the father, Taya?" asked Justine, reflecting painfully on Taya's earlier description of Shilaw entering her room at night, forcing himself on her. However, this was not the best first question.

Now it was Taya's turn to be shocked. "What?? What do you mean?"

Justine softened her voice. "Ricardo or your brother?"

"*Miss Justine*, please. Ricardo. I think."

Justine swept Taya into her arms, stroking the girl's hair as she started to sob.

"I promise, Miss Justine. Ricardo hasn't touched me since we talked last time at your house. Since I jumped out of the car . . . it must have been before." She trembled in Justine's arms, pulling away, looking around to see if anyone was watching.

"Are you sure?"

"I haven't had my period for two months, I've been throwing up."

Justine just nodded. "Have you been to the clinic or told your parents?"

Taya shook her head and kept shaking it. "No, no . . . . "

"Let's start at the beginning," Justine said gently, pulling a Kleenex out of her pocket to wipe Taya's face. "We'll go to the clinic and make sure." Justine held out her hand, helping the girl up. The two women walked toward her car; Justine gazed upward one last time. How hopeful and optimistic was the sight of balloons swelling the sky, like giant pans of bread. Now, all she could feel was trepidation, a sense of foreboding for the young woman by her side.

CHAPTER 28

⎯⎯∞⎯⎯

THE IMAGE OF A LETTER from her great grandmother to D. H. Lawrence flashed into Justine's mind. A letter her mother had given her before she left Italy. A child conceived by a man who was not your husband in a time when secrets could portend life and death. Those burdened with them lived out their lives holding on to lies, in quiet desperation, avoiding truths that might have set them free—or might have aborted any freedoms they currently possessed.

Apparently, Isabella had made a copy of her own last letter to Lawrence, although Justine had not found the original among the Lawrence letters. But she knew it, or some form of it, had been received since his last letter indicated he knew about the child. Thoughts of Isabella's dilemma, tragedy really, flooded her mind as she and Taya got into the car and set out for the Northern New Mexico Birth Center.

OCTOBER, 1929, FIESOLE, ITALY

> *Dear David,*
>
> *As I awoke this morning I imagined you beside me, watching me sleep with those all knowing blue eyes. I often dream of you, my love. In my dreams, you read poetry to me, touch me, gaze at me with curiosity; or we are walking side by side, holding hands like an old married couple.*

I have learned so much about the world from you, David. I name each bird now: buttonquail, grouse, corn crake – and notice a swan by the lake. Poppies, violets and many roses. I pay attention to each child who frolics by, looking for the wisdom you see there. When I write poetry, I stop at each word and inquire, is there a better one? I ask more questions, although they are rarely answered.

I have news, David, and I have delayed telling you. I am with child. Your child. It happened during your visit in July while Ahmed was in Egypt. Nearly four months now. I know you are not well and I don't want to worry you. Are you angry, my love? Write and tell me you are pleased. Once you spoke of wanting a child, but knew it was not to be.

My husband does not suspect and it will remain that way until the end of my days. He will be a good father, David, even if he is not my true love.

Don't be too hard on Frieda. She is loyal and has stayed with you, all the while longing for her own three children. She takes care of you when you are ill. I know you say she is difficult, but find forgiveness in your heart, if you can . . . she admires you so.

The trees are golden now and a few of your favorite flowers linger on. Everywhere I look, I think of you, I touch my growing stomach and smile. This child is ours, David. Please take care of yourself and return to me soon.

With love, your Bella

Justine had few actual words from Isabella herself. Other than this letter, just a poem or two, a few notes on photos, a family recipe. Most of what she knew about Isabella came from Lawrence himself.

CHAPTER 29

⬦

THE SAD NEWS OF Taya's pregnancy washed over Justine like cold rain. Curling up on her living room floor in front of the crackling fireplace, the scent of pinion logs floating into the still chilled air, she had to wonder if she hadn't failed as the young girl's mentor and friend. Tears moistened her eyes as she gazed at the distant mountains, once frosted with aspen gold, now gray and white, like the mane of an aging lion.

Freshly inspired to find new clues about Lawrence and Isabella, she dealt out his letters like a deck of fragile cards. She sought the passages she had highlighted in Italy—those that told her what he had found in Isabella that captivated him so, that allowed him to be himself with her. She had read these letters through many times, but none more reverently than now. Her eyes skimmed the words formed with lyrical exactness, searching for those telling phrases. One of the earliest love letters, in February of '28:

> *Your presence in my life is the fresh air of the mountains I love so well. What is it that you are feeling? . . . When first we met I felt an instant and holy sympathy and that is how we connect to those who are meant to reflect our lives back to us. That is one way we express ourselves---by instinctual sympathy with those to whom we are drawn, as I was immediately drawn to you, dear soul. The meaning of this intuitive connection may never be fully revealed. Never have*

I been in the presence of a woman who allowed the quiet
space inside my chest room to flourish uninterrupted.

So much is here, Justine realized once more. Comparing his feelings for Isabella to Lobo Mountain. She, somehow, reflecting his life back to him. Her allowance of the quiet space inside him to flourish uninterrupted. Later, he referred to the tenderness she evoked in him, reminiscent of his comments on "the tenderness of reciprocity."

Another:

Your body gives me heat and sustenance, you feed my very
being. I have never experienced such tender fire. Intimacy
without feeling you would own me.

Tenderness again, and that idea that she doesn't try to own him, to possess him. And later, after returning from Germany with Frieda:

I needed to escape the interminable Prussian atmosphere of
possessive, insistent women – except for you, my love, who
never lays claim to my soul and therefore owns it. I am not
afraid of you; I am not afraid when I'm with you. Women
are capable of causing men agony and you have no such will,
my love . . .

Justine stared into the fire with enhanced clarity. Lawrence had found a unique love with Isabella—one that afforded him the freedom to be himself while also becoming less anxious, more self-assured. This self-assurance was not arrogant, nor egotistical—charges that had earlier been logged against him—but relaxed and natural. Capable of tenderness and sympathy. Justine liked this man who was her great grandfather. She smiled to herself and gently gathered the letters into her arms, imagining the easy relationship her great-grandparents surely had with each other.

CHAPTER 30

※

APRIL 15, 1927, NEAR FLORENCE, ITALY

"Do you believe in magic?" she asked, the petals of her green silk skirt moving gently with each step, as though part of the verdant landscape. Tiny pearls trim the hem like miniature moons.

"Doesn't everyone?" He grinned, bending to poke gently at one of the purple spring violets carpeting the meadow behind Hotel Mirenda. In the distance, Fiesole perched high above the plain, Cathedral of Santa Maria del Fiore's ochre crown popping up from the center of the Renaissance city of Florence.

She tilted her head, ebony hair falling free, her confining Cloche hat intentionally left in the hotel parlor. Isabella's lively black eyes gazed into his. "Not everyone, I would think."

"How would you explain the glory of this violet. See the velvety lavender hue. I would paint it. Or the way your eyes sparkle when you dare me. Magic."

Isabella refused to swoon to his compliments. "Science, religion, don't they explain most things? Things that others call magic?" She pulled her black lace shawl across her bare arms. A modest flapper.

"Poppycock. Both rob life of its mysteries, its magic," Lawrence said definitively. He was often definite. Defiant. Standing even more erect, he straightened his gray tie.

She didn't mind. "Are you playing with me, Mr. Lawrence?" Isabella leaned forward and caressed the violet with two fingers, as though the touch of her warm skin might wilt it.

"Of course. But I play with the truth."

"But whose truth? What is truth?" she asked.

"Truth . . . ," he paused. "Truth is fidelity, fidelity of perception, knowing that an observation is real, even if instinctual or intuitive."

"I understand your unique instinctual sympathies. Yet perception is personal, is it not?" She gazed at the horizon as though lost in thought. Certainly the perceptions of her native Egyptians differed from those of the Italians, from all others she had met.

"It is personal, as everything is. The individual experience in communion with nature. Nature presents itself as the only real truth. Everything else is make believe."

She grinned in that sideways expression of enchantment, full lips turning ever so slightly upward at the corners. "I can accept that, David. Yet some would say that magic, that truth, come from Allah."

"Ah yes. Allah. By whatever name we call our god, I've come to consider him disinterested. Take the two of us. Is he sitting up there or wherever," Lawrence motions broadly to the heavens, "pondering our fate? Saying to himself, 'umm, I wonder what I will do with this heathen couple?'"

Isabella took no offense. She laughed fully—that dancing laugh that delighted him so. Then she turned as though to confront him, instead reaching out to touch his cheek as she had the violet. "You are a strange man, David Herbert Lawrence. I am beginning to treasure you, even if you are an infidel."

"You can be assured of that." His vivid turquoise eyes caught the color of the heavens. He stepped closer, reached out his hand and touched her ivory cheek. Her eyes softened, shifting from amusement to adoration. Without further words, they embraced, then reached for each other's hands, turned, and continued their walk.

CHAPTER 31

—◦◦◦—

BELLS RING AND CANDLES burn all night at the Saint Jerome Church in preparation for All Souls Day on November 2nd. Taya was confined to the house so couldn't participate. It was customary to feed and confer with one's deceased relatives on this day, but Justine knew that the young girl would not be able to seek advice from her deceased grandmother about her choices, what few there were.

November held itself in abeyance until after the All Souls Day parade and the Day of the Dead, then arrived with little fanfare other than a light snow salting the landscape. Justine found that everything in Taos changed in November. The Community Theater goes dark; the village falls asleep until awakened by skiers at Thanksgiving. Artists, weavers, balloonists, hibernate; few tourists are found in the galleries or museums or shops until ski season.

Some Thursday afternoons she spent with Nina at the Southwest Research Center reading the news clippings from the twenties about D. H., Mabel, and friends and the short stories in Spud Johnson's *The Laughing Horse*.

Her work at the Archaeology office took her into the Santa Fe offices three or four days a week, most often riding with Mike. She had fully explained Scott's theories on the Mesa Verde migration to him, even sharing portions of the manuscript of the coming text, *Winds from the North* that Scott had loaned her. His response was predictable: "Bunk. The evidence is thin at best—any number of interpretations could be made based on the same weak facts. Show me the evidence, that's what I still say."

Mike was extraordinarily direct, conservative, set in his ways. Justine wondered if any amount of evidence would be persuasive once he had made up his mind. And, while she found most of Scott's evidence to be remarkably convincing because it formed a coherent narrative, she also needed more when it came to the theories around religious revolution. For now, she spent some of her working hours reviewing the mountains of evidence Scott referred to in his manuscript.

Calls and Skype conferences with Amir were weekly occurrences. She yearned to be beside him now as he worked with Egypt's youth in what they hoped would be the build up to revolution. But she knew that wasn't possible, even if she decided to do so. She wasn't welcome in Egypt—yet.

Justine found running with Giovanna—and occasionally with Taya when her parents would let her out of the house—to be satisfying. Some days, it felt like she had a sister and a daughter. Giovanna escorted Justine to the murals of Taos history she'd painted near the city hall, explaining the history of the area in colorful forms, as though she was using a linguist paintbrush. Her descriptions of the harshness of the early Spaniards leading to the Pueblo Revolt led by Po'pay in 1680 were of the greatest interest to Justine, since they dovetailed with Scott's interpretations of the mission of this charismatic leader—his intent to obliterate the intruders and return to their ancient ways, particularly their religious beliefs.

Justine already knew the story of Our Lady of Guadalupe, but Giovanna offered a few more insights. As the legend goes, the Virgin had appeared to the Aztec Indian Juan Diego in 1531 near Mexico City. The Indians of Central and South Americas were overwhelmed by the appearance of the Virgin on their own continent, as were the Indians of New Mexico area, ultimately a major influence in their acceptance of Catholicism. Justine and her mother had visited the Church of Our Lady of Guadalupe in Mexico City where Juan's apron hangs behind glass. When the Virgin visited the poor peasant farmer, he ran to tell the story of the visit, and the Virgin's request to build a cathedral in that very spot. It wasn't surprising that no one believed him. In an effort to get rid of the insistent Juan, the local priest sent him back to the hill for more evidence. When Juan returned, his apron was filled with roses—

which were out of season—and, as he released his apron, roses tumbled to the church floor. The priest stood aghast. There on Juan's apron was a sketching of the Virgin in glorious color. Peering through the glass at the hanging apron, Justine saw nothing. She was fifteen then and left wondering about this thing called "evidence."

Evidence? Justine mused, staring out the kitchen window, observing her ravens arrive. The trees were bare by now, yet the morning sun turned the few remaining leaves and blades of grass into a sparkling tray of jewels. The familiar birds, in turn, slowly lifted one foot and then another, as though examining the bottom of their webbed feet for clinging snow. Earlier in the morning, she had left a small bowl of cat food and the usual granola for her regular guests. *Everyone is looking for "evidence"—the ravens, Mike, the Mexican priest, Scott, the Catholic Church investigating the miracles of Kateri. Myself in search of Lawrence. Evidence to confirm beliefs, evidence to substantiate theories, evidence to persuade, evidence as proof . . . what were the ravens looking for? If they'd found snow on their feet, would it have changed their behavior?*

The pursuit of evidence can be touchy, even disastrous. Justine looked down at her cold coffee and walked to the microwave to warm it up, then snuggled up on the couch. She involuntarily recalled a situation in pursuit of evidence when she was in graduate school at the University of Chicago. She had joined a team from Arizona State investigating an isolated Hopi tribe at the bottom of the Grand Canyon. The team leader had convinced the tribe elders to submit to DNA testing for the tribe, an exceptionally rare permission, promising that the samples would be used to investigate the unusually high incidence of diabetes. That really was the intent of the testing, she was sure of it. Well, as it happened, the samples were not considered private or sacrosanct at the University and they were used for many dissertations. When tribal members discovered this violation, all hell broke lose and they filed suit. While she had nothing to do with the promise of privacy or the violations, her name had appeared in the suit as one of the team members. Fortunately, when Justine applied for the position in Santa Fe, the Hopi project did not come to light. She was already "notorious" enough.

Lawrence didn't need evidence to draw quick conclusions from experience. His senses were instinctual, intuitive, almost physical. Justine knew he sought refuge from the world in nature. On Lobo Mountain. What he found there enabled him to burst forth as an artist, write *Lady Chatterley's Lover*, find love with Isabella, an exotic Egyptian woman of maturity and empathy.

What else have I learned? She wondered, staring at her watch. She was due to meet Judy Lynn at the courthouse in less than an hour.

PART TWO

Six Weeks Later

December 17, 2010

———∞∞∞———

CHAPTER 32

⁓⁓⁓

ALBUQUERQUE, NEW MEXICO, DECEMBER 17, 2010

JUSTINE WATCHED A STRIKING man of Mexican descent move confidently between parked cars in front of United arrivals at the Albuquerque International Airport. His swagger and broad shoulders, buckskin-toned felt hat pulled part way over his deeply tanned face, reminded her of Amir. She unconsciously moved her tongue to moisten her lips as a broad hand urgently reached for the door handle of her car. Amir asked frantically, "Have you heard the news? About Tunisia?" No greeting, no kiss, no other endearments.

"I have," she replied, startled but not surprised by the directness of his non-greeting. "On the radio on my drive down. Tragic."

"I shouldn't be here," he declared impatiently, paleness seeping into his temples. "I shouldn't have come." His nostrils flared as he threw two duffle bags into the back seat and climbed in beside Justine.

"I want you here, Amir." She leaned over, expecting a kiss.

Amir took a deep breath and turned, staring into Justine's golden eyes. A tired smile moved to his mouth, slowly growing into a wide grin; his eyes darkened, flashed with desire. He hadn't seen her for more than six months, since the day she left Italy. On that very day, he was taking his own flight back to Egypt, back to his job at the Egyptian Museum. He leaned over and met her lips with his; each experiencing a taste of intense pleasure, like dark chocolate.

They held the kiss interminably; she could feel the nervous tension drain from his body, aroused to a new sensation. She pulled away reluctantly, reaching out to caress his cheek just as a traffic cop knocked on her window, aggressively waving her on. She released the brake, shoved the car in gear, and pulled away from the curb. Turning onto University Avenue and heading for Interstate 25, she finally asked, "What really happened, Amir? What have you heard?" She handed him a bottle of Evian.

Swigging the water, he mumbled, "A young Tunisian street vendor set himself on fire. He'd been denied a permit to sell his goods—more than once—and when he set up his stand without a permit, a woman policeman yelled at him—then slapped him. Slapped him, Justine! The humiliation! He couldn't take it any longer." Amir's eyes were moist.

Tears moved down Justine's cheeks. She audibly gulped. "What will happen now?"

"I don't know . . . this could be the trigger . . . it could ignite the whole Middle East. Our countries are powder kegs. You know about the tensions, the turmoil. My work with Wael. You've witnessed it yourself, haven't you? The religious tension. The constant state of emergency. Young men picked up on the streets without reason. The broken economy. But, who knows, the tragedy might just blow over, just like every other insult. People turn away, go on with their lives."

"Can they be so complacent again? What will it take?"

"I need to get on Facebook as soon as I can." His shoulders slumped as he settled into the passenger seat; he hadn't shaved for two days, his rumpled sports jacket and sweater gaped open over his hairy chest, all of which, combined with his determined expression, added to his rugged sensuality.

North of Albuquerque, pools of sand and sparse vegetation escaped from under scattered layers of melting snow. Justine observed a few dozen graceful mustangs race across the frozen landscape. Wild by nature, fenced by man, these magical animals, silken manes and tails sailing into the crisp evening air, came to a wooden fence, a barrier topped with barbed wire. The herd split themselves into two halves, each turning to sprint in the opposite direction, like a flock of starlings. She wondered if the mustangs expected to be free at the end of the race or were playing a game—a game they knew they couldn't win.

He looks so tired, Justine observed now, *yet will he be able to sleep*? "Can you nap while I drive?" she asked.

"Not likely," he said, shaking his head as he leaned forward to turn on the radio, spinning the dial to catch the news in mid-sentence:

> . . . Tunisia. This morning Mohamed Bouazizi, a 27-year-old shopkeeper in Tunis, set himself on fire after a squabble with a policewoman, onlookers say. More than a hundred witnesses stood in horror as Bouazizi slowly sat down in the middle of the road and poured gasoline on himself. He paused only briefly, mumbling inaudibly before he lit the match. No one moved. People stood transfixed, unbelieving. A woman ran from the crowd screaming 'help him, help him.' She was later identified as his mother. What would motivate a young man to take his life in this horrible way? What will happen now? Across the world . . .

Amir turned off the radio. Tears flowed down his whiskered cheeks. "What pain could cause a man to take such drastic action? The pain will spread, Justine. Throughout the Arab world, we will feel what Mohammed felt. Take up his fight."

Justine was quiet for several moments as she considered his words. *Pain. Arab world. Take up his fight.* "We'll get on line as soon as we're home."

"Yes, yes. I must do that." He leaned back in his seat, closed his eyes.

What is he thinking? Feeling? Talk to me Amir.

His head rested on the passenger seat, eyes closed. A classic Arab face. *He is praying,* she realized, reflecting on his deep faith and the courage it took to sustain beliefs when you're in such a minority, for Coptic Christians now represented less than ten percent of the population of Egypt. If trouble comes, his family and thousands of others will be in grave danger.

North of Espanola, past Ohkay Owingeh, they began the climb into the Rio Grande Gorge. Amir opened his eyes, turned to Justine, managing a smile.

"Where were you?" she asked, her voice soft, coaxing.

"In prayer, Justine. I asked God for guidance. The road ahead will be difficult. People will be hurt, many will probably die. I don't know if freedom is even possible in Egypt." He took another deep breath, slowly releasing it. "I'm feeling the altitude, I think," he said. "How high are we?"

"About 2300 meters, seven thousand plus feet. It will take a few days to adjust." She reached out to brush a black curl from his perspiring forehead. "We'll be home soon," she said.

For the last half hour of the drive, they were quiet; she turned onto highway 110, shortly pulling into her driveway, wheels crunching on fragments of snow sounding like millions of saltine crackers.

Justine opened the back car door, grabbed one of Amir's duffle bags and made for the house, slipping the key out of her slacks pocket as she walked. Amir followed closely with his computer bag and backpack, careful to keep his balance on the splintered wooden stairs and uneven flagstones. It was cold, stars sprouted in the raven-colored sky from an encircling rim of purple mountains. She had left the porch light on; automatic floodlights flashed boldly as Amir reached the bottom step.

Inside, they briefly stood facing one another, as though seeing each other for the first time. Justine lifted one eyebrow, as though to ask, "What now?" She couldn't be sure where his mind and body were. *In Tunisia? Egypt? Enmeshed in desire for her body?* She waited.

Amir smiled broadly and dropped his luggage where he stood. Taking her in his arms, he kissed her fully, languidly, inhaling all of her like a sizzling feast, nuzzling his nose into her smooth neck, under her lavender-scented hair. His body warmed as he pressed against her, she responding with a tingling desire she had not known with anyone other than Amir. She released herself into his arms. *I am so needy . . . how I want him. Oh my god, it's been so long.*

Amir lifted her into his arms, his eyes scanning the room, this strange house. Justine pointed toward the bedroom, then rested her head on his chest, listening to his strong, steady heartbeat.

He gently laid her on the bed, removed her shoes, kissing her neck as he unbuttoned her blouse, one button at a time, she pulling his sweater over his head, his hair flaring wildly around his eager face. He kissed her mouth; her searching hands grazed across his taut belly. Then he grabbed her with a force that surprised her, caught her off guard, vulnerable. They made desperate love, a breathy rhythm taking over, seizing them with orgasmic release—intense, lusty desire consuming them both.

Moments later, Amir's breathing steadied and slowed. He didn't move. Soon, she realized what had happened. *He's asleep*! Quivering with the pleasure of her own satisfaction, she watched this beautiful man fast asleep on her stomach. *How I've looked forward to his sumptuous body, musky aroma—his penetrating dark eyes.* She allowed her mind to wander, recalling the years that brought them to this day. Their relationship, their doubts, the conflicts.

It was still early and she wasn't sleepy. Gently rolling Amir's head to the pillow, Justine slid out of bed and tucked him under the quilt. He mumbled, then resumed breathing deeply again.

Justine watched him sleep for a time, then pulled on a pair of faded jeans, sweatshirt, and headed for the kitchen to make some dinner. *He'll be hungry when he wakes*, she reasoned. Extracting two marinated filets of chicken from the refrigerator and grabbing a couple of sweet potatoes from the woven basket of vegetables, she placed them in the oven and cut up a salad.

In her office, she turned on the computer and pulled up a YouTube video on the Tunisian incident that had been posted by a bystander. She forced herself to watch Mohamed burn, his features contorted and blurred, the painful hysteria in his eyes unmistakable. She could almost smell the stench of burning flesh. He stared straight ahead and she felt as though they made direct eye contact. She slammed the computer lid closed and sat shaking, stunned by the immediacy of the tragedy. So intimate, so close. What does it mean when millions of people can witness such an experience first hand—and feel so helpless? *If I had been there . . . yes, if I had been there I would have done something. Why didn't others?? How could anyone stand back and do nothing when confronted with such a tragedy?*

Something, the terror probably, raced her mind back to Zachariah's violent murder in Cairo, his throat slit by a Brotherhood member during the burning of a Coptic Church. Her regrets arose, not from her affections for Zachariah, the man who had kidnapped and abused her in an attempt to keep the contents of the codex from coming to light, but for his brother, Amir, and grandfather, Ibrahim. Her thoughts lingered on the glorious man asleep in her bedroom and the tragedies he'd endured, including the murder of that beloved grandfather who had helped her escape Cairo with the codex on her lap. If she hadn't found Mary's diary . . . .

Justine was shaking as she opened her e-mail and addressed a message to her father. "Dad, You must know about the Tunisian suicide by now. What will it mean? Amir just arrived. Love, Justine."

By eleven, dinner was cold, Justine was in her well-chosen nightgown—warm enough for a Taos winter, clinging and sensuous enough to be inviting. She crawled into bed beside Amir who hadn't moved since 8:00.

⚬⚬⚬

At 2:00 a.m.—11:00 a.m. in Egypt—a wandering hand slid under her night-gown and slipped across her bare skin, slowing along her hipline, caressing her inner thigh. Deeply asleep, Justine was initially startled; after all, she'd lived alone for many months. *Amir.* Then she gave herself over to relishing his sensuous touch, permitting desire to sweep again through every morsel of her warm body.

"Hey," he said.

"Hey," she said in return, turning over slowly to stare into his darkened face, barely illuminated by the nightlight in the bathroom. "Welcome home."

Amir grinned, bracing his head with one hand and reaching out with the other to brush a stream of dark golden hair from her eyes. "It's great to be here, Darling."

She smiled, slipping her hand around Amir's neck and drawing him to her. Their lips met. Tenderly, without desperation this time. Each pulled back, gazing at one another as though their faces were new territory to be explored. A map of desire and familiarity, yet with mystery accrued by time and separation.

Amir lovingly ran his forefinger around her lips, then touched the end of her nose. She felt intense longing energize his hands, his tightening body. He drew her closer, kissing her eyes, nose, mouth, nuzzling his face between her breasts, her hair a warm drape of scented satin.

Justine responded with unfathomable, aching desire, moving slowly with his body, now charged flesh upon her own. He deftly slipped her nightgown over her head and pulled her on top of him, her hands around his waist as they rolled across the bed. He straddled her, moving his mouth again to her breasts, her soft stomach, before sliding back up along the length of her eager body. She feeling his hardness against her legs, before he entered her.

—∞—

When the light of dawn first crept across the thick ceiling timbers, Justine and Amir lay spent, holding each other, talking only briefly through the events in the Middle East. When Amir jumped out of bed, Justine led him to her office computer and logged in to Facebook. As expected, the Tunisian incident had gone viral, stirring emotions across the region, especially in Egypt. Hundreds, thousands of entries cried out in Arabic: "Now is our time!" "We'll take no more!" "We must be as brave as Mohamed!" Amir watched in silence as he scrolled through the words, finding a personal message from Wael: "Amir, we must talk. Call me."

When Amir managed to connect with Wael, his first question was: "When are you coming back?"

"Soon," Amir assured him. "Will the revolution happen?"

"I have no doubt. As soon as we are ready."

"How soon?" asked Amir, excitement tightening his chest. As an archaeologist employed by the Egyptian Museum, a man in his late thirties, Amir was one of the "elders" in the movement.

"When we reach a million—a million followers on our site."

"I'll be there," Amir said confidently. "In the meantime, we'll talk each night ."

CHAPTER 33

⁓⁓⁓

"D O THE RAVENS ALWAYS visit in the morning," Amir asked, coffee in one hand, the other arm around her waist. The reunited lovers stood by the kitchen window gazing at the frozen landscape sparkling under the morning sun. Bare trees and absent vegetation announced the wintry season. Ravens circled, chattering among themselves, flapping their wings.

"They're expecting to be fed," she smiled, "they're omnivorous, and would prefer mice or bats, but I'm not willing to indulge them." Turning to grab granola out of the cupboard and blueberries from the frig, she prepared breakfast for the ravens and stepped outside in her bare feet.

"Looks good," he called after her, pouring granola into two bowls, dividing the remaining blueberries between them.

"Cold as a well-digger's bottom out here!" she exclaimed through the open screen door, then hurried past him to fetch her slippers. "I'll be right back," she called from the hallway.

Amir placed the bowls, coffee, and one banana on the coffee table and stirred the smoldering embers in the fireplace left from the night before, encouraging a blaze with a couple of fresh logs. "Tell me what you've learned about Lawrence," he said, settling in for a long story. "Or should I say your great grandfather?"

"Either will do," she grinned, staring out the bay window to gather her thoughts. *Where do I start? So much to tell.* "One of the stunning observations, Amir, is how many people live here because Lawrence is here: his ghost, his spirit, his memory, something."

"Amazing. What is it now? Eighty years since he died?"

"And, eighty-five since he last lived here." They were both silent, he processing this information, she revisiting the awe she felt each time she was explicit about these years and the presence of Lawrence devotees.

"It shouldn't surprise me. As an Arab and archaeologist, I'm used to lingering ghosts and myths, part of our psyche. Please continue," he coaxed, suspending his granola in the air and shifting his frame so their bodies touched at certain curvatures.

"I've been to the closed D. H. Lawrence Ranch a few times—I'm taking you tomorrow—you have to see it. Bill Haller will go with us . . . . "

"Bill?"

"The President of the Friends of D. H. Lawrence. He's passionate about Lawrence," she said, sipping her cooling coffee, "I'll tell you his story later. Then, there is Judy Lynn, an eccentric attorney. We've met at the courthouse twice."

"And, what have you found?" He appeared surprised that after all these years the court records would have much to tell. "What are you looking for??"

"Some of our hunt is just pure curiosity . . . we've found Frieda Lawrence's will. By the way, she died a very rich woman. She had stocks in most major companies—plus Lawrence's burgeoning literary estate."

Amir lifted his right eyebrow in surprise, but waited for Justine to continue. He couldn't imagine Egyptians organized enough to retain such records in one place.

"As we know, she left the ranch to the University of New Mexico, conditionally as a conference center in the form of a quit claim."

"What does that mean?"

"It means 'I give you what I have.' Technically, the University should have filed a Quiet Title to assure that they owned the property outright, but we can't find it. But there's more. We found the warranty deed through which Mabel Dodge Luhan gave the ranch to Frieda. Lawrence didn't want it himself—he didn't want to own anything, and particularly, he didn't want to be indebted to Mabel."

"Does New Mexico recognize community property?"

"Now, there's the rub. It does—for more than a hundred years now. But the standard belief is that this was a personal gift, pure and simple—and a personal gift doesn't fall under 'community property.'"

"You sound as though you don't think it was just a gift."

"Frieda's biographers are of one mind about it: that it was a gift. However, in Frieda's single autobiography, *Not I, But the Wind*, she said she gave Mabel the original manuscript of *Sons and Lovers* for the ranch. But most historians of the families say that, while there was this exchange, both women knew the manuscript was not intended to be in exchange for the ranch . . . . However, the warranty deed says the exchange was for 'one dollar and other considerations.' It's that last phrase that intrigues me."

"'For other considerations?'" Amir rose to stoke the fire; Cairo University was printed in large letters across the back of his gray sweatshirt.

"If the 'other considerations' meant the manuscript, then it was not just a gift."

"And that would make all the difference in terms of community property, right?" He didn't wait for her to answer. "What's your intention? Do you plan to re-open the will, the probate—which took place where? In France?"

"In England actually. But Lawrence didn't have a will. At least it couldn't be found." She told him the story of the family friend Middleton Murray testifying that he had seen Lawrence's will and it left everything to Frieda. "And, no, I don't intend to challenge the will. Even if I wanted to, I wouldn't have a strong case. Too many years have passed. And Judy Lynn assures me that the statute of limitations took effect a long time ago."

"Then, why . . . ?"

"I haven't entirely worked that out. Perhaps leverage with the University to get the ranch reopened. If I could establish my credibility as a family member who has a stake in the proper execution of my step-great grandmother's— Frieda's—will, perhaps I could influence what is happening there. Rather, what is not happening. Right now, I view this exploration as an archaeologist would, Amir, digging into the past. I'm not sure what it all means yet, but I am curious about everything related to Lawrence," she paused. "You remember I told you about Frieda's Italian lover, Ravagli?"

He nodded.

"Frieda and Ravagli lived together here for twenty years before they were married. In '36, six years after Lawrence died, Frieda sent Ravagli to France to have Lawrence's remains exhumed, cremated and brought back to the ranch. You'll see the chapel tomorrow."

"Why didn't they marry?"

"I really have no idea, but here's a fascinating little tidbit: on July 3, 1941, Frieda gave the ranch to Ravagli . . . ."

"Why? They weren't even married."

"Listen to this: on December 18, 1941, he gave the ranch back to her. Both were legitimate warranty deeds. I'm sure it had to do with World War II—certainly Pearl Harbor—and his being an enemy non-combatant.

"Wasn't she? Being German."

"Frieda carried an English passport, so she was safe. But Ravagli wasn't. And newly enacted state law allowed the state to confiscate the property of enemy non-combatants."

"Curious indeed! Does all of this work into your portrait of Lawrence?"

She laughed. "Not really. But the extended search—and what happened to Lawrence's estate is fascinating. Especially in light of the value it held from the 50's onward. Frieda died in '56."

"What happened to Ravagli?"

"He returned to his Italian wife and children. Twenty years after he left! Turns out, you see, they had never divorced . . . . "

"I see." Amir was silent, trying to make connections, some of which did not appear to be there.

"Then, there is the key," she added coyly. "I found a key in Lawrence's cabin on the Ranch. I have no idea what it is for, but I've learned that there is an old bank in a tunnel underneath the square, the hotel actually."

"Whoa. Hold on . . . what are you proposing? To blow up the safe or something?" He laughed at the ridiculousness of the question, his pupils dilating with amusement.

"Exactly, to blow up the safe!" She threw her arms out, surrendering to the rationality of her plan.

"You are a rare gem, *Habibti*! But you're going to get yourself kicked out of New Mexico!" Amir shook his head and reached out to tussle her silken hair.

"But there is something else," she said slowly, gazing up into his eyes. "Something far less tangible, less verifiable, not measurable at all. As I've told you, an important part of my journey here is to find out who Lawrence really was, and why this place, this ranch, held such magic for him. Why he longed so to return. I'm persuaded that part of the answer lies not only in the land, but in his hunt for his spiritual self."

"He was raised a Protestant, right?"

"Yes, but fought against it all his life. He was contemptuous of the harsh moral codes, the need for an intermediate like Jesus. Anais Nin said he liberated literature, and that he sought to liberate himself as well. He found something inside himself, some new affinity for the land, on Lobo Mountain. And with Isabella. In that relationship he lived out his growing sense of liberation. I'm sure of it."

Amir narrowed his eyes, opened his mouth, ready to ask the next question, when they heard a soft knock. The front door opened slightly, revealing a single eye.

"Taya. Come in. Join us," said Justine, pulling her robe more tightly around her.

"Oh. You're busy. I'll just go."

"None of that. Come in and meet my friend. Have a cup of coffee."

Taya wedged her enlarging body through the door as though it couldn't open any further and walked meekly toward Justine's outstretched arms, keeping her eyes on Amir.

Sitting down in the chair opposite Justine and Amir, Taya's body and face transfiguring into that of a coquette. Her toes folded toward one another, her face flushed. She smoothed the sweatshirt Justine had given her, announcing "Return of Blue Lake." Her small breasts moved forward nearly indiscernibly as her forefinger made its unconscious way to the corner of her mouth. *Lolita*.

You little devil, Justine mused. *You're attracted to Amir—but can I blame you?* Justine gave Taya a reassuring smile, and turned to appraise her lover, to see him as Taya must: a full head of unruly chocolate hair with a brush of salt at the temples, dark, absorbed eyes, almost imperceptible fans of small wrinkles at the corners. More a Roman than Arab nose, lips sensuously full. Skin the color of newly-baked caramel. Amir's intense gaze suggested he understood more than was being said. *Ummm*, she mused, *he has that exotic demeanor, as though he came from a lost tribe of wandering Bedouins.*

Amir appeared to sense Taya's sexual shift at once and sought to put the young girl at ease. "I understand that you and Justine have been running together, Taya. Do you like that?"

"Yes, sir, I like it a lot. We run and talk."

How formal, uncomfortable. "Why don't you get yourself a cup of coffee, Taya," suggested Justine. "You know where everything is. We need to get dressed for the day."

At this, Taya blushed, staring first at Justine, then Amir. "Okay," she said.

Amir took Justine's hand and began to lead her toward the bedroom.

But as Justine noted Taya's confused face, she stopped, squeezed Amir's hand and said, "I'll have a coffee with Taya, Amir. Go ahead and take your shower."

Justine had told Amir about Taya during one of their Skype calls, so he understood her need for stability and support. "Sounds fine. See you girls in ten minutes."

The "girls" stood at the kitchen island and drained the coffee pot, Taya stirring in her usual generous amount of sugar and cream.

"Do you remember me telling you about Amir, Taya? We've known each other for more than four years and been close for more than a year."

"I remember," said Taya. "Are you going to get married?"

Justine was taken aback by the directness of her question. "I don't think so, Taya. We're from different worlds, different cultures. We're both pretty independent."

"But you told me you studied cultures, Miss Justine. Don't you understand him?"

Justine laughed. "I think I do, Taya." She paused. "Yes, I think I do. But sometimes people change when culture and tradition demand that they behave in certain ways."

"I don't understand," she said, dark expressive eyes peering over her cup.

"Let me put it this way: in Egypt, women are not considered equal to men. In our world now, in our relationship, Amir treats me with tremendous respect. We are equals. But what if we lived in Egypt? Would he be able to resist the expectation that women are put on this earth to serve men? And, for how long?"

"I see. Egyptians are a lot like the Tiwa, aren't they? If I marry a Tiwa boy, or a Spanish boy like Ricardo, what will my life be like?"

"It's good that you're seeing this, questioning your life ahead." Justine found it curious that their futures had some striking similarities. At least some shared questions. "Perhaps we can work that out together... Want to join us for lunch?" she asked, just as Amir appeared in the hallway.

CHAPTER 34

DECEMBER 22, 2010

"What will happen now, Amir?" Mike was staring over his cranberry martini.

"Social networks are alive with plans and counter plans. It will happen." Amir paused, his dark eyes moving from guest to guest, his expression slightly self-conscious. Justine had warned him: "These are folks with great curiosities. They'll want to know everything about you, the Middle East . . . figure out this man sleeping with Justine." She had laughed with that playful lilt that he loved, that grin, although the comment had not eased his tensions at all.

"Please tell us what's going on." Carmen was insistent.

Amir was fascinated with Carmen Johnson. Justine had told him that she was eighty, but he would have estimated no more than sixty. Sparkling and energetic, he could imagine her forging the river at Hupobi. "A revolution, perhaps, Mrs. Johnson. Thousands of young Egyptians are following on Facebook, Twitter. Since the Tunisian incident, there is a feeling of fierce intensity on the Internet, a pulsing energy, like nothing I've ever experienced before. It's just a matter of time." The corner fireplace glowed. In concert, blinking lights from a glorious Christmas tree nearly touching the ceiling formed an aura around Amir, alternating shades of red and blue encircling his white turtleneck.

"Call me Carmen. Please," she said, giving his arm a maternal pat. "What kind of action, Amir? Is revolution really possible?"

"Excitement doesn't necessarily translate into revolution though, does it?" Pablo asked. "When was the last time you had a real revolution?"

"Point well taken, Pablo," said Amir, pausing to consider the question, to remember. "Bread riots in the 80's. But a real revolution of ideas, about how we live our lives? Honestly, I don't know that we've ever had one. The '52 revolution was peaceful." Amir was the man of the hour—not only a stranger to New Mexico, but also a man of Arab descent and sensibilities.

"Yep, Nasser sent the King off for a life of luxury in Europe. A revolution sounds unlikely, doesn't it?" This was Mike, eyes flashing, mouth distorted, arms flailing. Justine had mentioned that Mike talked with intense physicality, with drama. "This probably will blow over too."

Scott's eyes surveyed the room, the guests. "Yet, you may have a historical moment here, Amir. A convergence of unique forces. A 'Zeitgeist' we would call it." He paused. "What forces do you see merging on the Internet?"

"Good question, Scott. Let me see . . . ." Amir cocked his head, his eyes betraying worry, concern. "The collapsing world economy has worsened conditions in Egypt: unemployment, of course, high prices, shortage of food, crowded, nearly unlivable conditions."

". . . more educated youth, thirty years of emergency powers, a brutal police force." Justine called from the kitchen as she prepared another pitcher of martinis and Giovanna opened the oven to baste the steaming turkey.

"Exactly. Exactly." Amir moved across the room to draw Justine and Giovanna into the conversation; the others followed, grouping themselves into a surrounding circle, like flocking birds. "But this time it *could* be different. Before social media, there was no way to organize, to communicate, to plan. Small groups would come together, spontaneous groups of unemployed discontents, but nothing substantial." Amir's growing excitement was palpable, his eyes sparkled in the glowing tree lights, convincing himself as well as others.

"Are Egyptians capable of self-determination?" asked Mike straightforwardly, innocently, as though his words were not abrasive.

Amir stared at Mike sharply; his nostrils flared. "What do you mean?" he asked accusingly. "Capable??"

"A poorly chosen word," confessed Mike. "But, I would ask the same question of any peoples who have been colonized for nearly their entire existence. Egyptians have never been free, have they?"

"Not entirely," Amir admitted, calmed by Justine's warning stare. "I'll respond in two ways. After the '52 revolution, when King Farouk was peacefully escorted to a ship waiting in the Alexandria harbor, Nasser granted major freedoms. Free education for all, rights for women, a socialist economy, construction projects, respect. These past sixty years have formed the foundation for the next step in our history—have prepared us."

"Your second point?" sang out Judy Lynn, standing near the front door, peeling off her leather gloves, and hanging her heavy woolen coat on the peg by the door. No one had seen her enter. "Hi!" she shouted, setting her casserole of sweet potatoes on the island, then walking directly toward Amir. She took his extended hand. "I'm Judy Lynn," she announced, as though that explained most things worth knowing.

Amir's admiring expression examined her festive red dress and matching hair, amused by the forcefulness by which she occupied her space in the room. He smiled down at her, "All humans have a deep longing for freedom, an inherent, God given right, don't you think, Miss Judy?"

"I agree," said Judy Lynn, showing no inclination to correct his use of her name. "There were those who asked whether Indians, having been treated as children for so long, could control their own fates. But, of course, they can. They do."

"Gracefully, peacefully," added Carmen, stepping forward to give Judy Lynn a hug.

"Will Mubarak have to go?" Giovanna called out, her back to the group while she stirred the gravy. "I don't see another way."

"Not willingly. Not without force . . . . " Amir halted himself mid-sentence, cautious not to reveal the content of his hurried conversations with Wael— their speculations about the road ahead. His eyes sought Justine's, meeting a flash of fear they shared.

Mike noted the exchange of glances, his own eyes squinting in accusation of the two lovers. "What are you not telling us? What's really happening over there?"

"I'm not sure he can tell us. Amir?" Scott asked, offering to protect information that should not yet be revealed. As a highly respected scientist, his investigations were deep and thorough, but respectfully not venturing into territory held sacred and secret by the peoples of any culture he was probing.

Amir nodded and stepped closer. "Thanks, Scott. Let's just say that plans are being made and I'm not at liberty to discuss details." He smiled weakly. "If you'll excuse me." Amir turned and walked down the hall toward the bathroom.

Justine watched Amir disappear down the hall. "Dinner will be ready soon," she announced, softening the edges of Amir's declaration. She shivered as she reviewed conversations with Amir over the past few days. Her own clashes with the Egyptian government and religious leaders haunted her, as well as her slips in judgment when it came to keeping secrets. She'd never been very good at keeping secrets.

Carmen touched Pablo's arm, and walked toward the fire, attempting to disband the circle into smaller conversations. Giovanna removed her apron and joined them.

Judy Lynn edged herself away from Mike to find Justine, who was talking with Scott about Mesa Verde. Scott was telling Justine, "I'm going to call the book *Winds from the North*, I think. Do you like it?"

"I do!" declared Judy Lynn, as she clutched Scott's arm. Without taking a breath, "By the way, I have news. In one of Mabel's psych reports from A.A. Brill—remember, her therapist in New York—she says that the ranch was in exchange for the *Sons and Lovers* manuscript. Lois Rudnick obtained the files for her new scathing bio on Mabel."

"Meaning?" asked Scott.

"Meaning that the ranch was not a gift, and therefore it was community property," said Justine quickly, temples flushed. "So Lawrence did own property in New Mexico and the will would come under this state's jurisdiction."

"The will adjudicated in England? Eighty years ago?" Amir had moved into the conversation, as had other guests.

"A little farfetched, don't you think?" suggested Mike. "What use is it?"

"Probably none," admitted Judy Lynn, taking a welcome gulp of her pomegranate martini. "Probably none."

Justine's eyes had a devilish twinkle. "Dinner is served," she announced.

Pensive guests picked up dinner plates and talked indistinctly among themselves as they walked to the buffet of elaborate steamy dishes: turkey and dressing, mashed potatoes, baked sweet potatoes, cranberries, green beans, hot rolls.

A regular Nebraskan Christmas, thought Justine, remembering those holidays with her grandparents when the world seemed so perfect, so hopeful. How naïve she had been. Was she being naïve again—did it matter that the ranch was not a gift? She turned to find Amir.

He stood near the blinking tree; his eyes distant, deep in a troubled pool of thought.

Justine knew then what was to come.

By midnight, after a renewed stream of questions about Egypt, a lively debate regarding Mesa Verde migration, differing opinions on D. H. Lawrence, and effusive praise for the meal, the guests had gone out into the snow and headed home. Dishes had somehow been done, and Justine and Amir now sat in the darkened living room watching light snow falling through the light of a waning moon.

"I have to go home," said Amir.

"I know," she said, touching him knowingly. The evening conversation had clearly moved Amir toward his decision, a decision nearing resolution ever since he had landed in Albuquerque five days ago. She knew when she saw his eyes—so expressive, with unfathomable depth, as though she could see his heart beating wildly against his chest wall. "When?"

"As soon as I can get a ticket to Frankfurt, then on to Cairo." He turned toward her, a mixture of light and dark, the face of the Phantom, reflecting the light of resolve and the murky shadow of doubt. He grabbed her to him, burying his head in her breasts.

"You need to be there, but can you wait until Christmas? Two more days?" That is all she would ask, for she knew the part he was to play in Egypt was vital to him, the youth, his country. Her admiration for Amir had grown exponentially during these last few days. His commitment to Egypt's future—and his role in it—seemed to have stirred a smoldering fire within him, a powerful determination, an intense devotion.

Amir stood and gazed at her with gratitude. "Not too much to ask, *Habibti.* Yes, of course. We'll have our Christmas and then I'll go. *Mish mushkilla.*" They both laughed at the classic Arab phrase for "no problem." He pulled her to him again, kissing her tenderly on the mouth, the nose. He picked her up, her ebony cocktail dress flowing over his arm as he carried her into the bedroom.

Just outside the window there grew a perfectly formed little evergreen, now a second blinking Christmas tree, lighting the bedroom with red, green, blue, and white. So perfect, she thought, as though placed there by magic, by someone transcending nature's tendency for irregularities, asymmetry, preferring the randomness of Picasso, the surprises insisted on by Taos climate. *Perfection often disappoints*, she mused, *masking Truths embedded in nature*. Then he was at her neck, and her thoughts melted into pure honeyed desire.

Amir unzipped her cocktail dress and lowered her onto the bed, slowly removing his own sweater and throwing it on the chair. They made love intently, almost desperately, more even than before, each muscle in their bodies instilled with revolutionary resolve.

CHAPTER 35

❦

DECEMBER 24, CHRISTMAS EVE, 2010

Tangerine flames flared into the night sky illuminating St. Jerome's Church and the adobe buildings encircling the Taos Pueblo plaza. Three white crosses above the church stood stark against the dark palette, announcing forthcoming events. Scores of bonfires licked the frigid air, the sizzling night pregnant with expectations for the arrival of the holy infant. Believer and non-believer alike swept into the expectant ritual. For many an allegory of hope, a parable of new beginnings. Tonight, everyone is Christian. So it seemed to Justine and Amir.

After the mass and the parade of the Virgin in her Christmas finery, the two lovers stood in the middle of the Plaza in awe, watching the flames frame the Matachine Dancers. The dancers—danzantes—appeared in front of the ancient five-story pueblo: a young girl in a communion gown or Virgin robe, a king or prince, two clowns, men hidden inside a bull costume, a score of masked dancers in crimson Medieval capes and Chimayo blanket vests. Gaunt Don Quixote faces carved into wooden masks held up by posts. Tall majestic hats were framed in velvet and bejeweled with silver and turquoise from which eight wide ribbons floated into the cold night sky.

Each Matachine dancer wore gloves and carried a carved wooden palma, akin to a fan, in one hand, a rattle in the other. The dancers wove in and out, creating an interlocking pattern around a pole. The musical beat lacked the haunting percussion of drums heard during the Pow Wow. Instead, something akin to the twang of an ancient mandolin.

Recognizing its familiarity in the preparation and characters immediately, Amir exclaimed, "Justine! This Matachine dance is Moorish. Arabs carried it to Spain more than a thousand years ago!"

Justine loved the animation in Amir's face, and the nearly macabre effect of reflected flames. "And brought to the Americas by the Spanish in the 1500s, I assume," said Justine excitedly, cuddling deeper into her fur-lined coat. The temperature was dropping. "Curious, it's the only dance that the Indians and Spanish perform together," she said. "I know it as a dance of transformation, of good against evil . . . but what does it really mean? To the Moors?"

"Many things! The variation is nothing short of astonishing. 'Matachine,' I believe, comes from the Arabic 'mudawajjihin,' which means 'those who put on a face.' A young girl or virgin converts the pagan king. The Moorish-Christian struggle, Montezuma and the Indians. It can even refer to the planets, Mars and Jupiter. Unfortunately, the browner peoples usually lose. White over dark—the eternal struggle with an unmistakable air of violence. It usually ends with the castration of the bull, the clowns offering the bull's testicles to the crowd," he paused in amusement.

<hr>

It was after one a.m. in the morning when Justine and Amir arrived home, lit a fire, turned on the tree lights, and snuggled under a quilt on the couch. They'd decided to exchange gifts tonight, get a few hours sleep and leave for the Albuquerque airport early, since Amir's plane for Frankfurt left at two in the afternoon.

Amir sat hauntingly still with two beautifully wrapped presents, one in each hand. His face revealed a peaceful resolve, yet his temples throbbed with tension.

Justine was puzzled. She couldn't infer his mood. *Pleasure? Indecision? Tension? He doesn't know what to expect when he gets to Egypt. But tonight?* "My turn?"

"One present." He handed her the box in his left hand.

She eagerly untied the fuchsia satin ribbon and tore back the parchment paper, revealing a stunning set of silver earrings. "The Tuareg cross! Where did you ever get these? Timbuktu?"

"A friend," he said mysteriously.

"Thank you so much, Amir. I love them!" She placed her arms around his neck, pulling him to her, kissing him passionately. "Your turn," she said as she pulled away and handed him an oblong box bound with a giant red ribbon.

A heavy turquoise bracelet of squash blossom design was nestled into a crimson and midnight blue woolen scarf studded with Kokopelli images. He unfurled the fringed scarf with flourish, winding it around his neck. "Perfect for this weather! Kokopellis?" he asked, picking up the bracelet and fitting it around his left wrist.

"The little humpbacked flute player called Kokopelli is found everywhere in the southwest—Gods who bring good luck, fertility, ensure good crops . . . ."

"*Gamila! Latifa!*" Amir broke into a litany of Arabic. "Fertility, huh?" he winked; leaning over to kiss her lightly on the lips, to ruffle her hair.

"And, now. The other box?" Justine claimed an innocent expression, raising her eyebrows in question above dilated pupils. In spite of the lateness of the hour, she wasn't impatient; she could gaze forever into those fiery images reflecting in his dark eyes.

"Marry me," he said, his voice tense, almost matter of fact. He was risking his delicate ego without any assurance that she would agree.

Justine blinked, cocking her head to one side, frozen in place, in memories. Perspiration formed on her upper lip as conflicting thoughts raced back four years. He had promised he would never propose again. When she rejected him in Italy, she thought he would never attempt it again—never risk the embarrassment he'd felt. They both felt. Until tonight, she was determined never to marry an Egyptian. "Yes," she said simply and smiled.

He went wild, grabbing her into a near-desperate embrace.

CHAPTER 36

—◆—

KIOWA RANCH, NEW MEXICO, AUGUST 22, 1925

Shades of crimson framed Sacred Mountain to the east, and the dry, hot air cooled as Rachel and Bill Hawk rode into the ranch on handsome bay horses. Tying the reins to the wooden rail fence on the south side of the Lawrence cabin, they admired once again the life-sized buffalo painted by Trinidad, the reliable hired hand from the Pueblo. The Hawks had come for dinner with the Lawrences, and brought the mail from San Cristobal.

Frieda and Lorenzo welcomed their neighbors warmly, inviting them to make themselves comfortable at the rickety wooden table. Dinner was almost ready. Frieda dried her hands on her apron, threaded through the short stack of mail, and eagerly tore open the steamship line envelope containing their tickets on the SS Resolute, sailing in September, the day before Lorenzo's fortieth birthday.

"Why the burr under your saddle this time, Lorenzo? It's only five months since you got back from Mexico sick as a dog." Bill was insistent. "Look at this place . . . you've tamed the wilderness, planted a field of alfalfa, irrigated your garden . . . you've got yourself a regular Garden of Eden here!" The Hawks liked having the Lawrences close by, hated to see them set off again so soon.

"*Wrote myself back to health, Bill. But Italy calls. Need to get back to my Etruscans at Volterra, Cortona, Tarquinia.*" He stared dreamily at his Ponderosa framed dazzling in the setting sun, the tree that beckoned him each morning as he leaned against it to write The Plumed Serpent. Yet he was restless. "*Besides,*" he said, forcing himself to turn back toward his guests, "*We've got to see Frieda's Mother. Good woman. And her children demand attention—let them grow up, I say!*" As he spoke, Lorenzo puttered with the plates, setting the table, while Frieda removed a half-baked chicken from the oven. Potatoes and squash done to perfection, the chicken oozed blood when she stabbed it sternly with her favorite butcher knife. She was notorious for careless cooking; Lorenzo never allowed her any quarter.

"*The ranch is too much for him now, Bill,*" said Frieda, her back toward Lorenzo and the Hawks. She continued to stab the chicken, intent on finding a finished portion. "*We need too much help. Thank goodness my nephew is here.*"

"*Speak for yourself, woman!*" Lorenzo yelled, his fierce eyes glistening, anger stiffening his spine like a poker. "*You can't even cook a chicken! You're as useless as my cow out there!*" The plate in his hand promised to sail against the wall, but didn't. After all, there were only five plates left.

"*Why don't we fry it up, Frieda?*" offered Rachel, forever the peacemaker. "*Bill likes it better that way.*" She grinned in anticipation of the coming row, since she and Bill were used to playing audience at a Lawrence performance. By now, they understood that scraps would flare up, vicious words would be exchanged, but tempers would dissipate just as quickly. Lorenzo had explained it once to Bill; his friend had just smiled indulgently. While he rarely understood Lorenzo, he had come to like him in spite of himself.

Lorenzo had told him: "*You see, Bill, we're all individuals. We have our individuality . . . especially true for men and women. If we didn't react against the other from time to time, we would lose our integrity. Conflict is necessary, otherwise we lose ourselves."*

"Thanks, Rachel, you're a jewel." But Frieda couldn't leave well enough alone. She picked up the tickets and waved them in the air, paper birds promising flight. "You know, Lorenzo, when we leave . . . ." Frieda left the sentence unfinished. They both knew what was coming, what couldn't be said.

"What!" Lorenzo screamed. "'When we leave'—what??"

"Nothing . . . ," said Frieda, voice volume dropping and fading out as she turned to help Rachel fry up the chicken. Unconsciously, both of the Lawrences knew that if they left America now, his tuberculosis would probably prevent him from securing a visa to return. Yet, they preferred denial, refusing to believe that his condition was fatal.

"We'll be back in the spring!" Lorenzo pronounced, clapping his hands together like a young child, even as fear flashed through those unruly turquoise eyes.

CHAPTER 37

———◦◦◦◦———

A MIR HADN'T ACTUALLY agreed to live in Taos after they were married, although he'd shown an uncharacteristic fascination with the Earthships built as a cluster on six hundred acres of high mesa west of town. "Bananas and figs bloom in the winter!" he exclaimed after talking with a resident. Made of discarded materials, wholly self-sufficient and sustainable, these structures had evolved into science fiction delights—fairy tale houses and spaceships with elaborate twists and turns, towers and turrets, finished with smooth adobe. Justine found it incredible that old tires, concrete blocks, Coke cans and recycling water systems could be coaxed into castles.

So, she'd decided to take another look the week after New Years. *Would it be necessary to build our own, which was the point after all, or would there be a few for sale?* The trick was to find and purchase a piece of land on the high mesa. That she could do.

The frigid weather had not abated, and by 5:30 a fuchsia ribbon of waning light lay on the distant horizon. While Amir had never seen car chains before, he had skillfully managed to attach them to her car several days earlier. As the chained wheels crunched over snowdrifts alongside the exit from the Earthship Visitors Center, Justine felt determined to get home before dark. She turned on her headlights and drove slowly eastward toward the gaping Rio Grande Gorge, ten miles west of the Blinking Light four corners in El Prado.

As her car eked along in the icy, packed snow, her mind wandered back to her stunned surprise when she had accepted Amir's proposal in the wee hours of Christmas morning. Hard to believe it was little more than a week ago. After fighting her cautionary feelings for four years, she felt that something had changed in him—perhaps in her as well. She knew how conflicted he had been with the discovery of Mary's diary—initially provoked by the archeological import of the discovery, yet he'd nonetheless harbored resistance to the reinterpretation of Mary's identity. His Coptic Christian roots ran deep, making it difficult for him to give himself over to the sheer thrill of such an earthshaking discovery. Abandoning the virginal myth of Mary had not been easy for him. Although he had soon overcome the tug of tradition and joined her in deciphering the meaning of the discovery, he also held back, something held him in check.

Yes, this time he was different. The possibility of a revolution in Egypt thoroughly captivated and energized him—there was no half-hearted response—no hesitancy, only intense resolve. This fierce clarity gave him strength and determination she'd never witnessed before. He was more sensual, gritty, fiery. She couldn't resist him, for now she saw his capacity to override his cultural bondage. *More like Lawrence*, she mused, surprised at this observation.

Pulling herself out of her reverie, she glanced several times into her rear view mirror, finally recognizing the familiar pickup coming up quickly behind her. Ricardo's pickup! *What could he want now? He had won, hadn't he? He'd gotten Taya pregnant and her father insisted on a wedding. As her husband, he would control her completely.* Justine felt tears form under her tawny eyelashes. *Taya. I've lost her. She has lost herself.*

In the rear view mirror, she could barely make out two images, no, three. Ricardo's lips were drawn tight, determined, his eyes shadowed by his ever-present baseball cap. On the passenger side— another young man? *Who?* She couldn't tell who it was through the icy passenger-side windshield. She glanced again, dividing her attention between the icy road ahead and the pursuing truck. In the middle, a large dog with floppy ears, brown and tan, a German Shepherd perhaps, sitting upright as though sharing the thrill of the chase with his master. *But who is that other man? This hunt seems more like a personal vendetta than just an effort to keep me away from Taya.* She shuddered, feeling fear grasp her chest.

Pressing hard on the gas pedal, Justine felt her fear turn into anger. Her own anger, but even more so, anger at the thought of the life that lies ahead for Taya. *Damn him! Another case of controlling a woman by taking away her choices. This is a man who will be abusive if he doesn't get his way. Oh, Taya, what have you gotten yourself into?* The speedometer hit 60, not fast under normal conditions, but irresponsibly fast on packed snow and ice. In spite of the chains, she felt her Prius slip and slide, jolting her, her control over it tenuous. She took her foot off the gas pedal, but resisted the brake, for she knew enough from her years in Chicago that braking under these conditions was exactly the wrong thing to do.

Before reaching the bridge, Justine swerved off the road onto the long driveway leading to the visitor's parking lot, where she could expect to find a ranger or someone who could help, whose presence would stop the chase. No other cars sat in the lot. The lights were off in the center.

The road looped to the right then circled the parking area in back of the visitor's center. The bare-tired pickup was swerving side to side, following much too close to Justine's bumper, and way too fast. When Justine realized she was drifting too far right in the loop, she jerked her car to the left, fishtailing a little on the ice. So close behind, Ricardo, too, misjudged the turn. He must have slammed on the brake, a tragic choice, because as Justine watched in horror, the pick-up skidded in a rapid forward thrust, the metal pole extending down from the picnic shelter ripping off his side mirror a heartbeat before the old truck. Ricardo and his passenger, and the shepherd careened sideward right on through the sagging chain-link fence, and took unobstructed flight over the edge of the gorge into a nose-heavy dive aimed into the Rio Grande River six hundred and fifty feet below. She could hear their screams. *Oh my God! No! No!*

Stopping nearby, Justine stared at the hole in the fence. She had witnessed the entire catastrophe through her rear-view mirror. Pressing the gearshift into park, she called 911. Then she screamed and screamed, after which her head fell upon the steering wheel as she began to sob.

CHAPTER 38

⸺⚬⚬⚬⸺

MARCH 1ˢᵀ, 1930, VENCE, FRANCE

ALDOUS HUXLEY, fellow writer and long-time friend of D. H. Lawrence, came to visit Lawrence the day before he died of tuberculosis.

"Hux. Good man. Come to visit your dying friend?" He could hardly talk, and began almost immediately to cough violently. His pale face flushed slightly as he coughed.

"Don't try to talk, old friend. This may not be the end. You've been through rough times before." Huxley watched his friend with deep sadness for he knew that indeed this was the end. That's why Frieda had cabled him.

Lawrence nodded weakly, pulling his light lap blanket up over his chest. "So these quack doctors say. Maria with you?"

"She'll be along."

Lawrence nodded again, his vivid blue eyes faded to powder, his skin nearly white. "Brewster was here. Talked of our Etruscans." Another hacking cough, blood coming up with the phlegm.

"Brewster's a good man. You've been fortunate with friends, Lorenzo. Better than you deserve. None as good as I have been though." As Hux suspected, he still knew how to solicit a narrow grin.

"Been lucky for sure. Now I need to ready myself. The Etrus-cans and the Red Man get it right. No more Hebraic monotheistic hogwash for me. We all live and die together in this vast uni-verse. Coyotes, deer, mountain lions, possum." He burst into another violent coughing spell. Hux rested his hand on Law-rence's shoulder while he struggled to continue. *"Me. Just wrap me in a warm blanket, Hux, and let Mother Earth take me home."*

"Sounds like a good journey, old friend. Have you spoken to Frieda about it?"

"Tried. I did. She gets hysterical. Given to that vapid German Protestantism, you know. Wants to ship me off to Heaven. I told her, 'Hell is my likely destination.'" He spoke in a mere whisper, a wheezing sound lingering beneath each word.

"I'll meet you there!" Hux laughed wholeheartedly. Lawrence joined in until his coughing put a halt to the pleasure. *"Say, I brought you my latest essay, "Vulgarity in Literature," part of a collection. I want to know what you think."*

Lawrence grinned again. *"About me?"*

"Now don't go thinking everything is about you . . . but yes, partly. And who could be a better reviewer."

"I'm sorry, Hux . . . ," his voice trailed off.

"What are you sorry for? You owe me no apologies."

"I was a damn harsh critic, Hux. My comments on Brave New World."

Hux walked to the bed and placed his hand on Lawrence's shoulder again, *"Always some truth in your words, my friend. I cherish the thoughts of the most interesting man I have ever known."*

Lawrence's eyes moistened, shifting to an expression of affec-tion and gratitude. *"Stay in touch with Frieda, please, my friend. She doesn't know it, but she'll need you."* Hux nodded as Law-rence began to cough and retch, fear clouding his eyes. His nurse rushed into the room with a shot of morphine.

"Hux . . . wait." Lawrence reached to his table, fumbling for an envelope, which he handed to Huxley, a letter addressed to Lady Brett. *"Please don't forget. Mail it for me?"*

Huxley nodded and turned away, tears brimming his eyes.

CHAPTER 39

———❦———

Taya opened the door. "Ricardo was my baby's father, Miss Justine! And my brother is dead too." Her eyes were red, her nose runny.

"I know." Justine stared at Taya and waited, letting herself droop in submission.

"The police have been here."

"Yes. The boys were driving fast. And the road was icy."

"Did you lead them over the cliff? Into the gorge?"

"Oh my God! Of course not!" She paused and squinted her weeping eyes, reaching out to touch Taya's shoulder. "I pulled into the Visitor Center to get help, but it was closed." Justine felt stung by Taya's accusation, but quickly realized that Taya needed to find a cause, an explanation, someone to blame. She stood still.

"Justine," said Sharon, stepping up from behind her daughter and laying her hand on Taya's shoulder. "Please come in. Join us. Have something to eat," she said as she approached her visitor and whispered into her ear, "she's taking it very hard, so am I. My only son . . . life is but the flash of a firefly."

Justine blinked, pain sweeping her chest, and grasped Sharon into her arms. Taya watched helplessly as the two women cried and comforted each other. Sharon held Justine at arm's length and said simply, "You have a good heart, Justine. I know you weren't responsible."

Taya stepped aside, then silently followed Justine as she walked into the room full of mourners. The younger woman motioned to her mentor—the only Anglo in the room—to a chair near the corner of the living room. In a nearby bedroom, the body of the maimed young man was laid out on his bed, his body fully covered. When the medics had pulled the men out of the twisted truck at the bottom of the canyon, the injuries had been extensive. Grandmother Thelma sat in a corner of the room rocking back and forth, ". . . good heart . . . good heart . . . good heart . . . ."

"Tell me what happened," Taya demanded, her voice flat, without tenderness or feeling.

Justine described the incident as well as she could, attempting to suggest more of an accident than a chase. "I know that if I hadn't pulled off into the Visitor's Center, if I had just kept going." She paused. "I would do anything not to hurt you, Taya."

Taya reached out, but drew her hand back before it touched Justine's cheek. "I should be with Ricardo now . . . " she said, letting her voice drift off. She closed her eyes.

Justine was silent, waiting respectfully until Taya took a deep breath and opened her eyes. "I was surprised that your brother and Ricardo were together," she said, allowing the comment to hover in the air between them.

Taya turned toward Justine and spoke sharply. "I don't know why they were together. They hated each another," she insisted, her eyes narrowing, as though she thought Justine should have an answer.

Justine stalled, permitting her eyes to move from one mourner to another, watching with fascination, though not surprise, the almost stoic expressions. She had witnessed similar gatherings among the Hopi. Acceptance came sooner to grievers who were certain of the fate of their fallen family members. On the fourth day, they would wrap him in a favorite light blanket and lay him gently into a shallow grave from which he would be welcomed back into the arms of Mother Earth, and his soul would be released into the spirit world. She felt a wave of envy. "Perhaps they shared a common goal," she finally said.

"A common goal?" Taya asked, her face twisting in puzzlement. "To stop you from seeing me—teaching me to stand up for myself?"

"Perhaps so, Taya. I'm sorry." *But is that enough? What else might have brought these natural enemies together? Peyote? Penitents? I didn't want them to die because of me!*

"I'm sorry that God let them die. They couldn't accept that I was getting stronger. Making my own decisions. Maybe I should have been more careful, less strong. It was me who broke with tradition. I was wrong."

Justine reached out and patted Taya's hand, touched her cheek. "No, Taya, you were right to assert yourself. It's not acceptable to be treated like a prisoner, or to have little to say about your own body.

Sharon was listening nearby; it was written all over her face that she knew that her son had violated Taya. Clearly, the pain was almost more that she could bear, for she hadn't told her husband. "You did good, Taya," her mother said in a whisper.

His death solves a problem for both of them, but admission will be slow in coming, then short-lived. How will they cope in the long run?

Tears welled up in the young girl's eyes as she began to sob. Justine wanted to hold her, but it was not time yet. She began to cry. Their grief emanated from a different source. Taya cried for her family, her confusion about her own efforts to liberate herself, and her uncertain future as a single mother. Justine wept for Taya and for herself, the misery she felt from participating, even as a victim, in the death of two young men. *What could I have done differently? If only . . . if only . . . .*

—⁜—

"It was terrible, Amir! They just slid into the gorge, dropping a thousand feet." A sob caught in her throat. "There wasn't anything I could do." Justine had called Amir on the night of the accident, explaining the horror of the event, then the visit to Taya's family, her deep sense of guilt.

For a long time, Amir was quiet, letting her talk, get it out, all the pain and self-recrimination. "It wasn't your fault, Justine. They, at least Ricardo, had been following you for a long time. You told me about the day at the tunnel, how persistent he was then."

"I know. I know. But I'm not sure Taya will ever be able to forgive me. Or that I can forgive myself." Phone in hand, Justine walked into the kitchen and picked up her tea, stared out at the moonlit sky, the orb like a hall monitor waiting for her next move. She sat down in front of the shimmering fire. "How are things going on your side of the world?" she asked gently, in a tone that let Amir know she had regrouped and was ready to move on. For the moment at least. "Tell me all of it."

She could hear Amir take a deep breath as though preparing for a physical trial of some sort. "It's moving forward. Our Facebook pages had more than a half million hits today, Twitter is chattering around the clock. We're getting close."

"Close to . . . ?"

"The revolution. The revolution when the current regime will be ousted from power."

"What about the police? The army? Will they let it happen?"

"They may have no choice. We will be a million strong. But I think Wael is overly optimistic."

"That would be extraordinary, almost unbelievable."

"We have reason to believe the army could be with us. They're quite different from the police, you know. They're respected and have the interest of the country more at heart while the police are blood-thirsty henchmen—carrying out the wishes of this abusive regime."

"If the army supports a revolution, watch out. They have much to lose by democratic reforms."

"I know you're right, Justine. We'll be careful."

CHAPTER 40

—◦◦◦—

CAIRO, JANUARY 25, 12:45 P.M.

THE WEATHER WAS CRISP, cool, and clear. Smog found low quarters and narrow passageways, the sand-beige glare now tinted with azure blue. A surprisingly beautiful day in Cairo. Tahrir Square was quiet, a pregnant stillness hanging in the air. After days of growing tension, the air felt remarkably calm.

A dozen scattered cars circled the perimeter, yet the Square itself was empty. To the north, the Egyptian Museum opened its doors. A half dozen tourists stepped out of the Hilton in concert, and turned left toward the Museum. Across the avenue to the south sat the giant government building and the administration building of American University, both closed for the day. Directly east, on the corner across from the university, sat a bustling Burger King, colorful with young people.

Nearby mosques, of course, were open on Fridays. Throughout Cairo, men gathered well before noon for the most important prayer day of the week. Row upon row of Muslim men knelt on green and red mats in long alleyways around the Square, facing east toward Mecca. The rhythmic calls of Imams chanting Koran surahs blared from strategically placed loudspeakers. On the street leading north from the Burger King, a few men and women, seemingly oblivious to the mood of worship in nearby alleys, went about their daily lives, selling newspapers. The smell of flowers and foul beans, thinly sliced lamb and roasted corn drifting through the air. Parallel worlds, parallel lives; neither embarrassed by the other. A typical Friday morning in Cairo.

Then from above, what looked like ants swarming in a rush of hunger toward Tahrir Square, streaming in from streets in every direction. The Burger King emptied on cue. Some came from the museum itself, laced around the side fences, along the boulevard from the bazaars and the classic blue and white train station. Buses drained their bulging human contents near the Hilton, along the Corniche, in front of the university. Too, they sprang from the ground, surfacing from subway stations as though rising from the dead. From all directions, hundreds. No, thousands. Muslim youth from mosques throughout the immense city. Christians from their homes and coffeehouses. Young men in Western dress—jeans and plaid cotton shirts; women, also in jeans, brightly colored rayon blouses, most wearing hijabs. They had no idea what lay ahead, but they had had enough. Enough of unemployment and low wages, living at home until the age of thirty, unable to get a place of their own, a place to bring a wife. Postponing a family, watching their friends rounded up and imprisoned without charges, barely recognizing their bruised faces once they returned to their neighborhoods with flat, unexpressive eyes.

But not today. Not today. Today, their eyes filled with resolve, bravery. Members of the gathering crowd glanced from side to side as they walked rapidly into the center of the square, surprised to find so many students, middle class businessmen, old women whose sons had not returned from the dungeons, women with burqas, others with flowing hair. Elderly men, whose media-savvy grandchildren had brought them along. Coptic Christians alongside moderate Muslims and extreme Salafists. In unison they walked, impatient to discover what awaited them.

Men in business suits and ties handed out signs and placards proclaiming: DOWN WITH MUBARAK. NO MORE EMERGENCY POWERS. 30 YEARS OF DICTATORSHIP. WE WANT FREE ELECTIONS. Banners with photos of missing men were strung up between makeshift wooden poles. Small boys, maybe between nine and twelve, waving miniature Egyptian flags. Later in the day, these same men would hand out water and set up security stations to ensure no firearms entered in the square. These orderly beginnings of the revolution appeared well planned.

By the hour their numbers burgeoned. The media went wild. Many, particularly Al Jazeera, knew that when it came, it would be on a Friday. It had to be a Friday, the day when Muslims didn't report to work; the primary day of worship in the mosques. Several television and radio stations had been disappointed when the revolution didn't happen a week earlier, on January 18. Late on the 17th, Wael had declared to millions of followers on Facebook that the process needed more time, more pressure. He would not call it—declare it was a "go"—until the pressure cooker was ready to explode. As it happened, it would be Amir who would give the signal to start the revolution. By the 25th, Wael was in prison.

For journalists, the delay meant another week at their computers in the nearby Hilton staying tuned to the social media, watching for inklings of evidence that D-day was imminent. On the morning of January 25, they were ready. Room after room of the Hilton and nearby Semiramesis and Shepheard hotels were occupied with media hounds from CNN, Al Italia, the International Herald Tribune, Al Jazerra English and Arabic, Chicago Tribune, London Times.

———

It was 4:45 a.m. on the 25th in Taos, 1:45 p.m. in Cairo, when Justine woke with a start, sat upright in bed, and blinked. It was still dark except for a waning moon and the ever-present lights on the university campus close by. She jumped out of bed, threw on her bathrobe, dialed up the heat and turned on the television. *My god, it's cold.* An exercise program, cosmetic ads, a preacher wailing about the wrath of God. Nothing about Cairo.

All Amir had said in his short call the night before: "Today, Justine. It's today!" and hung up.

She padded into the kitchen and turned on the coffee pot. "What's happening??" she said aloud. Just then, the cosmetic ad on the television faded, the screen went blank and the swarming colorful scene at Tahrir Square came into view. The Square was still filling with people for as far as she could see. She backed into the kitchen so as to not miss a beat, grabbed her coffee, and curled up in a reclining chair in front of the television.

Hours passed before she moved, except to dash to the bathroom, refill her coffee and grab an apple. Her eyes scanned the screen for signs of Amir. He hadn't told her what he would be doing to spur the revolution. *Is he still in his office monitoring the movement, encouraging people to get to the square? Is he in the square? Is he safe?* Justine was incredibly impatient, as though it would just happen and be over. Just like that. She knew better. Not only would it go into the night, into the weekend and the days to follow, but, perhaps, even weeks to follow. The regime ran a sophisticated operation, having perfected its suppression tactics and infrastructure since Nasser led the revolution of 1952. Nasser to Sadat to Mubarak. Fifty nine years of experience, nearly as compulsive and regimented as the British and Turks before them. So, yes, the overthrow of Mubarak would not end quickly.

By nightfall in Cairo, the Square was a smoldering mass of more than a million people. Placards moved up and down in rhythm with the chanting. On the streets encircling the Square, young men were no longer silent, but ran and yelled, as though their energies knew no bounds; they had to move, to scream, to demand. Small encampments had been erected near the center—trails of smoke from miniature cook stoves—demonstrators clearly intending to stay as long as necessary. No one left, although women quietly filed out from time to time, returning with sacks of warm food prepared by other women in nearby apartments. Baladi bread wrapped around foul (Egyptian beans), chicken, shwarma—whatever could be held in a tissue-thin napkin. Water bottles were drawn from boxes behind the security gates, small boys distributing them through the crowd. People shared generously. Traditionally, Egyptians, prepared by the deprivation of Ramadan and the example of their camels, drank little water. The chanting and yelling dried their mouths, accentuating their thirst for water. At first, observers had thought the support structures for the revolution had been planned by the instigators, but, as it turned out, it was mainly the proactive Muslim Brotherhood behind the scenes.

Justine had fallen asleep in the chair when she heard the phone ring. Amir. It was 1:30 a.m. on the 26ᵗʰ in Cairo. She was startled awake and glanced at her watch: 4:40 in the afternoon. *Where has the day gone? I haven't written a word on the revised grant proposal.* On the screen, bonfires and torches glowed around the Square.

"It's happening, Justine!" His voice was breathless, excited.

She laughed lightly. "It sure is! Congratulations to all of you!"

"How does it look? What do you see?"

"They're projecting more than a million. It looks beautiful, Amir. Thousands of excited people, energized by the crowd, the bonfires and torches! Placards and flags are waving. It's as though the whole throng is pulsing in concert with each other! A scene right out of Cecille B. DeMille!" *Did he know who that was?*

"Great! Whatever!" he nearly shouted.

She could almost see his flushed face, sparkling eyes, ruffled hair. Justine flashed on his nude body beside her in bed. "So, what next?" she asked, listening for background noise, but all she could hear was a few muffled voices. *Where is he?*

"What next? I don't know. Our efforts have been focused on getting this far. Soon the crowd will head for Mubarak's compound, I suppose, then we'll see."

"Please be careful, my love. There will be causalities. Are you prepared?" *Is anyone ever prepared?*

A long pause before he answered. "We know. I'm not sure we're ever prepared for death, for murder but it will happen, I know. The police thugs are still under the regime's control. Right now they seem stunned, caught off guard, but they'll get their bearings. And when they do, we have ambulances standing by." His voice lost some of its energy as he pondered the consequences of the events he helped organize.

Justine let her thoughts float back to the tragedy of the two boys speeding on the ice, finally sliding into the Rio Grande Gorge. *We will be in similar positions*, she realized, *indirectly responsible for the deaths of young people.* She shivered. "Amir. When this is over, you'll be coming home, right? Coming back to Taos?"

Another pause. "As soon as we lay claim to the testicles of the bull," he said with heavy sarcasm. "And throw them to the crowd. Then I will come home to you Justine. Not until then."

She grinned at the use of the metaphor from the Christmas eve Matachine dance at the Pueblo. "I understand. Just hope it happens soon."

"So do I. Gotta go. Love you." And then he was gone. The line buzzed in protest.

CHAPTER 41

———

66 "J USTINE, THIS IS KOSTA PAPAMANOLIS. I thought you'd like to know we've opened the safe."

"Oh my god, Kosta. I'm thrilled. I'll be right there. 30 minutes." She had just walked into the house from Santa Fe where she and Mike had completed the grant application. Justine was uncertain the funding would be forthcoming—even from Berkeley. They had tried to construct a newer, broader concept of "community." Community, as defined in their grant, would be explained as "The convergence of culture, history, consumption, and roles in habitable spaces. A culture of reciprocal responsibility." She liked it, but knew it was complex. It would take an algorithm to weigh the relative and interwoven influence of culture, history, consumption, and roles. But that is what anthropologists and archaeologists do. It was the nature of reciprocity that made this different—that changed the game. Lawrence, with his fondness of reciprocity, would be proud.

Driving into town, listening to NPR updates on the Egypt crisis, Justine thought for the thousandth time that day about what was happening in Cairo and Amir. He called less often now; busy maintaining the momentum of the revolution. And, she hadn't seen Taya, although she wasn't surprised. Her anger at and blaming of Justine was still palpable, even though they both knew it was unreasonable. Reason has little to do with perception. *So many loose ends—unfinished stories. Not least of all: what might we find in the safe? Will the key even fit one of the safe deposit boxes?*

Justine located a rare parking space right in front of the La Fonda Hotel. "Hello, Kosta," she called out as she entered the lobby of the hotel and saw him standing at the reception desk. The Greek looked up and smiled broadly.

"I'm excited about your call, Kosta! When did you get it open?"

"Just a couple of hours ago. We had to blow it open. A little dynamite does wonders." They both laughed. "Had to get city permission." Justine stepped forward to shake hands. "Shall we take a look?" he said, closing the reservation book he was examining. Business was not good.

"By all means. I can hardly wait," she said, brandishing the shiny key.

"Does it have a number? There are almost a thousand safe deposit boxes in there."

"911," she said.

"911?"

"His birthday."

"He was born on September 11?"

"Exactly. 1885."

Justine noticed Kosta shake his head in wonderment as he led her to the back stairs descending to the cellar. In spite of his bulky frame, Justine towered over him by a good three inches. He motioned her to follow.

They walked past hundreds of bottles of wine stacked in cellar cubicles until they came upon the ancient wooden door, which Kosta kicked open. "It sticks," he explained with a grin. They stepped onto the muddy tunnel floor, small puddles glistening under the makeshift string of lights—two on each side of the opening. Electrical cords wound through the mud, reminding her of the crypt in Cairo.

Looming to their left was the massive safe with its thick steel door hanging open. Burn spots near the handle flared out a few feet in each direction. Inside, several hundred safe deposits boxes surrounded a small table, not unlike Lawrence's table at the ranch or Van Gogh's table at the Casanova Restaurant in Carmel.

A shiver of delight and expectation ran through her body as she stood there in amazement at the sight before them. She glanced at Kosta. He was grinning like a Cheshire cat, gazing into the murky dark.

"Shall we?" he asked invitingly, handing her a flashlight. His perfect, feathery eyebrows raised, giving his eyes an expression of childlike excitement.

Justine bowed and placed her hand on top of his, like royalty entering a ballroom. They stepped inside the safe, each holding a flashlight. Shadowed images haunted the steel cavity. She swallowed hard, and stared at him, realizing that many of the numbers were difficult to distinguish. "This isn't going to be easy," she said.

Kosta moved boldly ahead, crouching to read the numbers that he could see, going from row to row. Undeterred. "Here! Justine, I've found 0874. Your number has to be on this side."

She grinned and crouched down beside him. "Here's 0889, and 0893," she said. "We have to be getting close! Look--0906. That's close enough, we can just count them off from here. 07, 08, 09, 10—it's got to be the next one!"

Kosta fumbled with the key, inserting it into the rusty, dirt-matted box door. It didn't turn. "Just a minute," he said, rushing back into the cellar to grab a can of WD40 that he kept on a shelf under the wine.

Justine stood alone in the vault. A momentary wave of panic washed through her, as though she was trapped once again in the Cairo crypt under St. Sergius. She placed her hands on the table to steady herself, closed her eyes, and took a deep breath.

Kosta returned and sprayed the WD40 onto the lock of the safe deposit box door and waited no more than a few seconds. He handed the key back to Justine and nodded. "This is your treasure."

She smiled and nodded in gratitude. This time the key turned slowly. She took a deep breath before pulling the long rectangular metal box from its sticky slot and plunking it on the wooden table.

"*Opa!*" cried Kosta, eyes flashing, cheeks flushing, his soft masculinity revealing the pleasure he took in small things.

"Let's take it back to your office," she suggested.

"Good idea." Tucking the treasure under his arm, he led the way.

"Would you like a little brandy?" asked Kosta as he pulled up a chair for Justine and set the rusty box on his desk. He reached into the bottom drawer of his file cabinet and pulled out a bottle of Metaxa 7-Star.

"Sure," she said, staring at the box, nearly afraid to approach it, to handle it. As though it might vanish. When he handed her a small rounded glass half full of brandy, she put her nose to the rim and inhaled deeply. "Quite lovely," she said, taking a sip before she placed it on the desk. "Ok, let's give it a try."

Kosta opened the lid more easily than either of them expected.

They both stared into the box for several moments. Two items stared back.

One yellowed envelope contained two hundred shares of Atchison, Topeka, and Santa Fe Railroad stock, dated 1923. Another envelope was addressed to Lady Brett. Justine recognized Lawrence's handwriting. It had been mailed from the south of France on March 5, 1930. *Two days after Lawrence died.*

"But how?" they both said almost at the same time. She opened the letter and read aloud:

March 2, 1930

> *My dearest Brett,*
> *I don't expect to live the week. This damned tuberculosis has had its way with me. I know this will be sad news and that you will grieve. Not everyone will do so, I am sure. I want you to know that your friendship has been of the highest importance to me.*
>
> *Hux is arriving tonight and I will give him this letter to mail. I have a few things to tell you and know I can trust you to keep my confidences.*
>
> *For the past few years, I have been close to Isabella Hassouna, a woman very dear to me. You may have suspected. She lately gave birth to a daughter and the child is mine. I am sure you will understand that I am pleased beyond words to have a child of my own. If only I could live to watch her grow up.*
>
> *Frieda does not know of Isabella — or the child. I am enclosing a new will that leaves most of my literary estate for*

my daughter, Laurence. You will need to show the will to Frieda and I know that will cause you difficulties, but it must be done. You will need to take a lawyer with you. If Frieda is still in London to settle the estate when you receive this letter, please contact my lawyer there, Edward Mc-Grath at 4 Piccadilly Square, and inform him of my request.

After you have established the legitimacy of the will, please write to Isabella and tell her that a great deal of my literary estate will be forthcoming to Laurence when she reaches the age of 20. You may write her at: Isabella Hassouna, Piazza del S. Uffizio 15, Rome, Vatican City, Italy.

I am also enclosing a key to my safe deposit box in the Jaramillo Bank on the Taos Plaza. There is an envelope in the box containing railroad shares. You may have them, my dear, in appreciation.

With my love always, Lorenzo

Justine fell back into the chair, tears streaming down her face. Kosta watched helplessly.

"I can't understand why the will isn't in here," she said finally. "And, the key. Why did it show up under a concrete slab in front of the fireplace in his cabin? Why didn't Brett take the railroad stocks? They would have been worth something then." She paused, then, "I have a story to tell you, Kosta . . . You see, Isabella Hassouna was my great grandmother . . . ."

Kosta listened without a word until Justine stopped talking.

CHAPTER 42

⁓

FEBRUARY 3, 2011

JUSTINE'S KNEES BUCKLED and she sank to the floor as the television camera momentarily focused on the crumpled body she knew must be Amir, then swung wide to pan the thundering crowd in Tahrir Square. She lay still. *He's dead. Dead. Amir is dead.* Her chilled body trembled.

Time passed. How long did she lie on the living room floor? She didn't know. Eventually, the warmth of the morning sun washed across her inert body. She opened her eyes, shuddered, and stared at the ceiling while the full scene came back to her. *The club. The blood. Amir's murderer on the camel.* Justine walked into the bathroom and threw up. She fumbled methodically through the bedroom closet to find lined ski pants, two sweaters, insulated, lightweight boots, which she drew over her woolen socks. Digging her car keys out of her purse, she grabbed her coat and headed for her frozen car. The windshield was a sheet of ice. She started the engine, placed both gloved hands on the wheel, her head resting against the steering column while the defroster worked to clear the windows.

Justine drove south without a destination. She couldn't feel. Or think. Her skin was clammy and pale; she felt lightheaded. Was she going to the airport? To a friend's house? Into a town? She glanced at the clock. It was after 7:00 a.m. and fragments of sunlight slipped behind thick darkening clouds tumbling in from the northwest. She turned west toward Pilar. Unaware of the gathering storm, she drove on while snow flurries hit and slid from the windshield. Forgetting entirely that she was due at the office this morning, Justine continued west, and nearly two hours later found herself at Hupobi, the unexplored Mesa near Ojo Caliente. She parked, grabbed her coat, jumped out of the car and ran across the frozen river surface to the base of the mesa. She envisioned the happy children, splashing in the rushing river. Her clumsy race up the mountainside was slippery, treacherous, yet she was relentless.

At the top of the mesa, already blanketed by snow and ice, hefty flakes began to fall once more, landing on her reddening face, melting on contact and riveting down her cheeks like tears. Justine ran across the frozen landscape, alongside the giant kiva to the crest of the hill facing the great canyon below. She moved swiftly along the edge of the icy elevated mound. Sweating beneath the parka, memories forced themselves into her consciousness. She was a little girl, it was a summer morning in Fiesole when she called out for her Grandmother Laurence who was to meet her for tea, but was nowhere to be found. The young Justine ran into the lush Italian garden, her grandmother's pride, and found her beloved Nana there slumped over a bed of pansies. Shaking her, she wailed, "Gramma, Gramma, wake up!"

But her Grandmother did not wake up.

Wake up. Amir! She cried out, *I want you back!* Tears formed, then froze, on her face. The temperature was dropping, the storm slamming in with deadly force. Her body trembled. She lost her stride, her balance. Her right foot began to slide in the loose, slippery snow. She tried to regain her footing, but abruptly, with a crack, the ice breaking, her whole body careened over the edge of the icy cliff, tumbling, rolling until she slammed into a crevasse a few hundred feet above the valley floor. She passed out, and woke to find her right foot caught, twisted, wedged into a chasm bounded by gnarled tree roots.

Her coat had ripped, and she'd seen the boot from the trapped ankle spin into the air like a frisbee, sailing down the canyon wall. She was now wide awake, even though her breathing was still irregular, pulse rapid, eyes dilated. She stared at her broken foot, the searing physical pain pushing against the pain of loss—the loss of Amir. She screamed out, "No! No! Amir! Please . . . I need you!"

After a time, she pulled back and assessed her situation: she was alone and worse, no one knew where she was. *How could I be so stupid?* Dehydrated, she picked up a handful of snow and ate it. Her foot was caught and surely broken, maybe worse. Her toes would freeze first. The storm was getting more severe by the moment. Why hadn't she called someone? Giovanna? Her father?

I am going to die here on the mesa. When I die, will I see Amir again? Is that what I'm seeking? Wanting? She had never believed in a hereafter, a heaven. *Heaven doesn't make any sense, but the Native notion of my soul returning to a spirit world, being one with an encompassing universe sounds compelling, hopeful anyway. Or is this my Easternized version of the hereafter?* Justine pondered this: the hereafter. The minutes ticked by, but she'd lost all sense of time. *Amir was so sure. I envied him. Nothing could shake him from his Coptic beliefs. And D.H.? A skeptic 'till the end, trying desperately to separate from his Protestant roots through his paintings, his poems, to claim the aliveness, the genuine wholeness he felt here. Both of them went away, leaving the loves of their lives in Taos—for D.H., a ranch, for Amir, me, a woman. They yearned to return, would have returned, but died prematurely.* Her foot was nearly frozen, although it was cuddled within a cavern of snow and roots.

She rattled her IPhone to get it to respond. No service up here. She slammed it back in her coat pocket and tried to extract her foot by digging the roots loose from around her ankle, resting intermittently, remembering the chilling film, *127 Hours*, in which the trapped young man cut off his own arm in order to escape. *Am I capable of cutting off my own foot?* She didn't think so, and was somewhat grateful that she didn't have a knife. Attempting to stay upright, and slide no further, she dug a cradle into the snow to hold her body firm, then removed the glove from her left hand, leaning forward to slip it onto her trapped, bootless foot.

The snow had covered her tracks, and of course it wouldn't occur to a search party formed after she didn't show up at the office in Santa Fe that she might have headed for Hupobi. The drive would be considered insane in this weather. No one knew about Amir and the events of Cairo's Bloody Wednesday, about why she had freaked out.

By evening she was slipping in and out of hypothermic consciousness, had been on the mesa for nearly ten hours and was bone chilled. Then gradually, like the intoxication of a good red wine, she became aware that she was feeling warmer. At first, she was grateful, then realized that getting warm meant she was freezing to death. She dug faster, even as the warmth mutated into a powerful sense of presence. *A calm. Yes, a calm, supportive presence.* She was once again sitting on her grandmother's lap, being hugged with reassuring affection, feeling that soft belly, the buttons from her housedress pressing gently into her back. *I'm hallucinating*, she realized. She blinked and shook herself, rubbing her legs as vigorously as she could, twisting her torso, flapping her arms, moving her whole body in order to keep herself from freezing. The presence became more distinct, distinguishable, like two persons sitting close by.

"Are you my guides?" she asked. Lucinda had said my guides could come in any form.

No answer.

"Are you my guides?" she gently asked again, then waited. She felt a touch on her face as though a warm hand had moved tenderly across her cheek. Justine began to cry, to sob softly. "Thank you. Thank you." With new resolve, and an unexplainably powerful confidence, she turned her attention to the stubborn roots claiming her foot, and pulled and twisted with all of her strength.

Justine knew her guides were with her when the roots gave way. With both hands she carefully extracted her foot and laid it down in the snow, feeling it was a strange appendage that didn't belong to her. Searing pain shot up her calf, causing her breath to catch in her throat, her head to spin into near unconsciousness. Her awareness began to seep through when she stared at the gap in the hillside—the snow cascading over it—from which her foot had been removed. She saw remnants of an ancient garbage dump: large and small sherds of pottery, arrowheads, a gourd rattle, a disintegrating squirrel doll, stuffing gone, the sinew stitching unraveled.

One object didn't belong in such a forlorn space: a black stone image about five inches tall, straight and flat, almost like a carved stone fetish. She could see it clearly now, and reached out her hand to extract the gift from its grave. She stopped herself in mid air, remembering her training as an anthropologist. The figure is a part of this place. It belongs here, not in some glassy cage. She could feel the sensitivity of her Lakota ancestors; her guides circled and embraced her, affirming her decision by moving closer, growing warmer. Vision blurred, she stared at the precious miniature, its rounded Bufano sculpture-like head, small eyes, and flat bottom. Little hands were scratched into either side, as though she were tenderly holding her stomach. Just as she withdrew her hand, Justine heard the snow above her break loose.

Fighting for consciousness, she rotated her throbbing head in a pirouette and gazed at the lovely white blanket of snow moving toward her. She turned back toward the wondrous find, urgently seeking the smooth fetish with her eyes as the avalanche erased the crevasse, immersing her in blindness.

Justine's near frozen body spun like a top, tumbling downward with the racing snow bank, pain searing through her entire body, her injured foot dragging along as though it were the disintegrating leg of that old squirrel doll. The brutal wave of snow catapulted her into a flash of violent memory of overturning her kayak in the Rogue River, the pressure of the water spinning and pulling at her . . . *water, wave—swimming. Swimming!* a voice inside her cried out. She managed to roll onto her stomach and began to swim as hard and fast as she could, forcing her body to move like a dolphin through the collapsing mountain of snow. Roots and trees tumbled alongside, slashing through her ski pants, a sharp rock tearing at her cheek, even as the thundering avalanche carried her downward.

CHAPTER 43

———⚬⚬⚬———

"HI," HE SAID, his fur-lined parka pulled up to shield his mouth. He stood in the blowing snow just outside the covered porch at Justine's house in Taos. "Where's Justine?" he asked the young girl shivering on the bench.

"I can't find her." Taya's voice trembled as she spoke, her words almost lost in the frigid wind. "She's gone."

"I'm her father," said Morgan Jenner, "just got in from Italy, flew all night. I need to find her quickly. Who are you?" He noted the girl's engorged stomach.

"Taya. Her friend." She pulled her coat more tightly around her stomach. "She usually leaves me a key."

"Do you know where she might be?" he asked. He could hear the chaos in Tahrir Square blaring through the locked door. His eyes squinted as a desperate tone crept into his voice. "Help me."

"Maybe at work in Santa Fe? Her car is gone." Redness from the cold wind blended with the redness in her weeping eyes. "She's mad at me, I think."
"I tried at her office. She didn't show up for work today . . . mad at you?"

"She thinks I blamed her when my boyfriend and brother were killed. They slid into the gorge, you see. They were chasing her. I guess I did blame her a bit."

"She told me. I think she blames herself too." Morgan's voice softened in the presence of such pain; he could only begin to imagine the anguish his own daughter was feeling. That's why he was here. "You're shivering—come sit in the car."

Morgan helped Taya up and guided her to the car, raising his voice to talk through the shrieking wind. "You see, something has happened. I think her friend Amir has been killed."

"Amir! Oh, no!" She began to cry.

Morgan was taken aback. "I'm sorry. I didn't know you knew him."

"Justine introduced me. She loves him a lot."

He flinched. "I know. We have to find her, Taya. Think."

Taya put her mind to the question. "Well, she talked a lot about the ranch, the mountain, and Hupobi. She thought Hupobi was a real mystery—like a storybook."

Within a half hour, Bill, Cheyenne, and Giovanna headed for the ranch and Lobo Mountain; Morgan and Pablo Williams were on their way to Hupobi. Too far and the weather was ferocious. Morgan left Taya in the lobby at BLM and asked the secretary to find her a ride home.

They knew it was a long-shot, but when Pablo told Morgan the story of the site, he convinced himself that it might have been her destination. The ranger station were called and the police were searching for her car. Helicopters were ready to be dispatched to the mountains around Ojo Caliente, or Lobo Mountain, when the storm cleared.

She must have seen him brutally beaten, Morgan knew, since he'd heard the television through Justine's front door when he was talking with Taya. But how would she know it was he in that crowd? For the first hour of the drive both Pablo and Morgan were surprisingly quiet, lost in silent worry and foreboding. Neither speculated on the possibilities of being lost in a snowstorm overnight. They sat, two archaeologists, both afraid to speculate on their next find. Gradually, the truck grew cozy, their feet warm. Pablo asked, "You say you just got in from Italy?"

"Yeah. I was watching the riots in Cairo from my place in Florence when I was almost certain I saw our family friend Amir El Shabry beaten, possibly killed. Justine's fiancé. He's like a son to me . . . . " His voice broke.

"Sorry to hear that—I didn't know."

"Tried to call Justine, then her mother."

"Justine's told me a lot about her mother . . . Lucrezia, isn't it? She with you?"

"No. Broke her ankle." Morgan paused, somehow feeling a need to explain more. "We have what Justine calls a modern partnership. We live apart, but close by. See each other often. I'd be willing to give it another go, but Lucrezia doesn't want to be married again."

"I see . . . ," Pablo said awkwardly. It was probably more than he wanted to know. "Your daughter is one special young woman."

Morgan paused again, tensed by Pablo's fast driving on slippery mountain roads. "I think so. Pablo, is this really feasible—could she have come this far? In this weather?"

Near blizzard velocity snow blew against the side of the truck like a white tornado.

"Wouldn't think so, although she's very fond of this place, determined to unravel its mysteries. For some reason, Taya was convinced that she might head here. We'll know soon."

"She told me about your trek to Hupobi—she was quite excited about the possibility of the Mesa Verde peoples migrating into the area."

"Quite credible, I think. Timing, dry farming, pottery design. Don't quite understand the resistance by some to the migration narrative." Pablo stared straight ahead, determined to stay in the one set of tire tracks on the snow-packed mountain road. The road flattened and came to a stop sign. "We turn left here. Not much further."

Morgan sat stiffly; the harrowing road conditions over the mountain had been worse than he'd experienced since he was a kid in Nebraska. But at least his homeland had been flat. He'd nearly given up hope of finding Justine at Hupobi—it was just too far, too treacherous. He regretted the day he first took her hiking, for it was the beginning of her risk taking. Into the mountains and rivers and old crypts alone. He worried about her often. His only child. "She takes the migration quite seriously," he managed, distracted, his voice wavering.

Pablo glanced at Morgan briefly, not sure what he'd intended to say. He turned right into what might have been a narrow country road, but was now indistinguishable. As though from habit, the sturdy truck negotiated the roads to Hupobi as far as the frozen river.

They pulled up beside Justine's Prius and stared at each other. It had now been nearly twenty-four hours since the bloody events in Cairo. Pablo picked up his phone and called the police to direct the helicopters into a more constricted area around the mesa, but of course that couldn't happen until the snow subsided. Pointing to the looming plateau, he strapped on his backpack, as did Morgan, and began the march. The two men crossed the frozen river, trekked the half mile to the base of the mesa and began climbing. It was rough going, the spindly trees providing little support. Morgan's boots, more designer than practical, slipping in the crunchy, dry snow; yet with Pablo's help they crested the top of the mesa.

Pablo drew out his binoculars and scanned the plateau. The snow had buried any evidence of human or animal presence. Morgan pointed at the trees at the edge of the giant kiva, and the two men headed in that direction. They stared into the cavity smoothly encircled with fresh snow like an immense bowl of vanilla ice cream. The wind howled, making speech nearly impossible.

Morgan shook his head in despair, restraining tears, clearly feeling desperate. They turned slowly, keenly observing the contours in the land, the frayed edges of the cliff, the hills beyond. Without speaking, they turned into the blowing snow and started the hike around the perimeter of the mesa.

Morgan stopped dead in his tracks. "Do you hear that? A high-pitched sound? I think there's a pattern . . . . "

Pablo shook his head. He hadn't heard anything unusual. "The wind." He obviously wasn't encouraged, turning to continue the difficult hike around the mesa perimeter.

—∞∞—

The danger of being enclosed in a small space, unable to escape . . . these were the familiar thoughts on Justine's mind as she lay within a bubble woven of snow at the bottom of the canyon cliff. Cheyenne had explained to her that the Navajo rug has a Weaver's Pathway—a way out—otherwise the weaver becomes sick and loses her mind, loses her way. The pathway is the road to liberation of the mind, the body, the spirit, and the designer within. Afraid of being trapped in the pattern, unable to escape the weaving, the Navajo weaver leaves a trail, a visible thread leading to an exit from captivity. *Will I find a thread?*

Once again she was in the crypt that had crumbled in Cairo during the earthquake, nearly buried by the collapse of the church around her. The fear of being buried alive a second time was mind-numbing. *How could this happen? At least in Cairo I only had a few scratches.* This time she couldn't move. Her legs felt numb when she tried to move; the pain took her breath away.

Remembering to swim within the avalanche had saved her life, but the excruciating pain of propelling downward with a broken foot had brought her to near hysteria. She floated in and out of consciousness until the oxygen in her cage of snow was nearly gone. She had to act.

Her eyes searched unsuccessfully for the weaver's pathway, the way out. Her IPhone still had a dim light, which she lifted into the air, face up, flat on her palm, and moved it around in a wide circle to project the meager light onto the ceiling of snow. "No Service" blared at her from the upper left corner of the phone; on the right, only a razor thin strip of black remained. *I will be completely in the dark soon.* She began to tremble from the fear of the dark, the pain, the cold. She shut her eyes and forced herself to meditate, then slowly opened them again. The light was still there. Justine fumbled with the phone.

Amir . . . Amir. Hadn't he shown her a few other functions on the phone? An alarm clock, a calendar—which she had used—different apps—music! She started rapidly pushing buttons, it was easier with her bare hand, although it had little grip left. The phone slid out of her hand and landed face down in the snow. A thin rectangular light beamed upward as though projecting from a miniature coffin. She picked it up and pushed "music"—she would find "Chicago." Grad school in Chicago. *Late again for forensics . . . run. Am I ready for the exam??* Renee Zellweger blared out "Roxie!" Justine pushed the volume until the sound vibrated in her ears. "They love me for lovin' them, we love each other . . . " pierced the air around her. She felt a thrill, her body yearned to move in time, but refused. "Give'm the old Razzle Dazzle," Richard Gere pleaded next. Justine knew only too well that no one was within hearing distance, yet she stared at the phone as though she could will it to continue indefinitely.

Five minutes later, "The Cellophane Man" gave up in mid-sentence, "invisible, inconsequential me . . . you can look right through me, walk right by me, and never know I'm there . . . . " Her ice womb went black and she started to cry. Justine wasn't sure about her alloyed fears of death—if she cared whether she died, or when she died. But she hadn't wanted to die like this: in a dark cave, freezing, alone. *Am I alone?*

Once again, she forced herself to take control. She now knew she wanted to live, the will to live prodding her on. Where were her guides? Now she would have to rely on natural forms of information: her intuition, the wisdom of the snow. *What can the snow tell me?* It was still dark outside—*no it couldn't be*—she forced herself to recall the image on the phone just before it went black: 1:00 P.M. She closed her eyes and opened them again, scanning the arch of her prison for the palest patches of light. The absence of air, compounded by the elevation, forced her to take short, shallow breaths. She could feel her blood pressure dropping. Her body no longer had the strength to shiver. She dozed off.

"Amir, I thought I'd lost you! Darling, you're here!" she uttered this as a whisper. She attempted to reach for his face, push the black curl out of his eyes. She was growing warm again. "Come to me. I'll learn to cook," she lied, humor warming her chest slightly. "What? I can't hear you." Justine rolled into a fetal position.

She was awakened by a growing patch of light filtering softly through a thinning ceiling of snow, transforming the crystals into pale pink. An outline of two small creatures—ravens—perched on the thinning snow above. Her ravens come to save her. She stared at the ravens, watching them circling a thin spot as though they were scatching the snow, seeking to open it. In spite of the constancy of fear, the near unconsciousness, the sureness that she was hallucinating again, for a moment she experienced a wave of enchantment, pure joy, as though she was once again floating in the grotto on the isle of Capri with her father. Only then the light was blue. Clarity focused her mind.

Justine rose on one elbow as far as she could stretch, made a fist of her one gloved hand and jammed it forcefully through the patch of pink. The pink gave way to azure blue as the sky stared down at her like a giant eye; her ravens took flight, cawing loudly, then resettled on the igloo. Oxygen flowed freely into her confined space. She inhaled deeply and smiled, but couldn't move. Something more than a broken foot was handicapping her mobility. *I'm going to die here,* she realized once again.

"You won't die here Justine," said a voice near her shoulder, a warm sense of comfort flooding through her.

"Did you see that?" Morgan screamed. "Like the spout of a whale shooting up from that mound of snow near the bottom. Two ravens perched near the spout!" He pointed. Patches of blue sky replaced the softly falling snow.

"Gotta be Justine!" shouted Pablo. "There's been an avalanche here. See this collapsed ledge." He grabbed his police radio and began shouting into it. "Yes—we've found her. A couple hundred feet down the western edge. Can you see us?" The massive man raised both hands in the air and jumped up and down. Morgan followed suit. The chopper pilot waved back. Immediately, Pablo barked, "Follow me and be careful where you step."

CHAPTER 44

———✦———

THE HELICOPTER HOVERED for several minutes before it could land on the freshly-plowed pad just south of the emergency entrance to Holy Cross Hospital in Taos. During the thirty-minute flight from Hupobi, the first responders cut off Justine's wet clothes, dried her nearly frozen body and covered her with heated blankets. They applied warm compresses to her neck, knowing full well that in cases of extreme hypothermia, treating her limbs first would draw blood away from her head and brain. Morgan sat beside her, cupping her hand in his; his face having lost its natural structure, reforming itself into a macabre mask of desperation. "Mom?" she asked nearly inaudibly through the oxygen mask.

"Broken ankle—couldn't travel—she'll be fine," Morgan assured his daughter. "Sends her love."

A small smile crept across Justine's pale blue lips.

———✦———

If she had a chance of living, it was within the care of this highly trained trauma staff, both in the helicopter and the hospital. As the nearest hospital to the massive Taos Ski Area, the staff was well equipped for tragedies brought on by cold, snow, injuries, and isolation.

Justine's gurney was unloaded with incredible dispatch and rushed through the automatic doors into the emergency room where two doctors and three nurses awaited. Morgan jumped out and ran after the gurney. Pablo had driven the truck back to the BLM offices, picked up his own car, and headed back for the hospital.

"Temperature is 88," cried the senior nurse. "Pulse slow—about 40—breathing shallow." Justine's body had given up shivering a few hours earlier, for the body possessed no further strength to try to warm itself. Although senior nurse Marina was experienced with patients brought off Taos Mountain suffering from hypothermia, rarely did anyone spend much time in the cold before being rescued. On only one other occasion had she dealt with such an extreme case—that time a few years ago when a nine-year old was lost on Lobo Mountain. He had been trying to find help when his father had fallen and broken his leg. Neither lived.

But she knew what to do—they all did: fill the IV with lukewarm salt water to heat Justine's blood, while her assistant dipped cloths into a pan filled with warmer salt water, lifted the heated blankets from Justine's inert body, and applied the cloths to the patient's lower stomach and upper thighs. The hypothermia would have to be treated before Justine could be wheeled in for an MRI of her skeletal frame and CT scan of her brain, all areas of possible damage. An anxious staff fought for patience.

Hours passed before the attending physician entered the waiting room to speak with Morgan. He scanned the room. Two women and another man watched him closely, hanging on every word. Dr. Fred Fernandez recognized the faces, but didn't socialize. A swarthy man of medium height, a slight case of sclerosis gave him a bent position that made him appear older than his forty-eight years. Fred had worked in this emergency room for nearly twenty years and had seen everything this country had to offer.

His words reassured Morgan at first. "Your daughter is one lucky girl, Mr. Jenner. Hypothermia, a broken foot and left shoulder. Her spinal vertebrae are essentially whole, and there's no trace of brain damage. However, there can still be serious complications from such a severe case of hypothermia: damage to nerves and small blood vessels, possibly in the hands and feet—a condition sometimes known as chilblains." Although a very exacting man, Fred was even more specific than usual. "The baby should be fine."

Morgan gasped, as did everyone else in the room.

Observing the sea of surprised faces, the physician flinched and apologized to Morgan, "Sorry. I thought you knew."

"Don't be sorry. I just arrived in the country and Justine and I haven't had a chance to talk. I couldn't be more pleased. When can I see her?"

"In a couple more hours. She is still pulling out of the hypothermia, and . . . may I ask you to step outside?" He walked into the hall, moving further into the inner sanctum of the hospital, turning back toward Morgan when they were out of hearing range. "Your daughter has had a prolonged and terrifying experience, Mr. Jenner. It's hard to know what to expect. I'm going to contact the hospital psychiatrist."

The tanned skin on Morgan's face drew tight across his cheekbones and around his mouth. Before he could reply, the emergency doors swung open and Fred's beeper began to wail. "If you'll excuse me," he said, already moving in the direction of the rolling gurney. Apparently, only one physician was on duty.

The new patient's face was pale, her lips ashen. Eyes closed. Then she doubled up in agony and began to scream.

"Find the midwife!" rang a voice from the hallway. The respectful relationship of Holy Cross Hospital to the Northern New Mexico Birth center was a rare one—unlike any in the country, thanks to the pioneering efforts of two women: an obstetrician and the founder of the center. The two institutions operated with unparalleled cooperation and admiration, a shared mission.

So, when a woman was brought in for delivery, it was second nature to call in the midwife, even though more babies were delivered at home or in the clinic on the pueblo than in the hospital. The hospital was for complicated cases, the outliers that didn't fit the usual, natural pattern. Complications required advanced technologies.

The midwife was already in the hallway taking care of admission by the time the call went out. The patient's mother had called ahead when her daughter began to double over in pain and bleeding, her lips turning blue. The receptionist at the midwifery center had urged her to head for the emergency room.

Taya had been bundled up and stuffed into the backseat of her mother's old Ford. During the fifteen-minute drive south, the young girl screamed, Sharon holding her daughter and praying while blood rushed out onto the floorboard. Lucinda, Sharon's elder sister, drove significantly over the speed limit. "We should have called an ambulance," cried Taya's mother. "Not even seven months along and all this blood!"

"Look at me!" insisted Fred Fernandez, the doctor turning to glance and nod as the midwife entered the room. Clearly grateful to see Lisa, for she would be familiar with Taya's history. The girl's lids were at quarter mast, unfocused, then they flew open and she screamed again. The bleeding was profuse.

"What's causing all the bleeding?" asked Lisa, her eyes narrowed with urgency.

"I don't know! Here's her file. Check her second trimester ultrasound."

"I can tell you without looking that there's nothing in the file. Fred, she didn't show up for the appointment." The midwife stared at Fred, a man whom she'd known and worked with for many years. Then she broke eye contact and looked away. It was usual practice to go out and find a patient if she didn't show up, especially if she were very young. Or at least call the parent.

Turning to the nurse, Fred spoke urgently. It wasn't in him to judge his colleague, for he had made his own mistakes. "We need an ultrasound right now." He said nothing about his suspicions, he could be wrong.

Lisa helped prepare Taya for transport to the lab. She and the nurse shifted the girl onto the gurney, the IV continuing to pump blood into her limp arm as the wheels of the gurney slid sideways in a puddle of blood and found traction.

No one noticed the lone woman, silent and terrified, sitting in the shadows. Sharon had found her daughter curled up on the floor of her room that afternoon, lying in a pool of blood, mumbling inaudibly. At times like this she sorely missed her husband, who had decided to live with his own tribe in South Dakota. He had returned home upon the death of their son, then turned and left without a word. Why couldn't they comfort each other? This time would be no different.

If the midwife Lisa hadn't been so distressed, she might have noticed Sharon in the darkened corner. It was the policy of the midwifery center to involve parents of under aged children in the pre-natal care of their daughter. Both of them, somehow, had fallen short of their responsibilities. For Sharon, it had been concerns for the troubled son—followed by his death—that had captured her attention. But how about Lisa herself?

"How far along did you say she is?" Fred asked while the ultrasound was being connected. The bleeding continued unabated as the IV supply of blood crept lower and lower. He stared at the hanging bag as though to ask, "Can the blood flow into her body as fast as it is flowing out?"

Before the midwife could tell him that Taya was less than thirty weeks along, Fred motioned to the nurse to rush and find a new supply. As the doctor spoke, he glanced up at the ultrasound screen and went pale. It was as though all the blood had drained out of his own body. He turned to the midwife, who was staring at the screen as well.

"The placenta is covering the cervix," said the midwife matter of factly, her voice disconnected, almost sterile. She held her breath as though that action alone would change the screen, move the placenta from the bottom of the uterus to the side where it belonged.

"So, that's causing the bleeding . . . get her to Op!" he yelled. "Now."

The IV bag gurgled its last drop of precious blood just as another nurse entered with a fresh supply. "Wait," she commanded, halting the movement of the gurney so that she could attach the bag.

Lisa, the midwife, asked the nurse: "Where's her mother? Sharon."

"In the patient's room. Been there for some time."

Lisa's face formed into a question. "She is?" She hurried down the hall and found Sharon seated where she had been since Taya was brought in."

"Sharon," she began urgently, pulling up a chair, leaning over to hug her. "I'm sorry to neglect you like this. We're concerned about Taya's bleeding."

"Is she going to be all right? And the baby? Is the baby okay?"

Lisa paused. "Let me explain. As you may know, during pregnancy, the placenta embeds itself on the side or top of the uterus. But that's not the case with Taya. Her placenta is at the bottom, covering the cervix. It's a condition called placenta previa."

"So the baby can't get out . . . . "

"Exactly."

"But why all the bleeding?"

"As the cervix expands, it rips the placenta. The blood is coming from that rip."

"She'll need surgery, won't she? A Caesarian?"

"They're prepping her right now."

"But she's not far enough along—will the baby live?" Sharon's eyes welled up. They were already red from the ride in, watching her little girl bleed onto the floorboard. Memories of her own difficult childbirths flooded through her mind. But at least, no blood—only intense pain. "She's only a child," she whimpered, almost inaudibly.

"I know . . . we can't know about the baby yet. We've been giving him corticosteroids to speed up his lung development. She didn't say, 'a little late to make any difference.' That's about all we can do right now . . . other than the Caesarian."

A boy. "Lisa. I didn't know. She had some pains—lower back, sometimes on the side of her stomach." Sharon placed her hand on her own stomach. "Then she would lie down and say she felt better. I didn't think it was anything . . . . "

"If we'd known, we would have had her on bed rest. If she'd had her second trimester ultrasound, we would have known what to do. Sometimes, as the stomach expands, the placenta can pull back into place. But neither of us knew. Please don't blame yourself. You've had enough grief lately . . . with your son . . . . "

A fountain of grief exploded inside Sharon, sobs welling up uncontrollably, as though this was the first time she'd allowed herself to cry.

Lisa would have comforted Sharon more, but needed to get to the operating room. She bundled Taya's mother in her arms for a moment, holding her as tight as she could. "Where's Lucinda? Where's your sister?" Lisa whispered into her ear.

"She let us off and went to pick up her son from a basketball game," Sharon said between sobs. "She'll be right back."

"Call her. Now," Lisa insisted and hurried back down the hall, a shiny white tunnel leading to the operating room where she washed up, donned a smock and mask and joined Fred and the nurses.

She was just in time to observe Fred gently lift the pale blue, inert baby from her mother's womb and hand him off to a waiting nurse who swaddled him in a towel and carried him to the sink, scales, and incubator. The child was as limp and translucent as a wilting lily.

Fred moved his hand gently around the inside of Taya's uterus, letting his fingers feel the contours of the flesh, wet and soft to his touch. When he finally looked up, he gazed into Lisa's penetrating eyes above the medical mask.

He shook his head, his eyes reflecting an uncharacteristic touch of terror. Something was terribly wrong. Finally, he stood upright and said, "It's not coming out, the placenta is embedded too deeply."

"Placenta accretia," Lisa said. It sounded like a death sentence.

He nodded again. The nurses were stunned into an eerie silence. The baby didn't cry. Only the sound of oxygen flowing to the pale patients could be heard above the myriad of nearly inaudible thoughts and prayers in the cold operating quarter.

Fred stretched his arms and fingers in preparation for the hysterectomy. It broke his heart to perform such a drastic procedure on a child. Her baby was unlikely to live and she would never have another. He looked up into the fading sunlight washing down from the skylight. When the hospital was constructed he'd opposed it. "I don't want nature controlling the light over the operating table," he'd insisted. They had placed a remote shade over the opening so that he could control it. He was satisfied and now found that he left it open more often than not.

"I'm going to talk to her mother again," Lisa said. "Fred, she has to give her permission for a hysterectomy."

He forced his shoulders back; he was steadfast. "I can't wait, Lisa. She is bleeding too heavily."

Throwing her smock and mask into a corner chair, the midwife rushed from the room. She knew that Fred would proceed with the surgery. What if Sharon didn't agree?

Nearly running down the hall, Lisa's hand caught the doorframe as she spun into the room, then slowed her pace. "It is a matter of her life, Sharon. We have no choice," she pleaded.

"But she'll never have another child, isn't that right? Will her baby live?"

The midwife gulped. She couldn't reassure Sharon that Taya would have at least this one child, that she would have at least one grandchild. But she couldn't—the chances were slim for both. "I don't know. I really don't know."

Sharon started to cry again, to mumble. It was an impossible decision to make. "Lucinda doesn't answer her phone. Is Justine awake?" She'd been informed about Justine's accident and rescue. Her presence in the hospital.

"Justine?" Lisa asked with surprise. "There is a Justine Jenner here. Is that who you mean? I'll find out."

Lisa returned quickly from the reception desk with the permission form in hand. "Justine is still unconscious, I'm afraid. Sharon, you have no choice. You have to sign this."

Taya's mother said nothing as she took the pen from Lisa's hand and signed the form. She turned away. The midwife quickly signed as witness and left the room. She couldn't take the time to comfort Sharon.

CHAPTER 45

⟨oœo⟩

A FEW HOURS LATER, well after midnight, Sharon stood at Justine's hospital room door, nodded to Giovanna who sat in the dark across the room and stared at the man near her bed.

Morgan looked up and walked toward Sharon. He knew without asking who she was. "Hello. I'm Justine's father," he said. "How is Taya?"

As Sharon's eyes welled up, Giovanna walked over and embraced her. Giovanna had helped in the hunt for Justine, searching with Bill in the direction of Lobo Mountain. Now fully exhausted, her spunky elfin demeanor was gaunt. She refused to leave Justine's side. Morgan had been welcoming when she'd insisted on being there, for his daughter had told him of her relationship with this woman, a believer in miracles.

"We're not sure," said Sharon finally. "The hysterectomy is over, but she's lost a lot of blood. Justine? How's Justine?"

"There may be some nerve damage around the blood vessels in the broken foot from the hypothermia. Too early to tell. She's still drifting in and out of consciousness. We can only hope. But she'll live." He trembled as he said those final words. Gazing at each woman in turn, he added. "She doesn't know about Taya."

Sharon nodded. She'd grown close to Justine over the past months, had come to rely on her, sometimes for advice about her daughter who had become more and more estranged from the family. "First I lose my son, then I seem to be losing Taya as well," she had told Justine. "I'm losing both children at once." During the past month, the girl had been angry with her as well.

"Sharon." Lisa stood at the door, addressing Sharon, yet gazing intensely, knowingly at Giovanna. "May I talk with you?"

Sharon stepped into the hall, fear flashing through her eyes, and followed the midwife to Taya's room.

Without explanation, Giovanna left the room and hurried toward the hospital exit.

Justine opened her uncomprehending, lusterless eyes and looked at her father. She stared at him for several moments while he massaged her hand, waiting for her to figure out where she was, why her father was beside her. Finally, she said, "Is he dead? Is Amir dead?" She glanced around the room as though she expected to find Amir there, waiting for her. Then, "Lucinda, where's Lucinda. I must tell her about my guides . . . . "

The psychiatrist had warned Morgan, "Once she realizes where she is, Dr. Jenner, she'll want to know about Amir. Be honest with her." Whatever that means, he had thought at the time. "His body hasn't been found," he said reluctantly. "There's still hope. I'll find Lucinda."

Her eyes focused on the wall behind him and she shivered. Her body was beginning to regulate its own temperature. That's a good sign. "How am I doing, Dad? Will I live?"

Her father started to cry. "We were so scared, Honey . . . but, you're going to be just fine. You were damned cold, some bones are broken in your foot and shoulder. But you're strong, the body of an athlete."

"I was so scared, Dad. I was sure I was going to die out there alone. How did you ever find me?"

Morgan explained about Taya—and Pablo—the hunt, hearing the pulsing sound of her IPhone, the ravens. Seeing her fist burst through the snow bubble. The weather and helicopter. He told the story slowly, lavishly, as though escorting her down a primrose path to sanity. "Everyone was great, Honey. You have many good friends here—and in so short a time."

Justine was only half listening. "Taya? I thought she would never speak to me again after . . . what did she want?"

"I'm not really sure. I didn't even ask when I found her there, sitting on your porch. I just needed to find you."

Justine flinched at the image of Taya sitting in the cold. "I just hope her baby will be fine."

"Both of your babies should be fine, Honey," he lied. " I . . . . "

Justine stiffened, then recoiled in pain when her body resisted. "Baby? I'm pregnant?!"

"I thought you knew, but I should have known better. You would have told your mother and me. I didn't think it through . . . . "

The senior nurse, standing unnoticed by the foot of the bed, stepped forward to check her IV, her pulse. "I think she needs to get a little rest now, Dr. Jenner. May I ask you to step out?"

Fred told Lisa there was little chance that Taya would survive the night. Her heartbeat and pulse were very slow, and the loss of blood, especially before she'd reached the hospital, had caused some veins to collapse. She was now in shock, lying in a private recovery room.

The curtains were pulled, and once again, a tense stillness permeating the air. The new supply of blood flown up from Santa Fe was seeping through the IV, the heart monitor showing an exceptionally weak pattern, the oxygen grinding away. Fred was standing by the door when Lisa came in with Sharon and Lucinda. It was 1:30 a.m.

Lisa pulled up two chairs for Taya's mother and aunt and drew in a quick breath. Tears rolled down her eyes. In her years as a midwife she had learned to cry quietly.

Fred approached the two women. "Taya's been through a great deal and her situation is very serious. Stay with her, be with her, say your goodbyes. Then you need to let go." This was Fred's way of telling a family that their loved one wouldn't live until morning. He had never found the right words to cushion this moment.

Before Sharon could respond, Giovanna quietly walked into the room, slid her hand into her jeans and grasped a black and amber stone shaped roughly like a heart, clutching it firmly, feeling warmth flood through her palm. She had found the precious artifact at the ancient homeland of Kateri Tekakwitha near Toronto and was convinced that it possessed special healing properties.

Then she walked over to Sharon, leaned down and whispered in her ear, slipping the stone under Taya's pillow. A brief flash of acceptance washed over Sharon's face; she turned and spoke to Lucinda in a hushed voice. Silent praying began. In concert, as though a new resolve had been thrust into the room by Kateri herself. Each woman believed in the Saint's agency in performing miracles. On her way back to the hospital, Giovanna had called the Center for the Blessed Kateri and activated a network of thousands of believers around the country, believers who would be sending their prayers and positive energies, vibrations, to this young woman near death.

The stone, the prayers brought together the energies in the room as though Kateri's blue blanket was being rewoven in the presence of such faith. The blue blanket wrapped around Kateri when she died, the blanket used to heal so many others. The hours passed.

Fred had been rescued from fully dealing with Sharon's response to his pronouncement of Taya's imminent death. By Kateri perhaps? He stared at Giovanna. When the Pope decided that Kateri was a saint, he would too. The doctor came to the door several times, often walking away, at other times quietly approaching the front of the bed and checking Taya's vitals. The midwife and the senior nurse were in and out as well. Both approaches to life— medicine and miracles—side-by-side throughout the night. Each person honoring and respecting whatever thoughts and prayers floated through the room. Taya lay there with few signs of life, paleness tinged with blue, breathing shallow. There was no visible change in her status.

Morning was sneaking up the rise from the east, kissing the frost on the lawn outside the window, warm rays of sunlight reaching the glass, catching a prism hanging from a rod, a prism left behind when a young child occupying this room had died before morning. Rainbows washed across the walls, catching the sleeping faces of the women. Taya.

Fred had grabbed a few hours sleep in the early hours of the morning. Lisa had driven home at 4:00 a.m. It was nearly 7:00 a.m. now and she was back.

Down the hall, Morgan shook himself awake. The sun brushed the top of his mix of sandy and gray hair, turning it to gold. He blinked, barely remembering where he was, what had happened. The flight from Italy, the hunt for Justine, and the hours in the hospital had taken its toll. His sixty-year old body hurt all over.

A chill washed through his aching body as he roused himself up and approached the bed. He stared at Justine's motionless face, not knowing whether she was asleep or unconscious.

Her eyes opened. "Hi, Dad," she said weakly, but clearly. "Were you here all night?"

"I was."

Tears ran down Justine's face. In spite of the sunlight on her face, a cloud of agony washed over it. "Taya. How is she? And, the baby?" Giovanna had come into the room while Morgan was asleep and asked Justine to pray to Kateri, to join the throngs of worshippers who were focusing their energies on Taya. She had done so, in her own way, focusing her meditation on Taya and her baby.

Morgan paused, not knowing how much she was ready to hear, even how she had learned of Taya's struggle. "It doesn't look good. For either of them. I'll find out." Morgan slipped on his sweatshirt and walked into the bathroom, splashing cold water on his face. He called out, "Do you need anything? Water? Help in getting to the bathroom."

"I'll help with that, Mr. Jenner," said the young nurse standing near the door, looking fresh and ready for her new shift. One of the few people in the hospital to have had a night's sleep.

"Thanks," he said. "If you think she'll be okay for awhile, I'll check on a friend. Get a cup of coffee." Morgan headed for the door.

"That will be fine. I'll check her vitals, bring her something to eat."

"I haven't eaten in two days," Justine exclaimed weakly, attempting to lift herself onto her elbow. She didn't succeed, falling back in pain.

Morgan turned and flinched as he saw his daughter grimace—he looked questioningly at the nurse. She waved him on.

Down the hall, Taya still lay unconscious. Then, suddenly, her eyes flew open and she focused above her mother's head, into the open space just below the ceiling; dust particles danced in the sunlight. "Ricardo. You're here. We have a child—a boy. You will be proud . . . . " Her voice was clear, determined, deeper than usual. What appeared to be a brief moment of lucidity was something else instead.

Lisa whispered to Fred, who stood beside her just inside the room. "She's having a near death experience."

"I've had a few cases in my time," said the doctor. "It can go either way now."

"Taya! I'm here. This is your mother." Sharon spoke loudly; Lucinda and Giovanna quietly continued in their prayers. The senior nurse rushed to the bed, checking her vitals, then motioned to Fred. The heart monitor jumped, peaked and dropped.

Taya's eyes flashed as her cadence increased; she rose and, almost as quickly, she fell back on the bed. The heart monitor flatlined.

"I'm afraid she's gone," said Lisa quietly, her eyes welling up.

"I've seen a case like this before. A colleague of mine in Italy. He cheated death . . . . " Morgan leaned against the doorframe behind Lisa.

Lisa turned around, raising an eyebrow. No words.

"I'm sorry," he whispered. "I'm Justine's father. May I stay?"

Lisa was too grieved to react. She just nodded, stilled by the gravity of the moment.

Taya's face was beatific, serene, as though she were seeing something or someone of great beauty. Several moments passed. Perhaps ten minutes. Then slowly she opened her eyes. "Hi, Mom," she said.

CHAPTER 46

⸺⸺⸺

ORGAN SET A SMALL tray with tea, toast, and strawberries on the table next to Justine's bed. It was her second day back home. He sat on the end of the bed, careful not to disturb her broken foot.

She opened her eyes and gazed lovingly at her father. "Have I told you how important you are to me? What a dear father you are?" Justine tried to sit up, but her cracked clavicle held together with screws made it difficult, right now, impossible.

He stepped forward and lifted her into a sitting position. "You're being delusional again, my dear girl," he accused playfully. They had both had nearly ten hours sleep. He was a new man. "I've built a fire—but it's still as cold as a well digger's ass in here."

"Dad. Taya. How is she? Will she make it? And the baby?"

"Too early to tell. She is with her mother and the baby is still in the hospital. But the surprised doctor is optimistic."

Justine raised a questioning eyebrow. "Surprised?"

"Let's say that Dr. Fernandez now believes in miracles."

Justine smiled. *Perhaps I do too.*

"I'll get dressed and carry you in by the fire."

"It's a deal. In the meantime, will you get me my supply of drugs? This foot is throbbing." She winced, managing a grin.

Within five minutes, Morgan scooped her up in his arms and toddled down the hall, careful not to bump her foot on either wall. She asked him to let her check in on her ravens first, so he sat her down on a chair near the glass door to the patio.

"My rapture of ravens," she intoned nostalgically. "They visit me every day, and, as you know, two of them found me in the snow. Showed me how to get out. Do we have Cheerios? A few blueberries? The ravens find their own protein. But after Hupobi, I may catch mice for them. "

He laughed at the sight of his daughter catching mice. "A rapture of ravens, huh? Love it. I've only heard of an 'unkindness of ravens'—don't like it much. I'll get their breakfast."

"An 'unkindness of ravens'—I find that cruel," she said. "From old British folklore, I imagine. For some mistaken reason, they must have thought ravens were unkind to their young. I'll take some Cheerios too."

"I'm cooking up some scrambled eggs and bacon for us. They may be able to find their own protein, but you can't. But first, let's get you to the couch, cover you up, feed you and the birds." He paused. "Why 'rapture'?"

Justine laughed. "Well, I wanted a word that would describe a group, and I feel a sense of intense pleasure when I watch them. Bliss. A kind of enchantment."

Morgan grinned and nodded. Just like his daughter.

She held out her arms so he could pick her up again and transport her to the couch where he had piled a couple of pillows and a handmade quilt. On the coffee table beside her sat a box of Kleenex, water, and two volumes by D. H. Lawrence, *Kangaroo* and *Boy in the Bush*, along with Mabel's *Taos in Winter.*

"Dad, what's happening in Egypt? Is Mubarak still in office?"

"Nope, he's been removed and is in custody someplace on the Sinai."

"Will they make it Dad? As a democracy, I mean?" Sadness washed across her peaked face.

"I don't know, Justine. It will take awhile. The military is in charge and the Brotherhood is waiting in the wings."

"I was afraid that the youth who led the revolution may be too naïve to put together a campaign. Especially with Amir gone." A cloud of pain distorted her features.

"You're probably right . . . we'll have to wait and see." Morgan redirected the conversation.

Justine's eyes were moist as she stared into the fire. "Looks like I'm all set, Dad. Lovely fire. Thank you."

Morgan was silent, watching his daughter, waiting for her to begin speaking again. He would not rush her. So much to process: Amir, her accident and frozen prison, the boys driving into the gorge. Egypt. She hadn't said anything about her own baby.

"Amir and I sat right here in front of this fire the night before he left. Christmas eve. It was late—we'd been to the ceremonies at the pueblo—and we exchanged gifts. Dad, it was the Kokopelli scarf I gave him that convinced me it was he I saw out there in the square being beaten . . . . " Justine broke down as images of that terrible moment traveled through her mind, pain rushing through her body, now racked with sobs.

"I didn't know about the scarf," Morgan said gently, "but I recognized the way he moved, his profile. I don't think we're mistaken."

She took several deep breaths and drew her good arm across her eyes, wiping the tears away with her flannel sleeve. She involuntarily shuddered. "They still haven't found his body?"

"That's right. I talked with his father last night. But as long as the body hasn't been found, there is still hope."

She flashed an accusatory expression at her father. "Don't try to humor me, Dad. If he were alive he would have been in touch. You know that."

Morgan nodded. It was clear to his daughter that he knew that was true, but found it nearly impossible to envision Amir dumped in some mass grave.

"I'm carrying his child, Dad." She shook her head as though to cleanse it of unwanted thoughts. "It's gratifying that part of him will always be with me. Our child. I only wish he could have known about the baby before."

This time, Morgan responded quickly, trying to keep her from falling back into the deep sadness that had haunted her for days. "Your mother and I are incredibly happy about the prospect of a grandchild. You must know that we are overjoyed."

Justine turned to her father, embracing him with her gaze, "I do, Dad. Yes, I appreciate that you had hoped for a grandchild and wasn't at all sure that your only daughter—an old woman of thirty two—would ever allow herself to get pregnant."

Morgan laughed fully. "Something like that."

Justine returned her gaze to the fire. "I have to shift my attention to the baby. My work. Lawrence. It's hard."

"It's got to be incredibly difficult. The psychiatrist said you would probably struggle with occasional bouts of depression, but you're a strong woman and have so many friends ready to give you support."

"People in Taos are remarkable, aren't they? The way they found me, supported us, brought the energies of the followers of Kateri to save Taya."

"Amazing indeed. I'll admit, I've never seen anything like it. If we get another casserole, we won't have room in the frig for anything else. Almost makes a believer of me."

"Dad. Why aren't you . . . a believer? Certainly, your Nebraska roots were firmly Christian. We haven't talked about this since I was a kid."

It was Morgan's turn to take his time staring into the fire. Then he got up to refill his tea, beginning to talk from the island in the kitchen. "During much of my childhood, I was pretty devout, even in high school. Then a couple things happened. You'll remember that my grandmother's wool house coat caught fire on an old space heater and she burned to death?"

Justine nodded without turning around. She had heard the story in detail. A terrible tragedy, two days before her dad was to graduate from high school. Too deeply grieved, he hadn't attended the ceremony.

Morgan returned to his seat by the fire. "Her death, the way she died, really shook me, made me question everything. Then the next year I went off to Berkeley and my anthropology professor said there have never been a people found who didn't have some form of religion. It struck me like an epiphany. I thought: sure, humans psychologically need religion, so they had to invent it. It was so clear to me and I've never lost that clarity."

"And Mom felt the same, as have I. I was indoctrinated with agnosticism." She smiled at her father. "Yet, I think I'm becoming spiritual. I'm shaky in that department, but I'm sure I encountered my guides on that mountain at Hupobi. And then when the ravens arrived I experienced a bolt of clarity."

"Tell me more." He slowly sipped his tea and stared straight ahead into the fire.

"I'll start with what I think Lawrence found on the mountain. He unearthed his center, an interior place of calm and joy. The mountain spoke to him and freed him from his own bondages, liberated his sensibilities. He labored in a very Zen-like way—baking bread each morning, chopping wood, fixing the plumbing. He came to understood well the magic of reciprocity, engagement with nature, his labors, his art, another human. In this case Isabella."

"Makes sense to me. Do you have more than your intuition to go on?" Morgan was a man who needed evidence—along with enlightened hunches.

Justine grinned. She knew her father well. "In the months after he left the ranch, he began to paint seriously—declaring himself a painter. He met Isabella and began Lady Chatterley. He talked of tenderness. A reciprocity of tenderness."

"Convincing," he admitted. "Certainly Chatterley turned out to be his best. Focused intensity and clarity."

"And mysticism. I don't think he could have written it without Isabella—and the mountain."

Morgan nodded. "How about my daughter? What did you find on Hupobi?"

"I think I found much of what Lawrence found: clarity, my own interior life force, a buoyant energy encircled me," she paused, gazing into her father's incredulous eyes. "Lucinda taught me about her guides, two supernatural entities who are with her always—making her feel safe, giving her confidence. She is never alone. I was never alone on that mountain. Physically, yes. But I could feel a presence, a warmth." She knew that her father would be skeptical, but not disrespectful. She waited.

He was silent for a long time. What he didn't say was a lot: that she had been delusionary, that hypothermia brings warmth. "I have never been able to find such comfort, Justine. But it's worth exploring, keeping an open mind."

She held his eyes with deep appreciation. "Thanks, Dad," is all she said. Cuddling her head deeper into the pillows, she fell into a sound sleep.

—∞∞∞—

Two hours later, Justine woke with a start, terrified, feeling that she was falling through snow. "Dad! Are you there??" she nearly screamed.

"I'm here, Honey." He had been working on his computer at the kitchen table on an interim report on the newest dig at Ceveteri, Italy. He rushed to her side.

"It was terrible. As though it was happening all over again. Being trapped in the snow keeps blending with the crypt in Cairo." Then she stopped. "How is it that I get into these messes, Dad? Get trapped in collapsing churches and mountains??"

He sat on the floor beside her and held her hand. "You're adventurous, my dear, one of the things I love about you. It's a virtue, not a fault."

"Ah, thanks, I needed that," she grinned. "Dad, go into my bedroom and get an old yellowed envelope out of my top drawer, will you?"

Morgan raised a questioning eyebrow, but did as he was told. Shortly, he returned with the fragile envelope in hand, the one she'd found that day with Kosta in the old Jaramillo Bank vault.

"Read it to both of us please. I need to hear it again." He read a few paragraphs, then, "It's this last part that is most enticing." He read on:

> . . . I am enclosing a new will that leaves most of my literary estate for my daughter, Laurence. You will need to show the will to Frieda and I know that will cause you difficulties, but it must be done. You will need to take a lawyer with you. If Frieda is still in London to settle the estate when you receive this letter, please contact my lawyer there, Edward McGrath at 4 Piccadilly Square, and inform him of my request.
>
> After you have established the legitimacy of the will, please write to Isabella and tell her that a great deal of my literary estate will be forthcoming to Laurence when she

reaches the age of 20. You may write her at: Isabella Has-
souna, Piazza del S. Uffizio 15, Rome, Vatican City, Italy.

I am also enclosing a key to my safe deposit box in the
Jaramillo Bank on the Taos Plaza. There is an envelope in
the box containing railroad shares. You may have them, my
dear, in appreciation.

"Astounding! A will? A key? Railroad shares? You haven't found a will, right?"

"Right. But you'll remember, Taya and I found the key at the ranch. Why wouldn't Brett have taken the railroad shares?"

"Remind me when Lawrence died," said Morgan. "1930 or so?"

"March, 1930."

"Five months after the crash. He probably didn't realize that the shares were worthless."

"Of course! Why didn't I think of that?"

Morgan waved off her self-doubt. "But why were they even in the safe? And, where is the will? Why didn't it ever come to light? Surely Brett would have tried to carry out Lawrence's requests."

"And, the literary estate would have been quite valuable in time. So many questions. Dad . . . sometimes I wonder if my great grandmother Isabella might have come to Taos, looking for Brett."

"I don't know. That's a long shot, but not impossible. We may never know," he paused. Giovanna will be here anytime with lunch. She'll stay with you while I take a run into town for groceries and gas, pick up a prescription."

———— ∞∞∞ ————

Before leaving for his errands, Morgan reminded his daughter, "You'll stay away from the news, right?"

Both Giovanna and Justine nodded in agreement. If Justine had been younger, she would have crossed her fingers behind her back.

As soon as Giovanna left for class, Justine opened her Mac and typed in "Al Ahram news" on Safari.

February, 2011-Hosni Mubarak resigns. President surrenders power to army and flies out of Cairo. Egypt rejoices as 18 days of mass protest end in revolution. Military pledges not to get in the way of 'legitimate' government. Egypt celebrates a new dawn.

Justine slowly lowered the lid as she heard her father's car, and used the tale of her housecoat to wipe away unwelcome tears. *If only Amir could have lived to see Mubarak resign . . . .*

CHAPTER 47

———— ✤ ————

MARCH 8, 2011

"So when did your dad leave?"

"Just last night, Mom. A few friends are taking turns staying with me; the physical therapist comes three times a week. I'm well taken care of."

"My damned ankle will take a couple more weeks, then I'll fly to Taos."

Justine paused. "You know, I'm thinking that it might be best if you came for my delivery and to help with the baby for a few weeks. Would that work for you?"

"You're thinking September? But, sure you don't need me now? I could do both. September's a while off."

"Yes. September. I think I'm doing okay and I'm going back to work later today. Part time at first." She wasn't really doing okay. Depression would often overtake her like a raincloud of psychic pain, sadness seeping into her limbs, as well, an inability to concentrate. She couldn't even conjure up interest in her usual passions. She felt empty inside and didn't want her mother to see her this way. "No word on Amir, I guess," her voice was tinged with hopelessness.

Lucrezia heard the inevitable symptoms sneaking through her words and chose not to press her daughter on her visit. She resolved to stay in touch continually and be ready to travel on the spur of the moment. "Your dad and I are on top of this. We're in regular contact with Amir's parents. When he is found, I'll call immediately."

"We're kidding ourselves, Mom. If his body were going to be found, it would have been found by now. I've no doubt that the regime has dumped him somewhere. I'm having so much trouble dealing with the uncertainty. Have you told his parents about the baby?"

Lucrezia paused. "I thought that you should tell them, Justine. Don't you agree?"

"You're right, of course. I'm apprehensive about what it will mean to them. Will it ease their loss?"

"I would think so. After all, they love you, and after losing both their sons, Zachariah and . . . . " Lucrezia stopped in mid-sentence. It sounded as though she had accepted the death of Amir. "I'm sorry," she attempted.

"Don't worry about it, Mom. I'm also certain that Amir is dead, so please don't try to edit your words. We both know he's gone."

"Are you still seeing the psychiatrist?" Lucrezia asked.

"I am. He thinks I'm doing pretty well under the circumstances. I don't want to take any drugs now, especially with the baby. Just wish I were up to running again. Got to get ready for work now. Talk with you later." Her mother was getting a little too close to the quick, too close to asking the difficult questions that she didn't want to answer.

Justine hung up. She needed to clear her head before Mike arrived. She hobbled into the kitchen and warmed her coffee. Her rapture of ravens gathered, waiting for breakfast. Justine grinned, propped her crutch near the back door and set a bowl of Cheerios and blueberries outside. She would buy more corn chips today.

—∞∞—

Justine heard Mike's familiar knock on the door. She glanced around the room and grabbed her coat from the hall closet. *When will this cold let up?* The thermometer outside the kitchen window said 38 degrees this morning. She found the cold depressing. But then she found most things depressing, including life itself. She paused by the hall mirror and registered her depressed demeanor, making an effort to animate herself, practice smiling, forcing life into her eyes.

"Good morning," she said, opening the door to Mike's smiling face. They both made a special effort to be cheery. "I'm ready."

He reached out to help her but she gave him a look that said, "I can do it myself."

Nothing resistant or offensive, just a mild rebuke. She handed him her briefcase as a consolation prize.

The lines around Mike's eyes and mouth tightened as he watched Justine slowly negotiate the flagstone pathway to his truck. "Let me help you in," he insisted.

She took a deep breath and relinquished control, permitting Mike to give her an extra lift into the high seat. "Thanks," she said sheepishly, looking longingly at her car that had sat there for several weeks. *I wonder if the battery has run down.*

"When did your father leave?" he asked as he pushed the gear into reverse and backed out of the tricky driveway. "You must miss him."

Justine appreciated Mike's capacity to get almost to the heart of her concerns. "Just yesterday. He'd stayed with me for nearly a month and had to get back to his project in Italy. Still working on Etruscan finds; those ancient tombs continue to give up their secrets."

"A lucky man. Exotic finds in exotic places. Sometimes I think I made a mistake just staying here at home where I was born and raised. Now I'll grow old and die here without ever having the Grand Adventure." He was pensive, staring straight ahead as he talked, turning right onto Highway 68 leading through the Rio Grande Gorge.

"The Grand Adventure isn't always so grand," she assured him. "I tend to romanticize life, then get disappointed."

"But look at you, Justine. Not much over thirty and you've had more adventures than most people have in a lifetime," insisted Mike.

Justine laughed with a tinge of bitterness. "But I keep getting myself into trouble, both physically and professionally. I need to dig deeper inside myself rather than the ground."

"Ah!" Mike laughed. "I suppose so—we could all benefit from more reflection. But I think it's harder for men somehow. We try to be rational, which is an exterior business."

She turned to Mike and placed her hand on his arm, feeling a wave of affection for this man who had begun, finally, to reveal himself to her. Either he was moving beyond his own gender bias, or he was being kind. Empathy had worked wonders. Either way, she found it therapeutic. "Thanks," is all she said. Then, "What's up for today?"

"Scott will be there. And, Sam. We'd like to debrief your experience, what you saw before the avalanche." Justine had shared a few random observations with each of them when they visited her in the hospital, although she wasn't at all sure that she had formed a gestalt herself.

Justine shivered. "Oh. Of course. Makes sense." She wasn't too keen about being cross-examined about her experience in the avalanche.

—◦◦◦—

"You were within arm's length?" asked Scott, as gently as he could manage.

"Well, yes," she admitted. "There was what appeared to be a small, black obsidian fetish figure. A fertility figure staring at me as though she was daring me to touch her."

"And you didn't. Touch her, I mean. You didn't pick her up," asked Sam, struggling to keep his voice even.

"No, no I didn't," she said simply, her eyes moving to each man in turn, returning their gazes, struggling to project a sense of clarity. During the balance of the drive from Taos, she had been preparing for the moment when one of the men would challenge her decisions. It was natural. An archaeologist might find her actions indefensible.

"Back off," Mike warned Sam and Scott. "Let her tell it her way. Go on Justine." He stood and refreshed her cup of tea.

She realized that Mike was treating her like a fragile doll. Justine glanced at him in appreciation. Several forces were stirring inside her: the desire to stand on her own, not to be coddled—at the same time, a surging desire to be cared for, protected. She took a deep breath and continued, "I want to make two points here. First, I responded as an anthropologist, not an archaeologist." She paused for affect. "As an anthropologist, I understand the native cultural feeling that the figure belongs to the land, to the place where it resides. It's sacrilegious to remove it from its sacred place. So I didn't."

"And the second point?" asked Scott.

"I've gotten myself into trouble before by unilaterally removing an important artifact from its resting place, thus making it an unprovenanced find. Professionally, this creates the biggest problem in the long run. As you all know by now, when I was trapped in the crypt in Cairo during that earthquake, I unconsciously picked up a codex that turned out to be the diary of Mary of Nazareth. The fact that it was unprovenanced provided ammunition for my being discredited and expelled."

Scott flinched; Sam stared at the table; Mike gazed at Justine, his eyes welling up.

Finally, Scott said, with unexpected lightness, "It would have been nice to see the figure, but that is just not to be . . . unless of course we can get state sponsorship to excavate."

"That might be possible," added Sam. "We've always wanted to dig at Hupobi, although our technologies may make thorough excavation unnecessary. And, of course, resources are always limited."

"But now there is evidence, at least personal testimony that could be persuasive," said Mike, glad to add to the speculations.

"Well . . . " Justine adopted a surprisingly teasing tone. "I do have a little something to show you." She opened her IPhone, pushed on the camera icon, then camera roll. A small blurry figure appears in the center of what appeared to be a frame of snow. Justine spread her fingers on the scene, continuing to pull the photo into a larger and larger view. The men crowded around, nearly overcome with excitement.

The crisp, distinct black stone image appeared to be about five inches tall. Straight and flat, clearly a stone fetish of some kind now staring back at the viewers. The photo vividly revealed the delicacy of the precious miniature, its rounded head, small eyes, and flat bottom. Little hands were scratched into either side, as though she were tenderly holding her stomach. Fine carving marks could be detected where the stone had been carefully chipped away.

"Sleeping Ute Mountain!" Scott proclaimed. "If I'm not mistaken, the stone could be from Sleeping Ute Mountain. That's the only place that contains stone that looks like that—of course, we're only looking at the photo, hard to be sure."

"It could be from Mesa Verde," Mike added reluctantly, to everyone's surprise, for he had been the most skeptical. Not only about Mesa Verde, but about most migration theories.

CHAPTER 48

———&&&———

JUSTINE CRAWLED OUT OF BED, pulled back the white muslin drapes and stared out at the late March day. Winter had not lifted and neither had her spirits. In spite of getting into work three days a week, she felt as though a veil of malaise clung to her mind like a wool shawl. She sat down on the edge of the bed and took three deep breaths, forcing the air deep into her chest as though pumping up her lungs would bring life to her limbs. She knew the value of breathing, centering herself, desperately attempting to exhale her depression. One in . . . one out . . . two in . . . two out . . . .

Six weeks after Bloody Wednesday in Cairo, she could only imagine Amir's fate. Every day she became more sure. Images of his probable fate cluttered her dreams, blackened her waking hours. Physically, she was growing stronger, the crutches had given way to a cane.

She limped into the kitchen and fiddled with the cone and ground coffee, heating water in the microwave. One cup would be enough. At this time of morning, the muted golden landscape and sky were as one, a scene that once would have inspired her, sent her off running toward the horizon as though she could grasp it. But not today. Today she felt empty as though there was nothing going on inside, no energy source, no spirit. But she knew that wasn't so, for she was carrying a life, Amir's life in her body.

So many unanswered questions—she didn't seem to be getting anywhere. She and Judy Lynn had read through Lawrence's letter to Brett over and over and couldn't find enough clues about a new will. But did it really matter? It wasn't the estate she was after, but an understanding of her great-grandfather and what he had found here and nowhere else.

And, then there was Egypt. She was encouraged by her next visit to Al Ahram: "Egypt referendum backs constitutional revisions. Next, the election."

Her phone rang. She drew it from her robe pocket and stared at the phone face announcing "Cheyenne." She really didn't feel like talking to anyone just now, but chose to move the bar to the right anyway, hit speaker and listened as she drew her steaming cup from the microwave.

"Justine. You remember Jody, the musician and sculptor, who lives in the Pink House. Lawrence's old haunt. Well, he's going to Australia for six months! The pink house will be available. Seems to be a good move for you right now."

Justine started to laugh, tings of bitterness seeping through the spaces in her speech. "Cheyenne, you are something else. I like Emily's house. Why would I move? I'm not up to a move."

"Because you need to tackle your malaise. Live in Lawrence's space, get directly in touch with his spirit." She paused. "You're not pulling out of this slump. I feel like donning a shroud whenever we're together."

Justine flinched. She hadn't given much consideration to the affect she was having on her friends, yet she had noticed that people were beginning to avoid her, even at the Santa Fe office. And, she needed to be more present for Taya. Justine forced her voice into a higher octave. "I'm sorry, Cheyenne. I don't mean to be such a wet blanket. When is Jody leaving?"

—∞∞—

The move took less than a week, especially with the help of Cheyenne, Giovanna, Bill, and Mike. It turned out that she didn't have that many possessions in Emily's Llano Quemado house, mostly what she'd brought from Italy in her suitcases. Justine arranged to rent the Pink House until the end of summer, assuming that she would prefer Emily's home when the baby came. More comfort, a predictable heating system, room for her mother. Until then, she would bask in the aura and spirit of Lawrence in the first place he stayed when arriving in Taos in 1922. All in all, she would have preferred the ranch, but it was too isolated—and the university would never have allowed it.

And, she was somehow grateful not to have a television, not to stay glued to the unfolding, unenlightened news from Egypt. No resolution. No Amir. Only the military in charge.

Justine was surprised to find the Pink House largely unchanged from its original 1920's design, which presented a few problems. The small, primitive kitchen was almost devoid of conveniences and furnished with a miniature wooden table and two fragile chairs that looked as though they would collapse under the weight of a cat, let alone a woman as bulky as Frieda. Justine walked gently on the creaking wood-plank floors, stepping over Jody's sheet-covered wooden sculptures. Adobe walls of broken plaster folded inward to encase small-latticed windows, some strung with sagging muslin drapes.

Justine stepped back into the kitchen and stood there, leaning on her cane, imagining Lawrence and Mabel sitting at the table trying to write while Frieda zealously swung her broom, pretending to clean the floor. She remembered from Mabel's autobiographies about her attempts to seduce Lorenzo, as both she and Frieda called him, into co-authoring a book with her. Justine shuddered when she thought about her great grandfather in his house. She sat down and started to cry. *Why do I cry so easily these days?*

She took a deep breath, stood up and hobbled to the sink, selecting the only sharp knife from the single drawer and began to peel a bowl full of apples Pablo had brought her. One by one. Slowly, methodically. After each apple, she placed the peelings in a Maxwell House compost tin and turned back to the next apple, like encountering a new friend. She turned on her precious IPhone and dialed to Julio Iglesias singing *La Vie en Rose*, his sensuous voice echoing through the room like French pigeons cooing in a primeval cave.

She held the knife gently, yet firmly, as though she and the knife were partners, neither forcing the other forward. As the blade entered the crispy fruit, the scent of sweet apple blossoms floated up into her nostrils. She stilled herself to enjoy the pleasure of each whiff. Placing her palms together, she lifted the chopped apples into a dented pan, unevenly warped on the bottom, took a small handful of sugar from a one-pound box and sprinkled it on the fruit. She then began her hunt for the cinnamon. *Thyme. Oregano. Salt. Pepper. Curry. Cinnamon.* Four shakes to freckle the apples. She picked up a lemon and massaged it with affection, holding it into the air, sunlight brushing its yellow luster. Julio's lush, lusty voice moved through her flesh, vibrations traveling down her arms, her hips undulating in sinuous rhythm, her body twisting in graceful dance. Her flushed cheeks tickled by her swishing honey-colored hair floating by. A sense of intense freedom, which was now just below the surface, permeated her being.

Pausing to slice through the lemon's supple skin, the juice squirted across her hand and onto the wooden cutting board. She squeezed one half of the lemon onto the apples, permitting the juice on her hand to drip into the pan, dissolving the remains of the untouched cinnamon. *Dribbles of fresh water.* "Now for a match," she said aloud, turning slowly, gazing around the room until her eyes lit on a partially full box of Diamond matches.

Lawrence's ghost accompanied her on this meditative journey toward applesauce, toward her inner calm. She imagined she'd learned it from him— the way he made bread each day, respected each ingredient, each tool. *What was it about this place, and the Ranch, that engendered such Zen practice?* Justine pulled up one of the fragile wooden chairs, placed her hands on either side of her stomach and lowered herself into a sitting position. She was mesmerized by the blue flame licking the bottom of the wobbly pan, moving it back and forth with the energy of fire. *After all, he's my great grandfather, his blood runs in my veins, I hear the same rhythms, the same spirits. I am the descendent of his startling curiosity, his impatience with life . . . .*

Then she felt it. A kick. *No, two. My baby is alive, dancing with me, telling me she enjoys the music.* Justine began to cry again, this time with joy. Pure joy—and gratitude, a remarkably wide wave of gratitude.

A knock sounded at the front door. She slowly glanced up to see Judy Lynn's flaming red head of hair —then looked back toward the drawer, rose and pushed it part way in. "I'll be right there," she said.

"It's Saturday, Justine. Time to get out and around. Go to lunch . . . see friends," Judy Lynn declared. Justine's friends had taken to coming around, rousing her on the days when she wasn't working in Santa Fe, getting her out.

They realized that limping around with an increasingly engorged stomach was not in keeping with her athletic self, so she had to be coaxed. Pushed was more like it.

"Come in!" Justine called blithely. "Want some applesauce?"

"Love applesauce! Hey, girl, look at those clear eyes! Happiness is becoming!"

The double entendre was not lost on Justine, who stood gazing at Judy Lynn. Her amber eyes were bright, expressive, alive. She just grinned. "Wanna feel the baby kick?"

"Sure," Judy Lynn giggled, walking up to Justine and tentatively placing a hand on her stomach.

"Here," Justine exclaimed, taking both of Judy Lynn's hands and placing them on both sides of her stomach.

"Oh! I felt it!" Judy Lynn was thrilled. She donned that toothy, exuberant smile that Justine loved.

"Say, you haven't seen the letter that Kosta and I found in the old safe—right?" She walked into the bedroom, opened her jewelry box and withdrew the letter from Lawrence to Brett. Returning to the kitchen, she thrust it into her friend's hands. "What do you think??"

"Give me a moment to read it—don't be so eager. I'm getting some applesauce." Judy Lynn's mouth curled as she read. "But none of this happened, Justine! No will was presented in court. Brett didn't have any resources, but she didn't cash the stocks—well, of course not; they were still in the safe deposit box!"

"Dad figured out the part about the railroad shares. Lawrence's letter was written just five months after the crash . . . they were worthless!"

"Sure—of course! While you get ready we'll brainstorm some more—then get some exercise." Judy Lynn walked ahead of Justine into the bedroom and plunked on the single cot. "This is no better than an army cot, girl! How can you get comfortable?"

"I guess I need to get a little sponge egg crate . . . do you think Wal Mart has one?"

"I'm sure. I'll pick one up," promised Judy Lynn. "Now, you get dressed."

"How cold is it?"

"Cold. About as cold as this damn drafty poky of yours. Now . . . how could it be that Brett didn't make the new will known?"

"Something happened with Frieda. She threatened Brett somehow. And if the shares were no longer good, she probably needed Frieda's support."

"That's credible," said Justine. "Frieda would do that. Surely she saw the letter."

"Surely Brett would have shown her the letter. After all, wasn't that what Lawrence wanted?" asked Judy Lynn.

"Yes, I think she would have shown her the letter and the will," said Justine. "It was probably torn up. By Frieda."

"If that's what it took. She was shrewd," said Judy Lynn, her nose wrinkling with her choice of words. "Remember her estate would be worth a couple million today."

"Let's assume that somehow Brett's efforts on Lawrence's behalf were blocked—either because she felt threatened, or because she made other choices."

"Enough. Off to the gym," Judy Lynn rose from the bed, stretched her arms above her head as far as she could reach, which wasn't far.

"Do we have to?" Justine copied the stretch and grinned. "Dinner after? I need strawberry ice cream."

"Yes. And, yes."

CHAPTER 49

❦

KIOWA (D. H. LAWRENCE) RANCH, LOBO MOUNTAIN, SEPTEMBER 15, 1935

Costumed dancers from the Pueblo moved slowly in rhythm to the drums. For hours now they had negotiated the uneven incline surrounding the tiny six by six Lawrence chapel 1000 feet up the side of the Lobo Mountain. The Red Willow dancers were honored to participate in the service for their friend Lawrence.

That morning, Frieda's lover, Ravagli, had prepared the wet cement into which Frieda had stirred her late husband's ashes, determined to keep Mabel Dodge Lujan from carrying them off. She had had enough trouble guarding the ashes already. First, she'd left the ashes at the train station at Lamy, then at the Fechin House when she went for tea with her friend Alexandria. Frieda could be a careless woman.

Were these even his ashes? She had her suspicions, since she didn't entirely trust Ravagli's commitment when he left for France to exhume her late husband's body. To his credit, he did return with the paperwork from the appropriate authorities. Like the questionable relics of St. Mark ensconced in Venice, Frieda knew that it really didn't matter whether they were authentic, as long as supplicants were willing to believe they were.

Frieda found Mabel's claim to her husband's ashes inconceivable. What chutzpah! Mabel thought she was more simpatico with Lorenzo than Frieda—or Brett. So Mabel pouted, refused to attend the actual service, and arrived late into the evening, only staying a short while. Frieda ignored her.

By late evening a chill drifted over the mountain and stars were flung across the night sky like casino dice. Frieda sat down on the damp grass in front of the white chapel. Huxley joined her. "Sorry that Maria couldn't make it, Hux," she said.

"She wanted to be here, Frieda. But her health has been unreliable lately. It's quite a trip you know."

A disingenuous grin crept across her lips. She knew Maria wasn't fond of her. "Good that you could be here. Lorenzo thought the world of you. It would have been his 50th birthday, you know. On the 11th. Couldn't get it all together until today."

Aldous Huxley nodded. "D. H. was a good friend—he would have enjoyed his birthday party. Danced some, no doubt. I brought you my book of letters. Sorry I didn't get it here earlier. I do a little analysis of my friend. I hope you'll find it accurate."

"No one knew him better than you did, Hux. I'm sure you did him justice."

"Frieda." He paused for several moments, gazing at the sky as though intending to count the stars. "The last time I saw him— the night before he died—he gave me a letter for Brett. I mailed it a couple days later. . . five years ago now."

Frieda stiffened and began to shiver. She wasn't cold. "Brett mentioned something about a letter. About his Italian whore."

Light from a smoldering bonfire flared across Huxley's face. She knew him well, recognized the raised eyebrow, the challenging expression.

"My dalliances were always just physical with me, Hux. You know that."

"Ravagli?"

"After Lorenzo died, I needed someone. Ravagli was there for me. My daughter couldn't hold it together. She was hysterical. I needed someone," she repeated, desperate to convince her friend.

"There is a child."

A bitter laugh rose from deep inside her ample chest. "Ha! Don't you think I know better? He couldn't even . . . . "

Huxley turned away, disgusted and deeply disappointed with her attempt to demean the man he had admired more than any other.

"I told Brett to tear up the letter," Frieda said. "You see, now that Lorenzo was gone, Brett needed me more than she needed to be obedient to a dead man. She was destitute; her family lost everything in the crash. Besides, the court was willing to believe that the will couldn't be found."

"The judge wouldn't have believed it if Murray hadn't convinced him," Hux responded.

"A good friend, Murray." Her pungent laugh echoed into the night air.

CHAPTER 50

———⊶⊷———

JUDY LYNN WAS A straightener. Pictures, flowers, dishes, closets. Anything that could be ordered, should be ordered. Things that were crooked or out of place burdened her sensibilities in the same way that combining brown and blue or red and orange would have sent Lucrezia into a fit. Justine found it curious that such order didn't apply to her dogs. She knew her friend's idiosyncrasies and allowed them full expression, enjoying those small things over which she had some remaining control, yet could observe with delight. Such was her response to the crooked, partially opened drawer in Justine's kitchen.

As they walked through the kitchen, Judy Lynn automatically verged toward the cabinets and reached out to shut the protruding drawer.

Before she touched it, Justine cried, "Watch out . . . . "

But it was too late. The drawer nearly crumbled in her hand, the slats and contents separating in air and splashing across the wooden floor like children's jacks, the off-white, peeling drawer box splitting into pieces and heading in all directions. An assortment of Royal Albert flatware followed: knives, forks, three soup spoons.

The two women watched the display as though it were a soccer match. Judy Lynn laughed, Justine rolled her eyes and plunked down in a nearby chair. She wasn't fond of bending over. "Now, see what you've done," she accused good humoredly.

Judy Lynn began to pick up the pieces "I don't think this drawer is worth saving. I'll get Joe to build you another." She picked up a yellowed envelope with tape sticking out of each side. "Yours?" she asked.

"Never seen it before," Justine said as her heart quickened. She handled the envelope as she would a newborn, more with her long fingers than with her whole hand. Turning it in every direction, she said, "Please stop what you're doing and sit down."

Justine spoke with a firmness that Judy Lynn was compelled to obey. She released the six or seven slats she held in her hands, watching them slide across the floor once more. Pulling up a chair, she sat down facing Justine. "Okay, let's see what you've got."

"There are two items in here," Justine observed, her voice trembling. "Just like in the safe." She held one in each hand, deciding to open the lighter one first. Unfolding the brittle paper that must have been taped under the drawer, she noted that it was not Lawrence's handwriting, nor Frieda's, nor Mabel's. She began to read, starting with the date:

September 22, 1952

My dear Lady Brett,

I want to thank you for your hospitality and generous time you allowed for our conversations during my recent visit to Taos. As you know, my mother had wanted to come with me, but in the end felt it inappropriate. On my return, she came to see me here in Paris, so eager to hear your stories.

We were both thrilled to have a copy of the letter my father wrote to you the day before he died. Mother had no word of him since Brewster's visit in February of that year. And, of course, Frieda had sent on the newspaper clipping announcing his death. How much she knew about their relationship was never clear.

Mother and I were both saddened to hear that the railroad stocks lost their value in the crash. I am certain my father would not have wanted you to be dependant on Frieda.

From his letters to mother, we knew that he understood your brave, independent soul and cherished your friendship.

In the situation that you found yourself, we appreciate your decision not to bring the new will to light. The original manuscript of Women in Love that you sent to my mother was of more value than any amount of money. My step-father and our own family are not without resources, although as you can understand, the crash and war affected us all. Our wounds are more emotional than physical, having lost my dear step-father in the north African campaign. Fortunately, he never knew about my real father. My mother only chose to tell me the day the war ended. I was 15.

You are welcome in my home anytime, Lady Brett. I wish you well with your beautiful paintings and thank you with all my heart for your friendship with my father.

With affection and appreciation, Laurence Hassouna

"Well! That confirms your father's hunch about the railroad stocks!" Judy Lynn had a way of cutting to the chase. She stopped and gazed at Justine whose eyes had filled with tears as she read.

"I can almost picture my great grandmother Isabella and my grandmother sitting in her Paris apartment talking over Lady Brett's stories, reading and re-reading that last letter," she said.

"Why was she in Paris? She would have been what? Twenty-two?"

"About that. Grandmother Laurence attended the Sorbonne and majored in literature. Became a journalist for the *Paris Match*. Then went home and married an Egyptian—my grandfather. That was the end of her career, I understand."

"Not unlike the fate of many women in the 50s—and married to an Egyptian to boot. Deadly combination."

"True." Justine said with a sad nostalgic grin. "That relationship convinced my mother not to marry an Egyptian, although she had plenty of chances. She went off to Berkeley instead!"

"From what you've told me, your father was a little controlling himself—more Nebraskan than Berkeley-like. I found him to be a real charmer." Judy Lynn had met Morgan a few times while he was in Taos tending to his daughter in the aftermath of her accident and injuries . . . her grieving.

"He's mellowed a lot since I was a kid. Let's take a look at this other item—I just can't wait any longer." She picked up the second document and opened it slowly, barely recognizing Lawrence's unsteady handwriting. Justine shivered as she began to read aloud:

Last Will and Testament of David Herbert Lawrence

I, David Herbert Lawrence, being of sound and disposing mind and memory and mindful of the uncertainties of life, hereby make, publish and declare this, my last will and testament, hereby revoking any and all former wills, codicils or bequests by me, at any time, made.

First-I direct the payment of my just debts, my funeral expenses and the expenses of my last illness, out of my personal estate, as soon as can conveniently be done.

Second-After the payment of my just debts, my funeral expenses and the expenses of my last illness, I give, devise and bequeath, as follows:

A. My personal bank accounts and properties to my wife, Frieda Lawrence, with the following exceptions.

B. The manuscripts of The Gipsy and the Virgin and all of my poetry to my step-daughter, Barbara Weekly.

C. Remaining royalties forthcoming from the sale of Lady Chatterley to my sister, Ada Lawrence.

D. My literary estate and all proceeds forthcoming (with the exception of Lady Chatterley) in a trust for my daughter, Laurence Hassouna, held in private until she is twenty years of age. The trust is to be administered by Pearn-Pollinger-Higham, Ltd., London.

Third-If my sister and/or step-daughter shall predecease my daughter, the remains of those estates will be granted to my daughter, Laurence Hassouna.

Fourth-I hereby order and direct that I be cremated and that my ashes be distributed on Lobo Mountain, Taos, New Mexico.

Fifth-I hereby nominate, constitute and appoint Lady Dorothy Brett to serve as Executor of this, my last will and testament. I also, herewith, nominate and constitute and appoint Mr. Lawrence Pollinger literary Executor and Pearn-Pollinger-Higham, Ltd., to deal with all of the matters stemming from my literary work.

IN WITNESS WHEREOF, I have hereunto set my hand and seal, to this, my last will and testament, consisting of three handwritten pages, to each of which I have subscribed my name, at Vence, France, this 5th day of February, A.D., 1930.

_____Bernard Dubois_____ ____Mrs. Bernard Dubois_____
      witness   witness

signature_ David Herbert Lawrence_____

Justine read with strange detachment, then rose and walked to the window, staring at the lone pine just outside. She blinked, the armature of her face rigid as a porcelain doll. *The literary estate to my grandmother! While worth little while Lawrence was alive, it would have been worth a fortune as the years passed. Grandmother found out about it when she saw Lady Brett. Grandfather was dead by then, so why didn't she pursue it?* She shivered and turned to gaze at Judy Lynn. She had almost forgotten that she was sitting there.

Her guest waited patiently, almost breathless, then, "It's a legal document, for sure. He had professional advice."

Justine took another deep breath, finding it difficult to process all that she had read. "Probably in the sanitarium," she said. "He was there until just a few days before he died. That's probably where he found the witnesses."

"And Barbara?" Judy Lynn wanted to know. "Who was she?"

"Barbara was Frieda's daughter. She often visited the couple in Italy and became quite close to Lawrence. He wrote *The Gipsy and the Virgin* for her. She was there with him at Vence at the end and was devastated by his death, I understand."

"I see. A sad corollary to the story. Never heard that before," Judy Lynn's eyes welled up, yet she went on, "Remember that Lawrence had no properties in New Mexico, so the estate cannot—perhaps could not—be reopened here. If it were, it would have to be in England and the statute of limitations could forbid that in both countries."

"That was probably part of the reason that my grandmother didn't pursue the will. For all we know, she sought legal advice. I'm not sure I would want to reopen the will. Even if I could."

Judy Lynn's eyebrows shot up, her mouth puckering like a cupie doll. "I realize it's a long shot, but after all this searching . . . hunting . . . pursuing? What will you do with the will now??"

Justine sighed, then released a genuine, relaxed smile. "I have a few thoughts." After a pause, "Shall we go?"

CHAPTER 51

⟨※⟩

JUSTINE HOBBLED INTO the office in Santa Fe with renewed vigor, a new lease on her life—at least a significant part of it. She now had proof, beyond the letters, that she was D. H. Lawrence's great granddaughter.

The town was still cold and stark, no sign of life springing from the trees or would-be lawns. Yet she knew that it was all there, life lying dormant. Like hers. She had driven to Santa Fe for the first time this morning. The cane was still her close companion, and would be for a while, but she didn't mind anymore. A pocket of sorrow resided in her heart for Amir. She had turned on BBC news as she drove.

> The Cairo Court for Urgent Matters ruled today to ban the 6 April Youth Movement Monday for "espionage" and "activities that distort Egypt's image". The court also ruled to shut down the headquarters of the movement, which was one of the main groups calling for protests ahead of the 25 January Revolution. Khaled Al-Masri, media director for 6 April Youth Movement said, however, that 6 April has no headquarters. "We are an idea, not a company. How would they ban people from assembling in coffee shops, clubs and other places?" he said. The group plans to appeal, he said. "It is a black era for the Egyptian judiciary," he said.

6 April, Amir's revolutionary group. Khaled, his friend and colleague.
Justine had pulled the car to the curb across from Ohkay Owingeh casino,
dropped her head on the steering wheel and started breathing deeply.

———oxo———

Sam nearly knocked her down opening the door.

"Whoa, Sam! Don't be quite so helpful!" she warned.

"I've great news. But I'll wait until you sit down." He stepped aside, held
the door and waited for her to start down the hall.

As she moved, men and women sitting at their desks waved to her. *Am I
some kind of local hero? The article in the New Mexican must have touched
a few readers. How ironic, hero worship . . . my god, I didn't cast myself off
that mesa in an avalanche on purpose. I shouldn't have even been there in the
first place!* She smiled and nodded.

Justine settled into the armchair held out for her at the end of the table. She
was being handled with kid gloves, as though she could easily break. "Hi,
Scott. Mike. Pablo—delighted to see you here. Sam seems a little excited.
Who's going to tell me the good news?"

"I think Sam has the honors," said Mike with generosity, then adding,
"Wish you'd have let me drive you."

Justine smiled and turned to hear what Sam had to say.

"Well, it's like this. Scott, please chime in at anytime," he began. Scott
nodded and grinned. "We—Scott and I—talked with the director of the Ar-
chaeological Institute of America at the conference two days ago and she
offered to support our efforts for a Cotsen Excavation Grant. Looks like our
own office will provide for the overhead. Just talked, mind you. No proposal,
no grant. She simply said, 'I'll get back to you.'"

"And, she did," added Pablo. "Right away."

"How soon could you get back on top of Hupobi, Justine?" inquired Sam
with the innocence of a high school coach asking when she could get back in
the game. In a way, he was her coach.

She began to laugh. Fully, expressively, playfully. "Are you kidding me?"
A pregnant woman with several broken parts—little chance.

The men stared at each other and joined in her obvious pleasure. "Okay, Okay," admitted Sam, slightly embarrassed, "a dumb question."

"We could lower her in by helicopter," offered Pablo. His sardonic manner never accusatory or sarcastic. "That's how we took her out." He sat back with his chipped coffee cup, a sly grin sneaking out from under his bushy mustache.

"I can work from maps," she offered, eager to please these generous men, friends really. "The site of the garbage dump will not be difficult to find."

"That should work," said Mike, jumping from his chair before anyone could remind him that map study was a bit premature. He sprinted toward his own cubicle.

"When will this funding arrive—and what do we have to do to secure it?" Justine asked as she watched Mike disappear down the hall.

"Good questions," acknowledged Scott, refilling his coffee. "While the initial support was amazingly easy—so far—the actual process will require a plan and a timeline."

Mike returned with maps of Taos and Rio Arriba Counties and threw them across the scarred, oblong table. "Here it is" he exclaimed, placing his index finger on Hupobi.

Pablo reached forward and moved Mike's finger a little to the left. Justine grinned, but said nothing.

"Justine. Mike. Can you draw up an excavation plan? Consult with Pablo here." Sam was focused, his exuberance giving way to practicalities.

"I'd like to include members of Santa Clara and Taos Pueblo. I have a couple in mind," suggested Justine, watching Mike from the corner of her eye. Not so long ago Mike declared that including local Indians would muddy the water, embellish reality with myth.

Mike swallowed hard, his left eyebrow shooting upward toward his receding hairline. "If you must," he grinned.

"It's settled then," said Sam before Mike could speak further.

Pablo's eyes danced with pleasure as though he were watching his granddaughter dance. "Lunch anyone? I know a great little dive off Old Santa Fe Trail. Not much to look at, but terrific burritos."

"Thanks, Pablo, but I've got to get back to the Institute. Let me know how I can help." Scott directed his comment to Justine, who understood that lunch with Mike would not be to his taste. While the two men had come to respect each other in recent months, their worldviews were vastly different. Until recently, Mike had thoroughly rejected what he considered to be Scott's far-flung notions about migration.

"We'll take you up on your offer," Justine said, confident that she saw amazing transformation in Mike. A new openness to alternative worldviews. "Now, how about a burrito? Baby and I are hungry."

—⁂—

The drive back to Taos took Justine a while. Although she preferred shopping in Taos, she had a few favorite things that she could find only at Sprouts on St. Francis. Then, she set about to leisurely make her way home. While driving couldn't quite replace running as a satisfying venue for reflection, increased meditation had helped, as well as some gentle dancing.

By the time she passed the Opera House and approached the Los Alamos turnoff, Justine had lassoed her mind around a few compelling questions: *What will I do with great grandfather's will? Who needs to know? What action—if any—will I take?* She knew that the easiest option was to take no action at all. While the value of the literary estate must still be significant, the proceeds trickle out to generations of Frieda's heirs.

The thought that a case could be made for reopening the will in New Mexico based on Frieda's personal testimony in her autobiography that the manuscript of *Sons and Lovers* was given to Mabel in exchange for the ranch was now more defensible. *Even though I'm persuaded that the Ranch wasn't a gift, and therefore the Ranch was community property, I don't think the case can be made that it was.* Lawrence biographers are certain that the ranch was a gift, although Mabel's journals suggest otherwise. *I will have Judy Lynn's quirky assistance if I decide to pursue it.* She laughed to herself as she envisioned the energetic attorney with the fiery red hair.

Do I owe it to my unborn daughter to reopen the will? What purpose would it serve? Judy Lynn had pointed out that unless sinister forces were afoot to keep the will from coming to light, the statute of limitations could not be overturned. Certainly the letters suggest that Frieda forced Brett to withhold the new will. *Any court would agree...wouldn't they?* And, what position would the University take? Certainly a reopening of Frieda's will, which would of course be done during the trial, would air their dirty laundry: their failure to fulfill the conditions of the will by establishing a foundation to keep the ranch as a continuing memorial to Lawrence.

A frantic horn blared at her when she began to roll through a red light at the Chimayo junction in Espanola. She slammed on the brakes and held her breath. Justine cleared her mind and turned to Seriously Sinatra on her satellite radio. Taya had once asked her, "Who is Frank Sinatra?"

"Just my grandmother's favorite singer," she had replied. "Only the world's best singer . . . along with Pavarotti." As a small child, she had sat on her Gramma Laurence's lap and rocked back and forth while Sinatra's voice crooned from her old phonograph. Her eyes welled up thinking of Taya and her premature baby. Her near death. Finally, Taya's forgiveness of Justine. Something happened to Taya in that hospital. She is a different girl from the one who had gone running with Justine, had shared her fears and sorrows with her, had been confused about who she was and how to deal with the two young men who wanted her.

Sinatra's melodic voice smoothly ventured into *Where or When*, "It seems we stood and talked like this before, we looked at each other in the same way then, but I can't remember where or when." Justine began to cry—for Amir and the life they would never have. The child he would never see. To remember their lovemaking, that lock of curly black hair that insisted on crossing his forehead. The way he gazed at her when she awoke. *Why did I wait so long to say yes?*

CHAPTER 52

—◦◦◦—

I T HAD BEEN A TUMULTUOUS NIGHT, nightmares intruding into her consciousness, seemingly in time with the repeated kicking of the active child, but
she was definitely better all around this morning. A natural resiliency was her
constant companion now; even though her capacity to bounce back had been
so often tested over the past four years. She was now confident that she would
make it. She knew that the major task ahead of her was to allow herself to let
go of Amir. But how could she with his child in her body?

She heard the footsteps and the knock she'd been waiting for. Gathering her
belongings, she turned off the burner under her teapot, picked up a file folder,
and shuffled to the door. The sunlight caught her feathered eyelashes as she advanced toward the front of the house and stared straight ahead to Mabel's house.

She wasn't sure that she was expecting a girl, although she talked to the
child as she would a daughter—cherishing the possibilities of bringing up a
woman as the next generation. Projecting the life ahead for Isabella, the name
she had already chosen.

"Good morning, Taya," she said, opening the door. "I'm ready. Is Ricky
with you?"

"He's in the car. I told him we'd be right out." She giggled, still appreciative of the opportunity to live, to have her own child. Although still a young
girl, she had matured, ripened. She no longer called Justine "Miss Justine."

Taya was free of the dominance of two men: her brother and the assumed father of her child. She could breathe, decide her own fate. Justine

detected that Taya was beginning to settle comfortably into this evolving persona.

"How ya doing young man," Justine touched Ricky on the nose, wiggling it slightly. The three-month old laughed fully, and so did she. Climbing into the passenger seat of Taya's old Ford, she held both sides of her stomach as though she was protecting a basket of eggs. "Don't you think I'm getting a little fat?" she asked.

"You are! Big mama, or I should say, Big Godmama," Taya agreed. Before leaving the hospital, she had asked Justine to be Ricky's godmother. Justine was extremely pleased, not only because she'd never been a godmother before, but, most importantly, because it meant that Taya had forgiven her, that she would still be a part of the young girl's life.

"Thanks a lot! About being fat, I mean. I was a fat child and never want to face that again. What will Amir . . . . " She stopped herself and turned to Taya. "Let's go."

Taya nodded and pushed the gear into reverse to back out of the yard of the Pink House. "How much longer will you stay here?" she asked.

"Until the end of August. I want to be back in Emily's house by September. I'm thinking of buying a place."

"Here? In Taos? You'll stay??"

"I'm planning on it. How could I leave my godson? My good friends. The work on Hupobi."

Taya laughed with pleasure. "In that order?" she inquired.

Justine paused and held her stomach as Taya negotiated the bumpy dirt road back to Kit Carson Road. "I think so. Yes. In that order. By the way, I had lunch with your mom and Lucinda yesterday. They seemed to be doing well. Strong women."

"Yes, strong women. I'll be strong some day," Taya said as she pulled up in front of the Northern New Mexico Midwifery Center on Maestas Road near the southeast corner of Holy Cross Hospital.

"You're strong now, Taya," Justine insisted. While she could have well made it to the appointment on her own, Taya had wanted to take her. *Who is the mentor now? Both of us.*

Justine wasn't fond of pink, having always considered herself too much of a feminist to endure the color, but now she lived in the Pink House and would give birth in the pink room of the midwifery center. She laughed to herself.

Taya walked around the car and helped Justine out of the car where she waited until Taya handed her baby Ricky and grabbed her diaper bag. "Okay. We're ready."

The midwife Lisa met them at the door, warmly hugging both women.

"I'd like to be with Justine for the ultrasound, if that's okay," said Taya.

"Sure," said Lisa, placing her arm around Taya, shivering at the memory of the young girl's struggle with life and death. Life had certainly triumphed. "Justine, if you will just bring Ricky into the nursery here, Madrona will watch him while we're in the lab. Such a good baby," she observed as Ricky's large black eyes moved around the room, drawn to the light and a dancing clown on a wire.

The three women walked together to the ultrasound room. Justine could hardly wait. While she assumed the child was a girl, she really had no idea. A boy would be just fine. She had already decided on his name as well: Amir Morgan. If a girl: Isabella, and for the middle name, either Laurence or Lucrezia. She would consult her mother. She liked cultural traditions that involved the child's grandmother in the process of naming a child. Justine had promised to call her mother as soon as she had the news—a boy or a girl—either was fine. *Just so the child is healthy,* she thought, *the mantra of all expectant mothers.*

Justine slipped into the hospital gown and sat on the cool metal table. The lights in the room were soft, subtle, reminding her of the aura of the entire center: gentle and caring. She lay quietly while the technician attached the machine's tentacles to her stomach. Justine gazed into the technician's enlarged eyes and recognized a flash of surprise. *She, too, thinks I'm a little large for six months*, Justine deduced. *I'd better give up pistachio ice cream!* "Taya, are you there? Can you see the screen?"

"Right here, Justine. I have a good view," answered the thrilled Taya.

"Okay," said the technician. "We're ready to see this darling little human being."

The image of a small child came into view, the head curled forward as though ready to play a flute. Small fingers and toes came into clear focus, no penis in sight. A girl. No one spoke.

Abruptly, a third foot protruded into sight. Justine gasped. *The child is deformed*, she immediately thought, a sob pushing itself up through her chest. Still, no one said a word. The camera moved slowly around the stomach, faithfully photographing the inside of the uterus, catching the back of the skull, the left arm. "What is that?" she cried. "A shadow? Can there be a shadow in there?"

"We're seeing a second head, Dr. Jenner. You're having twins. A girl . . . and . . . and . . . a boy," she said as the camera closed in on the second child.

—⦿—

Justine lay back on her primitive cot watching the waning sunlight dance across the adobe walls. She smiled. She couldn't keep from smiling. Her mother had been as pleased as she was, reminding her of the time in Cairo when the investigating team had discovered in the codex that Jesus had had a twin. A sister. She didn't need to be reminded. It was the very twinness of Jesus' life that had caused the major religious and political upheaval. She'd found it profoundly curious that the revelation that Mary was not a virgin was less disturbing than the notion that Jesus had shared his mother's womb with a female. *Had God made a mistake by coupling Jesus with a female? Unthinkable.*

It was as though her life had come full circle. Life was a circle, a never-ending cycle of discovery and possibilities. Once she came to trust the process, she could let go of controlling the future. *And the way we think about the world changes us forever. Lawrence had found peace here, and so will I.*

CHAPTER 53

⸺⸻⸺

AUGUST 21, 2011

"LOVE THIS RED pepper hummus! Cheyenne, did you make this?" Judy Lynn called across the forest of people standing in Justine's living room in Llano Quemado. The meager ceiling fan stirred the warm air like slow hot tub jets.

Justine's lease on the antiquated Pink House had run its course. She was eight months along and, besides, she was ready to return to the comforts of Emily's house. A comfortable bed, warm bath, modern kitchen. Thick adobe walls that partially guarded against the extreme August heat. Her adventurous spirit was tempered now by a touch of domesticity. She surprised herself by reading recipes and discussing lactose and gluten. The twins were active occupants of her body, waking her at all times of night and day. Such a strange and wondrous feeling, it never failed to captivate her totally, engage all of her senses.

On this lovely, hot, and dry August Sunday afternoon, she had invited her friends to join in celebration of the launching of the dig at Hupobi, her purchase of a home just off Blueberry Hill, and a few surprise announcements. She was judicious about her news. Building to a dramatic moment reminded her of her mother, who was due to arrive at any minute. Justine had offered to pick her up at the airport in Albuquerque, but Lucrezia had insisted that she would want her own car anyway. After all, she was staying for a month or more. Justine smiled to herself at her mother's familiar flourish of independence. They were so much alike, she realized—having fought the idea for many years.

Justine leaned on the island, sipping her champagne glass of fresh squeezed apple juice and surveying the crowd. She was overwhelmed by her mob of engaged friends. Loyal and diverse. Fascinating. Animated and eager.

Giovanna had arrived early to set up the catered buffet, supplemented by an array of favorite potluck dishes. Taya held Ricky, talking intently with her mother and Pablo. Scott, Lucinda, and Cheyenne were nearly whispering; all that Justine could pick up was something about Roxanne Swentzell's aunt at Santa Clara, an important colleague of Scott's in his pursuit of an explanation for the migration of the peoples from Mesa Verde. Apparently, Lucinda knew her. Bill Haller and his wife Jan were at the back door observing her ravens.

Mike waved his arms as he and Judy Lynn ranted playfully at each other. His wife watched in amusement. She was used to Mike's dramatics. "You must be kidding?!" declared Mike, perspiration beading at his temples. "Horses were brought here by the Spanish."

"Ah, ha," said Judy Lynn with characteristic aplomb, "they were indigenous here before the last ice age." She lifted her long reddish hair off her neck.

Now it was Mike who rolled his large eyes, deep brown orbs floating in pools of white.

Justine laughed as she watched the theatrics. A wave of gratitude lightened her body once again. It was past 3:00, past her naptime—*where is Mom?*

At that very moment, the door opened and her mother nearly sprang into the room, setting two large suitcases down in the hallway. Bill and two others rushed to help her with the load she had nearly dragged from the car. Otherwise, she was her glamorous self. White dress and jacket, chunky silver jewelry, tinted raven-black hair damp at the temples. Ivory skin. About a foot shorter than Justine, and with strikingly darker coloring, it was a challenge for anyone to think of them as mother and daughter.

"Mom!" Justine cried, swaying across the room to meet her. "Welcome!" Bill was wrestling her suitcases into the second bedroom.

Lucrezia threw her arms around her daughter and held on tight. It was a funny sight, both women arching their backs to lean across the protruding stomach. Lucrezia placed her hands on Justine's shoulders and held her at arm's length, then kissed both cheeks and lowered her hands to her generous stomach. "You look great!" she declared, the ultimate verdict now uttered.

"My mother," Justine announced proudly, turning to the room, her arm around Lucrezia's shoulders. "Now we can begin. But first, Mom, what can I get you?"

"Ice water followed by champagne," she said, walking with confidence into the crowd, introducing herself to each eager guest. "Yes," she was saying, "A good flight . . . Florence was just as warm . . . Oh, my girl sure was! Climbed the tallest trees, swam to the middle of lakes and could hardly get back. Smart as a whip. Her teachers said she could do anything . . . just like her great grandfather, I'm sure." The stream of questions and answers about her heroic daughter went on for several minutes, until Lucrezia switched from water to champagne.

"Now show me those ravens," she said to Justine, having taken the long path across the room. Justine and her mother stepped out the back door, as much to talk privately as to observe the birds. "Are you okay? You're carrying quite a load there."

A rainbow arched across the Sacred Mountain, a late summer rain that failed to dampen Taos itself.

"I tire out easily, especially by late afternoon when I indulge in naps. Working more at home right now. Did I tell you I'm on salary? I'm finding it difficult not to be up on the mesa with the team; but, Mom, the thrill of these children, Amir's babies, is all consuming. I'm well and as happy as could be." She didn't say, "under the circumstances."

Lucrezia heard the subtle qualifier and raised a sculpted eyebrow above her Etruscan green eyes, an expression that would have intimidated Justine at one time. Deep in thought, she asked, "Where did the ravens go when you weren't here?"

"Emily was here much of the time. She said they would crouch near the miniature evergreen out front and watch for my car." A raven stepped forward and cocked her head, as though to listen more closely.

"Watch for your car?!"

"Remarkable, isn't it? They recognize individuals. They're loyal too, Mom. Remember, they came searching for me, showed me the way out of the snow bubble."

Lucrezia apparently decided not to challenge what she considered her daughter's fantasy. She would have to learn for herself. Her eyes swept the mesa, the curvature of this magnificent land, embroidered with sage and cactus. Her daughter had not exaggerated its grandeur. She smiled and turned back to Justine. "When will you make the announcements?"

"Right away. I need to run down the hall, throw some water on my face first though. Mom, I'm glad you're here. This is going to be fun. Get yourself a plate of food and I'll be right back." Justine hadn't always felt such comfort in her mother's presence. As a teenager, she saw herself as gangly, fat, and homely beside her beautiful Egyptian mother and, even as a young adult, she was always too eager to please. But things had changed. Both women had matured.

"May I have your attention, everyone?" Justine asked, looking refreshed and buoyant, perched on a bar stool and the edge of revelation, holding an elaborately hand-carved chest.

"All of you know by now that one of my major motivations for coming to Taos was to learn about my great-grandfather, D. H. Lawrence. My mother's grandfather." Justine nodded to her mother. "I needed to know what mysteries he'd found here on the side of Lobo Mountain—how this magical place influenced the balance of his life, those pivotal three years. His inner muse that became more fully liberated on the mountain. Then, after returning to Italy in '25, he saw himself as a painter; he started to write with even more daring; and he met my great grandmother, Isabella. She became his muse, teaching him to love in new ways, to find tenderness inside, even a little patience. Now, I do believe that he loved and respected Frieda. His letters tell us so. Yet in Isabella he discovered a side of himself previously unknown, a side that he found here in Taos. A new capacity to love."

"The hunt for Lawrence in Taos has been the most important pursuit in my life. Many of you have been on this journey with me," she turned and bowed to Taya, who smiled. "It began with Bill and his generous efforts to open the Lawrence Ranch to me. Through Bill, I also discovered the Kiowa Trail and the Hawk Ranch, locales where Lawrence walked and discovered his thoughts—his creativity, and became spirituality whetted by nature and the peoples of the pueblo." Before she was done, she would acknowledge each person in the room.

"There, on the side of that mountain, I found my own spirituality as well." Her mother looked surprised. "The deepness of the divine in each of us, in nature, in the seasons." Justine gazed at Lucinda with gratefulness. "An understanding that the deliberate practice of simple things can bring an unexpected peace. And, on the side of the Hupobi mesa, I found hope in those simple things, in an unseen presence guiding me, in the sacredness of snow." Many eyes in the room began to well up.

"But, let me continue with the story . . . I came to Taos with many letters," she patted the ornate chest, "letters from D. H. Lawrence to Isabella that describe their unique relationship. His desire, his yearning to return to Lobo Mountain came through convincingly. It was those letters that led me here. Then—and this is a major confession, Bill—Taya and I discovered an old key under a concrete slab in front of the fireplace in Lawrence's cabin at the ranch." She paused. "But to what did the key belong?—or was it relevant at all? Enter Judy Lynn and Kosta onto the stage."

The two glanced at one another—grinned with a certain pride.

"Judy Lynn, the adventurous attorney that she is, led me to the courthouse and the records of sales, gifts, quit claim deeds. Meanwhile, Giovanna introduced me to Maria Jaramillo who told us of the bank underneath the plaza, and the owner of the Red Cat led me to the tunnel running underneath the plaza. I can tell you, it's a mess down there." Everyone laughed.

"Can you believe it Lucinda, I met Kosta Papamanolis when he tried to save me from the Tricksters on San Geronimo Day. Little did I know then that he owned the La Fonda Hotel, the Lawrence paintings, and the mysterious bank situated underneath." Justine bowed to the flamboyant Greek. "Kosta obliged by finding a little dynamite to help out. That's where we found Lawrence's safety deposit box, number 911, holding two

322   •   *A Rapture of Ravens: Awakening in Taos*

astounding items: 200 shares of Atchison, Topeka, and Santa Fe stock and a letter from Lawrence to Lady Brett referring to a new will. He told Brett that he expected her to bring it to the attention of the court. And Frieda."

"Good luck!" Cheyenne chimed in.

Bill gasped. The room was so quiet, it was hardly possible to hear any breathing, if there was any. The fan churned uselessly.

"That's not all. After my accident at Hupobi," she chose not to describe Amir's death, "Cheyenne called and persuaded me to rent the Pink House on Mabel's property for the summer. That was a fated move. When Judy Lynn came by to force me to get some exercise—yes, force," she persisted, as Judy Lynn opened her mouth to protest, "she was resolute on straightening an old drawer which immediately shattered into splinters. There at our feet were the two missing pieces of this puzzle." She paused, aware that almost no one in the room knew all of the pieces.

"Go on!" Mike demanded, his appetite for intrigue fully whetted.

A knock sounded at the door and Scott moved to open it. "Arturo, come in," Justine called. The short, distinguished Italian had been lost in the housing complex for the past thirty minutes and appeared aggravated. His white shirt clung to his moist back. "Do you all know Arturo Servosi, Director of the New Mexico State Historical Museum? Have some champagne, Arturo. I'm in the middle of a story. I think you'll be interested." She chose to ignore his exasperated demeanor, trusting he would cool down before the last segment of her ritual. He caught her eye and she pointed to the hallway.

"It is those two items found in the Pink House with which we concern ourselves today." She laid her left hand on the chest before her. "One was Lawrence's will, legally drawn, as Judy Lynn pointed out, leaving his literary estate, with the exception of the proceeds from Lady Chatterley—which he left to his sister, Ada—to his daughter, my grandmother, Laurence. Why this will was never made public or carried out was explained by the accompanying letter from Grandmother Laurence to Lady Brett. You see, my grandmother came to Taos, and met with Brett, Mabel and probably Frieda, although we don't know that. Lady Brett apparently explained to her that the shares were rendered worthless by the depression, that she was penniless and dependent upon Frieda. We learn of this in Laurence's letter."

"Which Lawrence?" asked Giovanna.

"Grandmother Laurence, spelled with a U instead of a W," Justine explained patiently.

Beside her on the island, the phone began to buzz again and dance across the granite. A text. She chose to ignore it. This was not the time to interrupt the flow of conversation, to divert her attention from the moment. She knew it was her father, but he would have to wait.

"Lady Brett was afraid of losing Frieda's sponsorship if she made the new will public," Justine added. "Understandable."

"Do you plan to reopen the will now Justine?" asked Kosta.

"That was never my intention, Kosta. I only wanted to understand—and make public—Lawrence's full story, his full life." Beside her on the island, Justine's phone began to buzz and dance across the granite once again. Another text. Taya picked up the phone, without looking, and casually handed it to Justine who laid it on the island. She took a deep breath, picked up the chest and walked toward Bill.

"This container holds the letters from D. H. Lawrence to Isabella Hassouna and to Lady Dorothy Brett written from 1927 to 1930, the railroad shares, a thank you letter from Grandmother Laurence to Lady Brett written in 1954, and his will. Bill, on behalf of our family, I give these treasures to the Friends of the D. H. Lawrence as per our agreement."

Bill beamed, thanked her profusely and kissed her on the cheek. He accepted the gift without equivocation, his eyes damp with emotion. Then he turned, as planned, and stepped across the room, presenting the treasure to Arturo, who bowed ceremoniously.

A usually taciturn man, on this momentous occasion, Arturo was so choked up he could hardly utter words of acceptance. "Thank you, Bill. Justine. These treasures will remain with us for the New Mexican exhibit on D. H. Lawrence, then returned to Taos for the new museum."

"New museum?" asked Mike. "What new museum?"

"The new D. H. Lawrence Museum to be built at the ranch on Lobo Mountain," Bill proudly announced. "A gift from Justine and her family estate to the community."

Heads turned toward Justine and her mother.

Justine smiled and surveyed the room of friends and colleagues—those individuals who had challenged and supported her through this year of her own evolution. They gazed at her in return, expressions of respect and affection, tinged with wonderment, surprise. Her mother's unparalleled expression of love warmed her further. It had only been a year, but it seemed like an eternity. Life as dramatic as New Mexico seasons: life and death and renewal. She slowly returned to the island and picked up her phone. The text screen announced: "Lost in coma from injuries. Coming home. Amir."

EPILOGUE

—◦◦◦—

APRIL 14, 2012, LAWRENCE RANCH

JUSTINE GAZES OUT OF Lady Brett's small cabin window while her mother brushes her long hair. Outside to her left, a thousand-foot cement staircase winds up to the Lawrence Chapel perched on the side of the mountain. Like a doll house, really, painted yellow with a single stained glass window and large wooden cross on top. Her great-grandfather's ashes are interred within, Frieda buried just out front. In the distance, the peaks of the Sacred Taos Mountain and Sangra de Cristo range rise majestically into a turquoise sky.

Justine thinks of Lady Dorothy Brett now, a nearly deaf single woman born into the British aristocracy who had been madly in love with Lawrence, yet could never fulfill his last wish—to make his will known. Still deep in contemplation, Justine slips on her simple emerald earrings, a gift from her father years ago. She and Lucrezia chose this miniature cottage, barely large enough for a small cot, two chairs, and a table as the perfect place to prepare for the big event. Amir had lugged in an ornate Mexican mirror framed in brightly colored tin from a furniture shop in El Prado. On the bed lay Justine's dress and matching shoes, which her mother brought from Florence. The pale blue organdy dress rose from the box like leavened bread. Lucrezia is already dressed in a simple cocktail dress and jacket in a complementing, darker blue.

"Are you happy?" asks her mother.

"Deliriously so," Justine says without hesitation.

"No more doubts?"

Slipping on her dress, Justine laughs. "I've learned that life can't be predicted, nor fully planned, so I have to let go of trying to guide the future. Like you, Mom, I've learned to like surprises."

Lucrezia raises a sculptured eyebrow, laying the brush on the table. She knows her daughter well. "Will Egypt let their notorious codex thief back into the country?"

Justine tilts her head and grins. "Amir's father has smoothed things out. Being married to an Egyptian makes a great difference, you know. As for doubts, Mom, these last months with the children and Amir have quieted the small doubts I had." She didn't say, *for now anyway*. Justine shakes her head as though to free her thoughts and reaches for her broad-brimmed matching hat, situating it askance on her caramel-colored hair. The two women await the arrival of Giovanna who will pass summary judgment on her readiness to be a bride.

Directly in Justine's line of sight sits the D. H. Lawrence cabin, the rooms scattered now with small, linen-topped tables. A crackling fire struggles to take the early spring chill off the four rooms that once housed Lawrence and Frieda, then dozens of writers in the 60s and 70s. The scent of piñon perfumes the air. O'Keeffe's Red Poppy poster no longer hangs in redemption of the aged kitchen, now refurbished for today's festivities. In the open field just over the eastern fence, near the Lawrence pine, a white tent stands ready for the evening events—dancing, singing, sharing, toasting. Nearby, a sizeable pit releases ribbons of steam from a roasting pig.

A perfect day for a wedding.

Fifteen miles away, Justine's father, Morgan, prepares to escort Amir from the couple's home off Blueberry Hill to the ranch for the 4:00 ceremony. Morgan rented a tux in Albuquerque for Amir, which the young man at first resisted, later relenting. "My God, Morgan, we are getting married in an Indian ceremony on the side of a hill and I must wear a tux!" But he is good-natured about it. Certain revolutions take longer than others. Amir, admittedly stunning in his black tux, knows what battles are worth fighting. The months of healing and learning to be a father to the twins has taught him important

lessons in patience. Working alongside local Taos and Hispanics on the acequia water system—originally an Arab invention, imported to New Mexico
through Spain—he has found peace, even if he still sometimes experiences
restlessness.

Back at the ranch, Justine watches as friends from the Taos Valley, Santa
Clara Pueblo, and Santa Fe file by the big house, then Brett's tiny cabin. They
curiously cross in front of the buffalo painting on the south side of Lawrence's cabin, now more vivid since Taya touched up the fading colors.

Chairs on the cabin lawn are arranged to face inward from the four directions, all focused toward the center where the ceremony will take place. As
guests arrive, they are cleansed and purified by the smoke from cones of
smoldering sage whisked on friends and family by Sharon and Lucinda. They
are then seated by direction: on the North, the elders; on the South, married
couples and children; to the East, the young men and warriors. And, this is
where the practice varies: to the West, the single women, instead of the traditional warriors. Family members sit in a small inner circle.

Several minutes before 4:00, Lucinda's daughter and her husband begin to
play haunting tribal melodies on long wooden flutes. Mystical ancient tones
float through the air, touching each person like a gentle tuning fork, evoking
memories of long ago ceremonies. A veil of silence floats down over the
crowd.

From the side of the cabin, Judy Lynn's niece, a lovely child of six wearing
a wreathe crown of marigolds and daisies, leads the procession. Her small
hands clutch a miniature white satin pillow with two rings tied on top. Next
comes Justine, holding her father's arm. Amir's sister, Samira, Taya, and
Giovanna, all maids of honor, walk behind. Justine stares at the celebrated
Lawrence pine, the ceremonial circle, then catches Amir's adoring eyes. He
stands with best men Bill Haller, Mike Sandoval, and Pablo Williams. Beside
the men stands Lucinda in traditional tribal dress, flowing soft leather with
fringed sleeves, small turquoise stones beaded across the white bodice. Her
long black hair is held back by small braids at the temples. Cheyenne and
Judy Lynn sit in the inner circle, eight month old Isabella on one lap and
Ibrahim on the other. The twins catch one another's fingers and giggle.

Justine and Amir face each other, then slowly turn toward Lucinda who initiates the ceremony. "Let us begin." She turns to the bride. "Justine, what do you provide for this union of marriage?"

Lucrezia steps forward and hands the Bride's basket, lined in cedar, to her daughter. Corn, peaches, strawberries, squash, beef jerky, and freshly baked bread protrude from under a red cloth covering.

"I provide these things to my husband and home," Justine says, gazing at Amir. "They are a symbol that I will care for you and love you always."

"Amir," says Lucinda, turning. "What do you provide for this union of marriage?"

Samira comes forward and hands the Groom's basket to her brother.

Amir nods to his sister and says, "I provide these things to my wife. They are a symbol that I will provide, love, and protect our family always."

"You may exchange baskets," directs Lucinda. Justine and Amir set their baskets in front of the other and join hands.

"I offer you this special blessing," says Lucinda:

> Above you are the stars, below you are the stones.
> As time does pass, remember;
> Like a star should your love be constant.
> Like a stone should your love be firm.
> Be close, yet not too close.
> Possess one another, yet be understanding.
> Have patience with the other, for storms will come, but they
> will go quickly. Be free in giving of affection and warmth.
> Make love often, and be sensuous to one another.
> Have no fear, and let not the ways of words of the unenlight-
> ened give you unease. For the Great Spirit is with you, now
> and always."

Then Lucinda quietly steps back as an evocative siren of flutes again fills the air. The guests stand or sit in stillness. After several moments, Lucinda nods and continues, "Please repeat after me--."

"I, Justine, take you, Amir, as my husband. I do solemnly avow my love for you. I will comfort you, keep you, love you, defend you in sickness or in health, in riches or poverty, in sorrow or joy, seeking only to be with you until death parts us. All these things I pledge upon my honor."

Justine continues. "This poem is one of my favorites from D. H. Lawrence, my great-grandfather." She recites words from *Mystery*:

> Now I am all one bowl of kisses,
> Such as the tall, slim votaresses of Egypt.
> I lift to you my bowl of kisses, and through
> The temple's blue recesses cry out to you
> In wild caresses . . . .
> And still before the altar I exult the bowl brimful,
> And cry to you to stoop and drink, most high.
> Oh drink me up that I may be within your cup like
> A mystery, like wine that is still in ecstasy.

A tear of gratitude moves down Justine's cheek, as Lucrezia and Samira step forward, each holding one edge of a blue wedding blanket, ready to wrap it around the bride and groom, an action that is not to be. Baby Isabella chooses this moment to slip off Cheyenne's lap and take wobbly first steps toward her mother, burying her face in Justine's full organdy skirt, swaying to and froe. "She's walking!" exclaims Justine, picking up her daughter. Seeming not to want to be undone, Ibrahim wiggles and squeals, plops on the ground, gets up and plops again. Amir laughs, reaches over and sweeps his son into his arms. With Ibrahim in hand, he continues. "I, Amir, take you, Justine, as my wife. I do solemnly avow my love for you—and you," he says ruffling Ibrahim's hair as he finishes his vow.

Samira glances at Lucrezia, grins, and folds the wedding blanket, laying it over her arm.

Lucinda, laughing, says, "Shall we?" She pauses. "Circles have no beginning and no end, and so in the long and sacred tradition of marriage, rings have come to symbolize eternal love and endless union of body, of mind, and of the spirit."

Handing Ibrahim back to Judy Lynn, Amir unties the rings from the small satin pillow, kisses Judy Lynn's niece on the cheek, and hands one ring to Justine. He continues, "This ring is a symbol of my love and faithfulness. And with all that I am, and all that I have, I honor you, Justine, and pledge to you my love and life." He places the ring on Justine's hand.

She smiles wide, repeats Amir's words, and positions the simple gold band on his third finger.

Then Lucinda concludes, "Father Sky and Mother Earth, creator and nurturer of all life, we give heartfelt thanks for the moment that brought Justine and Amir together in the Holy State of Marriage. Now as you both have consented together in matrimony and have pledged your faith to each other by the giving and the receiving of rings before your family and community, according to the powers invested in me by my own people and the state of New Mexico, I pronounce you husband and wife." Lucinda grins and whispers to Amir, "You may kiss the bride now."

———

Later, at the reception. "How about your work, Justine?" asks an Elder from Santa Clara standing before her in the reception line.

"The project is in good hands, my friend. The excavation of Hupobi is nearly complete, but the small fetish I saw hasn't turned up. Sometimes I think I was dreaming, in spite of the photo I took!"

"Best to leave it to Mother Earth," says the Elder, patting her hand.

Justine nods knowingly and returns the pat.

"When are you leaving?" asks Cheyenne, next in line, holding Isabella, fast asleep on her shoulder.

"At the beginning of June. We'll fly to Florence to see my parents, then on to Cairo. Amir is eager to return. His parents were not well enough to come to the wedding—and, of course, much remains to be done to fulfill the revolution . . . ."

"And you, Justine? Are you eager to return?" asks her father as he hands her a glass of champagne.

Factual Epilogue

—∞∞—

- The Muslim Brotherhood candidate for the Peace and Freedom Party, Mohamed Morsi, is elected President of Egypt in June, 2012. He is overthrown in a military coup in July, 2013 led by Abdel Fattah el-Sisi, who is elected President, May, 2014.
- Kateri Tekakwitha is made a Saint by Pope Benedict in December, 2012. Giovanna Paponetti, and representatives from Indian pueblos throughout North America, attend the ceremonies.
- Scott Ortman's *Winds from the North,* the text explaining the rationale for the sudden departure of the peoples of Mesa Verde is published in 2012.
- The D.H. Lawrence Ranch, Taos, is reopened in the spring of 2012.
- The Northern New Mexican Midwifery Center closed in the summer of 2014, reopening as the Womens' Health Clinic in January, 2015.

THE END OF THE JUSTINE TRILOGY

AUTHOR NOTES

—◦◦◦—

HISTORICAL, CULTURAL, AND RELIGIOUS CONTEXT OF THE ADVENTURES OF JUSTINE JENNER

While the exploits of Justine and Amir are fictional, these exploits are situated in truth: the struggles and fate of Egypt and the Lawrence Ranch; the successful return of Blue Lake and Sacred Mountain to the Tiwa; the canonization of Kateri Tekakwitha by Pope Benedict; the exploration of Hupobi led by Pablo Williams; the theories and understandings of the migration of Mesa Verde peoples held by the Tewa Pueblo peoples of Santa Clara and Scott Ortman; the history of D. H. Lawrence and Mable Dodge Luhan; the tunnels under Taos; the joint acequia project between the Taos Pueblo and the Taos Community; the remarkable relationship between the Northern New Mexico Birth Center and Holy Cross Hospital; and, the ravens, intelligent and strategic beings who recognize people, choose to eat with wolves, and are monogamous. The following individuals granted permission to be presented in this novel as actual characters: Giovanna Paponetti; Bill Haller; Paul (Pablo) Williams; Melissa Serfling, owner of Red Cat Melissiana; Kosta Papamanolis; and Scott Ortman. Other characters are amalgamations of Taosenos who have generously given of their time and knowledge.

Justine Jenner's Maternal Lineage:

- Lucrezia Cellini Jenner, mother; Morgan Jenner, father
- Laurence Bashour Cellini (formerly Laurence Hassouna), grand-mother; Anwar Bashour, grand-father; Benvenuto Cellini, step-grandfather who adopted Lucrezia after the death of her father
- Isabella Hassouna, great-grandmother; Ahmed Hassouna, great-grandfather of record; D. H. Lawrence, great-grandfather

D. H. Lawrence Language Choices:

Lawrence wrote more that 5000 letters, many of which were written during the period 1926-1930, right up to the time of his death. The created letters in this novel seek to be faithful to his voice, pre-occupations, his history, and language choices. For instance, he tended to use "sympathies" for what today might be expressed as "empathy." Lawrence felt that the deepest forms of human knowing were "instinctual" and "intuitive." "Phallic consciousness" meant the source of human emotion. He also used language that is ethnically and racially inappropriate, although not rare in his days, such as Mabel's "red man."

The Tiwa-Tewa Pueblo Indian distinction

The **Tiwa** are groups of related Tanoan pueblo peoples in New Mexico. They traditionally speak a Tiwa language, and are divided into the two Northern Tiwa groups, in Taos and Picuris, and the Southern Tiwa in Isleta and Sandia, around Albuquerque. The Taos group is frequently referred to as the Red Willow people.

The **Tewa** (or **Tano**) are a linguistic group of Pueblo Indians who speak the Tewa language, one of the five Tanoan languages, and share the Pueblo culture Tiwa. Their homelands are on or near the Rio Grande in New Mexico north of Santa Fe. The six Tewa-speaking pueblos are Nambe, Pojoaque, San Ildefonso, San Juan, Santa Clara, and Tesuque.

Chapter 17: The mountain lion story was inspired by a true story written by Kay Like. The 1923 Lawrence scene is adapted from his poem "Mountain Lion."

Chapter 29: D. H. Lawrence and his wife, Frieda, sailed for England on the SS Resolute on September 10, 1925, never to return. In his imagination and in his letters, the Kiowa Ranch, now known as the D. H. Lawrence Ranch, remained his home for the rest of his life.

ACKNOWLEDGMENTS

I WISH TO ACKNOWLEDGE and extent gratitude to the following generous individuals and groups: Bill and Jan Haller, Giovanna Paponetti, Paul Williams, Jeff Boyer, Linda Yardley, Dolly and Fred Peralta, Liz Cunningham, Skip Miller, Art Bachrach, Tessie Naranjo, Porter Swentzell, David Fernandez, David Farmer, Scott Ortman, Robin Collier, Roberta Myers, Ouray Myers, Mary Lane Leslie, Jan Mellor, Janice Razo, Gal Tabib, Nita Murphy, Heather Nelson, Melissa Serfling, C.J. Johnson, Norm Ferguson, and Anne Marie Petrokubi. The staffs of The Mable Dodge Luhan House, Taos Public Library, The Southwest Research Center, New Mexico Historical Museum, and the caretakers of the D. H. Lawrence Ranch have been remarkably giving of their time. Continuing support has been forthcoming from my California colleagues: Emily Nelson, Ida Egli, Kosta P'manolis, Judith Fisher, Peggy Berryhill, Alice Combs, Mary Gardner, and Julie Morita. And scores of Taosenas and members of the Mendonoma Coast communities.

A special thanks to my son, Tod Green, for his ingenious knowledge of social media, and to my invaluable editors: Ida Egli, Morgan Lambert, Judith Fisher, and Caitlin Alexander. I thank my publisher, Mark Bernstein, West Hills Press, for his support and faith in the Justine Trilogy.

Linda Lambert
Santa Rosa, California
www.lindalambert.com

ABOUT THE AUTHOR

LINDA LAMBERT, Ed.D., is a full time author of novels and texts on leadership and professor emeritus, California State University, East Bay. During Dr. Lambert's career, she has been a social worker, teacher, principal, director of county and district adult learning programs, as well as a university professor, state department envoy to Egypt, and international consultant. Her international consultancies have taken her to Egypt, Lebanon, Morocco, England, Thailand, Mexico, Canada, and Malaysia. Lambert is the author of dozens of articles and lead author of *The Constructivist Leader* (1995, 2002), *Who Will Save Our Schools* (1997), *Women's Ways of Leading* (2009), and *Liberating Leadership* (2015); she is the author of *Building Leadership Capacity in Schools* (1998) and *Leadership Capacity for Lasting School Improvement* (2003). The first novel in The Justine Trilogy, *The Cairo Codex* (2013) has been widely acclaimed. It was the winner of the Silver Nautilus Award, the Bronze IPPY Award, and a finalist in U.S.A. Best Books. The second novel in the trilogy, *The Italian Letters* was released in 2014. She lives with her husband, Morgan, a retired school superintendent, in Santa Rosa, California.